DATE DUE			
APR 2 '90	APR 16 '92	MY 24 '00	
APR 18 '90	MAY 18 '92	FE 15 '01	
MAY 10 '90	SEP 18 '92	JE 19 '01	
JUN 19 '90	JUL 15 '93	DEC 1 3 2005	
SEP 15 '90	OCT 2 '93	FEB 2008	
DEC 20 '90	MY 10 '94	JUN 11 2008	
APR 16 '91	OC 24 '94	SEP -2 2008	
MAY 21 '91	OC 3 '96	6-21-10	
AUG 22 '91	NO 28 '96	7-12-11	
NOV 30 '91	MR 19 '98		
DEC 30 '91	OC 15 '98		
FEB 13 '92	AP 13 '00		

Dragon
Wing

THE DEATH GATE CYCLE

VOLUME ♦ 1

Dragon Wing

MARGARET WEIS
AND
TRACY HICKMAN

BANTAM BOOKS
NEW YORK • TORONTO • LONDON • SYDNEY • AUCKLAND

DRAGON WING
A Bantam Spectra Book / February 1990

Library of Congress Cataloging-in-Publication Data
Weis, Margaret.
  Dragon wing.
  (The Death Gate cycle ; v. 1)
  1. Hickman, Tracy.   II. Title.   III. Series: Weis,
Margaret.   Death Gate cycle; v. 1.
PS3573.E3978D66   1990   813'.54   89-18250
ISBN 0-553-05727-8

Published simultaneously in the United States and Canada

Bantam Books are published by Bantam Books, a division of Bantam Doubleday
Dell Publishing Group, Inc. Its trademark, consisting of the words "Bantam
Books" and the portrayal of a rooster, is Registered in U.S. Patent and Trademark
Office and in other countries. Marca Registrada. Bantam Books, 666 Fifth Avenue,
New York, New York 10103.

PRINTED IN THE UNITED STATES OF AMERICA

DH   0 9 8 7 6 5 4 3 2 1

This work is dedicated to

the memory of my mother,

FRANCES IRENE WEIS

◆

—Margaret Weis

To Dezra and Terry Phillips

FOR ALL WE SHARED

◆

—Tracy Hickman

Self is the only prison

that can ever bind

the soul.

◆

—Henry Van Dyke

The World of Arianus

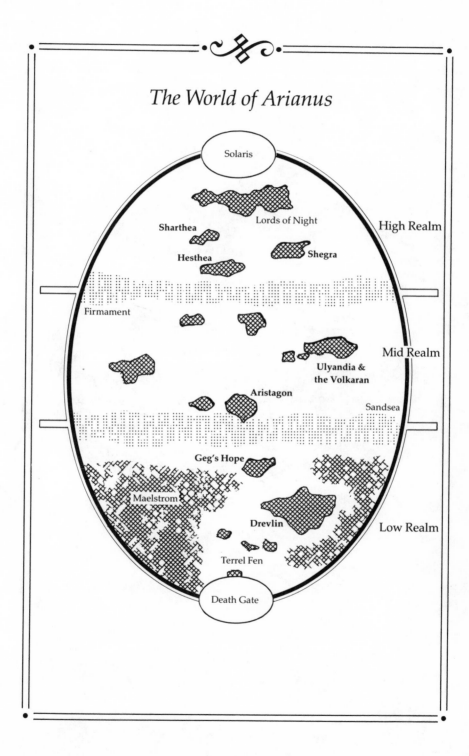

Mid Realm of Arianus

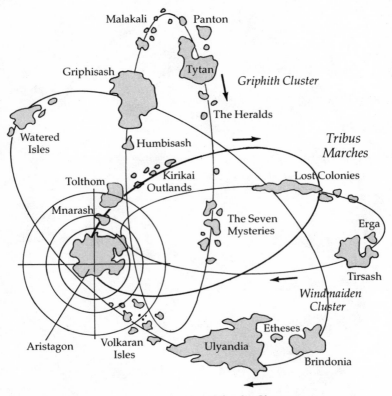

Malakali Panton

Griphisash

Tytan

Griphith Cluster

The Heralds

Watered
Isles

Humbisash

Tribus
Marches

Tolthom

Kirikai
Outlands

Lost Colonies

Mnarash

The Seven
Mysteries

Erga

Tirsash

Windmaiden
Cluster

Aristagon

Volkaran
Isles

Etheses

Ulyandia

Brindonia

Ulyndia Cluster

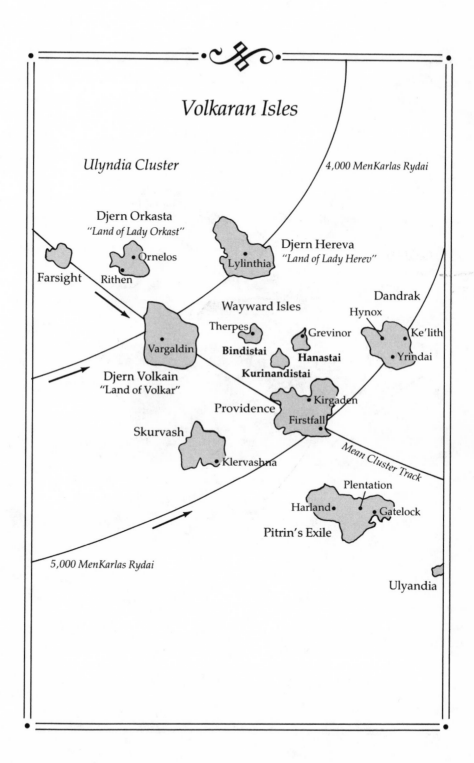

Volkaran Isles

Ulyndia Cluster

4,000 MenKarlas Rydai

Djern Orkasta
"Land of Lady Orkast"

• Ornelos

Djern Hereva
"Land of Lady Herev"

Lylinthia•

Farsight

Rithen

Dandrak

Hynox

Wayward Isles

Therpes•

•Grevinor

Ke'lith

Vargaldin•

Bindistai

Hanastai

•Yrindai

Djern Volkain
"Land of Volkar"

Kurinandistai

•Kirgaden

Providence

Firstfall•

Skurvash

Mean Cluster Track

•Klervashna

Plentation

Harland•

•Gatelock

Pitrin's Exile

5,000 MenKarlas Rydai

Ulyandia

Drevlin
Low Realm

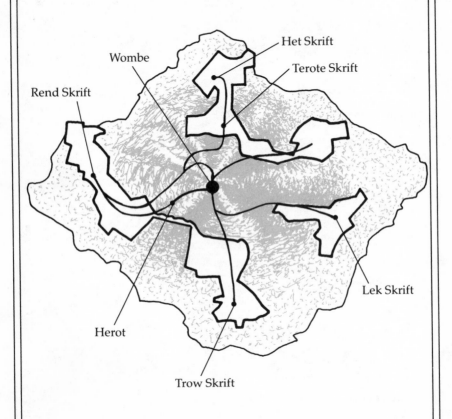

Het Skrift

Wombe

Terote Skrift

Rend Skrift

Lek Skrift

Herot

Trow Skrift

Dragon
Wing

PROLOGUE

"BE AT EASE, HAPLO. COME IN AND MAKE YOURSELF COMFORTABLE. Sit down. There are no formalities between us.

"Allow me to fill your glass. We drink what was once called the stirrup cup, a salute to your long journey.

"You like the port? Ah, my talents are many and manifold, as you know, but I begin to think that only time—not magic—can produce a truly fine port. At least that's what the old books teach. I've no doubt our ancestors were right about that . . . no matter how wrong they were in other things. There is something about the drink I miss, a warmth, a mellowness that comes with age. This port is too harsh, too aggressive. Fine qualities in men, Haplo, but not in wine.

"So, you are prepared for your journey? Is there any need or want I can satisfy? Say so, and it's yours. Nothing?

"Ah, I do envy you. My thoughts will be with you every moment, waking and sleeping. Another salute. To you, Haplo, my emissary to an unsuspecting world.

"And they must not suspect. I know we've been over this before, but I want to stress this again. The danger is great. If our ancient enemy catches even the slightest hint that we've escaped their prison, they will move land, sea, sun, and sky—as they did once—to thwart us. Sniff them out, Haplo. Sniff them out as that dog of yours sniffs out a rat, but never let them catch a whiff of you.

"Let me refill your glass. Another salute. This one to the Sartan. You hesitate to drink. Come. I insist. Your rage is your strength. Use it, it will give you energy. Therefore . . .

"To the Sartan. They made us what we are.

"How old are you, Haplo? You have no idea?

"I know—time has no meaning in the Labyrinth. Let me think. When I first saw you, you looked to be just over twenty-five years. A long life for those of the Labyrinth. A long life, and one that had almost ended.

"How well I remember that time, five years ago. I was about

to reenter the Labyrinth when you emerged. Bleeding, barely able to walk, dying. Yet you looked up at me with an expression—I will never forget it—Triumph! You had escaped. You had beaten them. I saw that triumph in your eyes, in your exultant smile. And then you collapsed at my feet.

"It was that expression which drew me to you, dear boy. I felt the same when I escaped from that hell so long ago. I was the first one, the first one to make it through alive.

"Centuries ago, the Sartan thought to defeat our ambition by sundering the world that was ours by rights and throwing us into their prison. As you well know, the way out of the Labyrinth is long and tortuous. It took centuries to solve the twisting puzzle of our land. The old books say the Sartan devised this punishment in hopes that our bounding ambition and our cruel and selfish natures would be softened by time and suffering.

"You must always remember their plan, Haplo. It will give you the strength you'll need to do what I ask of you. The Sartan had dared to assume that, when we emerged into this world, we would be *fit* to take our places in any of the four realms we chose to enter.

"Something went wrong. Perhaps you'll discover what it was when you enter Death Gate. It seems, from what I have been able to decipher in the old books, that the Sartan were to have monitored the Labyrinth and kept its magic in check. But, either through malicious intent or for some other reason, they forsook their responsibility as caretakers of our prison. The prison gained a life of its own—a life that knew only one thing, *survival*. And so, the Labyrinth, our prison, came to see us, its prisoners, as a threat. After the Sartan abandoned us, the Labyrinth, driven by its fear and hatred of us, turned deadly.

"When at last I found my way out, I discovered the Nexus, this beautiful land the Sartan had established for our occupation. And I came across the books. Unable to read them at first, I worked and taught myself and soon learned their secrets. I read of the Sartan and their 'hopes' for us and I laughed aloud—the first and only time in my life I have ever laughed. You understand me, Haplo. There is no joy in the Labyrinth.

"But I will laugh again, when my plans are complete. When the four separate worlds—Fire, Water, Stone, and Sky—are again one. Then I will laugh long and loudly.

"Yes. It's time for you to leave. You've been patient with the ramblings of your lord. Another salute.

"To you, Haplo.

"As I was the first to leave the Labyrinth and enter the Nexus, so you shall be the first to enter Death Gate and walk the worlds beyond.

"The Realm of the Sky. Study it well, Haplo. Come to know the people. Search out their strengths *and* their weaknesses. Do what you can to cause chaos in the realm, but always be discreet. Keep your powers hidden. Above all, take no action that will draw the attention of the Sartan, for if they discover us before I am ready, we are lost.

"Death first, before you betray us. I know you have the discipline and the courage to make that choice. But more important, Haplo, you have the skill and the wits to make such a choice unnecessary. This is why I've chosen you for this mission.

"You have one other task. Bring me someone from this realm who will serve as my disciple. Someone who will return to preach the word, *my* word, to the people. It can be someone of any race—elven, human, dwarven. Make certain that he or she is intelligent, ambitious, . . . and pliable.

"In an ancient text, I came across a fitting analogy. You, Haplo, shall be the voice of one crying in the wilderness.

"And now, a final salute. We will stand for this one.

"To Death Gate. 'Prepare ye the way.' "

CHAPTER ◆ 1

YRENI PRISON, DANDRAK,

MID REALM

◆

THE CRUDELY BUILT CART LURCHED AND BOUNCED OVER THE ROUGH
coralite terrain, its iron wheels hitting every bump and pit in
what passed for a road. The cart was being pulled by a tier, its
breath snorting puffs in the chill air. It took one man to lead the
stubborn and unpredictable bird while four more, stationed on
either side of the vehicle, pushed and shoved the cart along. A
small crowd, garnered from the outlying farms, had gathered in
front of Yreni Prison, planning to escort the cart and its shameful
burden to the city walls of Ke'lith. There, a much larger crowd
awaited the cart's arrival.

Dayside was ending. The glitter of the firmament began to
fade as the Lords of Night slowly drew the shadow of their
cloaks over the afternoon stars. Night's gloom was fitting for this
procession.

The country folk—for the most part—kept their distance from
the cart. They did this not out of fear of the tier—although those
huge birds had been known to suddenly turn and take a vicious
snap at anyone approaching them from their blind side—but out
of fear of the cart's occupant.

The prisoner was bound around the wrists by taut leather
thongs attached to the sides of the cart, and his feet were mana-
cled with heavy chains. Several sharp-eyed bowmen marched
beside the cart, their feathered shafts nocked and ready to be let
loose straight at the felon's heart if he so much as twitched the
wrong way. But such precautions did not appear to offer the
cart's followers much comfort. They kept their gaze—dark and

watchful—fixed on the man inside as they trudged along behind at a respectful distance that markedly increased when the man turned his head. If they'd had a demon from Hereka chained up in that cart, the local farmers could not have gazed on it with any greater fear or awe.

The man's appearance alone was striking enough to arrest the eye and send a shiver over the skin. His age was indeterminate, for he was one of those men whom life has aged beyond cycles. His hair was black without a touch of gray. Sleeked back from a high, sloping forehead, it was worn braided at the nape of his neck. A jutting nose, like the beak of a hawk, thrust forward from between dark and overhanging brows. His beard was black and worn in two thin short braids twisted beneath a strong chin. His black eyes, sunken into high cheekbones, almost disappeared in the shadows of the overhanging brows. Almost, but not quite, for no darkness in this world, it seemed, could quench the flame that smoldered in those depths.

The prisoner was of medium height, his body bare to the waist and marked all over with gashes and bruises, for he had fought like a devil to avoid his capture. Three of the sheriff's boldest men lay in their beds this day and would probably lie there for a week recovering. The man was lean and sinewy, his movements graceful and silent and swift. One might say, from looking at him, that here was a man born and bred to walk in the company of Night.

It amused the prisoner to see the peasants fall back when he glanced around at them. He took to looking behind him often, much to the discomfiture of the bowmen, who were constantly lifting their shafts, their fingers twitching nervously, their gazes darting for instructions at their leader—a solemn-faced young sheriff. Despite the chill of the fall evening, the sheriff was sweating profusely, and his face brightened visibly when the coralite walls of Ke'lith came in sight.

Ke'lith was small in comparison with the other two cities on Dandrak Isle. Its ill-kept houses and shops barely covered a square menka. In the very center stood an ancient fortress whose tall towers were catching the last light of the sun. The keep was constructed of rare and precious blocks of granite. In this day, no one remembered how it was built or who had built it. Its past history had been obscured by the present, by the wars that had been fought for its possession.

Guards pushed open the city gates and motioned the cart

forward. Unfortunately the tier took exception to a ragged cheer that greeted the cart's arrival in Ke'lith and came to a dead stop. The recalcitrant bird was alternately threatened and coaxed by its handler until it began moving again, and the cart trundled through the opening in the wall onto a smoothed coralite street known grandiosely as Kings Highway; no king in anyone's memory had ever set foot on the place.

A large crowd was on hand to view the prisoner. The sheriff barked out an order in a cracked voice and the bowmen closed ranks, pressing close around the cart, the front men in dire peril of being bitten by the nervous tier.

Emboldened by their numbers, the people began to shout curses and raise their fists. The prisoner grinned boldly at them, seeming to consider them more amusing than threatening until a jagged-edged rock sailed over the cart's sides and struck him in the forehead.

The mocking smile vanished. Anger contorted the blood-streaked face. His fists clenched, the man made a convulsive leap at a group of ruffians who had discovered courage at the bottom of a wine jug. The leather thongs that held the man fastened to the cart stretched taut, the sides of the vehicle quivered and trembled, the chains on his feet jangled discordantly. The sheriff screeched—the young man's voice rising an octave in his fear— and the bowmen swiftly lifted their weapons, although there was some confusion over their target: the felon or those who had attacked him.

The crudely made cart was strong, and the man inside, though he exerted all his energy, could neither break his bonds nor the wood that held them. His struggles ceased and he stared through a mask of blood at the swaggering ruffian.

"You wouldn't dare do that if I were free."

"Oh, wouldn't I?" the youth jeered, his cheeks flushed with drink.

"No, you wouldn't," replied the man coolly. His black eyes fixed themselves upon the youth, and such was the enmity and dire threat in their coal-fire stare that the young man blenched and gulped. His friends—who were urging him on, though they themselves stayed well behind him—took offense at the felon's remarks and became more threatening.

The prisoner turned, glaring at one side of the street, then the other. Another rock struck him in the arm, followed by rotting tomatoes and a stinking egg that missed the felon but caught the sheriff squarely in the face.

Having been prepared to kill the prisoner at the first opportunity, the bowmen now became his protectors, turning their arrows toward the crowd. But there were only six bowmen and about a hundred in the mob, and things appeared likely to go ill for both prisoner and guards, when a beating of wings and high-pitched screams from overhead caused most of those in the crowd to take to their heels.

Two dragons, guided by helmed and armored riders, swooped in low over the heads of the mob, sending them ducking into doorways and dashing down alleys. A call from their leader, still wheeling high overhead, brought the dragon knights back into formation. He descended and his knights followed him, the dragons' wingtips clearing the buildings on either side of the street by barely a hand's breadth. Wings tucked neatly at their flanks, their long tails lashing wickedly behind, the dragons alighted near the cart.

The knights' captain, a paunchy middle-aged man with a fiery-red beard, urged his dragon closer. The tier—terrified at the sight and smell of the dragons—was heaving and howling and going through all kinds of gyrations, causing its handler no end of grief.

"Keep that damn thing quiet!" snarled the captain.

The tiermaster managed to catch hold of the head and fixed his beast with an unblinking stare. As long as he could maintain this steady gaze, the stupid tier[1]—for whom out of sight was out of mind—would forget the presence of the dragons and calm down.

Ignoring the stammering, babbling sheriff, who was hanging on to the captain's saddle harness as a lost child hangs on to its newly found mother, the captain gazed sternly at the bloody, vegetable-stained prisoner.

"It seems I arrived in time to save your miserable life, Hugh the Hand."

"You did me no favor, Gareth," said the man grimly. He raised his shackled hands. "Free me! I'll fight all of you, and them too." He flicked his head at the remnants of the mob peeking out of the shadows.

---

[1]In the wild, these enormous birds are a dragon's favorite prey. Tiers' wings are large and covered with soft feathers and are almost completely useless. They can, however, run extremely fast on their powerful legs. They make excellent beasts of burden and are extensively used as such in the realms of the humans. Elves consider the tier repulsive and unclean.

The captain of the knights grunted. "I'll bet you would. That death's a damn sight better than the one you're facing now—kissing the block. A damn sight better and a damn sight too good for you, Hugh the Hand. A knife in the back, in the dark—that's what I'd give you, assassin scum!"

The curl of the Hand's upper lip was emphasized by a feathery black mustache and was clearly visible even in the failing light. "You know the manner of my business, Gareth."

"I know only that you are a killer for hire and that my liege lord met his end by your hand," retorted the knight gruffly. "And I've saved your head merely to have the satisfaction of placing it with my own hands at the foot of my lord's bier. By the way, they call the executioner Three-Chop Nick. He's never yet managed to sever a head from a neck at the first blow."

Hugh gazed at the captain, then said quietly, "For what it's worth, I didn't kill your lord."

"Bah! The best master I ever served murdered for a few barls.[2] How much did the elf pay you, Hugh? How many barls will you take now to restore my lord's life to me?"

Yanking on the reins, the captain—his eyes blinking back tears—turned the head of his dragon. He kicked the creature in the flanks, just behind the wings, and caused it to rise into the air, where it remained, hovering over the cart, its snakelike eyes daring any of those lurking in the shadows to cross its path. The dragon knights riding behind likewise took to the air. The tiermaster, his own eyes watering, blinked. The tier once more trod sullenly forward, and the cart clattered over the road.

It was night when the cart and its dragon escort reached the fortress keep and dwelling place of the Lord of Ke'lith. The lord himself lay in state in the center of the courtyard. Bundles of charcrystal soaked in perfumed oil surrounded his body. His shield lay across his chest. One cold, stiff hand was clasped around his sword hilt; the other hand held a rose placed there by his weeping lady-wife. She was not among those gathered around the body, but was within the keep, heavily sedated with poppy syrup. It was feared that she might hurl herself upon the flaming bier, and while such sacrificial immolation was customary on the

---

[2]The barl is the main standard of exchange in both elven and human lands. It is measured in the traditional barrel of water. An equivalent exchange for a barrel of water is one barl.

island of Dandrak, in this case it could not be allowed; Lord Rogar's wife having just recently given birth to his only child and heir. The lord's favorite dragon stood nearby, proudly tossing its spiky mane. Standing beside it, tears rolling down his face, was the head stablemaster, a huge butcher's blade in his hand. It wasn't for the lord he wept. As the flames consumed its master's body, the dragon which the stablemaster had raised from an egg would be slaughtered, its spirit sent to serve its lord after death.

All was prepared. Every hand held a flaming torch. Those milling about the courtyard awaited only one thing before they set fire to the bier: the head of the lord's murderer to be placed at his feet.

Although the keep's defenses had not been activated, a cordon of knights had been drawn up to keep the curious out of the castle. The knights drew aside to allow the cart entry, then closed ranks as it trundled past. A cheer went up from those standing in the courtyard when the cart was sighted rumbling beneath the arched gateway. The knights escorting it dismounted, and their squires ran forward to lead the dragons to the stables. The lord's dragon shrieked a welcome—or perhaps a farewell—to its fellows.

The tier was detached and led away. The tiermaster and the four men who had pushed the vehicle were taken to the kitchen, there to be fed and given a share of the lord's best brown ale. Sir Gareth, his sword loosened in its scabbard, his eyes noting every move the prisoner made, climbed into the cart. Drawing his sideknife, he cut the leather thongs attached to the wooden slats.

"We caught the elflord, Hugh," Gareth said in an undertone as he worked. "Caught him alive. He was on his dragonship, sailing back to Tribus, when our dragons overtook him. We questioned him and he confessed giving you the money before he died."

"I've seen how you 'question' people," said Hugh. One hand free, he flexed his arm to ease the stiffness. Gareth, loosing the other one, eyed him warily. "The bastard would've confessed to being human if you'd asked him!"

"It was your accursed dagger we took from my lord's back, the one with the bone handle with those strange markings. I recognized it."

"Damn right, you did!" Both hands were free. Moving swiftly, suddenly, Hugh's strong hands closed over the chain-mail armor that covered the knight's upper arms. The assassin's fingers bit deep, driving the rings of the chain mail painfully into the man's flesh. "And you know both how and why you saw it!"

Gareth sucked in his breath, his sideknife jerked forward. The blade was three-quarters the way to Hugh's rib cage when, with an effort of will, the knight halted his reflexive lunge.

"Get back!" he snarled at several of his fellows, who, seeing their captain accosted, had drawn their swords and were preparing to come to his assistance.

"Let go of me, Hugh." Gareth spoke through gritted teeth. His skin was a ghastly leaden hue, sweat beaded on his upper lip. "Your trick didn't work. You won't meet an easy death at my hand."

Hugh, with a shrug and a slight sardonic smile, released his grip on the knight's arms. Gareth caught hold of the assassin's right hand, jerked it roughly behind his back, and, grabbing his left, bound the two together tightly with the remnants of the leather thongs.

"I paid you well," the knight muttered. "I owe you nothing!"

"And what about her, your daughter, whose death I avenged—"

Spinning Hugh around by the shoulder, Gareth swung his mailed fist. The blow caught the assassin on the jaw and sent him crashing through the wooden slats of the cart. Sprawled on his back on the ground, the Hand lay in the muck of the courtyard. Gareth jumped down from the cart. Straddling the prisoner, the knight stared down at him coldly.

"You'll die with your head on the block, you murdering bastard. Bring him," he ordered two of his men, and kicked Hugh in the kidney with the toe of his boot. Gareth watched with satisfaction as the man writhed in pain. The knight added grimly, "And gag his mouth."

CHAPTER ♦ 2

KE'LITH KEEP, DANDRAK,

MID REALM

♦

"Here is the assassin, Magicka," said Gareth, gesturing to the bound-and-gagged prisoner.

"Did he give you any trouble?" asked a well-formed man of perhaps forty cycles, who gazed at Hugh with a sorrowful air, as though he found it impossible to believe that so much evil could reside in one human being.

"None that I couldn't handle, Magicka," said Gareth, subdued in the presence of the house magus.

The wizard nodded and—conscious of a vast audience— straightened to his full height and folded his hands ceremoniously over his brown velvet cassock; he was a land magus and so wore the colors of the magic he favored. He did not, however, wear in addition the mantle of royal magus—a title he had, according to rumor, long coveted but one which Lord Rogar, for reasons of his own, refused to grant.

Those standing in the muddy courtyard saw the prisoner being led before the person who was now—by default—the highest voice of authority in the fiefdom, and crowded around to hear. The light of their torches flared and danced in the cold evening breeze. The lord's dragon, mistaking the tenseness and confusion for battle, trumpeted loudly, demanding to be unleashed upon the enemy. The stablemaster patted it soothingly. Soon it would be sent to fight an Enemy that neither man nor even the long-lived dragon can finally avoid.

"Remove the gag from his mouth," ordered the wizard.

Gareth coughed, cleared his throat, and cast the Hand a

sidelong glance. Leaning near the wizard, the knight spoke in low tones. "You will hear nothing but a string of lies. He'll say anything—"

"I said, remove it," remonstrated Magicka in a commanding tone that left no doubt in the minds of anyone standing in the courtyard who was now the master of Ke'lith Keep.

Gareth sullenly did as he was told, yanking the gag from Hugh's mouth with such force that he wrenched the man's head sideways and left an ugly weal on one side of his face.

"Every man, no matter how heinous his crime, has the right to confess his guilt and cleanse his soul. What is your name?" questioned the wizard crisply.

The assassin, gazing over the wizard's head, did not answer. Gareth smote Hugh rebukingly.

"He is known as Hugh the Hand, Magicka."

"Surname?"

Hugh spit blood.

The wizard frowned. "Come, Hugh the Hand can't be your real name. Your voice. Your manners. Surely you are a nobleman! The *baton sinister*, no doubt. Yet, we must know the names of your ancestors in order to commend to them your unworthy spirit. You will not speak?" Reaching out a hand, the wizard caught hold of Hugh's chin and jerked the man's face to the torchlight. "The bone structure is strong. The nose aristocratic, the eyes exceedingly fine, although I seem to see something of the peasant in the deep lines in the face and the sensuality of the lips. But there is undoubtedly noble blood in your veins. A pity it runs black. Come, sir, reveal your true identity and confess to the murder of Lord Rogar. Such confession will cleanse your soul."

The prisoner's swollen mouth widened in a grin; there was a flicker of flame deep in the sunken black eyes. "Where my father is, his son will shortly follow," Hugh replied. "And you know better than any here that I did not murder your lord."

Gareth raised his fist, intending to punish the Hand for his speech. A glimpse of the wizard's face caused him to hesitate. Magicka's brow cleared in an instant, his face smooth as a pail of fresh cream. The sharp eyes of the captain, however, had noted the ripple that passed across its surface at Hugh's accusation.

"Insolence," the wizard said coldly. "You are bold for a man facing a terrible death, but we will hear you cry out for mercy before long."

"You better silence me and silence me quick," said Hugh, his tongue running across his cracked and bleeding lips. "Otherwise people might remember that you're now guardian of the new little lord, aren't you, Magicka? Which means you can run things around here until the kid's . . . What? Eighteen? Or maybe longer than that if you can keep your web wound tight around him. And I've no doubt you'll be a great comfort to the grieving widow. What mantle will you wear tonight—the purple of royal magus? And wasn't it strange, my dagger disappearing like that. *As if by magic—*"

The wizard lifted his hands. "The ground quakes in fury at this man's blasphemy!" he shouted. The courtyard began to shake and tremble. Granite towers swayed. People cried out in panic, huddling close together. Some fell to their knees, wailing and pressing their hands in the muck and mud, shouting in supplication to the magus to ease his anger.

Magicka glared down his long nose at the captain of the knights. A punch from Gareth, given somewhat reluctantly, it seemed, in the small of Hugh's back, caused the assassin to gasp and draw a painful breath. The Hand's gaze, however, never wavered or faltered, but remained fixed on the wizard, who was pale with fury.

"I have been patient," said Magicka, breathing heavily, "but I will not be subjected to such filth. I apologize to you, captain," the wizard continued, shouting to be heard above the rumbling of the ground and the cries of the people. "You were right. He will say anything to save his miserable life."

Gareth grunted but did not reply. Magicka raised his hands placatingly and, gradually, the ground ceased to shake. People drew deep breaths of relief and rose to their feet again. The knight's gaze flicked aside at Hugh, met the Hand's own intense, penetrating stare. Gareth frowned; his eyes went from the assassin to the wizard, and they were dark and thoughtful.

Magicka, speaking to the crowd, did not notice.

"I am sorry, truly sorry, that this man must leave this life with such black spots upon his soul," said the wizard in grieved and pious tones. "Yet so he chooses. All here are witness that I have given him ample opportunity to confess."

There were sympathetic, respectful murmurs.

"Bring forth the block."

The murmurs changed in aspect, becoming loud and anticipatory. People shifted around to get a good view. Two burly warders, the strongest that could be found, emerged from a small doorway leading to the dungeon of the keep. Between them they carried a huge stone—not the lacy and delicate coralite[1] of which almost everything in the city except the keep itself was constructed. Magicka, whose business it was to know the types and natures and powers of all rocks, recognized the stone as marble. It did not come from this island or from the larger, neighboring continent of Uylandia, for no such rock existed there. The marble, therefore, came from the larger, neighboring continent of Aristagon, which meant that this block had been dug out of the land of the enemy.

Either it was a very old piece of marble and had been brought over legitimately during one of the few periods of peace between the humans and the elves of the Tribus Empire—a theory the wizard discounted—or Three-Chop Nick, as he was known, had smuggled it over, which Magicka thought probable.

Not that it mattered. There were numerous diehard nationalists among the lord's friends, family, and followers, but the wizard doubted if there were any who would object to a piece of dung such as Hugh the Hand losing his head on an enemy rock. Still, they were a hotheaded clan and the wizard was thankful that the marble was so covered with dried blood that few of Rogar's kin would recognize the stone. None would think to question its origin.

The marble block was about four feet by four feet and had a groove cut out of one side that was almost exactly the size of the average human neck. The warders—staggering under the weight—hauled the block out into the courtyard and placed it in front of Magicka. The executioner, Three-Chop Nick, ducked out from beneath the doorway and a tremor of excitement rippled through the crowd.

---

[1]All the floating isles in the Realm of Sky are composed of coralite. The excretion of a small, harmless, snake-shaped creature known as the coral grubb, coralite is spongelike in appearance. When it hardens, it is as strong as granite, though it cannot be cut and polished. Coralite forms very fast; structures made of the substance are not built so much as grown. Coral grubbs give off a gas that is lighter than air. This keeps the isles suspended in the sky, but can be a nuisance when attempting to construct buildings. The magic of first-house land wizards is necessary to remove it.

Occasionally, deposits of iron and other minerals have been discovered embedded in the coralite. How they got there is not known, but it is presumed to have been a phenomenon that occurred during the Sundering.

Nick was a giant of a man and not one soul on Dandrak knew who he really was or what he looked like. Whenever he performed an execution, he wore black robes and a black hood over his head so that, when passing among the populace on a daily basis, he would not be recognized and shunned. Unfortunately, the result of his clever disguise was that people began to suspect every man over seven footspans in height of being an executioner and tended to avoid them all indiscriminately.

When it came time to deal out justice, however, Nick was the most popular and sought-after executioner on Dandrak. Whether an incredible bungler or the most talented showman of his time, Three-Chop certainly knew how to entertain an audience. No victim ever died swiftly, but lingered on in screaming agony as Nick hacked and chopped away with a sword that was as dull as his wits.

All eyes went from the hooded Nick to the black-haired prisoner, who—it must be admitted—had impressed most of those present with his coolness. But all those in the courtyard that night had either admired or actually been fond of their murdered liege lord, and it was going to be a distinct pleasure for them to see his killer die horribly. The people noted with satisfaction, therefore, that—at the sight of the executioner and the bloodstained weapon in his hand—Hugh's face set in masklike calm, and though he carried himself well and forbore to tremble, they could see his breath come quick and hard.

Gareth grabbed the Hand by the arms and, dragging him out of the wizard's presence, led the prisoner the few steps to the block.

"What you said about Magicka . . ." Gareth hissed the words in a low undertone, and, perhaps feeling the wizard's eyes boring into his back, let the sentence stand unfinished, contenting himself with interrogating the assassin with a glance.

Hugh returned his gaze, his eyes black hollows in the flickering torchlit night. "Watch him," he said.

Gareth nodded. His eyes were red-rimmed and bloodshot, his face unshaven. He had not slept since the death of his lord two nights previous. He wiped his hand across his sweat-rimed mouth; then the hand went to his belt. Hugh caught a flash of fire, reflecting off a sharp-edged blade.

"I can't save you, Hugh," Gareth mumbled. "They'd cut us both to ribbons. But I can end it for you quick. It'll likely cost me my captaincy"—the knight glanced back darkly at the wizard—

"but then, after what I've heard, it's likely I've lost that anyhow. You're right. I owe that much to her."

He shoved the Hand around to stand in front of the block. The executioner solemnly removed his black robes—he disliked having them fouled with blood—and handed them to a young boy standing nearby. Highly elated, the child stuck out his tongue at an unfortunate friend who had been hovering near, hoping for the same honor.

Grasping the sword, Nick took two or three practice swings to limber up his arms and then indicated, with a nod of his head, that he was ready.

Gareth forced Hugh to his knees before the block. The knight stepped back, but not far, only two or three paces. His fingers flexed nervously around the knife concealed in the folds of his cape. His excuse was framing itself in his mind. *When the blade sank into his neck, Hugh screamed out that it was you, Magicka, who killed my lord. I heard it clearly. The words of a dying man are, they say, always true. Of course, I know that he lied, but I feared the peasants—being a superstitious lot—would take it ill. I thought it best to cut his miserable life short.* Magicka wouldn't believe it. He'd know the truth. Ah, well, Gareth didn't have that much left to live for anyway.

The executioner grabbed hold of Hugh's hair, intending to position the prisoner's head on the block. But Magicka, perhaps sensing an uneasiness in the crowd that not even the excitement of a forthcoming execution could quite banish, raised a restraining hand.

"Halt," he cried. His robes swirling around him in the chill wind that had sprung up, the wizard walked toward the block. "Hugh the Hand," said Magicka in a loud, stern voice, "I give you one more chance. Tell us—now that you are near the Realm of Death—have you anything to confess?"

Hugh raised his head. Perhaps the fear of approaching oblivion had finally struck him.

"Yes. I have something to confess."

"I'm glad we understand each other," said Magicka gently. The smile of triumph on the thin, aesthetic face was not lost on the watchful Gareth. "What is it you have to regret in leaving this life, my son?"

The Hand's swollen mouth twisted. Straightening his shoulders, he looked at Magicka and said coolly, "That I never killed one of your kind, wizard."

The crowd gasped in pleasurable horror. Three-Chop Nick chuckled beneath his hood. The longer this death dragged out, the better the wizard would reward it.

Magicka smiled with cool pity.

"May your soul rot like your body," he said.

Casting Nick a look that plainly invited the executioner to have a good time, the wizard stepped back well out of the way, to keep the blood from spattering on his robes.

The executioner drew forth a black handkerchief and started to bind it around Hugh's eyes.

"No!" the assassin shouted harshly. "I want to carry that face with me."

"Get on with it!" Foam flecked the wizard's lips.

Nick grabbed his hair, but Hugh shook the hand free. Voluntarily the prisoner laid his head down upon the bloodstained marble. His eyes were wide open, staring unblinkingly, accusingly at Magicka. The executioner reached down, took hold of the man's short braid, and yanked it over to one side. Three-Chop liked a clear expanse of neck with which to work.

Nick raised his blade. Hugh drew a breath, gritted his teeth, and kept his eyes focused on the wizard. Gareth, watching, saw Magicka blench, swallow, and dart hasty glances here and there, as though seeking escape.

"The horror of this man's evil is too much!" the wizard cried. "Be swift! I cannot bear it!"

Gareth gripped his knife. Nick's arm muscles bulged, preparing for the downward stroke. Women covered their eyes and peeped out between their fingers, men craned to see over each other's heads, children were hastily lifted up to get a better view.

And then there came, from the gates, the clash of arms.

CHAPTER ✦ 3

KE'LITH KEEP, DANDRAK,

MID REALM

✦

A GIGANTIC SHAPE, BLACKER THAN THE LORDS OF NIGHT, APPEARED above the keep's towers. No one could see clearly in the gloom, but the flapping of huge wings was audible. The gate guards clashed sword against shield, sounding the alarm, causing everyone in the courtyard to turn his attention from the impending execution to the threat above. Knights drew their swords and shouted for their mounts. Raids by Tribus corsairs were commonplace, and one had been expected daily in retaliation for the abduction and subsequent death of the elflord who had allegedly hired Hugh the Hand.

"What is it?" bellowed Gareth, endeavoring vainly to see what was going on, torn between leaving his post at the side of the prisoner and rushing to the gates that were his responsibility.

"Ignore it! Get on with the execution!" snarled Magicka.

But Three-Chop Nick demanded an attentive audience, and he had lost this one. Half of the crowd was staring at the gate; the other half was running toward it. Lowering his blade with an air of wounded pride, Nick waited in hurt and dignified silence to see what all the fuss was about.

"It's a real dragon, fools! One of ours, not an elf ship. It's one of ours!" Gareth shouted. "You two, keep an eye on the prisoner." The captain raced to the gates to quell the spreading panic.

The battle dragon swooped low over the castle. A score of rope cables, glistening in the torchlight, snaked through the air. Men leapt from the dragon's back, slid down the cables, and landed in the courtyard. Everyone could see the silver insignia of the King's Own glittering on their panoply, and the crowd muttered ominously.

Swiftly the soldiers deployed, clearing a large area in the center of the courtyard and placing themselves in position around it. Shields in their left hands, spears in their right, they stood at relaxed attention, facing outward, refusing to meet anyone's eyes or answer anyone's questions.

A lone dragonrider appeared. Flying over the gate, the small, swift-flying dragon hovered over the circle cleared for it, wings holding it poised in the air while it scanned the area in which it would land. By now its rider's elegant livery, flashing red and golden in the flaring torchlight, could be easily recognized. The people caught their breath and glanced at each other with questioning eyes.

The riding dragon settled to the ground, wings trembling, its flanks heaving. Flecks of saliva dripped from its fanged mouth. Jumping from the saddle, the rider cast a swift glance around the courtyard. He was clad in the short gold-trimmed cape and red flared coat of a king's courier, and the people waited in breathless anticipation to hear the news he had to impart.

Almost everyone expected it to be a declaration of war against the elves of Tribus; some of the knights were already looking about for their squires so that they might be ready to muster at a moment's notice. It was, therefore, with considerable shock that those standing in the courtyard saw the courier raise a hand gloved in the finest soft and supple leather and point at the block.

"Is that Hugh the Hand you are about to execute?" he shouted in a voice as soft and supple as his gloves.

The wizard strode across the courtyard and was admitted into the circle through the ranks of the King's Own.

"What if it is?" answered Magicka warily.

"If it is Hugh the Hand, I command you, in the name of the king, to deliver him to me—alive," said the courier.

The wizard glowered at the man darkly. Ke'lith's knights looked questioningly in Magicka's direction, awaiting his orders.

Until recently, the Volkarans had never known a king. In the world's very early days, Volkaran had been a penal colony established by the inhabitants of the main continent Uylandia. The famous prison at Yreni held murderers and thieves; exiles, whores, and various other social embarrassments were shipped off to the surrounding isles of Providence, Pitrin's Exile, and the three

Djerns. Life was hard on these outer isles, and over the centuries, the isles produced a hard people. Each isle was ruled by various clans; each clan's lord spent his time either beating assaults off his own lands or attacking those of his neighbors on Uylandia.

Thus divided, the humans were easy prey for the stronger, wealthier elven nation of Tribus. The elves gobbled the humans up piecemeal, and for almost forty cycles, the elves ruled both Uylandia and the Volkaran Isles. Their iron grip on the humans had come to an end twenty cycles earlier, when a chieftain of the strongest clan on Volkaran married the matriarch of the strongest clan on Uylandia. Rallying their people, Stephen of Pitrin's Exile and Anne of Winsher formed an army that overthrew the elves and hurled them—some of them literally—off the isle.

When Uylandia and Volkaran were free of occupation, Stephen and Anne proclaimed themselves king and queen, murdered their most dangerous rivals, and, though it was rumored that they were now intriguing against each other, the two continued to be the most powerful and feared force in the realm. In the old days, Magicka would have simply ignored the command, carried out the execution, and done away with the courier if the man proved obstinate. Now, standing in the shadow cast by the pitch-black wings of the battle dragon, the wizard was reduced to quibbling.

"Hugh the Hand is the murderer of our lord, Rogar of Ke'lith, and it is the king's own law that we take his life in punishment."

"His Majesty fully approves and applauds your excellent and swift execution of justice within his kingdom," said the courier with a graceful bow, "and he regrets that he must interfere, but there is a royal warrant out for the arrest of the man known as Hugh the Hand. He is wanted for questioning in regard to a conspiracy against the state—a matter which takes precedence over all local affairs. Everyone knows," added the courier, looking directly into Magicka's eyes, "that this assassin has had dealings with the elflords of Tribus."

The wizard knew, of course, that Hugh *hadn't* had dealings with an elflord on Tribus. The wizard also knew, at that instant, that the courier knew this as well. And if the courier knew this, then he might know a number of other things—such as how Rogar of Ke'lith had truly met his death. Caught in his own net, Magicka flopped and floundered.

"Let me see the warrant," he demanded.

Nothing, it seemed, would give the king's courier greater pleasure than producing the king's warrant for Magicka's viewing. Thrusting his hand into a leather pouch that hung from the dragon's saddle, the courier withdrew a scrollcase. He removed the scroll inside and handed it to the wizard, who pretended to study it. The warrant would be in order. Stephen wasn't one to make a mistake like that. There was the name, Hugh the Hand, and it was sealed with the Winged Eye that was Stephen's device. Gnawing his lip until it was raw and bleeding, Magicka could do nothing but cast his people a much-suffering glance that said he had tried but greater powers were at work here. Placing his hand over his heart, he bowed coldly in silent, ungracious acquiescence.

"His Majesty thanks you," said the courier, smiling. "You, Captain!" He gestured. Gareth—his face carefully expressionless, though he, too, had followed the unspoken as well as the spoken—came up to stand behind the wizard. "Bring me the prisoner. Oh, and I'll need a fresh dragon for my return trip. King's business," he added.

Those two words—king's business—could commandeer anything from a castle to a flagon of wine, a roast boar to a regiment. Those who disobeyed did so at their extreme peril. Gareth looked at Magicka. The wizard literally shook with rage, but said nothing—merely gave a swift, short nod—and the knight left to obey the command.

The courier deftly retrieved the parchment, rerolled it, and slid it back into its scrollcase. As he glanced about idly, awaiting Gareth's return with the prisoner, his gaze alighted on the bier. Instantly his face assumed an expression of deep sorrow.

"Their Majesties extend their sympathy to Lady Rogar. If they can be of service, her ladyship can be assured that she has only to call upon them."

"Her ladyship will be most grateful," said Magicka sourly.

The courier, smiling once again, began to slap his gloves impatiently against his thigh. Gareth was leading the prisoner past the King's Own, but there was as yet no sign of a fresh mount. "About that dragon—"

"Here, my lord, take this one," cried the old stablemaster eagerly, offering the reins of the lord's dragon to the messenger.

"Are you certain?" queried the courier, glancing from the bier to the wizard. He was, of course, familiar with the custom of sacrificing the dragon—no matter how valuable—in honor of the fallen.

Magicka, with a furious snort, waved his hand. "Why not? Carry my lord's murderer away on my lord's most prized dragon! King's business, after all!"

"Yes, it is," said the courier. "King's business."

The King's Own suddenly shifted their stance, turning their spears point outward and locking shields to form a circle of steel around the courier and those who stood near him.

"Perhaps there are some aspects of the king's business you would be interested in discussing with His Majesty. Our gracious monarch will be happy to arrange for the governing of this province in your absence, Magicka."

The shadow of the wings of the circling battle dragon slid over the courtyard.

"No, no," protested the wizard hastily. "King Stephen has no more loyal subject than myself! You may assure him of that!"

The courier bowed and answered Magicka with a charming smile. The soldiers surrounding him remained attentive and on alert.

Gareth, sweating beneath his leather helm, entered the circle of steel. The captain knew how close he'd come to being ordered to fight the King's Own and his stomach was still clenching.

"Here's your man," Gareth said gruffly, shoving Hugh forward.

The courier took in the prisoner with one swift glance that noted the lash marks on the back, the bruises and cuts on the face, the swollen lip. Hugh, his dark sunken eyes seeming to have vanished completely in the shadows beneath his brows, regarded the courier with a detached curiosity that held no hope, only a sardonic expectation of further torment.

"Cut loose his arms and unlock those manacles."

"But, my lord, he is dangerous—"

"He cannot ride like that and I have no time to waste. Do not worry"—the courier waved a negligent hand—"unless he can sprout wings, I do not think he will try to escape by leaping from the back of a flying dragon."

Gareth drew his dagger and cut the bonds around Hugh's arms. The stablemaster, summoning his helpers with a cry, gingerly entered the ring of steel, removed the saddle from the courier's spent mount, and put it on the back of Lord Rogar's dragon. Patting the dragon's neck, the stablemaster cheerfully passed the reins to the courier. The old man would not see the dragon again; whatever came into King Stephen's hands never left. But it was far better to lose it than be forced to thrust a knife into the throat of a creature who loved and trusted him, then watch its life spill out, wasted on a man dead and gone.

The courier mounted. Reaching down his hand, he held it out to Hugh. The assassin appeared for the first time to comprehend the fact that he was freed, his head was not on the block, that terrible sword was not about to sever his life. Moving stiffly and painfully, he stretched out his hand, caught hold of the courier's, and let the man pull him up on the dragon's back.

"Bring him a cloak. He'll freeze," ordered the courier. Many capes were offered, and he selected one of thick fur and tossed it to Hugh. The prisoner wrapped the cloak around his shoulders, reached back and gripped firmly the rim of the dragon's saddle. The courier spoke a word of command and the dragon, with a trumpeting call, spread his wings and soared upward.

The leader of the King's Own gave an ear-piercing whistle. The battle dragon flew down until the ropes dangling from its back were within the soldiers' reach. Swiftly they climbed back up and took their places on the dragon's large flat back. The dragon lifted its wings, and within moments the shadow was lifted, the sky was empty, night's gray gloom returned.

In the courtyard below, men glanced at each other in silence, their faces grim. Women, eyeing their husbands and sensing the tense atmosphere, hurriedly rounded up children, sharply reprimanding or slapping those who whined.

Magicka, his face livid, stalked into the keep.

Gareth waited until the wizard had departed, then ordered his men to set fire to the bier. The flames crackled as the men and women gathered around and began to sing their lord's soul to his ancestors. The captain of the knights sang a song for the lord he had loved and loyally served for thirty years. When he finished, he watched the leaping, roaring flames consume the body.

"So you never killed a wizard? Hugh, my friend, you might yet get your chance. If I ever see you again . . . King's business!" Gareth grunted. "If you don't show up, well, I'm an old man with nothing left to live for." His eyes went to the wizard's quarters, where a robed silhouette could be seen looking out the window. Having his duties to attend to, the captain walked to the gate to make certain all was secure for the night.

Forgotten, an artist bereft of his art, Three-Chop Nick sat disconsolately upon the block.

CHAPTER ◆ 4

SOMEWHERE, VOLKARAN ISLES,

MID REALM

◆

THE COURIER KEPT HIS DRAGON UNDER TIGHT REIN. GIVEN ITS HEAD, the small riding dragon could swiftly outfly the larger battle dragon. But the courier did not dare fly unescorted. Elven corsairs often lurked in the clouds, waiting to snap up lone human dragonriders. And so the going was slow. But at length the torches of Ke'lith vanished behind them. The craggy peaks of Witheril soon obscured the smoke rising from the bier of the province's fallen lord.

The courier kept his dragon flying near the tail of the nightrae—the battle dragon. It was a sleek black wedge, cutting through night's gray gloom. The King's Own, strapped into their harnesses, were so many black lumps upon the nightrae's back.

The dragons flew over the small village of Hynox, visible only because its squat, square dwellings showed up plainly. Then they passed over Dandrak's shore and headed out into deepsky. The courier glanced up and down, this way and that, like a man who has not flown much before—an odd thing in a supposed king's messenger. He could see two of the three Wayward Isles, he thought. Hanastai and Bindistai showed up clearly. Even in deepsky, it was not truly dark—as dark as legend held night had been in the ancient world before the Sundering.

Elven astronomers wrote that there were three Lords of Night. And though the superstitious believed that these were giant men who conveniently spread their flowing cloaks over Arianus to give the people rest, the educated knew that the Lords of Night were really islands of coralite floating far above them, moving in an orbit that took them, every twelve hours, between Arianus and the sun.

Beneath these isles were the High Realm, purportedly where lived the mysteriarchs, powerful human wizards who had traveled there in voluntary exile. Beneath the High Realm was the firmament or day's stars. No one knew precisely what the firmament was. Many—and not just the superstitious—believed it to be a band of diamonds and other precious jewels floating in the sky. Thus, legends of the fabulous wealth of the mysteriarchs, who had supposedly passed through the firmament, evolved. There had been many attempts made by both elves and humans to fly up to the firmament and discover its secrets, but those who tried it never returned. The air was said to be so cold it would freeze blood.

Several times during the flight, the courier turned his head and glanced back at his companion, curious to note the reactions of a man who had been snatched from beneath the falling ax. The courier was doomed to disappointment if he thought he would see any sign of relief or elation or triumph. Grim, impassive, the assassin's face gave away nothing of the thoughts behind its mask. Here was a face that could watch a man die as coolly as another might watch a man eat and drink. The face was, at the moment, turned away from the courier. Hugh was intently studying the route of their flight, a fact that the courier noticed with some uneasiness. Perhaps sensing his thoughts, Hugh raised his head and fixed his eyes upon the courier.

The courier had gained nothing from his inspection of Hugh. Hugh, however, appeared to gain a great deal from the courier. The narrowed eyes seemed to peel back skin and carve away bone, and might have, in a moment, laid bare whatever secrets were kept within the courier's brain, had not the young man shifted his eyes to his dragon's spiky mane. The courier did not look back at Hugh again.

It must have been coincidence, but when the courier noted Hugh's interest in their flying route, a blanket of fog immediately began to drift over and obscure the land. They were flying high and fast and there was not much to see beneath the shadows cast by the Lords of Night. But coralite gives off a faint bluish light, causing stands of forests to show up black against the silvery radiance of the ground. Landmarks were easy to locate. Castles or fortresses made of coralite that have not been covered over with a paste of crushed granite gleam softly. Towns, with their shining ribbons of coralite streets, show up easily from the air.

During the war, when marauding elven airships were in the skies, the people covered their streets with straw and rushes. But there was no war upon the Volkaran Isles now. The majority of humans who dwelt there thought fondly that this was due to their prowess in battle, the fear they had generated among the elflords.

The courier, considering this, shook his head in disgust at their ignorance. A few humans in the realm knew the truth— among them King Stephen and Queen Anne. The elves of Aristagon were ignoring Volkaran and Uylandia because they had much bigger problems to deal with at the moment—a rebellion among their own people.

When that rebellion was firmly and ruthlessly crushed, the elves would turn their attention to the kingdom of the humans— the barbaric beasts who had stirred up this rebellion in the first place. Stephen knew that this time the elves would not be content with conquering and occupying. This time they would rid themselves of the human pollution in their world once and forever. Stephen was quietly and swiftly setting up his pieces on the great gameboard, preparing for the final bitter contest.

The man sitting behind the courier didn't know it, but he was to be one of those pieces.

When the fog appeared, the assassin, with an inward shrug, immediately gave up attempting to ascertain where they were going. Being a ship's captain himself, he had flown most of the airlanes throughout the isles and beyond. They had been taking a negative rydai,[1] traveling in the general direction of Kurinandistai. And then the fog had come and he could see nothing.

Hugh knew the mist had not sprung up by chance, and it only confirmed what he had begun to suspect—that this young "courier" was no ordinary royal flunky. The Hand relaxed and let the fog float through his mind. Speculating about the future did no good. Not likely to be much better than the present, the

---

[1]Navigational term used in the Tribus Standard. The center for all navigation is the Imperial Palace in Tribus, from which—since early days when the races were at peace—all navigational readings are referenced. A negative rydai refers to moving closer to the current position of Tribus, while a positive rydai refers to heading in the opposite direction.

future could hardly be worse. Hugh had done all he could to prepare for it; he had his bone-handled, rune-marked dagger—slipped to him at the last moment by Gareth—tucked into his belt. Hunching his bare, lacerated shoulders deep into the thick fur cape, Hugh concentrated on nothing more urgent than keeping warm.

He did, however, take a certain grim delight in noting that the courier seemed to find the fog a nuisance. It slowed their flight and he was continually having to dip down into clear patches that would suddenly swirl up before them, to see where they were. At one point it appeared that he had managed to get them lost. The courier held the dragon steady in the air, the creature fanning its wings to keep them hovering in the sky in response to the rider's command. Hugh could feel the courier's body tense, note the darting, shifting glances cast at various objects on the ground. It seemed, from muttered words spoken to himself, that they had flown too far in one direction. Altering course, the courier turned the dragon's head and they were once again flying through the mist. The courier cast an irritated glance at Hugh, as much as to say that this was his fault.

Early in his life, primarily for his own survival, Hugh had taught himself to be alert to all that happened around him. Now, in his fortieth cycle, such precaution was instinctive, a sixth sense. He knew the instant there was a shift in the wind, a rise or dip in the temperature. Though he had no timekeeping device, he could tell within a minute or two how much time had elapsed from one given periodo another. His hearing was sharp, his eyes sharper. He possessed an unerring sense of direction. There were few parts of the Volkaran Isles or the continent of Uylandia that he hadn't traveled. Adventures in his youth had taken him to distant (and unpleasant) parts of the larger world of Arianus. Not given to boasting, which was a waste of breath—only a man who cannot conquer his deficiencies feels the need to convince the world he has none—Hugh had always been confident in his own mind that, set him down where you would, he could within a matter of moments tell where upon Arianus he stood.

But when the dragon, at the courier's soft-spoken command, descended from the sky and landed upon solid ground, Hugh gazed around him and was forced to admit that for the first time in his life he was lost. He had never seen this place before.

The king's messenger dismounted from the dragon. Removing a glowstone from the leather pouch, he held the stone in his open palm. Once exposed to the air, the magical jewel began to give off a radiant light. A glowstone gives off heat as well, and it is necessary to place it in a container. The courier walked unhesitatingly to a corner of a crumbling coralite wall surrounding their landing site. Leaning down, he deposited the glowstone in a crude iron lamp.

Hugh saw no other objects in the barren courtyard. Either the lamp had been left in expectation of the courier's arrival or he himself had placed it there before he departed. The Hand suspected the latter, mainly because there was no sign of anyone else nearby. Even the nightrae had been left behind. It was logical to assume, therefore, that the courier had started his journey from this place and obviously expected to return—a fact that might or might not have much significance. Hugh slid down off the dragon's back.

The courier lifted the iron lamp. Returning to the dragon, he stroked the proudly arched neck and murmured words of rest and comfort that caused the beast to settle itself down in the courtyard, tucking its wings beneath its body and curling its long tail round its feet. The head fell forward on the breast, the eyes closed, and the dragon breathed a contented sigh. Once asleep, a dragon is extremely difficult and even dangerous to wake, for sometimes during sleep the spells of submission and obedience which are cast over them can be accidentally broken and you've got a confused, irate, and loudly vocal creature on your hands. An experienced dragonrider never allows his animal to sleep unless he knows there is a competent wizard nearby. Another fact Hugh noted with interest.

Coming close to him, the courier raised his lantern and stared quizzically into Hugh's face, inviting question or comment. The Hand saw no need to waste his breath in asking questions he knew would not be answered, and so stared back at the courier in silence.

The courier, nonplussed, started to say something, changed his mind, and softly exhaled the breath he had drawn in to speak. Abruptly he turned on his heel, with a gesture to the assassin to follow, and Hugh fell into step behind his guide. The courier led the way to a place that Hugh soon came to recognize, from early and dark childhood memories, as a Kir monastery.

It was ancient and had obviously been long abandoned. The flagstones of the courtyard were cracked and in many cases missing entirely. Coralite had grown over much of the standing outer structures that had been formed of the rare granite the Kir favored over the more common coralite. A chill wind whistled through the abandoned dwellings, where no light shone and had probably not shone for centuries. Bare trees creaked and dry leaves crunched beneath Hugh's boots.

Having been raised by the grim and dour order of Kir monks, the Hand knew the location of every monastery on the Volkaran Isles. He could not remember hearing of any that had ever been abandoned, and the mystery of where he was and why he had been brought here deepened.

The courier came to a baked-clay door that stood at the bottom of a tall turret. He fit an iron key into the lock. The Hand peered upward, but could not see a glimmer of light in any of the windows. The door swung open silently—an indication that someone was accustomed to coming here frequently, since the rusted hinges were well-oiled. Gliding inside, the courier indicated with a wave of his hand that Hugh was to follow. When both were in the cold and drafty building, the courier locked the door, tucking the key inside the bosom of his tunic.

"This way," he said. The direction was not necessary—there was only one possible way for them to go, and that was up. A spiral staircase led them round and round the interior of the turret. Hugh counted three levels, each marked by a clay door. All were locked, the Hand noted, surreptitiously testing each as they ascended.

On the fourth level, at another clay door, the iron key again made an appearance. A long narrow corridor, darker than the Lords of Night, ran straight and true before them. The courier's booted footsteps rang on the stone. Hugh, accustomed by habit to treading silently in his soft-soled, supple leather boots, made no more noise than if he had been the man's shadow.

They passed six doors by Hugh's count—three on his left and three on his right—before the courier raised a warning hand and they stopped at the seventh. Once again the iron key was produced. It grated in the lock and the door slid open.

"Enter," the courier said, standing to one side.

Hugh did as he was told. He was not surprised to hear the door shut behind him. No sound of a key turning in the lock, however. The only light in the room came from the soft glow given off by the coralite outside, but that faint shimmer illuminated the room well enough for the Hand's sharp eyes. He stood still a moment, closely inspecting his surroundings. He was, he discovered, not alone.

The Hand felt no fear. His fingers, beneath his cloak, were clasped around the hilt of his dagger, but that was only common sense in a situation like this. Hugh was a businessman and he recognized the setting of a business discussion when he saw it.

The other person in the room with him was adept at hiding. He was silent and kept himself concealed in the shadows. Hugh didn't see the person or hear him, but he knew with every instinct that had kept him alive through forty harsh and bitter cycles that there was someone else present. The Hand sniffed the air.

"Are you an animal? Can you smell me?" queried the voice—a male voice, deep and resonant. "Is that how you knew I was in the room?"

"Yeah, an animal," said Hugh shortly.

"And what if I had attacked you?" The figure moved over to stand by the window. He was outlined in Hugh's vision by the faint radiance of the coralite. The Hand saw that his interrogator was a tall man clad in a cape whose hem he could hear dragging across the floor. The man's head and face were covered by chain mail, only the eyes visible. But the Hand knew his suspicions had been correct. He knew to whom he was talking.

Hugh drew forth his dagger. "A hand's breadth of steel in your heart, Your Majesty."

"I am wearing a mail vest," said Stephen, King of the Volkaran Isles and the Uylandia Cluster. He was, seemingly, not surprised that Hugh recognized him.

A corner of the assassin's thin lips twitched. "The chain mail does not cover your armpit, Majesty. Lift your elbow." Stepping forward, Hugh placed thin, long fingers in the gap between the body armor and that covering the arm. "One thrust of my dagger, there . . ." Hugh shrugged.

Stephen did not flinch at the touch. "I must mention that to my armorer."

Hugh shook his head. "Do what you will, Majesty, if a man's determined to kill you, then you're dead. And if that's why you've brought me here, I can only offer you this advice: decide whether you want your corpse burned or buried."

"This from an expert," said Stephen, and Hugh could hear the sneer if he could not see it on the man's helmed face.

"I assume Your Majesty requires an expert, since you've gone to all this trouble."

The king turned to face the window. He had seen almost fifty cycles, but he was well-built and strong and able to withstand incredible hardships. Some whispered that he slept in his armor, to keep his body hard. Certainly, considering his wife's reputed character, he might also welcome the protection.

"Yes, you are an expert. The best in the kingdom, I am told."

Stephen fell silent. The Hand was adept at reading the words men speak with their bodies, not with their tongues, and though the king might have thought he was masking his turbulent inner emotions quite well, Hugh noted the fingers of the left hand close in upon themselves, heard the silvery clinking of the chain mail as a tremor shook the man's body.

So it often was with men making up their minds to murder.

"You also have a peculiar conceit, Hugh the Hand," said Stephen, abruptly breaking his long pause. "You advertise yourself as a Hand of Justice, of Retribution. You kill those who allegedly have wronged others, those who are above the law, those whom—supposedly—my law cannot touch."

There was anger in the voice, and a challenge. Stephen was obviously piqued, but Hugh knew that the warring clans of Volkaran and Uylandia were currently being held together only by a mortar composed of fear and greed, and he did not figure it worth his while to argue the point with a king who undoubtedly knew it as well.

"Why do you do this?" Stephen persisted. "Is it some sort of attempt at honor?"

"Honor? Your Majesty talks like an elflord! Honor won't buy you a cheap meal at a bad inn in Therpes."

"Ah, the money?"

"The money. Any knife-in-the-back killer can be had for the price of a plate of stew. That's fine for those who just want their man dead. But those who've been wronged, those who've suffered at the hands of another—they want the one who brought them grief to suffer himself. They want him to know, before he dies, who brought about his destruction. They want him to experience the pain and the terror of his victims. And for this satisfaction, they're willing to pay a high price."

"I am told the risks you take are quite extraordinary, that you even challenge your victim to fair combat."

"If the customer wants it."

"And is willing to pay."

Hugh shrugged. The statement was too obvious for comment. The conversation was pointless, meaningless. The Hand knew his own reputation, his own worth. He didn't need to hear it recited back to him. But he was used to it. It was all part of business. Like any other customer, Stephen was trying to talk his way into committing this act. It amused the Hand to note that a king in this situation behaved no differently from his humblest subject.

Stephen had turned and was staring out the window, his gloved hand—fist clenched—resting on the ledge. Hugh waited patiently, in silence.

"I don't understand. Why should those who hire you want to give a person who has wronged them the chance to fight for his life?"

"Because in this they're doubly revenged. For then it's not my hand that strikes the killer down, Your Majesty, but the hands of his ancestors, who no longer protect him."

"Do you believe this?" Stephen turned to face him; Hugh could see the moonlight flash on the chain mail covering the man's head and shoulders.

Hugh raised an eyebrow. His hand moved to stroke the braided, silky strands of beard that hung from his chin. The question had never before been asked of him and proved, so he supposed, that kings *were* different from their subjects—at least this one was. The Hand moved to the window to stand next to Stephen. The assassin's gaze was drawn to a small courtyard below them. Covered over with coralite, it glowed eerily in the darkness, and he could see, by the soft blue light, the figure of a man standing in the center. The man wore a black hood. He held in his hand a sharp-edged sword. At his feet stood a block of stone. Twisting the ends of his beard, Hugh smiled.

"The only things I believe in, Your Majesty, are my wits and my skill. So I'm to have no choice. I either accept this job or else, is that it?"

"You have a choice. When I have described the job to you, you may either take it or refuse to do so."

"At which point my head parts company from my shoulders."

"The man you see is the royal executioner. He is skilled in his work. Death will be quick, clean. Far better than what you were facing. That much, at least, I owe you for your time." Stephen turned to face Hugh, the eyes in the shadow of the chain-mail helm dark and empty, lit by nothing within, reflecting no light from without. "I must take precautions. I cannot expect you to accept this task without knowing its nature, yet to reveal it to you is to place myself at your mercy. I dare not permit you to remain alive, knowing what you will shortly know."

"If I refuse, I'm disposed of by night, in the dark, no witnesses. If I accept, I'm entangled in the same web in which Your Majesty currently finds himself twisting."

"What more do you expect? You are, after all, nothing but a murderer," Stephen said coldly.

"And you, Your Majesty, are nothing more than a man who wants to hire a murderer." Bowing with an ironic flourish, Hugh turned on his heel.

"Where are you going?" Stephen demanded.

"If Your Majesty will excuse me, I'm late for an engagement. I should've been in hell an hour previous." The Hand walked toward the door.

"Damn you! I've offered you your life!"

Hugh didn't even bother to turn around. "The price is too low. My life's worth nothing, I don't value it. In exchange, you want me to accept a job so dangerous you've got to trap a man to force him to take it? Better to meet death on my own terms than Your Majesty's."

Hugh flung open the door. The king's courier stood facing him, blocking his way out. At his feet stood the glowlamp, and it cast its radiance upward, illuminating a face that was ethereal in its delicacy and beauty.

He's a courier? And I'm a Sartan, Hugh thought.

"Ten thousand barls," said the young man.

Hugh's hand went to the braided beard, twisting it thoughtfully. His eyes glanced sideways at Stephen, who had come up behind him.

"Douse that light," commanded the king. "Is this necessary, Trian?"

"Your Majesty"—Trian spoke with respect and patience, but it was the tone of one friend advising another, not the tone of a servant deferring to a master—"he is the best. There is no one else to whom we can entrust this. We have gone to considerable trouble to acquire him. We can't afford to lose him. If Your Majesty will remember, I warned you from the beginning—"

"Yes, I remember!" Stephen snapped. He stood silent, inwardly fuming. He would undoubtedly like nothing better than to order his "courier" to march the assassin to the block. The king would probably, at this moment, enjoy wielding the executioner's blade himself. The courier gently drew an iron screen over the light, leaving them in darkness.

"Very well!" the king snarled.

"Ten thousand barls?" Hugh couldn't believe it.

"Yes," answered Trian. "When the job is done."

"Half now. Half when the job is done."

"Your life now! The barls then!" Stephen hissed through clenched teeth.

Hugh took a step toward the door.

"Half now!" Stephen's words were a gasp, almost incoherent.

Hugh, bowing in acquiescence, turned back to face the king.

"Who's the victim?"

Stephen drew a deep breath. Hugh heard a clicking, catching choke in the king's throat, a sound vaguely similar to the rattle in the throats of the dying.

"My son," said the king.

CHAPTER ◆ 5

KIR MONASTERY, VOLKARAN ISLES,

MID REALM

◆

Hugh was not surprised. It had to be somebody close to his Majesty, to account for all the intrigue and secrecy. The Hand knew Stephen had an heir to the throne, nothing more than that. Judging by the king's age, the kid must be eighteen, twenty cycles. Old enough to get into serious trouble.

"The prince is here, in the monastery. We"—Stephen paused, trying to moisten a dry tongue—"have told him his life is in danger. He believes you are a nobleman in disguise, hired to take him to a secret hiding place where he will be safe." Stephen's voice cracked. Angrily he cleared his throat and resumed speaking. "The prince will not question this decision. He knows well enough what we say is true. There are those who are a threat to him—"

"Obviously," said Hugh.

The king stiffened, the chain mail clinked, and Stephen's sword rattled in its sheath.

The courier, with a whispered, "Restrain yourself, Your Majesty!" swiftly interposed his body between that of the king and the assassin.

"Remember, sir, whom you are addressing!" Trian rebuked.

Hugh ignored him. "Where am I to take the prince, Majesty? What am I to do with him?"

"I will provide you with the details," Trian answered.

Stephen had apparently had enough. His nerve was failing him. He stalked past Hugh toward the door, turning his body slightly so that he avoided touching the assassin. He probably did it unconsciously, but the Hand, recognizing the affront, smiled grimly in the darkness and struck back.

"There is a service I offer all my clients, Majesty."

Stephen paused, hand on the door handle. "Well?" He did not look around.

"I tell the victim who is having him killed and why. Shall I so inform your son, Majesty?"

The chain mail jingled softly; a tremor shook the man's body. But Stephen's head remained unbowed, his shoulders straight. "When the moment comes," he said, "my son will know."

Stiff-backed, straight-shouldered, the king walked into the corridor; Hugh heard his footsteps receding in the distance. The courier moved to stand next to the Hand, not speaking until he heard—in the distance—the sound of a door slam shut.

"There was no call to say that," said Trian softly. "You wounded him deeply."

"And who is this 'courier,' " returned Hugh, "who hands out the monies of the royal treasury and worries about a king's feelings?"

"You are right." The young man had turned slightly toward the window and Hugh could see him smile. "I am not a courier. I am the king's magus."

Hugh raised an eyebrow. "Young, aren't you, Magicka?"

"I am older than I appear," answered Trian lightly. "Wars and kingship age a man. Magic does not. And now, if you will accompany me, I have clothing and supplies for your journey, as well as the information you require. This way."

The wizard stood aside to allow Hugh to pass. Trian's manner was respectful, but the Hand noted that the wizard was deftly blocking the corridor down which Stephen had passed with his body. Hugh turned in the direction indicated. Trian paused to pick up the glowlamp, removed the screen, and walked near Hugh, hovering close at his elbow.

"You must, of course, look and act the part of a nobleman, and we have provided suitable costume. One reason you were chosen is the fact that you are gently born, though not acknowledged. There is a true air of aristocracy about you that is inbred. The prince is highly intelligent and would not be fooled by a clod in expensive clothes."

After a short walk of no more than ten steps, the wizard brought Hugh to a halt outside one of the many doors lining the corridor. Using the same iron key, Trian inserted it into the lock and the door opened. Hugh stepped inside, and they traversed a corridor that ran at an angle to the first. This corridor was not as well-kept as the former. The walls were crumbling. Footing was treacherous on the cracked floor, and both Hugh and the wizard trod carefully and cautiously. Turning left, they entered another corridor; another left turn brought them to a third. Each successive corridor was shorter than the one previous. They were, Hugh recognized, moving deeper into the building's interior. After this, they began a series of zigs and zags—turns taken seemingly at random. Trian talked the entire way.

"It was advisable that we learn all we could about you. I know that you were born on the wrong side of the sheets following your father's liaison with a serving wench, and that your noble father—whose name, by the way, I was unable to discover—cast your mother out into the streets. She died during the elven attack on Firstfall and you were taken in and raised by Kir monks." Trian shuddered. "It must not have been an easy life," he said in a low undertone with a glance at the chill walls that surrounded them.

Hugh saw no need to comment and so kept silent. If the wizard thought to confuse or distract him by this conversation and the circumvolved route they were taking, Trian was not succeeding. Kir monasteries are built generally along the same plans—a square inner courtyard surrounded on two sides by the monks' cells. On the third side were housed those who served the monks or, like Hugh, orphans taken in by the order. Here, too, were the kitchens, the "study" rooms, and the infirmary. . . .

. . . The boy lying on the straw pallet on the stone floor tossed and turned. Though it was bitterly cold in the dark, unheated room, the child's skin burned with an unnatural heat and he had, in his convulsive struggles, thrown aside the thin blanket used to cover his bare limbs. A second boy, some years older than the sick child, who appeared to be about nine cycles, entered the chamber and stared pityingly down at his friend. In his hands, the older boy carried a bowl of water. Placing it carefully upon the floor, he knelt beside the sick child and, dipping his fingers into the water, dabbled the liquid onto the dry, fever-parched lips.

This seemed to ease the child's suffering. His thrashings stopped and his glazed eyes turned to see who cared for him. A wan smile spread over the thin, pale face. The older boy, with an answering smile, tore a piece of fabric from his ragged clothes and placed it in the water. Wringing it out, careful not to waste a drop, he sponged the child's hot forehead.

"It'll be all right—" the older boy started to say, when a dark shadow loomed over them, a cold and bony hand grasped his wrist.

"Hugh! What are you doing?" The voice was chill and dank and dark as the room.

"I— I was helping Rolf, Brother. He has the fever and Gran Maude said that if it didn't break he'd die—"

"Die?" The voice shook the stone chamber. "Of course he will die! It is his privilege to die an innocent child and escape the evil to which mankind is heir. That evil which daily must be scourged from our weak shells." The hand forced Hugh to his knees. "Pray, Hugh. Pray that your sin in attempting to thwart the ancestor's will by performing the unnatural act of healing be forgiven you. Pray for death—"

The sick child whimpered and stared up at the monk in fear. Hugh flung aside the hand that held him down. "I'll pray for death," he said softly, rising to his feet. "I'll pray for *yours!*"

The blow of the monk's staff caught Hugh across his upper body. He staggered. The second blow knocked him to the floor. Blows rained down upon the boy's body until the monk grew too tired to lift the weapon. Then he stalked out of the infirmary. The water bowl had been broken during the beating. Bruised and battered, Hugh groped about in the darkness until he found the rag—wet with water or his own blood, he didn't know which. But it was cool and soothing and he placed it gently on the forehead of his friend.

Lifting the thin body in his arms, Hugh held the sick boy close, rocking him awkwardly, soothing him until the body in his arms ceased to twitch and shiver and grew still and cold. . . .

"At the age of sixteen," Trian was continuing, "you ran away from the Kir. The monk to whom I spoke said that before you left, you broke into their record rooms and learned the identity of your father. Did you find him?"

"Yeah," answered the Hand, inwardly thinking: So this Trian has gone to some trouble over me. The magus has actually been to the Kir. He has questioned them, extensively, it seemed. Which means . . . Yes, of course. Now, isn't *that* interesting? Who will learn more about whom during this little walk?

"A nobleman?" Trian probed delicately.

"So he called himself. He was, in reality—how did you phrase it?—a clod in expensive clothes."

"You speak in the past tense. Your father is dead?"

"I killed him."

Halting, Trian stared at him. "You chill me to the bone! To speak of such a thing so carelessly—"

"Why the hell *should* I care?" Hugh kept walking and Trian had to hurry to catch up. "When the bastard found out who I was, he came at me with his sword. I fought him—bare-handed. The sword ended up in his belly. I swore it was an accident, and the sheriff believed me. After all, I was only a boy and my 'noble' father was well-known for his lecherous ways—girls, youths, it didn't matter to him. I didn't tell anyone who I was, but let them think I was someone my father had abducted. The Kir had seen to it that I was well-educated. I can sound high-bred when I want to. The sheriff assumed I was some nobleman's son, stolen to feed my father's lust. He was more than willing to hush up the old lech's death, rather than start a blood feud."

"But it wasn't an accident, was it?"

A stone turned under Trian's foot. He reached out instinctively to Hugh, who caught the wizard's elbow and steadied him. They were descending, moving deeper and deeper into the monastery's interior.

"No, it wasn't an accident. I wrested the sword from him; it was easy, he was drunk. I spoke my mother's name, told him where she was buried, and stuck the blade in his gut. He died too quick. I've learned, since then."

Trian was pale, silent. Lifting the glowlamp in its iron lantern, he flashed it into Hugh's deeply lined, grim face. "The prince must not suffer," the wizard said.

"So, back to business." Hugh grinned at him. "And we were having such a pleasant chat. What did you hope to find out? That I'm not as bad as my reputation? Or the opposite? That I'm worse."

Trian was apparently not to be drawn off onto any side paths. Keeping his hand on Hugh's arm, he leaned close, speaking softly, though the only ones to hear them that the assassin could see were bats.

"It must be swift and clean. Unexpected. No fear. Perhaps, in his sleep. There are poisons—"

Hugh jerked his arm from the man's touch. "I know my business. I'll handle it that way, if that's what you want. You're the customer. Or rather, I take it you speak for the customer."

"That is what we want."

Reassured, sighing, Trian walked only a short distance further, then halted before another locked door. Instead of opening it, he placed the glowlamp on the floor and indicated with a motion of his hand that Hugh was to look inside. Stooping, placing his eye to the keyhole, the assassin peered into the room.

The Hand rarely felt emotion of any sort, never showed it. In this instance, however, his bored and disinterested glance through the keyhole at his intended victim sharpened to an intense, narrow-eyed stare. He was not looking at the plotting, scheming youth of eighteen who had sprung from Hugh's reasoning. Curled up on a pallet, fast asleep, was a towheaded, wistful-faced child who could not be older than ten.

Slowly Hugh straightened. The wizard, lifting the glowlamp, scanned the assassin's face. It was dark and frowning, and Trian sighed again, his delicate brows creased in worry. Placing a finger on his lips, he led Hugh to another room two doors down from the first. He unlocked it with the key, drew Hugh inside and softly shut the door.

"Ah," the wizard said softly, "there's a problem, isn't there?"

Hugh gave the room in which they stood a swift and comprehensive glance, then looked back at the anxious magus. "Yeah, I could use a smoke. They took my pipe away from me in prison. Got another?"

CHAPTER ◆ 6

KIR MONASTERY, VOLKARAN ISLES,

MID REALM

◆

"BUT YOU FROWNED, YOU SEEMED ANGRY. I ASSUMED—"

"—that I was feeling squeamish about butchering a small child?"

It is his privilege to die an innocent child, and escape the evil to which mankind is heir. The words came to him from the past. It was this dark and chill room, the cracked stone walls that brought the memory back to him. Hugh drove it down into the depths of his mind, sorry he'd recalled it. A warming blaze burned in the firepit. He lifted a coal with the tongs and held it to the bowl of a pipe the magus had produced from a pack lying on the floor. Stephen, it seemed, had thought of everything.

A few puffs and the sterego[1] glowed and old memories faded. "The frown was for myself, because I'd made a mistake. I'd misjudged . . . something. That sort of mistake can be costly. I *would* be interested to know, however, what a kid that age could have done to earn an early death."

"One might say . . . he was born," answered Trian, seem-

---

[1]Sterego is a fungus found on the isle of Tytan. Humans of that land have long used crushed sterego as a healing balm. Elven explorers during the First Expansion noticed that the slow-burning, pungent sterego was far superior to their own pipethorn plant, and was less expensive to grow. They transported it to their own plantations, but there is apparently something special about Tytan. No other variety can match the original in flavor and aroma.

ingly before he thought, because he cast Hugh a swift furtive glance to see if he'd heard.

There was very little the assassin missed. Hugh paused, the hot coal held over the smoking bowl, and stared quizzically at the wizard.

Trian flushed. "You are being paid well enough not to ask questions," he retorted. "In fact, here is your money."

Fumbling in a purse that hung at his side, he produced a handful of coins and counted out fifty one-hundred-barl pieces.

"I trust the king's marker will be sufficient?" Trian held it out.

Hugh, raising an eyebrow, tossed the coal back into the fire. "Only if I can collect on it."

Puffing on the pipe to keep it lit, the Hand accepted the money and inspected it carefully. The coins were genuine, all right. A water barrel was stamped on the front, a likeness (though not a good one) of Stephen's head adorned the back. In a realm where most things were obtained by either barter or stealing (the king himself was a notorious pirate whose ravages committed among the elven shipping had helped him win his throne), the "double barl" coin as it was called was rarely seen, much less used. Its value was exchangeable in the precious commodity—water.

Water was scarce in the Mid Realm. Rain fell infrequently and, when it did fall, was immediately soaked up and retained by the porous coralite. No rivers or streams ran through the coralite isles. Various plant life growing there trapped water. The cultivation of crystaltrees and cupplants was an expensive, laborious means of obtaining the precious liquid, but it was the main source (other than stealing from the elves) of water for the humans of the Mid Realm.[2] This job would make Hugh's fortune. He would never have to work again, if he chose. And all for killing one little kid.

---

[2]There is an abundance of water in the Low Realm—those isles in the heart of a perpetual storm known as the Maelstrom. But no dragon has yet been found who will fly into the Maelstrom. The elves, with their magical, mechanical dragonships, are able to sail the storm-tossed route and consequently hold a virtual monopoly on water. The prices the elves charge—when they'll sell it to humans at all—are exorbitant. Therefore, the raiding of elven transport ships and of water storage ports is not only financially lucrative for humans, it is a matter of life or death.

It didn't make sense. Hugh balanced the coins in his hand and stood looking at the wizard.

"Very well, I suppose you must know something," Trian admitted reluctantly. "You are, of course, familiar with the current situation between Volkaran and Uylandia?"

"No."

On a small table stood a pitcher, a large bowl, and a mug. Tossing the money on the table, the assassin lifted the water jug and, pouring its contents into the mug, tasted it critically. "Low Realm stuff. Not bad."

"Water for drinking *and* washing. You must at least appear to be a nobleman," returned Trian irritably. "In looks *and* smell. And what do you mean, you know nothing of politics?"

Casting off his cloak, Hugh leaned over the bowl and plunged his face into the water. Laving it over his shoulders, he picked up a bar of lye soap and began to scrub his skin, wincing slightly when the lather stung the raw lash marks on his back. "You spend two days in Yreni prison and see how you smell. As for politics, they have nothing to do with my business, beyond providing the occasional customer or two. I didn't even know for certain Stephen had a son—"

"Well, he does." The wizard's voice was cold. "And he also has a wife. It is no secret that their marriage is strictly one of convenience, to keep their two powerful nations from going for each other's throats and leaving us at the mercy of the elves. The lady would like very much, however, to have power consolidated in her hands. The crown of Volkaran cannot be passed on to a female, and the only way Anne can take control is through her son. We recently discovered her plot. My king barely escaped with his life this time. We fear he would not a next."

"And so you get rid of the kid. That solves your problem, I guess, but leaves your king without an heir."

Pipe clamped firmly between his teeth, Hugh stripped off his pants and splashed water abundantly over his naked body. Trian turned his back, either from modesty or perhaps sickened by the sight of numerous weals and battle scars—some fresh—that marred the assassin's skin.

"Stephen is not a fool. That problem is being resolved. When we declare war upon Aristagon, the nations will unite, including the queen's own. During the war, Stephen will divorce Anne and marry a woman of Volkaran. Fortunately His Majesty is of an age that he can still father children—many children. The war will force the nations to remain united despite Anne's divorce. By the time peace comes—if ever—Uylandia will be too weakened, too dependent on Stephen to break the ties."

"Very clever," Hugh conceded. Tossing the towel aside, he drank two mugs of the cool, sweet-tasting Low Realm water, then relieved himself in a chamber pot in a corner. Refreshed, he began to look over the various articles of clothing that were folded neatly upon a cot. "And what'll make the elves go to war? They've got their own problems."

"I thought you knew nothing of politics," muttered Trian caustically. "The cause of war will be the . . . death of the prince."

"Ah!" Hugh drew on the underclothing and the thick woolen hose. "All very neat and tidy. That's why you must trust the deed to me, rather than handle it yourself with a few magics in the castle."

"Yes." Trian's voice broke on the word; he nearly choked. The Hand paused in the act of drawing a shirt on over his head to give the magus a sharp glance. The wizard kept his back turned, however. Hugh's eyes narrowed. Laying the pipe aside, he continued to dress himself, but more slowly, paying keen attention to every nuance of the wizard's words and tone.

"The child's body must be found by our people on Aristagon. Not a difficult task. When the word goes forth that the prince has been taken captive by the elves, there will be raiding parties sent to look for him. I will provide you with a list of locations. We understand you have a dragonship—"

"Of elven make and design. Isn't that convenient?" Hugh responded. "You had this well-thought-out, didn't you? Even to the point of framing me for Lord Rogar's murder."

Hugh pulled on a velvet doublet, black, braided in gold. A sword lay on the bed. Picking it up, examining it critically, Hugh slid the blade from the sheath and tested it with a quick, deft flick of his wrist. Satisfied, he replaced the blade and buckled the sword belt around his waist. He slipped his dagger into the top of his boot.

"And not only framing me for murder. Maybe committing the murder, as well?"

"No!" Trian turned to face him. "The house wizard murdered his lord, as you, I gather, have already guessed. We were on the watch and merely took advantage of the situation. Your dagger was 'appropriated' and substituted for the one in the body. The word was whispered to that knight friend of yours to the effect that you were in the neighborhood."

"You let me lay my head on the blood-slimed stone, let me see that maniac standing above me with his dull sword. And then you save my life and think that fear alone will buy me."

"It would have another man. With you, I had my doubts and—as you may have gathered—I had already expressed them to Stephen."

"So I take the kid to Aristagon, murder him, leave the body for the grieving father to find, who then shakes his fist and vows vengeance on the elves, and all humankind marches off to war. Won't it occur to someone that the elves aren't really that stupid? They don't need war with us right now. This rebellion of theirs is serious business."

"You seem to know more about the elves than you do your own people! Some might find that interesting."

"Some might, who don't know that I have to have my ship overhauled by elven shipbuilders and that its magic must be renewed by elven wizards."

"So you trade with the enemy—"

Hugh shrugged. "In my business, everyone's an enemy."

Trian licked his lips. The discussion was obviously leaving a bitter taste in his mouth, but that's what happens, thought Hugh, when you drink with kings.

"The elves have been known to capture humans and taunt us by leaving the bodies where they may easily be discovered," Trian said in a low voice. "You should arrange matters so that it appears—"

"I know how to arrange matters." Hugh placed his hand on the wizard's shoulder and had the satisfaction of feeling the young man flinch. "I know my business." Reaching down, he picked up the coins, studied them again, then dropped two into a small inner pocket of the doublet. The remainder he tucked away carefully into his money pouch and stored that in a pack. "Speaking of business, how will I contact you for the rest of my pay, and what assurance do I have that I'll find it and not a feathered shaft in my ribs when I return?"

"You have our word, the word of a king. As for the feathered shaft"—now it was Trian who experienced satisfaction—"I assume you can take care of yourself."

"I can," said Hugh. "Remember that."

"A threat?" Trian sneered.

"A promise. And now," said the Hand coolly, "we'd best get going. We'll need to do our traveling by night."

"The dragon will take you to where your ship is moored—"

"—and then return and tell you the location?" Hugh raised an eyebrow. "No."

"You have our word—"

Hugh smiled. "The word of a man who hires me to murder his child."

The young wizard flushed in anger. "Do not judge him! You cannot understand—" Biting his tongue, he silenced himself.

"Understand what?" Hugh flashed him a sharp, narrow-eyed glance.

"Nothing. You said yourself you have no interest in politics." Trian swallowed. "Believe what you want of us. It makes little difference."

Hugh eyed him speculatively, decided that no more information would be forthcoming. "Tell me where we are and I will find my way from here."

"Impossible. This fortress is secret! We worked many years to make it a safe retreat for His Majesty."

"Ah, but you have my word," Hugh mocked. "It seems we're at an impasse."

Trian flushed again, his teeth clenched over his lip so tightly that, when at last he spoke, Hugh could see white marks upon the flesh.

"What of this? You provide me with a general location—say the name of an isle. I'll instruct the dragon to take you and the prince to a town on that isle and leave you. That's the best I can do."

Hugh considered this, then nodded in agreement. Knocking the ashes from the pipe, he tucked the long, curved stem with its small rounded bowl into the pack and inspected the remainder of the pack's contents. He evidently approved what he saw, for he cinched it tightly.

"The prince carries his own food and clothing, enough for"— Trian faltered, but forced the words out—"for a . . . a month."

"It shouldn't take that long," said the Hand easily, throwing the fur cloak over his shoulders. "Depending on how close this town is to where we're bound. I can hire dragons—"

"The prince must not be seen! There are few who know him, outside of the court, but if by chance he were recognized—"

"Relax. I know what I'm doing," Hugh said softly, but there

was a warning in the black eyes that the wizard thought best to heed.

Hugh hefted the pack and started for the door. Movement glimpsed from the corner of an eye drew his attention. Outside, in the courtyard, he saw the king's executioner bow in apparent response to some unheard command and then quit his post. The block alone remained standing in the courtyard. It gleamed with a white light strangely inviting in its coldness and purity and promise of escape. The Hand paused. It was as if he felt, for a brief instant, the invisible filament, cast out by Fate, wrap itself around his neck. It was tugging him away, dragging him on, entangling him in the same vast web in which Trian and the king were already struggling.

One swift, clean stroke of the sword would free him.

One stroke against ten thousand barls.

Twisting the braid of his beard, Hugh turned to face Trian.

"What token shall I send to you?"

"Token?" Trian blinked, not understanding.

"To indicate the job is done. An ear? A finger? What?"

"Blessed ancestors forfend!" The young wizard was deathly white. He swayed unsteadily on his feet and was forced to lean against a wall to retain his balance. And so he did not see Hugh's lips tighten in a grim smile, the assassin's head incline ever so slightly, as if he'd just received an answer to a very important question.

"Please . . . forgive this weakness," Trian muttered, brushing a shaking hand across his damp skin. "I haven't slept in several nights and . . . and then the dragon ride up rydai and back again in such haste. Naturally, we want a token.

"The prince wears"—Trian gulped and then, suddenly, seemed to find some inner reserve of strength—"the prince wears an amulet, the feather of a hawk. It was given him when he was a babe by a mysteriarch from the High Realm. Due to its magical properties, the amulet cannot be removed unless the prince is"— here Trian faltered once again—"dead." He drew a deep, shivering breath. "Send us this amulet, and we will know . . ." His voice trailed off.

"What magic?" Hugh asked suspiciously.

But the wizard, pale as death, was silent as death. He shook his head, whether physically unable to speak or refusing to answer, Hugh couldn't tell. At any rate, it was obvious he wasn't going to find out any more about the prince or his amulet.

It probably didn't matter. Such magically blessed objects were commonly given to babes to protect them from disease or rat bites or keep them from tumbling headfirst into the firepit. Most of the charms, sold by roaming charlatans, had as much magical power in them as did the stone beneath Hugh's feet. A king's son, of course, was likely to have a real one, but Hugh knew of none—even those with true power—who could protect a person from, say, having his throat cut. Long ago, so legend told, there had been wizards who possessed such skill in their art, but not now. Not for many years, since they had left the Mid Realm and gone to dwell on the isles that floated high above. And one of these wizards had come down and given the kid a feather?

This Trian must take me for a real fool. "Pull yourself together, wizard," said Hugh harshly, "or the kid will suspect."

Trian nodded and gratefully drank the mug of water the assassin poured for him. Closing his eyes, the wizard drew several deep breaths, centered himself, and within a few moments managed to smile calmly and normally. Color returned to his ashen cheeks.

"I am ready now," Trian said, and led the way down the corridor to the chamber where the prince lay sleeping.

Inserting the key in the lock, the wizard silently opened the door and stepped back.

"Farewell," Trian said, tucking the key into the breast of his doublet.

"Aren't you coming? To introduce me? Explain what's going on?"

Trian shook his head. "No," he said softly. He was, Hugh noted, careful to keep his gaze straight ahead, not so much as glancing into the room. "It is now in your hands. I'll leave you the lamp."

Turning on his heel, the wizard practically fled down the corridor. He was soon lost in the shadows. Hugh's sharp ears caught the sound of a lock click. There was a rush of fresh air, swiftly shut off. The wizard was gone.

Shrugging, fingering the two coins in his pocket with one hand, the other reassuringly touching the hilt of his sword, the assassin entered the chamber. Holding the lamp high, he shone it on the child.

The Hand cared nothing for and knew less about children. He had no memory of his own childhood—little wonder, it had been brief. The Kir monks had no use for the state of blissful, carefree childish innocence. Early on, each child was exposed to the harsh realities of living. In a world in which there were no gods, the Kir worshiped life's only certainty—death. Life came to mankind haphazardly, at random. There was no choice, no help for it. Joy taken in such a dubious gift was seen to be a sin. Death was the bright promise, the happy release.

As part and parcel of their belief, the Kir performed those tasks which most other humans found offensive or dangerous. The Kir were known as the Brothers of Death.

They had no mercy for the living. Their province was the dead. They did not practice healing arts, but when the corpses of plague victims were tossed out into the street, it was the Kir who took them, performed the solemn rites, and burned them. Paupers who were turned from the doors of the Kir when they were alive gained entrance after death. Suicides—cursed by the ancestors, a disgrace to their families—were welcomed by the Kir, their bodies treated with reverence. The bodies of murderers, prostitutes, thieves—all were taken in by the Kir. After a battle, it was the Kir who tended to those who had sacrificed their lives for whatever cause was currently in vogue.

The only living beings to whom the Kir extended any charity at all were male children of the dead, orphans who had no other refuge. The Kir took them in and educated them. Wherever the monks went—to whatever scene of misery and suffering, cruelty and deprivation, they were called upon to attend—they took the children with them, using them as their servants and, at the same time, teaching them about life, extolling the merciful benefits of death. By raising these boys in their ways and grim beliefs, the monks were able to maintain the numbers of their dark order. Some of the children, like Hugh, ran away, but even he had not been able to escape the shadow of the black hoods under whose tutelage he had been reared.

Consequently, when the Hand gazed down at the sleeping face of the young child, he felt no pity, no outrage. Murdering this boy was just another job to him, and one that was likely to prove more difficult and dangerous than most. Hugh knew the wizard had been lying. Now he only had to figure out why.

Tossing his pack on the floor, the assassin used the toe of his boot to nudge the child. "Kid, wake up."

The boy started, his eyes flared open, and he sat up, reflexively, before he was truly awake. "What is it?" he asked, staring through a mass of tousled golden curls at the stranger standing above him. "Who are you?"

"I'm known as Hugh—Sir Hugh of Ke'lith, Your Highness," said the Hand, remembering in time he was supposed to be a nobleman and naming the first land holding that came to his mind. "You're in danger. Your father's hired me to take you to someplace where you'll be safe. Get up. Time is short. We must leave while it is still night."

Looking at the impassive face with its high cheekbones, hawk nose, braided strands of black beard hanging from the cleft chin, the child shrank back amidst the straw.

"Go away. I don't like you! Where is Trian? I want Trian!"

"I'm not pretty, like the wizard. But your father didn't hire me for my looks. If you're frightened of me, think how your enemies'll feel."

Hugh said this glibly, just for something to say. He was prepared to pick up the kid—kicking and screaming—and carry him off bodily. He was therefore somewhat surprised to see the child consider this argument with an expression of grave and keen intelligence.

"You make sense, Sir Hugh," the boy said, rising to his feet. "I will accompany you. Bring my things." He waved a small hand at a pack lying next to him on the straw.

It was on Hugh's tongue to tell the kid to bring his own things, but he recalled himself in time. "Yes, Your Highness," he said humbly, bending down.

He took a close look at the child. The prince was small for his age, with large pale blue eyes; a sweetly curved mouth; and the porcelain-white complexion of one who is kept protectively within doors. The light glistened off a hawk feather hanging from a silver chain around the child's neck.

"Since we are to be traveling companions, you may call me by my name," said the boy shyly.

"And what might that be, Your Highness?" Hugh asked, lifting the pack.

The child stared at him. The Hand added hastily, "I've been out of the country many years, Your Highness."

"Bane," said the child. "I am Prince Bane."

Hugh froze, motion arrested. Bane! The assassin wasn't superstitious, but why would anyone give a child such an ill-omened name? Hugh felt the invisible filament of Fate's web tighten around his neck. The image of the block came to him—

cold, peaceful, serene. Angry at himself, he shook his head. The choking sensation vanished, the image of his own death disappeared. Hugh shouldered the prince's pack and his own.

"We must be going, Your Highness," he said again, nodding toward the door.

Bane lifted his cloak from the floor and threw it clumsily over his shoulders, fumbling at the strings that fastened it around his neck. Impatient to be gone, Hugh tossed the packs back to the ground, knelt, and tied the strings of the cloak.

To his astonishment, the prince flung his arms around his neck.

"I'm glad you're my guardian," he said, clinging to him, his soft cheek pressed against Hugh's.

The Hand held rigid, unmoving. Bane slipped away from him. "I'm ready," he announced in eager excitement. "Are we going by dragon? Tonight was the first time I'd ever ridden one. I suppose you must ride them all the time."

"Yes," Hugh managed to say. "There's a dragon in the courtyard." He lifted the two packs and the lamp. "If Your Highness will follow me—"

"I know the way," said the prince, skipping out of the room.

Hugh followed after him, the touch of the boy's hands soft and warm against his skin.

CHAPTER ✦ 7

KIR MONASTERY, VOLKARAN ISLES,

MID REALM

✦

THREE PEOPLE WERE GATHERED IN A ROOM LOCATED IN THE UPPER levels of the monastery. The room had been one of the monks' cells and was, consequently, cold, austere, small, and windowless. The three—two men and one woman—stood in the very center of the room. One man had his arm around the woman; the woman had her arm around him, each supporting the other, or it seemed both might have fallen. The third stood near them.

"They are preparing to leave." The wizard had his head cocked, though it was not with his physical ear he heard the beating of the dragon's wings through the thick walls of the monastery.

"Leaving!" the woman cried, and took a step forward. "I want to see him again! My son! One more time!"

"No, Anne!" Trian's voice was stern; his hand clasped hold of the woman's and held it firmly. "It took long months to break the enchantment. It is easier this way! You must be strong!"

"I pray we have done right!" The woman sobbed and turned her face to her husband's shoulder.

"You should have gone along, Trian," said Stephen. He spoke harshly, though the hand with which he stroked his wife's hair was gentle and loving. "There is still time."

"No, Your Majesty. We gave this matter long and careful consideration. Our plans are sound. We must follow through on them and pray that our ancestors are with us and all goes as we hope."

"Did you warn this . . . Hugh?"

"A hard man such as that assassin would not have believed me. It would have done no good and might have caused a great deal of harm. He is the best. He is cold, he is heartless. We must trust in his skill and his nature."

"And if he fails?"

"Then, Your Majesty," said Trian with a soft sigh, "we should prepare ourselves to face the end."

CHAPTER ◆ 8

HET, DREVLIN,

LOW REALM

◆

AT ALMOST PRECISELY THE SAME TIME HUGH LAID HIS HEAD ON THE block in Ke'lith, another execution—that of the notorious Limbeck Bolttightener—was being carried out thousands of menka[1] below on the isle of Drevlin. It would seem at first that these executions had nothing in common except the coincidence of their time. But the invisible threads cast by that immortal spider, Fate, had just wrapped around the soul of each of these oddly disparate people and would slowly and surely draw them together.

On the night that Lord Rogar of Ke'lith was murdered, Limbeck Bolttightner was seated in his cozy, untidy dwelling in Het—the oldest city on Drevlin—composing a speech.

Limbeck was, in his own language, a Geg. In any other language in Arianus, or in the ancient world before the Sundering, he would have been known as a dwarf. He stood a respectable four feet in height (without shoes). A full and luxuriant growth of beard adorned a cheerful, open face. He was developing a slight paunch, unusual in a hardworking young adult Geg,

---

[1]Menka or, more precisely, menkarias rydai, is the elven standard form of measurement. Classically, it was said to be "one thousand elf hunters high." In modern times, this has been standardized by establishing that elf hunters are six feet tall, thus making the menka equal to six thousand feet. This has led to considerable confusion between the races, due to the fact that elven feet are somewhat smaller than those of humans.

but that was due to the fact that he sat a great deal. Limbeck's eyes were bright, inquisitive, and extremely nearsighted.

He lived in a small cavern amid hundreds of other caverns that honeycombed a large mound of coralite located on the out-skirts of Het. Limbeck's cave was different in certain respects from those of his neighbors, which seemed fitting since Limbeck himself was certainly an unusual Geg. His cave was taller than the others, being almost two Gegs high. A special platform, built of knobwood planks, allowed Limbeck to climb up to the ceiling of his dwelling and enjoy another of the cavern's oddities—windows.

Most Gegs didn't need windows; the storms that buffeted the isle made windows impractical, and in general, the Gegs were far more concerned with what was going on inside than outside. A few of the city's original buildings—the ones that had been built long, long ago by the hallowed and revered Mangers—had win-dows, however. Small panes of thick, bubble-filled glass set into recessed holes in the sturdy walls, the windows were perfectly suited to a lifetime of battering wind, rain, and hail. It was windows such as these that Limbeck had confiscated from an unused building in the center of town and transported to his cavern. A few turns of a borrowed bore-hoogus created the perfect-size openings for two windows on the ground floor and four more up above.

In this, Limbeck established the major difference between himself and the majority of his people. They looked only within. Limbeck liked to look without—even if looking without only brought visions of slashing rain and hail and lightning or (during those brief periods when the storms subsided) the vat-things and hummer coils and blazing bluezuzts of the Kicksey-winsey.

One other feature of Limbeck's dwelling made it posi-tively unique. On the front door, which faced the interior of the mound and its interconnecting streets, was a sign with the letters WUPP painted in red, marching along boldly at a definite uphill slant.

In all other aspects, the dwelling was a typical Geg dwelling—the furniture was functional and made out of whatever material the Gegs could find, there were no frivolous decorations. None could be found that would stay put. The walls and floors and ceiling of the snug cavern shook and quivered with the thump-ing, throbbing, whumping, zizzt, crackle, and clanging of the Kicksey-winsey—the dominant feature, the dominant force on Drevlin.

Limbeck, the august leader of WUPP, did not mind the noise. He took comfort in it, having listened to it, albeit somewhat muffled, in his mother's womb. The Gegs revered the noise, just as they revered the Kicksey-winsey. They knew that if the noise ceased their world would come to an end. Death was known among the Gegs as the Endless Hear Nothing.

Wrapped in the comforting banging and drumming, Limbeck struggled with his speech. Words came easily to him. Writing them down did not. What sounded fine and grand and noble when it came out of his mouth looked trite and pretentious when he saw it on paper. At least it did to Limbeck. Jarre always told him he was far too critical of himself, that his speeches read just as well as they sounded. But, as Limbeck always replied with a fond kiss on her cheek, Jarre was prejudiced.

Limbeck talked aloud as he wrote, in order to hear his words spoken. Being extremely nearsighted and finding it difficult to focus properly when he wore his spectacles, Limbeck invariably took them off when writing. His face pressed close to the paper, his quill scratching away, he got nearly as much ink up his nose and down his beard as he did on his speech.

"It is therefore our purpose, as Worshipers United for Progress and Prosperity, to bring to our people a time of good living *now*, not sometime in a future that may never come!" Limbeck, carried away, banged his fist on the table, sloshing ink out of the inkwell. A small river of blue crept toward the paper, threatening to inundate the speech. Limbeck stemmed the tide with his elbow; his frayed tunic soaked up the ink thirstily. Since the tunic had long ago lost any color it might have once possessed, the purple splotch on the sleeve was a cheerful improvement.

"For centuries we have been told by our leaders that we were placed in this realm of Storm and Chaos because we were not deemed worthy to take our place with the Welves above. We who are flesh and blood and bone could not hope to live in the land of the immortals. When we are worthy, our leaders tell us, then the Welves will come from Above and pass judgment on us and we shall rise up into the heavens. In the meantime, it is our duty to serve the Kicksey-winsey and wait for that great day. I say"—here Limbeck raised a clenched and inky fist above his head—"I say that day will never come!

"I say that we have been lied to! Our leaders deluded! It is easy enough for the high froman and the people of his scrift to talk of waiting for change until Judgment comes. *They* do not need a better life. *They* receive the God's payment. But do *they* disperse it equally among us? No, *they* make us pay, and pay dearly, for our share that we have already earned by the sweat of our brow!"

(I must pause here for cheering, Limbeck decided, and put a blot that was supposed to be a star to mark the place.)

"It is time to rise up and—" Limbeck hushed, thinking he heard a strange sound. Now, how anyone could hear anything in this land, other than the noise of the Kicksey-winsey and the buffeting and roaring of the storms that swept daily over Drevlin, was a mystery to the Welves who came monthly for their shipment of water. But the Gegs, accustomed to the deafening noises, minded them no more than the rush of air through the leaves of a tree would bother an elflord of Tribus. A Geg could sleep soundly through a ferocious thunderstorm and start bolt upright at the rustle of a mouse in his pantry.

It was the sound of distant shouting that aroused Limbeck's attention and, stricken by sudden consciousness, he peered up at a timekeeping device (his own invention) set in a hollow of the wall. A complex combination of whirly-wheels and spokey-spikes, the device dropped one bean every hour on the hour into a jar below. Each morning, Limbeck emptied the jar of beans into the funnel above, and the measuring of the day began again.

Leaping to his feet, Limbeck peered nearsightedly into the jar, hastily counting up the beans. He groaned. He was late. Grabbing a coat, he was heading out the door when, at that moment, the next line in his speech occurred to him. He decided to take just a second to record it and sat back down. All thoughts of his appointment went clean out of his mind. Ink-bedaubed and happy, he once more lost himself in his rhetoric.

"We, the Worshipers United for Progress and Prosperity, advocate three tenets: The first, all of the scrifts should come together and pool their knowledge of the Kicksey-winsey and learn how it operates so that we become its masters, not its slaves. [Blot for cheering.] The second, worshipers quit waiting for a day of Judgment and start to work now to better the quality of their own lives. [Another blot.] The third, worshipers should go to the froman and demand a fair share in the Welves' payment. [Two blots and a scribble.]"

At this juncture, Limbeck sighed. He knew, from past experience, that his third tenet would be the most popular with the young Gegs impatient over serving long hours for inadequate pay. But of the three, Limbeck himself knew it to be the least important.

"If only they had seen what I saw!" Limbeck mourned. "If only they knew what I know. If only I could tell them!"

The sound of shouting broke in on his thoughts again. Raising his head, Limbeck smiled with fond pride. Jarre's speech was having its usual effect. She doesn't need me, Limbeck reflected, not sadly but with the pleasure of a teacher who takes pride in seeing a promising student blossom. She's doing fine without me. I'll just go ahead and finish.

During the next hour, Limbeck—smeared with ink and inspiration—was so absorbed in his project that he no longer heard the shouts and therefore did not notice that they changed in tone from cheers of approval to roars of anger. When a sound other than the monotonous whump and whuzzle of the Kicksey-winsey did finally attract his attention, it was only because it was the sound of a door banging. Occurring some three feet away from him, it startled him immensely.

"Is that you, my dear?" he said, seeing a dark and shapeless blur that he assumed was Jarre.

She was panting as if from an undue amount of exertion. Limbeck patted his pocket for his glasses, couldn't find them, and groped with his hand over the table. "I heard the cheers. Your speech went well tonight, I gather. I'm sorry I wasn't there as I promised, but I got involved . . ." He waved a vague and ink-splattered hand at his work.

Jarre pounced on him. The Gegs are small in stature, but wide of girth, with large strong hands and a tendency to square jaws and square shoulders that give a general overall impression of squareness. Male and female Gegs are equally strong, since all serve the Kicksey-winsey until the marrying age of about forty years, when both are required to retire and stay home to bear and raise the next generation of Kicksey-winsey worshipers. Jarre was stronger even than most young women, having served the Kicksey-winsey since she was twelve. Limbeck, not having served it at all, was rather weak. Consequently, when Jarre pounced on him, she nearly carried him out of his chair.

"My dear, what is the matter?" Limbeck said, gazing at her myopically, aware for the first time that something *was* the matter. "Didn't your speech go well?"

"Yes, it went well. Very well!" Jarre said, digging her hands into his tattered and ink-stained tunic and attempting to drag him to his feet. "Come on, we've got to get you out of here!"

"Now?" Limbeck blinked at her. "But my speech—"

"Yes, that's a good idea. We shouldn't leave it behind for evidence." Letting loose of Limbeck, Jarre hastily caught up the sheets of paper that were a by-product (no one knew why) of the Kicksey-winsey and began stuffing them down the front of her gown. "Hurry, we haven't much time!" She glanced around the dwelling hastily. "Is there anything else lying around that we should take?"

"Evidence?" questioned Limbeck, bewildered, searching for his glasses. "Evidence of what?"

"Of our Union," said Jarre impatiently. Cocking an ear, she listened and ran over to peer fearfully out one of the windows.

"But, my dear, this is Union Headquarters," began Limbeck when she shushed him.

"There! Hear that? They're coming." Reaching down, she picked up his glasses and stuck them hastily and at a precarious slant on his nose. "I can see their lanterns. The coppers. No, not the front. The back door, the way I came in." She began to push and hustle Limbeck along.

Limbeck stopped, and when a Geg stops dead in his tracks, it is almost impossible to shift or budge him. "I'm not going anywhere, my dear, until you tell me what's happened." He calmly adjusted his spectacles.

Jarre wrung her hands, but she knew the Geg she loved. Limbeck had a stubborn streak in him that not even the Kicksey-winsey could have knocked out. She had learned to overcome this on former occasions by moving fast and not giving him time to think, but, seemingly, that wasn't going to work tonight.

"Oh, very well," she said in exasperation, her eyes darting constantly to the front door. "We had a big crowd at the rally. Bigger than anything we'd expected—"

"That's marvel—"

"Don't interrupt. There isn't time. They listened to my words and—oh, Limbeck, it was so wonderful!" Despite her impatience and fear, Jarre's eyes shone. "It was like setting a match to saltpeter. They flared up and exploded!"

"Exploded?" Limbeck began to get uneasy. "My dear, we don't want them to explode—"

"*You* don't!" she said scornfully. "But now it's too late. The fire's burning and it's up to us to guide it, not try to put it out again." Her fist clenched, her square chin jutted forward. "Tonight we attacked the Kicksey-winsey!"

"No!" Limbeck stared, aghast. So shaken was he by this news that he sat down quite suddenly and unexpectedly.

"Yes, and I think we damaged it permanently." Jarre shook her thick mane of short-cut curly brown hair. "The coppers and some of the clarks rushed us, but all of our people escaped. The coppers'll be coming to the Union Headquarters in search of you, my dear, and so I came to take you away. Listen!" Sounds of blows could be heard hammering on the front door; hoarse voices were shouting to open up. "They're here! Quickly! They probably don't know about the back—"

"They're here to take me into custody?" Limbeck said, pondering.

Jarre, not liking the expression on his face, frowned and tugged at him, trying to pull him back up on his feet. "Yes, now come—"

"I'll stand trial, won't I?" he said slowly. "Most likely before the high froman himself!"

"Limbeck, what are you thinking?" Jarre had no need to ask. She knew all too well. "Punishment for hurting the Kicksey-winsey is death!"

Limbeck brushed this aside as a minor consideration. The voices grew louder and more persistent. Someone called for a chopper-cutter.

"My dear," said Limbeck, a look of almost holy radiance illuminating his face, "at last I'll have the audience I've sought all my life! This is our golden opportunity! Just think, I'll be able to present our cause to the high froman and the Council of the Clans! There'll be hundreds present. The newssingers and the squawky-talk—"

The blade of the chopper-cutter smashed through the wooden door. Jarre turned pale. "Oh, Limbeck! This is no time to play at being a martyr! Please come with me now!"

The chopper-cutter wrenched itself free, disappeared, then smashed through the wood again.

"No, you go ahead, my dear," said Limbeck, kissing her on the forehead. "I'll stay. I've made up my mind."

"Then I'll stay too!" Jarre said fiercely, entwining her hand around his.

The chopper-cutter crashed into the door, and splinters flew across the room.

"No, no!" Limbeck shook his head. "You must carry on in my absence! When my words and my example inflame the worshipers, you must be there to lead the revolution!"

"Oh, Limbeck"—Jarre wavered—"are you sure?"

"Yes, my dear."

"Then I'll go! But we'll spring you!" She hastened to the doorway, but could not forbear pausing for one final glance behind her. "Be careful," she pleaded.

"I will, my dear. Now, go!" Limbeck made a playful shooing motion with his hand.

Blowing him a kiss, Jarre disappeared through the back door just as the coppers crashed through the splintered door in the front.

"We're looking for one Limbeck Bolttightner," said a copper, whose dignity was somewhat marred by the fact that he was plucking splinters of wood out of his beard.

"You have found him," said Limbeck majestically. Thrusting out his hands, wrists together, he continued, "As a champion of my people, I will gladly suffer any torture or indignity in their names! Take me to your foul-smelling, blood-encrusted, rat-infested dungeon."

"Foul-smelling?" The copper was highly incensed. "I'll have you know we clean our jail regular. And as for rats, there ain't been one seen there in twenty years, has there, Fred?" He appealed to a fellow copper, who was crashing through the broken door. "Ever since we brought in the cat. And we washed up the blood from last night when Durkin Wrenchwielder come in with a split lip on account of a fight with Mrs. Wrenchwielder. You've no call," added the copper testily, "to go insultin' my jail."

"I . . . I'm very sorry," stammered Limbeck, taken aback. "I had no idea."

"Now, come along with you," said the copper. "What have you got your hands stuck in my face for?"

"Aren't you going to shackle me? Bind me hand and foot?"

"And how would you walk? I suppose you'd expect us to carry you!" The copper sniffed. "A pretty sight we'd look, haulin' you through the streets! And you're no lightweight, neither. Put your hands down. The only pair of manacles we had busted some thirty years ago. We keep 'em for use when the young'uns get outta hand. Sometimes parents like to borrow 'em to throw a scare into the little urchins."

Having been threatened with those manacles often in his own turbulent urchinhood, Limbeck was crushed.

"Another illusion of youth fled," he said to himself sadly as he allowed himself to be led away to a prosaic, cat-patrolled prison.

Martyrdom was not starting out well.

CHAPTER ◆ 9

HET TO WOMBE, DREVLIN,

LOW REALM

◆

LIMBECK WAS LOOKING FORWARD TO THE FLASHRAFT RIDE ACROSS Drevlin to the capital city of Wombe. He had never ridden a flashraft before. Nobody in his scrift had, and there were more than a few mutterings among the crowd about common criminals getting privileges to which ordinary citizens weren't entitled.

Somewhat hurt at being referred to as a common criminal, Limbeck climbed up the steps and entered what resembled a gleaming brass box fitted with windows and perched on numerous metal wheels that ran along a metal track. Taking his spectacles from his pocket, Limbeck hooked the frail wire stems over his ears and peered at the crowd. He easily located Jarre among the throng, though her head and face were hidden in the shadows of a voluminous cloak. It was too dangerous for any sort of sign to pass between them, but Limbeck did not think it would hurt if he brought his thick fingers to his lips and blew her a small kiss.

A couple standing alone at the far end of the platform caught his attention and he was astounded to recognize his parents. At first it touched him that they would come to see him off. However, a glimpse of his father's smiling face, half-hidden by a gigantic muffler he had wound around his neck to ensure that no one knew him, made Limbeck understand that his parents had not come out of filial devotion but probably to make certain they were actually seeing the last of a son who had brought them nothing but turmoil and disgrace. Sighing, Limbeck settled back in the wooden seat.

The flashraft's driver, commonly known as a flasher, glared back at his two passengers, Limbeck and the copper who accompanied him, in the only compartment on the vehicle. This unusual stop in the station of Het had put the flasher way behind schedule and he didn't want to waste any more time. Seeing Limbeck start to stand up—the Geg thought he saw his old teacher in the crowd—the flasher threw both sections of his carefully parted beard over his shoulders, grasped two of the many tin hands before him, and pulled. Several metal hands sticking up from the compartment's roof reached out and grabbed hold of a cable suspended above them. An arc of blue lightning flared, a whistle-toot shrilled loudly, and, amidst crackling zuzts of electricity, the flashraft jolted forward.

The brass box rocked and swayed back and forth, the hands above them that clung to the cable sparked alarmingly, but the flasher never seemed to notice. Grasping another tin hand, he pushed it clear to the wall and the vehicle picked up speed. Limbeck thought he had never in his life experienced anything so marvelous.

The flashraft was created long ago by the Mangers for the benefit of the Kicksey-winsey. When the Mangers mysteriously disappeared, the Kicksey-winsey took over the operation and kept the flashraft alive just as it kept itself alive. The Gegs lived to serve both.

Each Geg belonged to a scrift—a clan that had lived in the same city and had worshiped the same part of the Kicksey-winsey since the Mangers first brought the Gegs to this realm. Each Geg performed the same task his father performed before him and his grandfather before him and *his* grandfather before him.

The Gegs did their work well. They were competent, skilled, and dexterous, but unimaginative. Each Geg knew how to serve his or her particular part of the Kicksey-winsey and had no interest in any other part. Further, he never questioned the reasons for doing what he did. Why the whirly-wheel had to be turned, why the black arrow of the whistle toot should never be allowed to point to red, why the pull-arm needed to be pulled, the push-arm pushed, or the cranky-clank cranked were questions that did not occur to the average Geg. But Limbeck was not an average Geg.

Delving into the whys and wherefores of the great Kicksey-winsey was blasphemous and would call down the wrath of the clarks—the ecclesiastical force on Drevlin. Performing his or her act of worship as taught by the scrift teachers and doing it well was the height of ambition for most Gegs. It would gain them (or their children) a place in the realms above. But not Limbeck.

After the novelty of moving at a terrific rate of speed wore off, Limbeck began to find riding in the flashraft extremely depressing. The rain dashed against the windows. Natural lightning—not the blue lightning created by the Kicksey-winsey—streaked down from the swirling clouds and occasionally fought the blue lightning, causing the brass box to buck and jolt. Hail clattered on the roof. Lumbering around, beneath, above, and through huge sections of the Kicksey-winsey, the flashraft seemed to be smugly exhibiting—to Limbeck, at least—the enslavement of the Gegs.

The flames from gigantic furnaces lit the oppressive and everlasting gloom. By their light, Limbeck could see his people— nothing more than squat, dark shadows against the glowing red— tending to the Kicksey-winsey's needs. The sight stirred an anger in Limbeck, an anger that he realized remorsefully had been banked and nearly allowed to die out as he'd grown absorbed in the business of organizing WUPP.

He was glad to feel the anger again, glad to accept its offer of strength, and was just pondering on how he could work this into his speech when a comment from his companion brought a momentary interruption to his thoughts.

"What was that?" asked Limbeck.

"I said, it's beautiful, ain't it?" repeated the copper, staring at the Kicksey-winsey in reverent awe.

That does it, thought Limbeck, thoroughly outraged. When I come before the high froman, I will tell them the truth. . . .

. . . "Get out!" shouted the teacher, his beard bristling with rage. "Get out, Limbeck Bolttightner, and never let me see those weak eyes of yours in this school again!"

"I don't understand why you're so upset." Young Limbeck rose to his feet.

"Out!" howled the Geg.

"It was a perfectly sound question."

The sight of his instructor rushing at him, upraised wrench

in hand, caused the pupil to beat a swift and undignified retreat from the classroom. Fourteen-turn Limbeck left the Kicksey-winsey school in such haste that he didn't have time to put on his spectacles, and consequently, when he reached the red creaking cog, he took a wrong turn. The exits were marked, of course, but the nearsighted Limbeck couldn't read the writing. He opened a door he thought led to the corridor that led to the marketplace, got a blast of wind right in the face, and realized that this particular door opened on Outside.

The young Geg had never been Outside. Due to the fearsome storms that swept over the land on the average of one or two an hour, no one ever left the shelter of the town and the comforting presence of the Kicksey-winsey. Rife with tunnels and covered walkways and underground passages, the cities and towns of Drevlin were constructed in such a way that a Geg could go for months without ever feeling a raindrop splash on his face. Those who had to travel used the flashraft or the Gegavators. Few Gegs ever, ever walked Outside.

Limbeck hesitated on the doorstoop, peering nearsightedly into the windswept, rain-drenched landscape. Though the wind blew strongly, there was a lull between storms and a feeble gray light was strained through the perpetual clouds—as close as Drevlin ever came to basking in the rays of Solarus. The light made the ordinarily gloomy landscape of Drevlin almost lovely. It winked and blinked on the many whirling and pumping and turning arms and claws and wheels of the Kicksey-winsey. It glistened in the clouds of steam rolling up to join their cousins in the skies. It made the dreary and drab landscape of Drevlin, with its gouges and slag heaps and pits and holes, seem almost attractive (particularly if all one could see was a kind of pleasant, fuzzy, mud-colored blur).

Limbeck knew at once he had taken a wrong turning. He knew he should go back, but the only place he had to go was home, and he was aware that by now word of his getting kicked out of Kicksey-winsey school would have reached his parents. Braving the terrors of Outside was far more attractive than braving the wrath of his father, and so Limbeck, without a second thought, walked Outside, letting the door slam shut behind him.

Learning to walk in mud was an experience all in itself. On his third step, he slipped and plunked down heavily in the muck. Upon rising, he discovered that one boot was firmly mired, and it took all his strength to tug it out. Peering dimly around, Limbeck concluded that the slag heaps might provide better walking. He slogged his way through the muck and eventually reached the piles of coralite that had been tossed aside by the strong digger hands of the Kicksey-winsey. Climbing up on the hard, pocked surface of the coralite, Limbeck was pleased to note he was right—walking was much easier up here than in the mud.

He guessed, too, that the view should be spectacular, and thought he really should see it. Pulling out his spectacles, he hooked them over his ears and gazed around.

The smokestacks and holding tanks, lightning-flinging arms and huge revolving wheels of the Kicksey-winsey thrust up from the flat plains of Drevlin; many of them towering so far into the sky that their steaming heads were lost in the clouds. Limbeck stared at the Kicksey-winsey in awe. One tended, when one served only one portion of the gigantic creation, to concentrate on just that one part and lose sight of the whole. The old saying about not seeing the wheel for the cogs came to Limbeck's mind.

"Why?" he asked (which was, by the way, the very question that had caused him to be thrown out of school). "Why is the Kicksey-winsey here? Why did the Mangers build it, then leave it? Why do the immortal Welves come and go every month and never fulfill their promise to lift us up into the shining realms above? Why? Why? Why?"

The questions beat in Limbeck's head until either these resounding whys or the wind rushing past him or the act of staring up at the gleaming structure of the Kicksey-winsey or all three together began to make him dizzy. Blinking, he took off his spectacles and rubbed his eyes. Clouds were massing on the horizon, but the Geg judged it would be some time yet before another storm swept over the land. If he went home now, a storm of a different sort would sweep over him. Limbeck decided to explore.

Fearing he might fall and break his precious spectacles, Limbeck tucked them carefully into the pocket of his shirt and began to make his way across the slag heap. Being short and stocky and deft in their movements, Gegs are remarkably surefooted. They clump across narrow catwalks built hundreds of feet above the ground without turning a hair in their beards. Gegs desiring to go from one level to another will often catch hold of the spokes of one of the huge wheels and ride it up, dangling by their hands, from the bottom to the top. Despite the fact that he couldn't see very clearly, Limbeck soon figured out how to traverse the cracked and broken piles of coralite.

He was just moving really well and making some headway when he stepped on a loose chunk that tilted and threw him sideways. After that, he had to concentrate on watching his footing, and it was undoubtedly due to this that he forgot to watch the approach of the clouds. It was only when a gust of wind nearly blew him off his feet and drops of rain splattered into his eyes that he remembered the storm.

Hastily Limbeck pulled out his spectacles, put them on, and looked around. He had traveled quite a distance without knowing it. The clouds were swooping down on him, the shelter of the Kicksey-winsey was some distance away, and it would take him a long time to retrace his route among the broken coralite. The storms on Drevlin were fierce and dangerous. Limbeck could see blackened holes blown in the coralite from the deadly lightning strikes. If the lightning didn't get him, there was no doubt that the giant hailstones would, and the Geg was just beginning to think that he wouldn't have to worry about facing his father ever again when, turning completely around, he saw a large Something on the fast-darkening horizon.

Just what the Something was, he couldn't tell from this distance (his spectacles were covered with water), but there was a chance that it might offer shelter from the storm. Keeping his spectacles on, knowing that he would need them to help locate the object, Limbeck tottered and stumbled over the slag heap.

Rain began pouring down, and Limbeck soon discovered he could see better without spectacles than he could with them, and pulled them off. The object was now nothing but a blur in front of him, but it was a blur that was rapidly growing larger, indicating he was getting nearer. Without his spectacles, Limbeck couldn't see what it was, until he was actually standing right in front of it.

"A Welf ship!" he gasped.

Though he had never seen one, the Geg recognized the ship instantly from the descriptions given by those who had. Made of dragon skin stretched over wood, with huge wings that kept it soaring in the air, the ship was monstrous in both appearance and size. The magical power of the Welves kept it afloat, carrying them from the heavens to the lowly realm of the Gegs below.

But this ship wasn't flying or floating. It was lying on the ground, and Limbeck, staring at it nearsightedly through the driving rain, could have sworn—if such a thing were possible for a ship of the immortal Welves—that it was broken. Pieces of sharp wood jutted up at odd angles. The dragon skin was torn and rent, leaving gaping holes.

A bolt of lightning striking quite near him, and the resultant thunder, caused the Geg to remember his danger. Hurriedly he leapt into one of the holes that had been torn in the side of the ship.

A sickening smell made Limbeck gag.

"Ugh." He grasped his nose with his hand. "It reminds me of the time the rat crawled up the chimney and died. I wonder what's causing it."

The storm had settled in; the darkness inside the ship was intense. The lightning strikes were almost continuous, however, providing brief flashes of illuminating light before the ship was once again plunged into pitch-darkness.

The light didn't help Limbeck much. Nor did his spectacles, when he finally remembered to put them on. The interior of the ship was strange and made no sense to him. He couldn't tell up from down or what was floor or wall. Objects were scattered about, but he didn't know what they were or what they did and was reluctant to touch them. He had a fear, in the back of his mind, that if he bothered anything the strange craft might suddenly rise up and fly off with him. And though the thought of such an adventure was somewhat exciting, Limbeck knew that if his father had been mad before, he would positively foam at the mouth to hear that his son had in any way annoyed the Welves.

Limbeck resolved to keep near the doorway, holding his nose, until the storm ended and he could find his way back to Het. But the whys and whats and wherefores that were continually plunging him into trouble in school began buzzing in his brain.

"I wonder what those are," he muttered, staring at a number of fascinating-looking blurs lying scattered about on the floor just a few feet in front of him.

Cautiously he drew nearer. They didn't look dangerous. In fact, they looked like . . .

"Books!" said Limbeck in astonishment. "Just like the ones the old clark used to teach me to read."

Before Limbeck quite knew what was happening, the "why" was propelling him forward.

He was very near the objects and could see, with growing excitement, that they *were* books, when his foot struck against something that was soft and squishy. Leaning down, gagging at the foul smell, Limbeck waited for another lightning flash to show him the obstacle.

It was, he saw in horror, a bloated and decaying corpse. . . .

"Hey, wake up," said the copper, poking Limbeck in the side. "Wombe's the next stop."

CHAPTER ◆ 10

WOMBE, DREVLIN,

LOW REALM

◆

An ordinary felon on Drevlin would have been brought before his local froman for judgment. Petty thefts, drunk-and-disorderlies, the odd brawl—these were considered to fall under the domain of the head of the defendant's own scrift. A crime against the Kicksey-winsey, however, was considered high treason and therefore the defendant was required to go before the high froman.

The high froman was head of the most important scrift in Drevlin—at least that was how his clan viewed themselves and that was how other Gegs were expected to view them. It was their scrift which was in charge of the Palm—the hallowed altar where, once a month, the Welves descended from the heavens in their powerful winged dragonships and accepted the homage of the Gegs, given in the form of holy water. In return, the Welves left behind ''blessings'' before they departed.

The capital city of Wombe was very modern, compared to other cities on Drevlin. Few of the original buildings constructed by the Mangers remained standing. The Kicksey-winsey, needing to expand, had leveled and built over them, thus destroying much of the existing housing of the Gegs. Nothing daunted, the Gegs had simply moved into sections of the Kicksey-winsey that the Kicksey-winsey had abandoned. It was considered quite fashionable to live in the Kicksey-winsey. The high froman himself had a house in what had once been a holding tank.

The high froman held court inside a building known as the Factree. A huge structure, one of the largest on Drevlin, the Factree was made of iron and corrugated steel and was, so legend had it, the birthplace of the Kicksey-winsey. The Factree had long since been abandoned and partially demolished, the Kicksey-winsey having fed parasitically off that which gave it birth. But here and there, standing silent and ghostly within the eerie light of the glimmerglamps, could be seen the skeleton of a clawlike arm.

The Factree was a sacred and holy place to the Gegs. Not only was it the Kicksey-winsey's birthplace, but it was in the Factree that the Gegs' most hallowed icon was located—the brass statue of a Manger. The statue, which was the figure of a robed and hooded man, was taller than the Gegs and considerably thinner. The face had been carved in such a way that it was shadowed by the hood. There was a suggestion of a nose, and the outlines of lips and prominent cheekbones and the rest blended into the metal. In one of its hands the Manger grasped a huge, staring eyeball. The other arm, held in a crooked position, was hinged at the elbow.

Standing on a raised dais next to the statue of the Manger was a tall overstuffed chair. It had obviously been constructed for those built along different dimensions than the Gegs, for its seat was some three Geg-feet off the floor, its back was nearly as tall as the Manger, and it was extremely narrow. This chair was the high froman's ceremonial sit-up-high, and he squeezed his large body into it on occasions of state. He overlapped the sides and his feet dangled well above the dais, but these minor detractions in no way reduced his dignity.

The froman's audience sat cross-legged on the concrete floor beneath the dais or perched on ancient limbs of the Kicksey-winsey or stood around on the balconies overlooking the main floor. On this day, a considerable crowd had jammed into the Factree to witness the trial of the Geg who was a reputed trouble-maker, the leader of an insurrectionist, rebellious group which had finally gone so far as to inflict injury on the Kicksey-winsey. Most of the night scrifts for every sector were present, as were those Gegs over forty who were no longer working on the Kicksey-winsey but were staying home raising young. The Factree was filled over and beyond capacity, and those who could not see or hear directly were kept informed of the proceedings by the squawky-talk—a sacred and mysterious means of communication developed by the Mangers.

A whistle-toot, blowing three times, called for relative silence. That is, the Gegs kept quiet, the Kicksey-winsey didn't.

The proceedings were interspersed with whoosh, thump, whang, zizzt, occasional sharp cracks of thunder, and howling gusts of wind from Outside. Being accustomed to these noises, the Gegs considered that quiet had descended and the ceremony of Justick could be commenced.

Two Gegs—one's shaved face painted black, the other white—stepped out from behind the statue of the Manger, where they had been standing, waiting for the signal. In their hands they held between them a large metal sheet. Casting their stern gazes over the crowd to see that all was in order, the two Gegs began to vigorously shake the metal, creating the effect of thunder.

Real thunder was not in the least impressive to the Gegs, who heard it every day of their lives. Artificial thunder, reverberating through the Factree over the squawky-talk, sounded eerie and wonderful and drew gasps of awe and murmurs of approval from the crowd. When the last vibrations of the quivering sheet had faded away, the high froman made his appearance.

A Geg of some sixty turns, the high froman was from the wealthiest, most powerful clan in Drevlin—the Longshoremans. His family had held the title of high froman for several generations, despite attempts by the Dockworkers to wrest it from them. Darral Longshoreman had given his years of service to the Kicksey-winsey before taking over the duties of his office upon his own father's death. Darral was a shrewd Geg, nobody's fool, and if he enriched his own clan at the expense of others in Drevlin, he was merely carrying on a time-honored tradition.

High Froman Darral was dressed in the ordinary working clothes of the Gegs—baggy trousers falling over thick, clumping boots, and a high-collared smock that fit rather tightly over his stout middle. This plain outfit was incongruously topped by a crown of cast iron—a gift from the Kicksey-winsey—which was the high froman's pride (despite the fact that after about fifteen minutes it gave him a pounding headache). Around his shoulders he wore a cape made of large and ugly bird feathers—the feathers of the tier—(a gift from the Welves), which signified the Gegs' symbolic desire to fly upward to heaven. In addition to the feathered cape, which appeared only at trials of Justick, the high froman had painted his face gray, a symbolic blending of the black and white faces of the Geg warders now standing on either side of him and designed to prove to the Gegs that Darral—in all things—was neutral.

In his hand, the high froman held a long stick from which

dangled a long, pronged tail. At a signal from Darral, one of the warders took the end of this tail and inserted it reverently and with muttered words of prayer to the Manger into the base of the statue. A bulbous glass ball affixed on top of the stick hissed and sputtered alarmingly for an instant, then sullenly began to glow with a bluish-white light. The Gegs murmured appreciatively, many parents drawing the attention of children in the audience to similar glimmerglamps that hung upside-down like bats from the ceiling and lit the Gegs' storm-ridden darkness.

After the murmurs again died down, there was a brief wait for a particularly violent whoosh-whang from the Kicksey-winsey to subside; then the high froman launched into his speech.

Facing the statue of the Manger, he raised his flashglamp. "I call upon the Mangers to descend from their lofty realm and guide us with their wisdom as we sit in judgment this day."

Needless to say, the Mangers did not respond to the call of the high froman. Not particularly surprised at the silence—the Gegs would have been tremendously astounded if anyone *had* answered—High Froman Darral Longshoreman determined that it was his duty by default to sit in judgment, and this he did, clambering up into the seat with the assistance of the two warders and a footstool.

Once he was wedged into the extremely uncomfortable chair, the high froman gestured for the prisoner to be led forward, inwardly hoping—for the sake of his squeezed posterior and his already aching head—that the trial would be a short one.

A young Geg of about twenty-five seasons who wore thick bits of glass perched on his nose and carried a large sheaf of papers, stepped respectfully into the presence of the high froman. Darral stared—narrow-eyed and suspicious—at the pieces of glass covering the young Geg's eyes. It was on the tip of his tongue to ask what the samhill they were, but then it occurred to him that fromans were supposed to know everything. Irritated, the high froman took out his frustration on the warders.

"Where's the prisoner?" he roared. "What's the delay?"

"Begging the froman's pardon, but *I* am the prisoner," said Limbeck, flushing in embarrassment.

"You?" The high froman scowled. "Where's your Voice?"

"If the froman pleases, I am my own Voice, Yonor," said Limbeck modestly.

"This is highly irregular. Isn't it?" asked Darral of the warders, who appeared perplexed at being thus addressed and could only shrug their shoulders and look—in their face paint—incredibly stupid. The froman snorted and sought help in another direction.

"Where's the Voice for the Offense?"

"I have the honor of being the Offensive Voice, Yonor," said a middle-aged Geg, her shrill tones carrying clearly over the distant whumping of the Kicksey-winsey.

"Is this sort of thing—" the froman, lacking words, waved a hand at Limbeck—"done?"

"It is irregular, Yonor," answered the Geg, coming forward and fixing Limbeck with a grim, disapproving stare. "But it will have to do. To be honest, Yonor, we couldn't find anyone willing to defend the prisoner."

"Ah?" The high froman brightened. He felt immensely cheered. It was likely to be a *very* short trial. "Then carry on."

The Geg bowed and returned to her seat behind a desk made out of a rusting iron drum. The Voice of the Offense was dressed in a long skirt,[1] and a smock tucked in tightly at the waist. Her iron-gray hair was coiled into a neat bun at the nape of her neck and was held in place with several long, formidable-appearing hairpins. She was stiff-backed, stiff-necked, stiff-lipped, and reminded Limbeck—much to his discomfiture—of his mother.

Subsiding into his seat behind another iron drum, Limbeck felt his confidence oozing from him and was suddenly conscious that he was tracking mud all over the floor.

The Voice of the Offense called the high froman's attention to a male Geg seated beside her. "The head clark will be representing the church in this matter, Yonor," said the Offensive Voice.

The head clark wore a frayed white shirt with a starched collar, sleeves whose arms were too long, breeches tied by rusty ribbons at the knees, long stockings, and shoes instead of boots. He rose to his feet and bowed with dignity.

The high froman ducked his head and squirmed uncomfortably in his seat. It was not often that the church sat in on trials, rarer still for them to be part and parcel of the Offense. Darral might have known his self-righteous brother-in-law would be in on this, since it was a blasphemous crime to attack the Kicksey-

---

[1] Female Gegs wear skirts—traditional dress—only on formal occasions and only when the whirling gears of the Kicksey-winsey are far away. At all other times female Gegs wear loose-fitting trousers bound by bright-colored ribbons.

winsey. The high froman was wary and suspicious of the church in general and his brother-in-law in particular. He knew that his brother-in-law thought that he himself could do a better job running the nation than he—Darral. Well, he wouldn't give them an opportunity to say that about this case! The high froman fixed Limbeck with a cold stare, then smiled benignly at the Prosecution.

"Present your evidence."

The Offensive Voice stated that for several years the Worshipers United for Progress and Prosperity—she pronounced the name in severe and disapproving tones—had been making a nuisance of themselves in various small towns among the northern and eastern scrifts.

"Their leader, Limbeck Bolttightner, is a well-known troublemaker. From childhood, he has been a source of grief, sorrow, and disappointment to his parents. For example, with the aid of a misguided elderly clark, young Limbeck actually learned to read and to write."

The high froman took advantage of the opportunity to cast a reproachful glance at the head clark. "Taught him to read! A clark!" said Darral, shocked. Only clarks learned to read and write, in order that they could pass the Word of the Mangers in the form of the Struction Manal on to the people. No other Gegs, it was assumed, had time to bother with such nonsense. There were murmurs in the courtroom, parents pointing out the unfortunate Limbeck to any children who might be tempted to follow his thorny path.

The head clark flushed, appearing deeply chagrined at this sin committed by a fellow. Darral, grinning despite his pounding head, shifted his pinched bottom in the chair. He did not succeed in making himself comfortable, but he felt better, having the satisfactory knowledge that in the contest between himself and his brother-in-law he was ahead one to nothing.

Limbeck gazed around with a smile of faint pleasure, as if finding it entertaining to relive the days of his childhood.

"His next act broke his parents' heart," continued the Offensive Voice sternly. "He was enrolled in Prentice School for Bolttightners and one infamous day, during class, Limbeck, the accused"—she pointed a quivering finger at him—"actually stood up and demanded to know *why.*"

Darral's left foot had gone numb. He was endeavoring to work some feeling into it by wriggling his toes when he heard that tremendous *why* shouted by the Voice of the Offense and came back to the trial with a guilty start.

"Why what?" asked the high froman.

The Offense, considering she had made her point, appeared taken aback and uncertain how to proceed. The head clark rose to his feet with a supercilious sneer that promptly evened the score between church and state. "Just 'why,' Yonor. A word that calls into question all our most cherished beliefs. A word that is radical and dangerous and could, if carried far enough, lead to a disruption of government, the downfall of society, and very possibly the end of life as we know it."

"Oh, *that* 'why,' " said the high froman knowingly, frowning at Limbeck and cursing him for having given the head clark an opportunity to score a point.

"The accused was thrown out of school. He then upset the town of Het by disappearing for an entire day. It was necessary to send out search parties, at great expense. One can imagine," said the Voice feelingly, "the anguish of his parents. When he wasn't found, it was believed that he had fallen into the Kickseywinsey. There were some who said at the time that the Kickseywinsey, angered at the 'why,' had seen fit to deal with him itself. Just when everyone believed he was dead and all were busy planning a memorial, the accused had the audacity to turn up alive."

Limbeck smiled deprecatingly, and appeared embarrassed. The froman, after an indignant snort, returned his attention to the Offense.

"He said he had been *Outside*," said the Voice in hushed and awe-filled horror that carried well over the squawky-talk.

The assembled Gegs gasped.

"I didn't mean to be gone that long," Limbeck put in mildly. "I got lost."

"Silence!" roared the froman, and instantly regretted yelling. The pounding in his head increased. He turned the flashglamp on Limbeck, nearly blinding him. "You'll get your chance to speak, young man. Until then you'll sit quietly or you'll be taken from the court. Do you understand?"

"Yes, sir. Yonor," Limbeck answered meekly, and subsided.

"Anything else?" the high froman asked the Offense peevishly. He couldn't feel his left foot at all, and the right one was beginning to tingle strangely.

"It was after Limbeck's return that the accused formed the aforementioned organization known as WUPP. This so-called

union advocates, among other things: the free and equal distri-
bution of the Welves' payment, that all worshipers get together
and pool their knowledge about the Kicksey-winsey and so learn
'how' and 'why—' "

"Blasphemy!" cried the shuddering head clark in hollow tones.

"And that all Gegs cease to wait for the Judgment day and
work to improve their lives themselves—"

"Yonor!" The head clark leapt to his feet. "I ask that the
court be cleared of children! It is appalling that young and impressionable minds should be subjected to such profane and
dangerous notions."

"They're not dangerous!" protested Limbeck.

"Hush up!" The froman scowled and gave the matter some
thought. He hated to concede another point to his brother-in-
law, but this did offer an ideal way to escape from his chair.
"Court recessed. No children under the age of eighteen will be
allowed back in. We'll break for lunch and return in an hour."

With help from the warders—who had to literally pull him
free—the high froman heaved his bulk out of his chair. He
removed the iron crown from his head, rubbed life back into his
tortured posterior, stomped on his foot until he could feel it
again, and breathed a sigh of relief.

CHAPTER ♦ 11

WOMBE, DREVLIN,

LOW REALM

♦

COURT RESUMED, MINUS CHILDREN AND THOSE PARENTS WHO WERE forced to stay home and take care of them. The high froman, with a resigned and martyred expression, put on his crown and once more wedged himself into the torturous chair. The prisoner was brought in, and the Voice of the Offense concluded her case.

"These dangerous ideas, so seductive to impressionable minds, actually swayed a group of young people as rebellious and discontented as the accused. The local froman and the clarks—knowing, Yonor, that young people are by nature somewhat rebellious, and hoping that this was just a phase through which they were passing—"

"Like pimples?" suggested the high froman. This brought the desired laugh from the crowd, although they seemed somewhat uncertain about chuckling in the presence of the frowning head clark, and the laughter ended in a sudden spate of nervous coughing.

"Er . . . yes, Yonor," said the Voice, resenting the interruption. The head clark smiled with the patient air of one who tolerates a dullard in his presence. The high froman, seized with the sudden urge to throttle the head clark, missed a considerable portion of the Offensive Voice's speech.

"—incited a riot during which the Kicksey-winsey, Sector Y-362, sustained minor damage. Fortunately, the Kicksey-winsey was able to heal itself almost immediately and so no lasting harm was done. At least to our revered idol!" The Offensive Voice rose to a screech. "What harm may have been done to those who dared do such a thing cannot be calculated. It is, therefore, our demand that the accused—Limbeck Bolttightner—be removed from this society so that he can never again lead our young people down this path that can only take them to doom and destruction!"

The Voice of the Offense, having rested her case, retired behind the iron drum. Thunderous applause reverberated throughout the Factree. Here and there, however, came hisses and a boo, which caused the high froman to look stern and brought the head clark to his feet.

"Yonor, this outburst only goes to prove that the poison is spreading. We can do one thing to eradicate it." The head clark pointed at Limbeck. "Remove the source! I fear that if we do not, the Day of Judgment that many of us feel to be at last close to hand will be postponed, perhaps indefinitely! I would urge you, in fact, Yonor, to prohibit the accused from speaking in this assembly!"

"I don't consider four hisses and a boo an outburst," said Darral testily, glaring at the head clark. "Accused, you may speak in your own defense. But take care, young man, I'll tolerate no blasphemous harangues in this court."

Limbeck rose slowly to his feet. He paused, as if pondering a course of action, and finally, after profound deliberation, laid the sheaf of papers down on the iron drum and removed his spectacles.

"Yonor," said Limbeck with deep respect. "All I ask is that I be allowed to relate what happened to me the day that I was lost. It was a most remarkable occurrence and it will, I hope, serve to explain why I have felt the need to do what I have done. I have never told this to anyone before," he added solemnly, "not my parents, not even the person I hold most dear in all the world."

"Will this take long?" asked the froman, putting his hands on the arms of the chair and endeavoring to find a certain amount of relief from his cramped situation by leaning to one side.

"No, Yonor," said Limbeck gravely.

"Then proceed."

"Thank you, Yonor. It happened the day I was thrown out of school. I had to get away, to do a lot of thinking. You see, I didn't consider that my 'why' had been blasphemous or dangerous. I don't hate the Kicksey-winsey. I revere it, truly. It fascinates me! It's so wonderful, so big, so powerful." Limbeck waved his arms, his face lit by the holy radiance. "It draws its source of energy from the storm and does it with incredible efficiency. It can even take raw iron from the Terrel Fen below and turn that iron into steel and mold that steel into parts so that it is continually expanding. It can heal itself when it is injured.

"It accepts our help gladly. We are its hands, its feet, its eyes. We go where it can't, help it when it gets into trouble. If a claw gets stuck on Terrel Fen, we have to go down and shake it loose. We push bleepers and turn whirly-wheels and raise the raisers and lower the lowers and everything runs smoothly. Or seems to. But I can't help," added Limbeck softly, "wondering *why.*"

The head clark, scowling, rose to his feet, but the high froman, pleased to have an opportunity to gain one on the church, regarded him with a stern air. "I have given this young man permission to speak. I trust our people are strong enough to hear what he has to say without losing their faith. Don't you? Or has the church been derelict in its duties?"

Biting his lip, the head clark sat back down and glared at the high froman, who smiled complacently.

"The accused may proceed."

"Thank you, Yonor. You see, I've always wondered why there are parts of the Kicksey-winsey that are dead. In some sectors it sits idle, rusting away or getting covered over with coralite. Some parts haven't moved in centuries. Yet the Mangers must have put them there for a reason. Why? What were they supposed to do and why aren't they doing it? And it occurred to me that if we knew *why* the parts of the Kicksey-winsey that are alive *are* alive, and if we knew *how* they were doing it, then we might be able to understand the Kicksey-winsey and its true purpose!

"And that's one reason that I think all the scrifts should get together and pool their knowledge—"

"Is this leading somewhere?" asked the high froman irritably. His headache was starting to make him nauseous.

"Er, yes." Limbeck nervously put his spectacles back on. "I was thinking these thoughts and wondering how I could make people understand, and I wasn't paying much attention to where I was going, and when I looked around, I discovered I had wandered completely outside of the Het town limits. Quite by accident, I assure you!

"There weren't any fierce storms in the area just then, and I thought I'd take a little look around, sort of distract myself from my trouble. It was difficult walking and I guess I was concentrating on keeping my footing, because suddenly a storm struck. I needed shelter and I saw a large object lying on the ground, so I ran for it.

"You can imagine my surprise, Yonor," said Limbeck, blinking at the high froman from behind the thick glass lenses, "when I discovered that it was one of the Welves' dragonships."

The words, echoing from the squawky-talk, resounded in the Factree. Gegs stirred and muttered among themselves.

"On the ground? Impossible! The Welves never land on Drevlin!" The head clark was pious, smug, and self-satisfied. The high froman appeared uneasy, but knew—from the reaction of the crowd—that he had allowed this to proceed too far to stop now.

"They hadn't landed," Limbeck explained. "The ship had crashed—"

This created a sensation in the court. The head clark leapt to his feet. The Gegs were talking in excited voices, many shouting, "Shut him up!" and others answering, "You shut up! Let him talk!" The high froman gestured to the warders, who shook the "thunder," and order was resumed.

"I demand that this travesty of Justick stop!" boomed the head clark.

The high froman considered doing just that. Ending the trial now accomplished three things: it would rid him of this mad Geg, end his headache, and restore the circulation in his lower extremities. Unfortunately, however, it would appear to his constituents as if he had caved in to the church, plus, his brother-in-law would never let him forget it. No, better to let this Limbeck fellow go ahead and speak his piece. He would undoubtedly string together enough rope to hang himself before long.

"I have made my ruling," said the high froman in a terrible voice, glaring at the crowd and the head clark. "It stands!" He transferred the glare to Limbeck. "Proceed."

"I admit that I don't know for certain the ship had crashed," amended Limbeck, "but I guessed that it had, for it was lying broken and damaged among the rocks. There was nowhere to go for shelter except inside the ship. A large hole had been torn in the skin, so I entered."

"If what you say is true, you were fortunate that the Welves did not strike you down for your boldness!" cried the head clark.

"The Welves weren't in much position to strike anyone down," returned Limbeck. "These immortal Welves—as you call them—were dead."

Shouts of outrage, cries of horror and alarm, and a muffled cheer rang through the Factree. The head clark fell back into his seat, stricken. The Offense fanned him with her handkerchief and called for water. The high froman sat bolt upright in shock and managed to wedge himself firmly and inextricably in his chair. Unable to rise to his feet to restore order, he could only wriggle and fume and wave the flashglamp, half-blinding the warders, who were attempting to pull him free.

"Listen to me!" Limbeck shouted in the voice that had quelled multitudes. No other speaker in WUPP, Jarre included, could be as compelling and charismatic as Limbeck when he was inspired. This speech was the reason he had allowed himself to be arrested. This was, perhaps, his last chance to bring his message to his people. He would make the most of it.

Jumping onto the iron drum, scattering his papers beneath his feet, Limbeck waved his hands to attract the crowd's attention.

"These Welves from the realms above are not gods, as they would have us believe! They are not immortal, but are made of flesh and blood and bone like ourselves! I know, because I saw that flesh rotting away. I saw their corpses in that twisted wreckage.

"And I saw their world! I saw your 'glorious heavens.' They had brought books with them, and I looked at some of them. And truly, it *is* heaven! They live in a world of wealth and magnificence. A world of beauty that we can only begin to imagine. A world of ease that is supported by *our* sweat and *our* labor! And let me tell you! They have no intention of ever 'taking us up to that world' as the clarks keep telling us they will, 'if we are worthy'! Why should they? They have us to use as willing slaves down here! We live in squalor, we serve the Kicksey-winsey so that they can have the water they need to survive. We battle the storm every day of our miserable lives! So that they can live in luxury off our tears!

"And that is why I say," shouted Limbeck over the rising tumult, "that we should learn all we can about the Kicksey-winsey, take control of it, and force these Welves, who are not gods at all, but mortals, just like us, to give us our proper due!"

Chaos broke out. Gegs were yelling, screaming, shoving, and pushing. Appalled at the monster he'd unwittingly unleashed, the froman—finally freed from his chair—stomped his feet and pounded the butt-end of his flashglamp on the concrete with such ferocity that he yanked the tail free of the statue and doused the light.

"Clear the court! Clear the court!"

Coppers charged in, but it was some time before the excited Gegs could be made to leave the Factree. Then they milled around in the corridors for a while, but fortunately for the high froman, the whistle-toot signaled a scrift change and the crowds dispersed—either going to perform their service for the Kicksey-winsey or returning home.

The high froman, the head clark, the Offensive Voice, Limbeck, and the two warders with smeared face paint were left alone in the Factree.

"You are a dangerous young man," said the high froman. "These lies—"

"They're not lies! They're the truth! I swear—"

"These lies would, of course, never be believed by the people, but as we have seen this day when you recite them, they lead to turmoil and unrest! You have doomed yourself. Your fate is now in the hands of the Manger. Hold on to the prisoner and keep him quiet!" the high froman ordered the warders, who latched on to Limbeck firmly, if reluctantly, as though his touch might contaminate them.

The head clark had recovered sufficiently from his shock to appear smug and pious again, this expression mingling with righteous indignation and the certain conviction that sin was about to be punished, retribution exacted.

The high froman, walking somewhat unsteadily on feet to which the circulation was only now returning, made his way with aching head over to the statue of the Manger. Led along by the warders, Limbeck followed. Despite the danger, he was, as usual, deeply curious and far more interested in the statue of the Manger itself than in whatever verdict it might hand down. The head clark and the Voice crowded close to see. The high froman, with many bowings and scrapings and mumbled prayers that were echoed reverently by the head clark, reached out, grasped the left hand of the Manger, and pulled on it.

The eyeball that the Manger held in the right hand suddenly blinked and came to life. A light shone, and moving pictures began to flit across the eyeball. The high froman cast a triumphant glance at the head clark and the Voice. Limbeck was absolutely fascinated.

"The Manger speaks to us!" cried the head clark, falling to his knees.

"A magic lantern!" said Limbeck excitedly, peering into the eyeball. "Only it isn't really magic, not like the magic of the Welves. It's mechanical magic! I found one on another part of the Kicksey-winsey and I took it apart. Those pictures that seem to move are frames revolving around a light so fast that it fools the eyes—"

"Silence, heretic!" thundered the high froman. "Sentence has been passed. The Mangers say that you shall be given into their hands."

"I don't think they're saying any such thing, Yonor," protested Limbeck. "In fact, I'm not certain what they're saying. I wonder why—"

"Why? Why! You will have a lot of time to ask yourself why as you are falling into the heart of the storm!" shouted Darral.

Limbeck was watching the magic lantern that was repeating the same thing over and over and did not clearly hear what the high froman had said. "Heart of the storm, Yonor?" The thick lenses magnified his eyes and gave him a buglike appearance that the froman found particularly disgusting.

"Yes, so the Mangers have sentenced you." The high froman pulled the hand and the eyeball blinked and went out.

"What? In that picture? No, they didn't, Yonor," Limbeck argued. "I'm not certain what it is, but if you'd only give me a chance to study—"

"Tomorrow morning," interrupted the high froman, "you will be made to walk the Steps of Terrel Fen. May the Mangers have mercy on your soul!" Limping, one hand rubbing his numb backside and the other his pounding head, Darral Longshoreman turned on his heel and stalked out of the Factree.

CHAPTER ◆ 12

WOMBE, DREVLIN,

LOW REALM

◆

"Visitor," said the turnkey through the iron bars.

"What?" Limbeck sat up on his cot.

"Visitor. Your sister. Come along."

Keys jangled. The closer clicked and the door swung open. Limbeck, considerably startled and extremely confused, rose from the cot and followed the turnkey to the visitors' vat. As far as he knew, Limbeck didn't have a sister. Admittedly, he'd been gone from home a number of years, and he didn't know all that much about rearing children, but he had the vague impression that it took a considerable length of time for a child to be born, then be up walking about, visiting brothers in jail.

Limbeck was just performing the necessary calculations when he entered the visitors' vat. A young woman flung herself at him with such force that she nearly knocked him down.

"My dear brother!" she cried, wrapping her arms around his neck and kissing him with more attachment than is generally displayed between siblings.

"You've got till the whistle-toot blows the next scrift change," said the turnkey in bored tones as he slammed shut and locked the closer behind him.

"Jarre?" said Limbeck, blinking at her. He'd left his spectacles in the cell.

"Well, of course!" she said, hugging him fiercely. "Who else did you think it would be?"

"I . . . I wasn't sure," Limbeck stammered. He was extremely pleased to see Jarre, but he couldn't help experiencing a slight twinge of disappointment at the loss of a sister. It seemed that family might be a comfort at a time like this. "How did you get here?"

"Odwin Screwloosener has a brother-in-law who serves on one of the flashraft runs. He got me on. Didn't it make you furious," she said, releasing her grip on Limbeck, "to see the enslavement of our people exhibited before your eyes?"

"Yes, it did," answered Limbeck. He was not surprised to hear that Jarre had experienced the same sensations and thought the same thoughts he had during the flashraft journey across Drevlin. The two often did this.

She turned away from him, slowly unwinding the heavy scarf from around her head. Limbeck wasn't certain—Jarre's face was pretty much a blur to him without his spectacles—but he had the feeling that her expression was troubled. It might be, of course, the fact that he was sentenced to be executed, but Limbeck doubted it. Jarre tended to take things like that in stride. This was something different, something deeper.

"How is the Union getting along?" Limbeck asked.

Jarre heaved a sigh. Now, Limbeck thought, we're getting somewhere.

"Oh, Limbeck," Jarre said, half-irritable, half-sorrowful, "why did you have to go and tell those ridiculous stories during the trial?"

"Stories?" Limbeck's bushy eyebrows shot up into the roots of his curly hair. "What stories?"

"You know—the ones about the Welves being dead and books with pictures of heaven in them—"

"Then the newssingers sang them?" Limbeck's face glowed with pleasure.

"Sang them!" Jarre wrung her hands. "They shouted them at every scrift change! Those stories were all we heard—"

"Why do you keep calling them *stories*!" Then, suddenly, Limbeck understood. "You don't believe them! What I said in court was true, Jarre! I swear by—"

"Don't swear by anything," Jarre interrupted coldly. "We don't believe in gods, remember?"

"I swear by my love for you, my dear," said Limbeck, "that all I said was true. All those things really happened to me. It was that sight and the knowledge it brought—the knowledge that these Welves aren't gods at all, but mortals just like us—that gave me the inspiration to start our Union. It's the memory of that sight which gives me the courage to face what I am facing now," he said with a quiet dignity that touched Jarre to the heart.

Weeping, she threw herself into his arms again.

Patting her comfortingly on her broad back, Limbeck asked gently, "Have I hurt the cause a great deal?"

"No-o-o," hedged Jarre in a muffled voice, keeping her face buried in Limbeck's now-tear-sodden tunic. "Actually, uh . . . You see, my dear, we let it . . . um . . . be known that the torture and hardship you suffered at the hands of the brutal imperialist—"

"But they haven't tortured me. They've really been very nice to me, my dear."

"Oh, Limbeck!" cried Jarre, pushing away from him in exasperation. "You're hopeless!"

"I'm sorry," said Limbeck.

"Now, listen to me," Jarre continued briskly, wiping her eyes. "We don't have much time. The most important thing we've got going for us right now is this execution of yours. So don't mess that up! Don't"—she raised a warning finger—"say anything more about dead Welves and suchlike."

Limbeck sighed. "I won't," he promised.

"You're a martyr for the cause. Don't forget that. And for our cause's sake, try to look the part." She cast a disapproving eye over his stout figure. "I believe you've actually gained weight!"

"The prison food is really quite—"

"Think of someone besides yourself at a time like this, Limbeck," Jarre scolded. "You've got only tonight left. You can't look emaciated by that time, I suppose, but do the best you can. Could you manage to bloody yourself up?"

"I don't think so," Limbeck said abjectly, aware of his limitations.

"Well, we'll have to make the best of it." Jarre sighed. "Whatever you do, try to at least *look* martyred."

"I'm not sure how."

"Oh, you know—brave, dignified, defiant, forgiving."

"All at once?"

"The forgiving part is *very* important. You might even say something along those lines as they're strapping you onto the lightning bird."

"Forgiveness," muttered Limbeck, committing it to memory.

"And a final defiant shout when they shove you off the edge. Something about 'WUPP forever . . . they'll never defeat us.' And you returning, of course."

"Defiance. WUPP forever. Me returning." Limbeck peered at her myopically. "Am I? Returning?"

"Well, of course. I said we'd get you out and I meant it. You didn't think we'd let them execute you, did you?"

"Well, I—"

"You're such a druskh," Jarre said, playfully ruffling up his hair. "Now, you know how this bird thing works—"

The whistle-toot went off, its blast resounding through the city.

"Time!" shouted the turnkey. His fat face pressed against the iron bars of the door to the visitors' vat. He began to rattle the opener in the closer.

Jarre, a look of annoyance on her face, walked over to the door and peered through the bars. "Five more tocks."

The turnkey frowned.

"Remember," said Jarre, holding up a formidable-looking fist, "that you'll be letting *me* out."

The turnkey, muttering something unintelligible, walked away.

"Now," said Jarre, turning around again, "where was I? Oh, yes. This bird contraption. According to Lof Lectric—"

"What does *he* know about it?" demanded Limbeck jealously.

"He's with the Lectriczinger scrift," replied Jarre in lofty tones. "They fly the lightning birds to harvest lectric for the Kicksey-winsey. Lof says that they'll put you on top of what looks like two giant wings made out of wood and tier feathers with a cable attached. They strap you to this thing and then shove you off above the Steps of Terrel Fen. You float around in the storm and get hit by hail and driving rain and sleet—"

"Not lightning?" asked Limbeck nervously.

"No." Jarre was reassuring.

"But it's called a lightning bird."

"It's only a name."

"But with my weight on it, won't it sink instead of fly up into the air?"

"Of course! Will you stop interrupting me?"

"Yes," said Limbeck meekly.

"The contraption will begin to fall, snapping the cable. The lightning bird will eventually crash into one of the isles of the Terrel Fen."

"It will?" Limbeck was pale.

"But don't worry. Lof says that the main frame is almost certain to withstand the impact. It's very strong. The Kicksey-winsey produces the wooden sticks—"

"Why, I wonder?" mused Limbeck. "Why should the Kicksey-winsey make wooden sticks?"

"How would I know!" Jarre shouted. "And what does it

matter anyway! Now, listen to me." She put both hands on his beard and tugged until she saw tears in his eyes, long experience having taught her that this was one sure way of getting his mind off its latest tangent. "You'll land on one of the islands of the Terrel Fen. These islands are being mined by the Kicksey-winsey. When the dig-claws come down to dig up the ore, you must put a mark on one of them. Our people will be watching for it, and when the dig-claw comes back up, we'll see your mark and know which island you're on."

"That's a very good plan, my dear!" Limbeck smiled at her in admiration.

"Thank you." Jarre flushed with pleasure. "All you have to do is stay away from the dig-claws so that you won't get mined yourself."

"Yes, I'll do that."

"The next time the dig-claws come down, we'll make certain that a help-hand is lowered." Seeing Limbeck look puzzled, Jarre patiently explained. "You know—one of the claws with a bubble clutched in it that carries a Geg down to the isle to free a stuck claw."

"Is that how they do it?" Limbeck marveled.

"I wish you'd served the Kicksey-winsey!" Jarre said, tugging on his beard in irritation. "There, I'm sorry. I didn't mean it." She kissed him and rubbed his cheeks to erase the pain. "You're going to be all right. Just remember that. When we bring you up, we'll put it out that you were judged innocent. It will be obvious that Mangers support you, and that therefore they support our cause. We'll have Gegs flocking to join us! The day of revolution will dawn!" Jarre's eyes gleamed.

"Yes! Wonderful!" Limbeck was caught up in her enthusiasm.

The turnkey, nose thrust between the bars, coughed meaningfully.

"All right, I'm coming!" Jarre wound her scarf back around her head. With some difficulty, muffled by the scarf, she kissed Limbeck a final time, leaving fuzz in his mouth. The turnkey opened the door. "Remember," Jarre said mysteriously, "martyred."

"Martyred," Limbeck agreed good-naturedly.

"And no more stories about dead gods!" The last was said in a piercing whisper as the turnkey hustled her away.

"They're not"—Limbeck began—"stories."

He said the last with a sigh. Jarre was gone.

CHAPTER • 13

WOMBE, DREVLIN,

LOW REALM

•

THE GEGS, A VERY GENTLE AND GOOD-NATURED PEOPLE, HAD NEVER, in their entire history (that they could remember), been to war. Taking another Geg's life was unheard-of, undreamt-of, unthinkable. Only the Kicksey-winsey had the right to kill a Geg, and that was generally by accident. And, although the Gegs had execution down on their lawbooks as a punishment for certain terrible crimes, they couldn't ever bring themselves to actually put another one of their fellows to death. Therefore they dumped it in the laps of the Mangers, who weren't around to protest. If the Mangers wanted the condemned to live, they'd see to it that he lived. If they didn't, he didn't.

Walking the Steps of Terrel Fen was the Gegs' term for this method of ridding themselves of undesirables. The Terrel Fen are a series of small islands that float beneath Drevlin, revolving downward in a never-ending spiral until they eventually vanish into the swirling clouds of the All-dark. It was said that in the ancient days, just after the Sundering, it was actually possible to "walk" the Terrel Fen, the islands being close enough to Drevlin that a Geg could leap from one to the other. The ancient Gegs presumably forced their criminals to do this very thing.

Over the centuries, however, the islands had gradually been pulled deeper and deeper into the Maelstrom, so that now one could—during pauses in the storm—only vaguely make out the shape of the nearest island drifting down below. As one of their more ingenuous high fromen pointed out, a Geg would have to sprout wings in order to survive long enough for the Mangers to judge him on the way down. This led, quite naturally, to the Gegs thoughtfully providing wings for the condemned, which led to the development of the "bird contraption" that Jarre had described.

"The "Feathers of Justick" was its formal appellation. It was made of the finely shaped and neatly trimmed wood pieces spit out by the Kicksey-winsey for use in the lectriczingers.

The wooden frame, four feet wide, had a wingspan of about fourteen feet. The frame was covered with a woven material (another product of the Kicksey-winsey) that was then decorated with tier feathers, held in place by a sticky substance made of flour and water. Ordinarily, a strong cable attached to the lectriczinger allowed it to zoom up into the heart of the storm and harvest lightning. But, of course, it couldn't very well do this with a two-hundred-rock Geg weighing it down.

During a lull in the storms, the offending Geg was taken to the edge of Drevlin and placed in the center of the Feathers of Justick. His wrists were strapped securely to the wooden frame, his feet dangled out over the back end. Six clarks lifted the contraption and, at the order of the high froman, ran with it to the edge of the isle and cast it off.

The only Gegs present to witness the execution were the high froman, the head clark, and six minor clarks necessary to send the Wings of Justick into the air. Long ago, all Gegs not serving the Kicksey-winsey had attended executions. But then had come the sensational "walking" of the notorious Dirk Screw. Drunk on the job, Dirk fell asleep, and didn't notice the tiny hand on the whistle-toot attached to the bubble-boiler waving at him wildly. The resultant explosion parboiled several Gegs and— what was worse—seriously damaged the Kicksey-winsey, which was obliged to shut itself down for a day and a half to effect repairs.

Dirk, though severely steam-burned, was taken alive and was sentenced to Walking the Steps. Crowds of Gegs came to witness the execution. Those at the back, complaining that they couldn't see, began to push and shove their way to the front, with the tragic result that numerous Gegs standing on the edge of the isle took unexpected "walks." The high froman banned all further public viewing of executions from that time forward.

On this occasion, the public didn't miss much. Limbeck was so fascinated by the proceedings that he completely forgot to look martyred, and highly annoyed the clarks, who were strapping his hands to the wooden frame, with his endless string of questions.

"What is this stuff made from?" Referring to the paste. "What holds the frame together? How big are the sheets of fabric wrapped around the frame? Do they come that big? Really? Why does the Kicksey-winsey make fabric?"

Finally the head clark, in the interests of protecting the innocent, decreed that a gag be placed in Limbeck's mouth. This was done, and the Feathers of Justick was ready to be cast off into the air without ceremony at the hurried command of the high froman, who—crown on his head—had a splitting headache and wasn't able to enjoy the execution in the slightest.

Six stout clarks grasped the main-frame section of the Feathers and hoisted it up over their heads. At the signal from the head clark, they broke into a lumbering run, dashing down a ramp, heading for the edge of the isle. Suddenly and unexpectedly, a gust of wind caught the Feathers, snatched it from their hands, and lifted it into the air. The Feathers bucked and lurched, spun around three times, then crashed down to the ground.

"What the samhill are you doing out there?" shouted the high froman. "What the samhill are they doing out there?" he demanded of his brother-in-law, who—looking harassed—ran to the edge to find out.

The clarks extricated Limbeck from the broken lectriczinger and brought him, dizzy and spitting feathers out of his mouth, back to the starting platform. Another Feathers of Justick was procured—the high froman fuming at the delay—and Limbeck was strapped on. The clarks received a stern lecture from their superior about the need to hold on tightly to the frame, and then they were off.

The wind lifted the Feathers at just the right moment and Limbeck sailed gracefully into the air. The cable snapped. The clarks, the head clark, and the high froman stood at the edge of the isle watching the feathered contraption glide slowly outward and sink slowly downward.

Somehow or other, Limbeck must have managed to yank the gag from his mouth, because Darral Longshoreman could have sworn that he heard a last "Whyyyyy?" trail off into the heart of the Maelstrom. Removing the iron crown off his head, he fought back an impulse to hurl it over the edge of the isle, and—heaving a vast sigh of relief—returned to his home in the holding tank.

*   *   *

Limbeck, floating on the air currents swirling him gently round and round, twisted his neck to look at the isle of Drevlin above him. For many moments he enjoyed the sensation of flying, circling lazily beneath the isle, peering up at the coralite formations that appeared unique from this viewpoint—much different than when seen from up above. Limbeck wasn't wearing his spectacles (he had them wrapped in a handkerchief tucked safely away in a pocket of his trousers), but having been caught in an updraft, he found himself swept quite close to the bottom of the isle and therefore had an excellent view.

Millions and millions of holes bored up into the interior. Some were extremely large—Limbeck could easily have sailed into one if he had been able to manage the wings. He was quite startled to see thousands of bubbles drifting out of these holes. They burst almost immediately when they hit the open air, and Limbeck realized in a flash that he had happened on a remarkable discovery.

"The coralite must produce some sort of gas that is lighter than air and so keeps the island afloat." His mind went to the picture he'd seen on the Eyeball. "Why would some islands float higher than others? Why would the island that the Welves live on, for example, be higher than ours? Their island must weigh less, that's logical. But why? Ah, of course." Limbeck didn't notice, but he was rapidly descending in a spiral that would have made him dizzy if he had thought about it. "Mineral deposits. That would account for the difference in weight. We must have more mineral deposits—such as iron and so forth—on our island than the Welves do on theirs. Which is probably why the Mangers built the Kicksey-winsey down here instead of up there. But that still doesn't explain why it was built in the first place."

Moved to write down his latest observation, Limbeck was irritated to find that his hands were tied to something. Looking to see what, he was recalled to his current interesting, if desperate, situation. The sky around him was growing rapidly darker. He could no longer see anything of Drevlin. The wind was blowing harder and had taken on a distinct circular motion; the ride was growing considerably more bumpy and erratic. He was tossed this way and that way, upward and downward and around and around. Rain began to pelt down on him, and Limbeck made another discovery. Although not as momentous as the first, this one had rather more impact.

The paste solution holding the feathers to the fabric dissolved in water. Limbeck watched in growing alarm as, one by one and then in clumps, the tier feathers began sliding off. Limbeck's first impulse was to loosen his hands, although what he would do when his hands were loose wasn't exactly obvious. He gave a violent tug at his right wrist. This had the effect—and a startling effect it was—of causing the contraption to flip completely over in midair.

Limbeck found himself hanging by his wrists from the rapidly defeathering wings, staring down at his feet. After the first moment of sickening panic subsided and Limbeck was fairly certain he wasn't going to throw up, he noticed that his situation had improved. The fabric, now missing most of the feathers, billowed out above him, slowing his rate of descent, and though he was still getting tossed around considerably, the motion was more stable and less erratic.

The laws of aerodynamics were just beginning to emerge from Limbeck's fertile mind when he saw, materializing out of the storm clouds below him, a darkish blob. Squinting, Limbeck ascertained at length that the blob was one of the islands of the Terrel Fen. It had seemed to him that when he was among the clouds, he was drifting down very slowly, and he was astonished to note that the isle appeared to be rising up to meet him at an alarming rate of speed. It was at this point that Limbeck discovered two laws simultaneously: the theory of relativity being one, the law of gravity being another.

Unfortunately, both laws were driven clean out of his head by the impact.

CHAPTER ◆ 14

SOMEWHERE, UYLANDIA CLUSTER,

MID REALM

◆

THE MORNING LIMBECK WAS GLIDING DOWNWARD INTO THE TERREL FEN, Hugh and the prince were flying dragonback into the nightside somewhere over the Uylandia Cluster. The flight was cold and cheerless. Trian had given the dragon its directions, so that Hugh had nothing to do but sit in the saddle and think. He could not even tell what track they were flying, for a magical cloud accompanied them.

The dragon would occasionally dip down below the cloud to get its bearings, and then Hugh tried to glean, from the softly glowing coralite landscape moving smoothly beneath them, some idea of where he was and where he had been. Hugh had no doubt but that he'd been double-crossed, and he would have given half the money in his purse to know the whereabouts of Stephen's hideout in case he decided to complain about his treatment in person. It was useless, however, and he soon gave up.

"I'm hungry—" began Bane, his childish high voice splitting the still night air.

"Hold your tongue!" snapped Hugh.

He heard a swift intake of breath. Glancing around, he saw the boy's eyes widen and shimmer with tears. The kid had probably never been yelled at in his entire life.

"Sound carries clearly in the night air, Your Highness," said the Hand softly. "If someone is following us, we don't want to make it easy for him."

"Is someone following us?" Bane was pale but undaunted, and Hugh gave the kid credit for courage.

"I think so, Your Highness. But don't worry."

The prince pressed his lips tightly together. Timidly he slid his arms around Hugh's waist. "That doesn't bother you, does it?" he whispered.

Small arms tightened around Hugh, he felt a warm body nestle against his, and the child's head rested lightly on his strong back. "I'm not afraid," Bane added stoutly, "it's just nicer when you're close."

A strange sensation swept over the assassin. Hugh felt suddenly dark and empty and abhorrently evil. Gritting his teeth, he resisted the impulse to free himself of the kid's touch by concentrating on their immediate danger.

Someone *was* following them. Whoever it was, he was good at it, too. Twisting around in the saddle, Hugh searched the sky, hoping that their shadow—fearful of losing sight of them—might grow careless and show himself. Hugh saw nothing, however. He couldn't even have told exactly how he knew they had company. It was a prickling at the back of his neck, instinct reacting to a sound, a smell, something glimpsed from the corner of the eye. He quietly accepted the warning, his one thought: Who was trailing them and why?

Trian. There was that possibility, of course, but Hugh discounted it. The wizard knew their destination better than they did. He might have been following them to make certain the Hand didn't attempt to subvert the dragon and make off with it. That would have been foolish in the extreme. Hugh was no wizard, he knew better than to meddle with a spell, especially one laid on a dragon. Ensorceled, dragons were obedient and tractable. Break the enchantment, and they regained their own will and intelligence and became totally erratic and unpredictable. They might continue to serve you, but they might also decide to make you their evening repast.

If it wasn't Trian, who was it?

Someone from the queen, no doubt. Hugh cursed the wizard and his king long and hard beneath his breath. The bungling fools had let slip their plans. Now, undoubtedly, Hugh had to contend with some baron or earl attempting to rescue the child. The Hand would have to rid himself of this nuisance, which meant laying a trap, cutting a throat, hiding a body. The kid would probably recognize the man, know him to be a friend. He would grow suspicious. Hugh would have to convince the prince that the friend had been an enemy; that his enemy was truly his friend. It looked to be a lot of bother, and all because Trian and his guilt-ridden king had been careless.

Well, thought Hugh grimly, it'll cost them.

The dragon began spiraling down, without guidance from Hugh, and the Hand guessed that they had reached their destination. The magical cloud disappeared and Hugh glimpsed a patch of forest, dark black against the blue-glowing coralite, and then a large cleared area and the sharply defined and delineated shapes that were never found in nature but were created by man.

It was a small village, nestled in a valley of coralite and surrounded by heavy forests. Hugh knew of many such towns that used the hills and trees to hide themselves from elven attack. They paid the penalty by being well off the major airlanes, but if it came to a question of living well or living at all, some people gladly chose poverty.

Hugh knew the value of life. Measuring it against good living, he considered them fools.

The dragon circled the sleeping village. Seeing a glade in the forest, Hugh guided the beast to a smooth landing. As he unpacked their gear from the dragon's back, he wondered where their shadow had set down. He did not spend much time considering the question. The Hand had laid his snare. It required only baiting.

The dragon left them immediately after it was unloaded. Rising into the air, it disappeared above the treetops. Casually, taking his time, Hugh shouldered the packs. Motioning to the prince to follow, he was heading off into the woods when he felt a tug at his sleeve.

"What is it, Your Highness?"

"Can we talk out loud now?" The child's eyes were wide.

Hugh nodded.

"I can carry my own pack. I'm stronger than I look. My father says someday I'm going to grow up to be as tall and strong as he is."

Stephen said that, did he? To a kid he knew would never grow up. If I had that bastard in front of me, it'd be a pleasure to twist his neck.

Silently Hugh handed Bane the pack. They reached the edge of the forest and plunged into the deep shadows beneath the hargast trees. Soon they would be lost to sight and hearing, their feet making no sound on the thick carpet of fine dustlike crystals.

The Hand felt another tug at his sleeve.

"Sir Hugh," said Bane, pointing, "who's that?"

Startled, the Hand glanced around. "There's no one there, Your Highness."

"Yes, there is," said the child. "Don't you see him? It's a Kir monk."

Hugh halted and stared at the boy.

"It's all right if you don't see him," added Bane, shifting his pack to lie more comfortably across his small shoulders. "I see lots of things other people don't. But I've never seen a Kir monk walk with anyone before. Why is he with you?"

"Let me carry it, Your Highness." Hugh took the pack from the prince and, propelling the child in front of him with a firm grip of his hand, resumed walking.

Damn Trian! The blasted wizard must have let something else slip. The kid had picked up on it and now his imagination was running wild. He might even guess the truth. Well, there was nothing to be done about it now. It only made the assassin's job that much more difficult—and therefore that much more expensive.

The two spent what was left of the night in a water harvester's warming shed.[1] The sky was lightening; Hugh could see the faint glimmer of the firmament that presaged dawn. The edges of the Lords of Night glistened a fiery red. Now he could determine the direction in which they were moving and could at last orient himself. Inspecting the contents of his pack before leaving the monastery, he'd ascertained that he had all the proper navigational equipment—his own having been taken from him in Yreni prison. He removed a small leather-bound book and silver baton topped by a quartz sphere. The baton had a spike on the end and Hugh shoved it into the ground.

All such sextants are of elven make—humans possessing no mechanical magic skills. This one was practically new and he guessed it was a trophy of war. Hugh gave the baton a tap with

---

[1]The scarcity of water in the Mid Realm means that much of it must be harvested from plant life. Water farmers raise such water-producing plants; water harvesters go foraging for the liquid.

his finger and the sphere rose into the air, much to the delight of Bane, who was watching in wide-eyed fascination.

"What's it doing?" he demanded.

"Look through it," Hugh offered.

The prince hesitantly placed his eye level with the sphere. "I just see a bunch of numbers," he said, disappointed.

"That's what you're supposed to see." Hugh made a mental note of the first number, turned a ring at the bottom of the baton, read off the second, and finally a third. Then he began flipping pages in the book.

"What are you looking for?" Bane squatted down on his haunches to peer over Hugh's arm.

"Those numbers you saw are the position of the Lords of Night, the five Ladies of Light, and Solarus, all in relation to each other. I find the numbers in this book, match them with the time of year, which tells me where the islands are located at this particular moment, and it should tell me within a few menkas where we are."

"What funny writing!" Bane turned his head nearly upside-down to see. "What is it?"

"It's elvish. Their navigators were the ones who figured all this out and came up with the magical device that takes the readings."

The boy frowned. "Why didn't we use something like that when we flew on the dragon?"

"Because dragons know instinctively where they are. No one's sure how, but they use all their senses—sight, hearing, smell, touch—plus some we probably don't even know exist to guide them. Elf magic won't work on dragons, so they had to build dragonships and they had to make things like this to tell them where they were. That's why"—Hugh grinned—"elves consider us barbarians."

"Well, where are we? Do you know?"

"I know," said Hugh. "And now it's time, Your Highness, for a nap."

They were on Pitrin's Exile, probably about 123 menkas backtrack[2] from Winsher. Hugh felt more relaxed, once this was

---

[2]Backtrack, trackward, kiratrack, and kanatrack are terms used in the isles to indicate direction. Track refers to the Mean Cluster Track or the path which the cluster takes in its orbit through the sky. To move trackward is to travel in the same direction; backtrack, in the direction precisely opposite. Kiratrack and kanatrack refer to moving at right angles to the track.

in his mind. It had been unsettling, not being able to tell up from down, so to speak. Now he knew and he could rest. It wouldn't be full light for another three hours.

Rubbing his eyes, yawning, and stretching, like a man who has traveled far and is bone-tired, Hugh—shoulders slumped and feet dragging—marched the prince into the shed. Seeming half-asleep, the assassin gave the door a push to close it. It didn't shut all the way, but he was, apparently, too tired to notice.

Bane took a blanket from his pack, spread it, and lay down. Hugh did the same, shutting his eyes. When he heard the child's breathing fall into a slow and steady rhythm, he swiftly twisted, catlike, to his feet and crept silently across the floor of the shed.

The prince was already fast asleep. Hugh looked at him closely, but the boy did not appear to be shamming. Curled up in a ball, lying on top of his blanket, he would freeze in the chill predawn air.

Fishing another blanket out of his pack, Hugh tossed it over the kid, then moved silently back to the opposite side of the shed, the side near the door. He slipped off his tall boots and laid them on the floor, carefully arranging them so that they were turned sideways, one resting on top of the other. He dragged his pack over and laid it just above his boots. Removing the fur cloak, he wrapped it in a ball and placed it next to the pack. A blanket, spread over the cape and pack, left the soles of the boots showing. Anyone looking in from the doorway would see the feet of a blanket-wrapped man fast asleep.

Satisfied, Hugh drew his dagger from his boot and squatted down in a dark corner of the shed. Eyes on the door, he waited.

Half an hour passed. The shadow was giving Hugh ample time to fall into deep sleep.

The Hand waited patiently. It wouldn't be too long now. Day had dawned fully. The sun was shining. The man must fear they would waken and start on their way again. The assassin watched the thin ribbon of gray light streaming in through the partially shut door. When that ribbon began to widen, Hugh's hand tightened its grip on the dagger.

Slowly, silently, the door swung open.

A head thrust inside. The man looked long and carefully at the supposedly slumbering figure of Hugh beneath the blanket, then turned the same careful scrutiny to the boy. Hugh held his breath. Apparently satisfied, the man entered the shed.

Hugh expected the man to be armed and to immediately attack the dummy of himself. The assassin was disconcerted to see that the man carried no weapon in his hand and was padding soft-footed over to the boy. It was just to be a rescue, then.

Hugh leapt, wrapped an arm around the man's neck, and put the dagger to his throat.

"Who sent you? Tell me the truth and I'll reward you with a quick death."

The body in Hugh's grasp went limp and the assassin saw, in astonishment, that the man had fainted.

CHAPTER ♦ 15

PITRIN'S EXILE, VOLKARAN ISLES,

MID REALM

♦

"Not exactly the sort of person I'd send out on a mission to rescue my son from the hands of an assassin," muttered Hugh, stretching out the comatose man on the floor of the shed. "But then, maybe the queen's having trouble finding bold knights these days. Unless he's shamming."

The man's age was indeterminable. The face appeared care-worn and haggard. He was bald on the top of his head; wispy gray hair hung in a long fringe around the sides. But his cheeks were smooth, and the wrinkles around the mouth came from worry, not age. Tall and gangly, he appeared to have been put together by someone who had run out of the correct parts and been forced to substitute. His feet and hands were too big; his head, with its delicate, sensitive features, seemed too small.

Kneeling beside the man, Hugh lifted a finger and bent it back until it almost touched the wrist. The pain was excruciating, and a person feigning unconsciousness would invariably betray himself. The man didn't even twitch.

Hugh gave him a sound smack on the cheek to bring him around, and was about to add another when he heard the boy coming up to his side.

"Is that who was following us?" The prince, keeping close to Hugh, stared curiously. "Why that's Alfred!" The boy grasped hold of the collar of the man's cape, jerked his head up, and shook him. "Alfred! Wake up! Wake up!"

Bang! went the man's head against the floor.

The prince shook him again. The man's head bumped the floor again, and Hugh—relaxing—sat back to watch.

"Oh, oh, oh!" Alfred groaned each time his head hit the floor. Opening his eyes, he stared dazedly at the prince and made a feeble effort to remove the small hands from his collar.

"Please . . . Your Highness. I'm quite awake, now . . . Ouch! Thank you, Your Highness, but that won't be necess—"

"Alfred!" The prince threw his arms around him, hugging the man so tightly he nearly smothered him. "We thought you were an assassin! Have you come to travel with us?"

Rising to a sitting position, Alfred gave Hugh—and particularly Hugh's dagger—a nervous glance. "Uh, traveling with you may not be quite feasible, Your—"

"Who are you?" interrupted Hugh.

The man rubbed his head and answered humbly, "Sir, my name—"

"He's Alfred," interrupted Bane, as if that explained everything. Noting from Hugh's grim face that it didn't, the boy added, "He's in charge of all my servants and he chooses my tutors and makes certain my bathwater's not too hot—"

"My name is Alfred Montbank, sir," the man said.

"You're Bane's servant?"

" 'Chamberlain' is the correct term, sir," said Alfred, flushing. "And that is your prince to whom you are referring in such a disrespectful manner."

"Oh, that's all right, Alfred," said Bane, sitting back on his heels. His hand toyed with the feather amulet he wore around his neck. "I told Sir Hugh he could call me by my name, since we're traveling together. It's much easier than saying 'Your Highness' all the time."

"You're the one who's been following us," Hugh said.

"It is my duty to be with His Highness, sir."

Hugh raised a black eyebrow. "Obviously somebody didn't see it that way."

"I was mistakenly left behind." Alfred lowered his gaze, staring fixedly at the floor of the shed. "His Majesty the king flew off so quickly, he undoubtedly overlooked me."

"And so you followed him—and the boy."

"Yes, sir. I was almost too late. I had to pack some things I knew the prince would need, which Trian had forgotten. I was forced to saddle my own dragon, and then I had an argument with the palace guards, who didn't want to let me leave. The king and Trian and the prince had disappeared by the time I was through the gates. I had no idea what to do, but the dragon seemed to have some notion of where it wanted to go and—"

"It would follow its stablemates. Go on."

"We found them. That is, the dragon found them. Not wanting to presume to thrust myself into their company, I kept a proper distance. Eventually we landed in that dreadful place—"

"The Kir monastery."

"Yes, I—"

"Could you get back there again if you had to?"

Hugh put the question casually, easily, out of curiosity. Alfred answered, never dreaming his life hung in the balance.

"Why, yes, sir, I think I could. I've a good knowledge of the countryside, especially the lands surrounding the castle." Lifting his gaze, he looked directly at Hugh. "Why do you ask?"

The assassin was tucking the dagger back into his boot. "Because that's Stephen's secret hideout you stumbled across. The guards will tell him you followed him. He'll know you found it—your disappearance clinches it. I wouldn't give a drop of water for your chances of living to a ripe old age if you went back to court."

"Merciful Sartan!" Alfred's face was the color of clay—he might have been wearing a mask of silt. "I didn't know! I swear, noble sir!" Reaching out, he grasped Hugh's hand pleadingly. "I'll forget the way, I promise—"

"I don't want you to forget it. Who knows, it might come in handy one day."

"Yes, sir . . ." Alfred hesitated.

"This is Sir Hugh." Bane introduced them. "He has a black monk walking with him, Alfred."

Hugh stared at the child in silence. No expression shifted the stone facade of the face except perhaps for a slight narrowing of the dark eyes.

Alfred, flushing red, reached out his hand and smoothed Bane's golden hair. "What have I told you, Your Highness?" said the chamberlain, gently rebuking. "It is not polite to tell people's secrets." He glanced apologetically at Hugh. "You must understand, Sir Hugh. His Highness is a clairvoyant and he has not quite learned how to handle his gift."

Hugh snorted, rose to his feet, and began to roll up his blanket.

"Please, Sir Hugh, allow me." Leaping up, Alfred sprang to snatch the blanket from Hugh's hand. One of the chamberlain's huge feet obeyed him. The other seemed to think it had received different orders and turned the opposite direction. Alfred stumbled, staggered, and would have pitched headfirst into Hugh had not the assassin caught his arm and shoved him upright.

"Thank you, sir. I'm very clumsy, I'm afraid. Here, I can do that now." Alfred began struggling with the blanket, which seemed suddenly to have gained a malevolent life of its own. Corners slid through his fingers. He folded one end, only to unfold its opposite. Wrinkles and bumps popped up in the most unlikely places. It was difficult to tell, during the ensuing tussle, who was going to come out on top.

"It's true about His Highness, sir," Alfred continued, wrestling furiously with the strip of cloth. "Our past clings to us, especially people who influenced us. His Highness can see them."

Hugh stepped in, throttled the blanket, and rescued Alfred, who sat back, panting and wiping his high domed forehead.

"I'll bet he can tell my fortune in the wine lees, too," Hugh said in a low voice, pitched so that the child wouldn't hear. "Where would he get that kind of talent? Only wizards beget wizards. Or maybe Stephen's not really this kid's father."

Hugh shot this verbal arrow aimlessly, not expecting to hit anything. His shaft found a target, however, burying itself deep, from the looks of it. Alfred's face went a sickly green, the whites of his eyes showed clearly around the gray iris, and his lips moved soundlessly. Stricken, he stared speechless at Hugh.

So, thought the Hand, this is beginning to make sense. At least it explains the kid's strange name. He glanced over at Bane. The child was rummaging through Alfred's pack.

"Did you bring my sweetmelts? Yes!" Triumphantly he dug the candy out. "I knew you wouldn't forget."

"Get your things together, Your Highness," ordered Hugh, throwing his fur cloak over his shoulders and hefting his own pack.

"I'll do that, Your Highness." Alfred sounded relieved, glad for something to occupy his mind and his hands and keep his face averted from Hugh's. Out of three steps across the floor, he missed only one, which brought him to his knees, where he needed to be anyway. With great goodwill he set to do battle with the prince's blanket.

"Alfred, you had a view of the landscape when you traveled. Do you know where we are?"

"Yes, Sir Hugh." The chamberlain, sweating in the chill air, did not dare look up, lest the blanket take him unawares. "I believe this village is known as Watershed."

"Watershed," repeated the Hand. "Don't wander off, Your Highness," he added, noticing the prince starting to skip out of the door.

The boy glanced back. "I just want to look around outside. I won't go far and I'll be careful."

The chamberlain had given up attempting to fold the blanket and had at last stuffed it bodily into the pack. When the boy had disappeared out the door, Alfred turned to face Hugh.

"You will allow me to accompany you, won't you, sir? I won't be any trouble, I swear."

Hugh gazed at him intently.

"You understand that you can never go back to the palace, don't you?"

"Yes, sir. I've set fire to my bridge, as they say."

"You haven't just set it on fire. You've cut it from the bank and dumped it down the gorge."

Alfred ran a trembling hand over his bald pate and stared at the floor.

"I'm taking you with me to look after the kid. You understand, he's not to go back to the palace either. I'm very good at tracking. It would be my duty to stop you before you did anything foolish, like trying to sneak him away."

"Yes, sir. That's understood." Alfred raised his eyes and looked directly into Hugh's. "You see, sir, I know the reason the king hired you."

Hugh flicked a glance outside. Bane was gleefully throwing rocks at a tree. His arms were thin, his throw clumsy. He continually fell short of the mark, but patiently and cheerfully kept at it.

"You know about the plot against the prince's life?" Hugh questioned easily, his hand, beneath his cloak, moving to the hilt of his sword.

"I know the reason," repeated Alfred. "It's why I'm here. I won't get in the way, sir, I promise you."

Hugh was confounded. Just when he thought the web was unraveling, it got more tangled. The man knew the reason, he said. It sounded as if he meant the *real* reason! He knows the truth about the kid, whatever that is. Has he come to help or hinder? Help, that was almost laughable. This chamberlain couldn't dress himself without help. Yet, Hugh had to admit, he'd done an extremely efficient job of tailing them; not an easy matter on a dark night made darker by enchanted fog. And, at the Kir monastery, he had managed to conceal not only himself but also his dragon from a wizard's six senses. But someone that skilled in tracking, hiding, and tailing had fainted dead away when he felt a knife at his throat.

There was no doubt this Alfred was a servant—the prince obviously knew him and treated him as such. But whom was he serving? The Hand didn't know, and he meant to find out. Meanwhile, whether Alfred was truly the fool he appeared or a cunning liar, the man had his uses, not the least of which would be to take charge of His Highness.

"All right. Let's get started. We'll circle around the village, pick up the road about five miles outside it. Not likely anyone around here would know the prince by sight, but it'll save questions. Has the kid got a hood? Get it on him. And keep it on him." He cast a disgusted glance at Alfred's satin-coated, knee-breeched, beribboned, and silk-stockinged finery. "You stink of the court a mile off. But it can't be helped. Most likely they'll take you for a charlatan. First chance we get, I'll bargain with some peasant for a change of clothes."

"Yes, Sir Hugh," Alfred murmured.

Hugh stepped out the door. "We're leaving, Your Highness."

Bane danced up eagerly and caught hold of Hugh's hand. "I'm ready. Are we going to stop at an inn for breakfast? My mother said we might. I've never been allowed to eat at an inn before—"

He was interrupted by a crash and a stifled groan behind him. Alfred had encountered the door. Hugh shook the boy's hand free. The child's soft touch was almost physically painful.

"I'm afraid not, Your Highness. I want to get clear of the village while it's still early, before people are up and stirring."

Bane's mouth drooped in disappointment.

"It wouldn't be safe, Your Highness." Alfred emerged, a large knot forming on his glistening forehead. "Especially if there is someone plotting to . . . uh . . . do you harm." He glanced at Hugh as he said this, and the assassin wondered again about Alfred.

"I suppose you're right," the prince said with a sigh, accustomed to the problems of being famous.

"But we will make a picnic under a tree," added the chamberlain.

"And eat sitting on the ground?" Bane's spirits lifted, then fell. "Oh, but I forgot. Mother never allows me to sit on the grass. I might catch a chill or get my clothes dirty."

"I don't think that this time she will mind," Alfred replied gravely.

"If you're sure . . ." The prince put his head on one side and looked intently at Alfred.

"I'm sure."

"Hurrah!" Bane darted forward, skipping lightheartedly down the road. Alfred, clutching the prince's pack, hurried after him. He'd make better time, thought Hugh, if his feet could be persuaded to travel in the same general direction as the rest of his body.

The assassin took his place behind them, keeping both under careful surveillance, hand on his sword. If Alfred so much as leaned over to whisper into the kid's ear, that whisper would be made with his last breath.

A mile passed. Alfred seemed completely occupied with the task of staying on his own two feet, and Hugh, falling into the easy, relaxed rhythm of the road, let his inner eye take over guard duty. Freed, his mind wandered, and he found himself seeing, superimposed over the body of the prince, another boy walking along a road, though not with cheerful gaiety. This boy walked with an air of defiance; his body bore the marks of the punishment he had received for just such an attitude. Black monks walked along at his side. . . .

. . ."Come, boy. The lord abbot wants to see you."

It was cold in the Kir monastery. Outside the walls, the world sweat and sweltered in summer heat. Inside, death's chill stalked the bleak hallways and kept court in the shadows.

The boy, who was not a boy any longer, but standing on the threshold of manhood, left his task and followed the monk through the silent corridors. The elves had raided a small village nearby. There were many dead, and most of the brothers had gone to burn the bodies and do reverence for those who had escaped the prisonhouse of their flesh.

Hugh should have gone with them. His task and that of the other boys was to search for charcrystal and build the pyres. The brothers pulled the bodies from the wreckage, composed the twisted limbs and staring eyes, and placed them upon the heaped oil-soaked faggots. The monks said no word to the living. Their voices were for the dead, and the sound of their chanting echoed through the streets. That chant had come to be a music everyone on Uylandia and Volkaran dreaded to hear.

Some of the monks sang the words:

> . .°. each new child's birth,
> we die in our hearts,
> truth black, we are shown,
> death always returns . . .

The other monks chanted over and over the single word "with." Inserting the "with" after the word "returns," they carried the dark song full-cycle.

Hugh had accompanied the monks since he was six cycles old, but this time he'd been ordered to stay and complete his morning's work. He did as he was told, without question; to do otherwise would be to invite a beating, delivered impersonally and without malice, for the good of his soul. Often he had silently prayed to be left behind when the others went on one of these grim missions, but now he had prayed to be allowed to go.

The gates boomed shut with an ominous dull thunder; the emptiness lay like a pall on his heart. Hugh had been planning his escape for a week. He had spoken of it to no one; the one friend he had made during his stay here was dead, and Hugh had been careful never to make another. He had the uneasy impression, however, that his secret plot must be engraved on his forehead, for it seemed that everyone who glanced at him kept looking at him with far more interest than they had ever before evinced.

Now he had been left behind when the others were gone. Now he was being summoned into the presence of the lord abbot—a man he had seen only during services, a man to whom he had never spoken and who had never before spoken to him.

Standing in the chamber of stone that shunned sunlight as something frivolous and fleeting, Hugh waited, with the patience that had been thrashed into him since childhood, for the man seated at the desk to acknowledge not only his presence but also his very existence. While Hugh waited, the fear and nervousness in which he'd lived for a week froze, dried up, and blew away. It was as if the cold atmosphere had numbed him to any human emotion or feeling. He knew suddenly, standing in that room, that he would never love, never pity, never feel compassion. From now on, he would never even know fear.

The abbot raised his head. Dark eyes looked into Hugh's soul.

"You were taken in by us when you were six cycles. I see in the records that ten cycles more have passed." The abbot did not speak to him by name. Doubtless he didn't even know it. "You are sixteen. It is time for you to make preparation for taking your vows and joining our brotherhood."

Caught by surprise, too proud to lie, Hugh said nothing. His silence spoke the truth.

"You have always been rebellious. Yet you are a hard worker, who never complains. You accept punishment without crying out. And you have adopted our precepts—I see that in you clearly. Why, then, will you leave us?"

Hugh, having asked himself that question often in the dark and sleepless nights, was prepared with the answer.

"I will not serve any man."

The abbot's face, stern and forbidding as the stone walls around him, registered neither anger nor surprise. "You are one of us. Like it or not, wherever you go, you will serve, if not us, then our calling. Death will always be your master."

Hugh was dismissed from the abbot's presence. The pain of the beating that followed slid away on the ice coating of the boy's soul. That night, Hugh made good his plans. Sneaking into the chamber where the monks kept their records, he found, in a book, information on the orphan boys the monks adopted. By the light of the stub of a stolen candle, Hugh searched for and discovered his own name.

"Hugh Blackthorn. Mother: Lucy, last name unknown. Father: According to words spoken by the mother before she died, the child's father is Sir Perceval Blackthorn of Blackthorn Hall, Djern Hereva." A later entry, dated a week after, stated: "Sir Perceval refuses to acknowledge the child and bids us 'do with the bastard as we will.' "

Hugh cut the page from the leather-bound book, tied it up in his ragged scrip, snuffed the candle, and slipped out into the night. Looking back at the walls whose grim shadows had long ago shut out any of the warmth or happiness he had known in childhood, Hugh silently refuted the abbot's words.

"I will be death's master."

CHAPTER 16

STEPS OF TERREL FEN,

LOW REALM

♦

LIMBECK REGAINED CONSCIOUSNESS AND FOUND THAT HIS SITUATION had improved, going from desperate to perilous. Of course, it took him, in his confused state, a considerable amount of time to remember just exactly what the situation was. After giving the matter serious thought, he determined he was *not* hanging by his wrists from the bedposts. Wriggling and grunting at the pain in his head, he looked about him as best he could in the gloom of the storm and saw that he had fallen into a giant pit, undoubtedly dug by the dig-claws of the Kicksey-winsey.

Further examination revealed that he had not fallen *into* a pit but was suspended *over* a pit—the giant wings having straddled it neatly, leaving him dangling down below. From the pain, he deduced that the wings must have inflicted a smart rap on his head during the landing.

Limbeck was just wondering how he was going to free himself from this awkward and uncomfortable position when the answer came to him rather unpleasantly in the form of a sharp crack. The weight of the Geg hanging from it was causing the wooden frame to break. Limbeck sank down about a foot before the wings caught and held. His stomach sank a good deal further, for—due to the darkness and the fact that he didn't have his spectacles on—Limbeck had no idea how deep this pit was. Frantically he attempted to devise some means of escape. A storm was raging above, water was pouring down the sides of the pit, making it extremely slippery, and at that moment there was another crack and the wings sagged down another foot.

Limbeck gasped, squinched his eyes tightly shut, and shook all over. Again, the wings caught and held, but not very well. He could feel himself slowly slipping. He had one chance. If he could free a hand, he might be able to catch hold of one of the coralite holes that honeycombed the sides of the pit. He jerked on his right hand . . .

. . . and the wings snapped.

Limbeck had just time enough to experience overwhelming terror before he landed heavily and painfully at the bottom of the pit, the wings crashing down all around him. First he shook. Then, deciding that shaking wasn't improving the situation, he extricated himself from the mess and peered upward. The pit was only about seven or eight feet deep, he discovered, and he could easily climb out. Since it was a coralite pit, the water that was streaming into it was draining just as swiftly through it. Limbeck was pleased with himself. The pit offered shelter from the storm. He was in no danger.

No danger until the dig-claws came down to mine.

Limbeck had just settled himself beneath a huge piece of torn wing fabric, to protect himself from the rain, when the terrible thought of the dig-claws occurred to him. Hastily he leapt to his feet and peered upward, but couldn't see a thing except for a black blur that was probably storm clouds and flashes of fuzzy lightning. Having never served the Kicksey-winsey, Limbeck had no idea if the dig-claws operated during storms or not. He couldn't see why they wouldn't, yet on the other hand he couldn't see why they would. All of which was no help.

Sitting back down—being careful to first remove several sharp splinters of wood and drop them down the holes of the coralite— Limbeck considered the matter as best he could through the pain in his head. At least the pit offered protection from the storm. And, in all probability, the dig-claws—which were huge, cumbersome things—would move slowly enough that he would have time to get out of the way.

Which turned out to be the case.

Limbeck had been squatting in the pit for about thirty tocks or so, the storm was showing no signs of abating, and he was wishing he'd had the foresight to stuff a couple of muffins down his pants, when there was a large thump and the pit in which he was sitting gave a tremendous shudder.

Dig-claws, thought Limbeck, and began to climb up the sides of the pit. It was easy going. The coralite offered numerous hand- and footholds, and Limbeck reached the top in moments. There was no use putting on his spectacles—the rain streaming over the glass would have blinded him. And he didn't need them anyhow. The dig-claw, its metal gleaming in the incessant flashes of lightning, was only a few feet from him.

Glancing upward, Limbeck could see other claws dropping out of the sky, descending on long cables lowered from the Kicksey-winsey. It was an awesome spectacle, and the Geg stood staring, headache forgotten, his mouth gaping wide open.

Made of bright and shining metal, ornately carved and fashioned to resemble the foot of some huge killer bird, the dig-claws dug into the coralite with their sharp talons. Closing over the broken rock, the claws carried it upward as a bird's claw grasps its prey. Once back on the isle of Drevlin, the dig-claws deposited the rock they had mined from the Terrel Fen into large bins, where the Gegs sorted through the coralite and retrieved the precious gray ore on which the Kicksey-winsey fed, and without which—so legend had it—the Kicksey-winsey could not survive.

Fascinated, Limbeck watched the dig-claws come smashing down all around him, biting into the coralite, digging down deep, scooping it up. The Geg was so interested in the procedure—which he'd never seen—that he completely forgot what he was supposed to do until it was almost too late. The claws were shaking free of the coralite and starting to rise back up when Limbeck remembered he was to put a mark on one of them to let Jarre and her people know where he was.

Broken bits of coralite, dropped out of the rising claws, would serve as a writing tool. Grabbing up a chunk, Limbeck made his way through the driving rain, stumbling over the rock-strewn ground, heading for one of the claws that had just come down and was burying itself in the coralite. Reaching the dig-claw, Limbeck was suddenly daunted by his task. The claw was enormous; he'd never imagined anything so big and powerful. Fifty Limbecks would have fitted comfortably inside its talons. It shook and jabbed and clawed the surface of the coralite, sending sharp shards of rock flying everywhere. It was impossible to get close to it.

But Limbeck had no choice. He had to get near. Gripping his coralite in one hand and his courage in the other, he had just started forward when a bolt of lightning struck the claw, sending blue flame dancing over its metal surface. The simultaneous thunder blast knocked Limbeck off his feet. Dazed and terrified, the Geg was about to give up in despair and run back to his pit—where he figured he would spend the remainder of a short and unhappy life—when the claw came to a shuddering stop. All the claws around Limbeck stopped—some in the ground; others hanging in midair on their way back up; others with talons wide open, waiting to descend.

Perhaps the lightning had damaged it. Perhaps there was a scrift change. Perhaps something had gone wrong above. Limbeck didn't know. If he had believed in the gods, he would have thanked them. As it was, he scrambled over the rocks, chunk of coralite in hand, and cautiously approached the nearest claw.

Noticing lots of scratch marks where the claw dipped into the coralite, Limbeck realized that he would have to make his mark on the upper part of the dig-claw, a part that didn't sink into the ground. That meant he had to choose a claw which was already buried. Which meant there was every possibility that it would start up again, yank itself out of the ground, and spill tons of rock down on the Geg's head.

Gingerly Limbeck touched the side of the dig-claw with the coralite, his hand shaking so that it made a ringing sound, like the clapper of a bell. It didn't leave a mark. Gritting his teeth, desperation giving him strength, Limbeck bore down hard. The coralite screeched over the metal side of the claw with a sound that made Limbeck think his head would split apart. But he had the satisfaction of seeing a long scratch mar the claw's smooth unblemished surface.

Still, someone might take that one scratch for an accidental occurrence. Limbeck made another mark on the claw, this one perpendicular to the first. The dig-claw shivered and shook. Limbeck dropped his rock in fright and scrambled backward. The claws were functioning once again. Pausing a moment, Limbeck gazed proudly on his work.

One dig-claw, rising into the stormy sky, was marked with the letter L.

Dashing through the rain, Limbeck returned to his pit. No claws seemed likely to descend on him, this time at least. He climbed back down the sides and, reaching the bottom, made himself as comfortable as possible. Pulling the fabric over his head, he tried not to think about food.

CHAPTER ✦ 17

STEPS OF TERREL FEN,

LOW REALM

✦

THE DIG-CLAWS CARRYING THEIR ORE LIFTED BACK UP INTO THE STORM clouds, on their way to the Drevlin dumps. Limbeck, watching them ascend, pondered how long it might take them to unload the coralite and return for more. How long would it take someone to notice his mark? *Would* someone notice his mark? If someone did notice his mark, would it be someone friendly to his cause or would it be a clark? If it was a clark, what was the clark likely to do about it? If it was a friend, how long would it take to attach the help-hand? Would that happen before he froze to death or died of starvation?

Such gloomy wonderings were unusual to Limbeck, who was not, ordinarily, a worrier. His disposition was naturally cheerful and optimistic. He tended to see the best in people. He held no malice toward anyone for his having been tied to the Feathers of Justick and tossed down here to die. The high froman and the head clark had done what they considered to be best for the people. It wasn't their fault that they believed in those who claimed to be gods. It was no wonder that the froman and his followers didn't believe Limbeck's story—Jarre herself didn't believe it either.

Perhaps it was thinking about Jarre that made Limbeck feel sad and discouraged. He had fondly assumed that she, at least, would believe in his discovery that the Welves weren't gods. Limbeck, huddling, shivering, in the bottom of his pit, could still not quite accept the fact that she didn't. This knowledge had nearly ruined his entire execution. Now that the initial excitement was over and he had nothing to do but wait and hope things went right and try not to notice that there was an incredible number of things that could go wrong, Limbeck began to reflect seriously on what would happen when (not if) he was rescued.

"How can they accept me as their leader if they think I lie?" Limbeck asked a stream of water running down the side of the pit. "Why would they even want me back at all? We've always said, Jarre and I, that truth was the most important virtue, that the quest for truth should be our highest goal. She thinks I've lied, yet she's obviously expecting me to continue as leader of our Union.

"And when I go back, then what?" Limbeck saw it all clearly, more clearly than he'd seen anything in years. "She'll humor me. They all will. Oh, they'll keep me as head of the Union—after all, the Mangers have judged me and let me live. But they'll know it's a sham. More important, I'll know it's a sham. The Mangers haven't had a damn thing to do with it. It's Jarre's cleverness that will bring me back, and she'll know it and so will I. Lying! That's what we'll be doing!"

Limbeck was growing increasingly upset. "Oh, sure, we'll get a lot of new members, but they'll be coming to us for the wrong reasons! Can you base a revolution on a lie? No!" The Geg clenched his thick wet fist. "It's like building a house on mud. Sooner or later, it's going to slip out from under your feet. Maybe I'll just stay down here! That's it! I won't go back!

"But that won't prove anything," Limbeck reflected. "They'll just think the Mangers did me in, and that won't help the cause at all. I know! I'll write them a note and send it up with the help-hand instead of going myself. There are tier feathers lying around. I can use those as a pen." He jumped to his feet. "And silt for ink. 'By choosing to stay down here and perhaps dying down here'—yes, that sounds well—'I hope to prove to you that what I said about the Welves was the truth. I cannot lead those who do not believe me, those who have lost faith in me.' Yes, that's quite good."

Limbeck tried to sound cheerful, but he found his pleasure in his speech rapidly draining. He was hungry, cold, wet, and frightened. The storm was blowing itself out, and an awful, terrible silence was descending over him. That silence reminded him of the big silence—the Endless Hear Nothing—and reminded him that he was facing that Endless Hear Nothing, and he realized that the death of which he spoke so glibly was liable to be a very unpleasant one.

Then, too, as if death wasn't bad enough, he pictured Jarre receiving his note, reading it with pursed lips and that wrinkle which always appeared above her nose when she was displeased. He wouldn't even need his spectacles to read the words of the note she'd send back. He could hear them already.

" 'Limbeck, stop this nonsense and get up here this instant!' Oh, Jarre!" he murmured to himself sadly, "if only *you* had believed me. The others wouldn't have mattered—"

A bone-jarring, teeth-rattling, earth-shaking thud jolted Limbeck out of his despair and simultaneously knocked him down.

Lying on his back, dazed, staring up at the top of the pit, he thought: Have the dig-claws come back? This soon? I don't have my note written!

Flustered, Limbeck staggered to his feet and stared up into the grayness. The storm had passed over. It was drizzling rain and foggy, but it was not lightninging, hailing, or thundering. He couldn't see the claws descending, but then, he couldn't see his hand in front of his face. Fumbling for his spectacles, he put them on and looked back up into the sky.

By squinting, he thought he could just barely distinguish numerous fuzzy blobs materializing out of the clouds. But if they were the dig-claws, they were far above him yet, and unless one had come down prematurely or fallen—which seemed unlikely, since the Kicksey-winsey rarely allowed accidents like that to happen—the dig-claws couldn't have been the cause of that tremendous thud. What, then, was it?

Hurriedly Limbeck began to climb the sides of the pit. His spirits were rising. He had a "what" or a "why" to investigate!

Reaching the rim of the pit, he peeped cautiously over the edge. At first he saw nothing, but that was because he was looking in the wrong direction. Turning his head, he gasped, marveling.

A brilliant light, shimmering with more colors than Limbeck had ever imagined existed in his gray and metallic world, was streaming out of a gigantic hole not more than thirty feet from him. Never stopping to think that the light might be harmful or that whatever had created the humongous thud might be lethal or that the dig-claws might be slowly and inevitably descending, Limbeck clambered up over the edge of the pit and made for the light as swiftly as his short, thick legs would carry his stout body.

There were numerous obstacles blocking his path; the surface of the small isle was pockmarked with holes dug by the claws. He had to avoid these, as well as heaps of broken coralite dropped when the dig-claws carried the ore upward. Making his way up and over and around these took some time, as well as considerable energy. When Limbeck finally reached the light, he was out of breath, both from the unaccustomed exertion and from excitement. For as he drew nearer, Limbeck could see that the colors in the light were forming distinct patterns and shapes.

Intent on the wonderful pictures he could see in the light, Limbeck stumbled almost blindly over the rocky ground and was saved from tumbling headfirst into the hole by tripping over a chunk of coralite and falling flat on his face at the hole's edge. Shaken, he put his hand to his pocket to feel if his spectacles were broken. They weren't there. After a horrible moment of panic, he remembered that they were on his nose. Crawling forward, he stared in amazement.

For a moment, he couldn't see anything but a brilliant, multicolored, ever-shifting radiance. Then forms and shapes coalesced. The pictures in the light were truly fascinating, and Limbeck gazed at them in awe. As he watched the constantly shifting and changing images, that portion of his mind which continually interrupted important and wonderful thoughts with mundane matters such as "Mind you don't walk into that wall!", "That pan's hot!", and "Why didn't you go before we left?", said to him urgently, "The dig-claws are coming down!"

Limbeck, concentrating on the pictures, ignored it.

He was, he realized, seeing a world. Not his own world, but somebody else's world. It was an incredibly beautiful place. It reminded him some, but not quite, of the pictures he'd seen in the books of the Welves. The sky was bright blue—not gray—and it was clear and vast, with only a few puffs of white sailing across it. Lush vegetation was everywhere, not just in a pot in the kitchen. He saw magnificent structures of fantastic design, he saw wide streets and boulevards, he saw what might have been Gegs, only they were tall and slender with graceful limbs . . .

Or had he? Limbeck blinked and stared into the light. It was beginning to fragment and break apart! The images were becoming distorted. He longed for the people to come back. Certainly, he'd never seen anyone—not even the Welves—who looked like what he thought he'd glimpsed in that split second before the light winked out, then blinked back on, and shifted to another picture.

Trying to make sense of the flickering images that were beginning to make his eyes burn and ache, Limbeck pulled himself farther over the lip of the hole and saw the light's source. It was beaming out of an object at the bottom of the hole.

"That was what made the thump," said Limbeck, shielding his eyes with his hand and staring at the object intently. "It fell from the sky, like I did. Is it part of the Kicksey-winsey? If so, why did it fall? Why is it showing me these pictures?"

Why, why, why? Limbeck couldn't stand not knowing. Never thinking of possible danger, he crawled over the edge of the hole and slid down the side. The nearer he drew to the object, the easier it was to see it. The light pouring out of it was diffused upward and was less brilliant and blinding approached from this angle.

The Geg was, at first, disappointed. "Why, it's nothing but a hunk of coralite," he said, prodding chunks of it that had broken off. "Certainly the largest hunk of coralite I've ever seen—it's as big as my house—and then, too, I've never known coralite to fall out of the sky."

Slithering closer, displacing small bits of rock that skittered out from under him and went bouncing down the side of the crater, Limbeck drew in his breath. Delighted, awed, and astounded, he immediately squelched the mental prod that was reminding him, "The dig-claws! The dig-claws!" The coralite was just a shell, an outer covering. It had cracked open, probably in the fall, and Limbeck could see inside.

At first he thought it must be part of the Kicksey-winsey, and then he thought it wasn't. It was made of metal—like the Kicksey-winsey—but the metal body of the Kicksey-winsey was smooth and unblemished. This metal was covered with strange and bizarre symbols, and it was from cracks in the metal that the bright light was streaming. And it was because of the cracks—or so Limbeck reasoned—that he couldn't see the complete picture.

"If I open the cracks wider, then perhaps I could see more. This is really exciting!" Reaching the bottom of the crater, Limbeck hurried toward the metal object. It was about four times taller than he was and—as he'd first noticed—as big as his house. Gingerly he reached out his hand and made a swift tapping motion with the tips of his fingers on the metal. It wasn't hot to the touch—something he'd feared due to the bright light pouring from it. The metal was cool, and he was able to rest his hand on it and even trace the symbols engraved there with his fingers.

A strange and ominous creaking noise sounded above him, and that irritating part of his brain was shrieking at him something about dig-claws coming down, but Limbeck ordered it to shut up and quit bothering him. Putting his hand on one of the cracks, he noticed that the cracks ran all around the symbols but never intersected one. Limbeck started to tug at the crack to see if he could widen it.

His hand seemed reluctant to perform its assigned task, however, and Limbeck knew why. He was suddenly and unpleasantly reminded of the fallen Welf ship.

"Rotting corpses. But it led me to the truth."

The thought passed through his mind swift as a heartbeat, and, refusing to let himself think about it further, he gave the metal a good hard tug.

The crack widened, the entire metal structure began to shiver and tremble. Limbeck snatched his hand away and jumped backward. But the object was only, apparently, settling itself more firmly into the crater, for the movement ceased. Cautiously Limbeck approached again, and this time he heard something.

It sounded like a groan. Pressing his ear to the crack, wishing angrily that the creaking sounds of the dig-claws descending from the skies would cease so that he could hear better, Limbeck listened intently. He heard it again, louder, and he had no doubt that there was something alive inside the metal shell, and that it was hurt.

Gegs, even the weak ones, have a tremendous amount of strength in their arms and upper body. Limbeck put his hands on either side of the crack and pushed with all his might. Though they bit into his flesh, the metal sides split wide open and the Geg was able, after a brief struggle, to squeeze inside.

The light had been brilliant out there. In here, it was blinding, and Limbeck at first despaired of seeing anything. Then he detected the light's source. It was radiating outward from the center of what the Geg had come to think of—by past association—as a ship. The groaning sound came from somewhere to the right, and Limbeck, by using his hand as a shield, was able to block out most of the light and search for whatever it was that was in pain.

Limbeck's heart jumped. "A Welf!" was his first excited thought. "And a live one at that!" Squatting down beside the figure, the Geg saw a large amount of blood beneath the head, but no signs of blood anywhere else on the body. He also saw—rather to his disappointment—that it wasn't a Welf. Limbeck had seen a human only once before, and that was in pictures in the Welf books. This creature looked something like a human, yet not quite. There was one thing certain, however. The creature, with its great height and thin, muscular body, was definitely one of the so-called gods.

At that moment, the screaming warnings in Limbeck's brain became so insistent that he was forced—reluctantly—to pay attention to them.

He looked up through the crack in the ship's structure and found himself staring into the wide-open maw of a dig-claw, directly above him, and descending rapidly. If Limbeck hurried, he could just manage to escape the ship before the claw smashed into it.

The god-who-wasn't groaned again.

"I've got to get you out of here!" Limbeck said to him.

The Gegs are a softhearted race and there is no doubt that Limbeck was moved by unselfish considerations in determining to risk his own life to save that of the god. But it must also be admitted that the Geg was moved by the thought that if he took back a live god-who-wasn't, Jarre would *have* to believe his story!

Grasping the god by the wrists, Limbeck started to pull him across the debris-strewn floor of the shattered ship, when he felt—with a shiver—hands grasp him back. Startled, he looked down at the god. The eyes, almost covered in a mask of blood, were wide open and staring at him. The lips moved.

"What?" With the claw's creaking, Limbeck couldn't hear. "No time!" He jerked his head upward.

The god's eyes glanced up. His face was twisted in pain, and it was obvious to Limbeck that the god was holding on to consciousness by a supreme effort. It seemed he recognized the danger, but it only made him more frantic. He squeezed Limbeck's wrists hard; the Geg would have bruise marks for weeks.

"My . . . dog!"

Limbeck stared down at the god. Had he heard right? The Geg glanced hastily around the wreckage and suddenly saw, right at the god's feet, an animal pinned beneath twisted metal. Limbeck blinked at it, wondering why he hadn't seen it before.

The dog was panting and squirming. It was stuck and couldn't free itself, but it didn't appear to be hurt and it was obviously trying, in its struggles, to reach its master, for it paid no attention to Limbeck.

The Geg looked upward. The claw was coming down with a rapidity that Limbeck found quite annoying—considering how slowly they had descended the last time he'd seen them. He looked from the claw to the god to the dog.

"I'm sorry," he said helplessly. "There just isn't time!"

The god—eyes on the dog—tried to wrench his hands from the Geg's grip. But the effort apparently taxed the god's remaining strength, for suddenly the arms went limp and the god's head lolled back. The dog, looking at its master, whimpered and increased its efforts to free itself.

"I'm sorry," Limbeck repeated to the dog, who paid no attention to him. Gritting his teeth, hearing the sound of the claw coming closer and closer, the Geg pulled the body of the god across the debris-strewn floor. The dog's struggles became frantic, its whimperings changed to yelps, but that was only— Limbeck saw—because it was watching its master being taken away and it couldn't get to him.

A lump in his throat that was both pity for the trapped animal and fear for himself, Limbeck heaved and pulled and strained and finally reached the crack. With a great effort he dragged the god through. Depositing the limp body on the floor of the crater, Limbeck threw himself down beside the god just as the dig-claw smashed into the metal ship.

There was a shattering explosion. The concussion lifted Limbeck off the ground and slammed him back into it, driving the breath from his stout body. Small bits of shattered coralite fell down around him like rain, the sharp edges biting painfully into his skin. When that ceased, all was quiet.

Slowly, dazedly, Limbeck lifted his head. The dig-claw was hanging motionless, probably injured in the explosion. The Geg looked around to discover what had happened to the ship, expecting to see it a mass of twisted wreckage.

Instead, he didn't see it at all. The explosion had destroyed it. No, that wasn't quite right. There were no pieces of metal lying about; no remnant of the ship remained. It wasn't only destroyed, it had vanished as though it had never been!

But there was the god to prove that Limbeck hadn't lost his

mind. The god stirred and opened his eyes. Gasping in pain, he turned his head, staring about.

"Dog," he called feebly. "Dog! Here, boy!"

Limbeck, glancing at the coralite that had been blown to smithereens in the blast, shook his head. He felt unaccountably guilty, though he knew there'd been no way he could have saved the dog and themselves.

"Dog!" called the god, and there was a panicked crack in the voice that made Limbeck's heart ache. Reaching out his hand, he started to try to soothe the god, fearful that he would do himself further injury.

"Ah, dog," said the god with a deep, relieved sigh, his gaze fixed on the place where the ship had been. "There you are! Come here. Come here. That was quite a ride, wasn't it, boy?"

Limbeck stared. There was the dog! Dragging itself out of the broken rock, it hobbled, limping on three paws, to its master. Its eyes shining brightly, its mouth open in what Limbeck could have sworn was a pleased grin, the dog gave its master's hand a lick. The god-who-wasn't relapsed into unconsciousness. The dog, with a sigh and a wriggle, sank down beside its master, laid its head on its paws, and fixed its intelligent eyes on Limbeck.

CHAPTER ◆ 18

THE STEPS OF TERREL FEN,

LOW REALM

◆

"I'VE COME THIS FAR. WHAT DO I DO NOW?"

Limbeck wiped his hand over his sweating forehead, rubbed his fingers under the wire rims of the spectacles that kept slipping down his nose. The god was in pretty bad shape, or so Limbeck thought, being uncertain as to the physical properties of gods. That deep gash on the head would have been critical in a Geg, and Limbeck had no choice but to assume it was critical in a god.

"The help-hand!"

Limbeck jumped up and, with a backward glance at the comatose god and his very remarkable dog, the Geg scrambled up the side of the crater. Reaching the edge, he saw all the dig-claws hard at work. The noise was ear-splitting—gouging and scraping, creaking and screeching: all very comforting to the Geg. Looking up quickly, ascertaining that there were no more dig-claws coming down, Limbeck crawled out of the crater and ran back to his own pit.

It was logical to assume that whatever WUPP Geg found the L mark on the dig-claw would send down the help-hand to the same location or as near as he or she could get. Of course, there was every possibility that no one had seen the L, or that they couldn't get the help-hand ready in time, or countless other dire occurrences. Running along, tripping and stumbling over the heaps of broken coralite, Limbeck tried to prepare himself to accept without disappointment the fact that no help-hand would be there.

But it was.

The wave of relief that broke over Limbeck when he saw the help-hand sitting on the ground right near his pit nearly drowned the Geg. His knees went weak; he grew light-headed and had to sit down a moment to recover.

His first thought was to hurry, for the dig-claws were about to rise again. Staggering to his feet, he headed back for the crater at a run. His legs informed him in no uncertain terms that they were on the verge of rebellion against this unusual amount of exercise. Pausing a moment for the pain to subside, Limbeck reflected that he probably didn't have to hurry after all. Surely they wouldn't bring up the help-hand until they were certain he was in it.

The pain drained from his legs but seemed to take all his strength with it. His limbs felt six times heavier than normal, and in addition, instead of his legs supporting him, Limbeck had the distinct impression that he was dragging them along. Wearily, stumbling and falling, he made his slow way back to the crater. He slid down the sides almost reluctantly, certain that, in his absence, the god-who-wasn't had died.

The god was still breathing, however. The dog, huddled as closely as possible next to its master's body, had rested its head on the god's chest, its eyes keeping watch over the pallid, blood-covered face.

The thought of dragging the god's heavy body up out of the crater and across the cracked and pitted landscape sank Limbeck's heart and left his spirits as heavy as his legs.

"I can't do it," he muttered, collapsing next to the god, his head resting on his propped-up knees. "I don't think . . . I can even make it back . . . myself!"

His spectacles steamed up from the vast heat he had worked up. Sweat chilled on his body. Adding another blow to his already numb mind and body, a rumble of thunder indicated a storm brewing. Limbeck didn't care. Just as long as he didn't have to get to his feet again.

"But this god-who-isn't will prove you were right!" nagged that irritating voice. "At last you will have the power to persuade the Gegs that they've been deluded, used as slaves. This could be the dawning of a new day for your people! This could start the revolution!"

The revolution! Limbeck lifted his head. He couldn't see a thing, due to the mist over his spectacles, but that didn't matter.

He wasn't looking at his surroundings anyway. He was back on Drevlin, the Gegs were cheering him. What was even more beautiful, they were doing as he advised.

They were asking "why"!

Limbeck could never afterward clearly recall the next harrowing span of time. He remembered that he tore up his shirt to make a crude bandage to wrap around the head of the god. He remembered glancing askance at the dog, being uncertain how the dog would react to anyone moving its master. He remembered that the dog licked his hand and looked at him with its liquid eyes and stood aside, watching anxiously as the Geg lifted the limp body of the god and began hauling him up the side of the crater. After that, Limbeck remembered nothing but aching muscles and sobbing for breath and dragging himself and the body a few feet, then collapsing, then crawling forward, then collapsing, then struggling on again.

The dig-claws went back up into the sky, though the Geg never noticed. The storm broke, increasing his terror, for he knew that they could not hope to survive its full fury out in the open. He was forced to remove his spectacles, and between his myopia, the blinding rain, and the gathering gloom, Limbeck lost sight of the help-hand. He could only keep traveling in what he hoped was the general direction.

More than once, Limbeck thought the god was dead, for the rain chilled the body, the lips turned blue, the skin ashen. The rain had washed away the blood, and the Geg could see the deep and ugly-looking head wound, a thin trickle of red oozing from it. But the god still breathed.

Perhaps he *is* immortal, Limbeck thought dazedly.

The Geg knew that he was lost. He knew that he had traveled halfway across this blasted isle at least. They had missed the help-hand, or perhaps the help-hand, growing tired of waiting, had gone back up. The storm was worsening. Lightning flared around them, blasting holes in the coralite and deafening Limbeck with the concussive thunder. The wind kept him flattened to the ground—not that the Geg had the strength to stand. He was about to crawl into a pit and escape the storm (or die, if he was lucky) when he noticed blearily that the pit he was contemplating was *his* pit! There was the broken wooden frame of the wings. And there was the help-hand!

Hope lent the Geg strength. He made it to his feet. Buffeted by wind, he nevertheless managed to drag the god the last few remaining feet. Lowering the god to the ground, Limbeck opened the door to the glass bubble and looked curiously inside.

The help-hand had been designed to allow the Gegs to come to the assistance of the dig-claws, should that be necessary. Occasionally a claw got stuck in the coralite, or broke, or malfunctioned. When this occurred, a Geg entered the help-hand and was lowered down onto one of the isles to effect repairs.

The help-hand looked like what it was named—a gigantic hand made of metal that had been severed at the wrist. A cable attached to the wrist allowed the hand to be raised and lowered from above. The hand was slightly cupped; thumb and fingers forged together, it held in its secure grip a large protective glass bubble in which rode the repair Gegs. A hinged door allowed entrance and egress, and a brass horn, attached to a tube that ran back up the cable, permitted the Gegs to communicate with those above.

Two stout Gegs could fit comfortably inside the glass bubble. The god, being considerably taller than a Geg, presented a problem. Limbeck dragged the god over to the bubble and thrust him inside. The god's legs hung out over the edge. The Geg finally fit in the god, tucking his legs up so that the knees rested against his chin and folding his arms over his chest. Limbeck climbed in wearily himself, and the dog jumped in after. It would be a tight fit with all three of them, but Limbeck wasn't about to leave the dog behind—not again. He didn't think he could stand the shock of seeing it come back from the dead a second time.

The dog curled itself up against the body of its master. Limbeck, reaching over the god's limp form, struggled against the roaring wind in a futile effort to shut the glass door. The wind whipped around to attack from another direction, and suddenly the door slammed shut on its own, throwing Limbeck back against the side of the bubble. For long moments he lay there, panting and groaning.

Limbeck could feel the hand rock and quake in the storm. He had visions of it breaking, snapping off the cable, and suddenly the Geg wanted only one thing—to get off this rock. It took a supreme effort of will to move, but Limbeck managed to reach over and grasp the horn.

"Up!" he gasped.

No response, and he realized that they must not be able to hear him.

Drawing in a lungful of air, Limbeck closed his eyes and concentrated all his waning strength.

"*Up!*" he yelled so loudly that the dog sprang to its feet in alarm, the god stirred and groaned.

"Xplf wuf?" came a voice, the words rattling down the tube like a handful of pebbles.

"*Up!*" Limbeck shrieked in exasperation, desperation, and sheer panic.

The help-hand gave a tremendous lurch that would have knocked the Geg off his feet had he been on them. As it was, he was already scrunched up against the side to allow room for the god. Slowly, with an alarming creaking sound, swinging back and forth in the gale winds, the help-hand began to rise into the air.

Trying not to think what would happen *now* if the cable snapped, Limbeck leaned back against the side of the bubble, closed his eyes, and hoped he wouldn't be sick.

Unfortunately, closing his eyes made him dizzy. He felt himself spinning round and round, about to fall into a deep black pit.

"This won't do," said Limbeck shakily. "I can't pass out. I've got to explain to them up above what's going on."

The Geg opened his eyes and—to keep from looking out—set himself to studying the god. He had, he realized, thought of the creature as male. At least it looked more like a male Geg than a female Geg, which was all Limbeck had to go on. The god's face was rough-cut: a square, cleft chin covered with a stubbly growth of beard; firm lips, tightly drawn, tightly closed, never relaxing, appearing to guard secrets that he would take with him to death. A few fine lines around the eyes seemed to indicate that the god, though not an old man, was no youngster. The hair, too, added an impression of age. It was cut short—very short—and though matted with blood and rain-soaked, Limbeck could see patches of pure white at the temples, above the forehead, and around the back where it grew at the base of the neck. The god's body seemed made of nothing but bones and muscle and sinew. He was thin—by Geg standards, too thin.

"That's probably why he's wearing so many clothes," said Limbeck to himself, trying hard not to look out the sides of the bubble, where lightning strikes were making the stormy night brighter than any day the Gegs, in their sunless world, ever knew.

The god wore a thick leather tunic over a shirt with a draw-string collar that encircled his throat. He had wrapped a strip of cloth around his neck, the ends tied in a knot at the base of his throat and thrust into the tunic. The shirt's long, full sleeves covered his wrists; drawstrings held them fast. Soft leather trousers were tucked into knee-high boots that fastened up the sides of the legs with buttons made of what appeared to be the horn of some animal. Over all this, he wore a long collarless coat with wide sleeves that came to the elbows. The colors of his clothes were drab—browns and whites, grays and dull black. The fabric was well-worn, frayed in places. The leather tunic, trousers, and boots had softened around the body, fitting it like a second skin.

Most peculiarly, the god wore rags around his hands. Startled by this, which he must have noticed, but hadn't thought about until now, Limbeck looked at the god's hands more closely. The rags were skillfully applied. Wrapping around the wrist, they covered the back of the hand and the palm and were twined around the base of the fingers and thumb.

"Why?" Limbeck wondered, and reached forward to find out.

The dog's growl was filled with such menace that Limbeck felt the hair rise on his head. The animal had jumped to its feet and was gazing at the Geg with a look that said plainly, "I'd leave my master alone, if I were you."

"Right," Limbeck gulped. He shrank back against the side of the bubble.

The dog gave him an approving glance. Settling itself more comfortably, it even closed its eyes, as much as to say, "I know you'll behave now, so if you'll excuse me, I'll take a short nap."

The dog was right. Limbeck was going to behave. He was paralyzed, afraid to move, almost scared to breathe.

The practical-minded Gegs liked cats. Cats were useful animals who earned their keep by catching mice and who took care of themselves. The Kicksey-winsey liked cats, at least so it was supposed, since it had been the creators of the Kicksey-winsey—the Mangers—who first brought cats down from the realms above to dwell with the Gegs. There were, however, few dogs on Drevlin. Those who kept them were generally the wealthy Gegs—such as the high froman and members of his clan. The dogs were not pets, but were used to protect the wealth. Gegs would not take each other's lives, but there were a few who had no aversion at all to taking each other's property.

This dog was different from Geg dogs, which tended to resemble their owners—short-legged, barrel-chested, with round, thick-nosed, flat faces . . . and an expression of vicious stupidity. The dog holding Limbeck at bay was sleek-coated and slim-bodied. It had a longish nose, its face was exceptionally intelligent, and the eyes were large and liquid brown. Its fur was a nondescript black with patches of white on the tips of the ears, and white eyebrows. It was the eyebrows, Limbeck decided, that made the dog's face unusually expressive for an animal.

Such were Limbeck's observations of god and beast. They were detailed, because he had a long time to study them during his ride in the help-hand back up to the isle of Drevlin.

And all the time, he couldn't help wondering: What? . . . Why? . . .

CHAPTER ◆ 19

LEK, DREVLIN,

LOW REALM

◆

Jarre waited impatiently for the Kicksey-winsey to slowly and laboriously wind up the cable from which dangled the help-hand. Occasionally, if some other Geg happened by, she would pull her scarf low over her face and stare with intense and frowning interest at a large round glass case in which lived a black arrow that did practically nothing all its life but hover uncertainly between a great many black lines all marked with strange and obscure symbols. The only thing the Gegs knew about this black arrow—known fondly as the pointy-finger—was that when it flopped over into the area where the black lines all turned red, the Gegs ran for their lives.

This night the pointy-finger was behaving, giving no indication that it was about to unleash blasting gusts of steam that would parboil any Geg caught within reach. Tonight everything was fine, just fine. The wheels were turning, the gears shifting, the cogs cogging. Cables came up and went down. The dig-claws deposited their loads of ore into carts pushed by the Gegs, who dumped the contents into the gigantic maw of the Kicksey-winsey, which chewed up the ore, spit out what it didn't want, and digested the rest.

Most of the Gegs working tonight were members of WUPP. During the day, one of their crew had sighted the dig-claw with Limbeck's L on it. By extraordinary good fortune, the claw belonged to the part of the Kicksey-winsey located near the capital city of Wombe. Jarre, traveling—with the aid of WUPP members—

by flashraft, had arrived in time to meet her beloved and re-nowned leader.

All the dig-claws had come up except one which appeared to have broken down on the isle below. Jarre left her supposed work station and came over to join the other Gegs, peering anxiously down into the gap—a large shaft that had been bored straight through the coralite isle, opening out onto the sky be-low. Occasionally Jarre glanced around nervously, for she wasn't supposed to be on this work crew, and if she was caught, there would be a lot of explaining to do. Fortunately, other Gegs rarely came into the help-hand area, doing so only if there was trouble with one of the claws. She looked up uneasily at the carts being rolled around on the level above her.

"Don't worry," said Lof. "If anyone looks down here, they'll just think we're helping to fix a claw."

Lof was a comely young Geg. He admired Jarre immensely and hadn't been exactly deeply grieved to hear of Limbeck's execution. Lof squeezed Jarre's hand and seemed inclined to hang on to it, but Jarre needed her hand herself and took it back.

"There it is!" she cried excitedly, pointing down into the gap. "That's it!"

"You mean that thing that just got struck by lightning?" asked Lof hopefully.

"No!" Jarre snapped. "I mean yes, but it wasn't hit."

They could all see the help-hand, clutching its bubble, rising up out of the gap. Never before had it seemed to Jarre that the Kicksey-winsey was so slow. Several times she wondered if it hadn't broken down, and looked at the giant winder-upper, only to see it crankily winding away.

And, at length, the help-hand rose up into the Kicksey-winsey. The winder-upper screeched to a halt, the gap closed beneath the hand with a rumble, floor plates sliding across to provide safe footing.

"It's him! It's Limbeck!" exclaimed Jarre, who could see a blurry blob through the glass of the bubble that was streaming with rain.

"I'm not sure," said Lof dubiously, still clinging to a frag-ment of hope. "Does Limbeck have a tail?"

But Jarre didn't hear. She rushed across the floor before the gap had quite closed all the way, the other Gegs hastening after her. Reaching the door, she began to yank on it impatiently.

"It won't open!" she cried, panicked.

Lof, sighing, reached up and turned the handle.

"Limbeck!" shrieked Jarre, and jumped inside the bubble, only to tumble out again with undue haste.

There came from inside a loud and unfriendly-sounding wuff.

The Gegs, noting Jarre's pale face, backed away from the bubble.

"What is it?" questioned one.

"A d-dog, I think," stammered Jarre.

"Then it's *not* Limbeck?" said Lof eagerly.

A weak voice came from inside.

"Yes, it's me! The dog's all right. You startled it, that's all. It's worried about its master. Here, give me a hand. This bubble's a tight fit with all of us in here."

Tips of fingers could be seen waggling from the door. The Gegs glanced at each other apprehensively and, with one accord, took another step back.

Jarre paused expectantly, looking for help from each Geg in turn. Each Geg, in turn, looked at the winder-upper or the munching-chopper or the rumble-floor—anywhere but at the bubble that had wuffed.

"Hey, help me get out of this thing!" shouted Limbeck.

Her lips pursed together in a straight line that boded no good for anyone, Jarre marched up to the bubble and inspected the hand. It looked like Limbeck's hand—ink stains and all. Somewhat gingerly she grasped hold of it and tugged. Lof's hopes were dashed, once and for all, when Limbeck—face flushed and sweating—appeared in the doorway.

"Hullo, my dear," said Limbeck, shaking hands with Jarre, completely ignoring, in his distraction, that she had held her face up to be kissed. Stepping out of the bubble, he immediately turned back around and appeared to be entering it again.

"Here, now help me get him out," he called from inside, his voice echoing weirdly.

"Who's him?" asked Jarre. "The dog? Can't it get out by itself?"

Limbeck turned around to beam at them. "A god!" he said triumphantly. "I've brought back a god!"

The Gegs stared at him in amazed and suspicious silence.

Jarre was the first to recover her power of speech. "Limbeck," she said sternly, "was that really necessary?"

"Why, uh . . . yes! Yes, of course!" he answered, somewhat

taken aback. "You didn't believe me. Here, help me get him out. He's hurt."

"Hurt?" demanded Lof, seeing, once more, hope glimmer. "How can a god be hurt?"

"Aha!" shouted Limbeck, and it was such a mighty and powerful "Aha" that poor Lof was blown off the track and was completely, finally, and forever out of the race. "That's my point!" Limbeck vanished back into the bubble.

There was some difficulty with the dog, which was standing in front of its master and growling. Limbeck was more than a little concerned at this. He and the dog had developed an understanding on the ride up in the bubble. But this understanding—that Limbeck would remain unmoving in his corner and the dog wouldn't rip out his throat—didn't seem likely to be useful in placating the animal and persuading him to move. "Nice doggy"'s and "There's a good boy"'s didn't get him anywhere. Desperate, fearful his god would die, Limbeck attempted to reason with the beast.

"Look," he said, "we don't want to hurt him. We want to help him! And the only way we can help him is to get him out of this contraption and to a place where he'll be safe. We'll take very good care of him, I promise." The dog's growling lessened; the animal was watching the Geg with what appeared to be wary interest. "You can come along. And if anything happens that you don't like, then you can rip out my throat!"

The dog cocked his head to one side, ears erect, listening intently. When the Geg concluded, the dog regarded him gravely.

I'll give you a chance, but remember that I still have my teeth.

"It says it's all right," shouted Limbeck happily.

"What says?" demanded Jarre when the dog, jumping lightly out of the bubble, landed on the floor at Limbeck's feet.

The Gegs instantly scrambled for cover, dodging behind those parts of the Kicksey-winsey that seemed likely to be proof against sharp fangs. Only Jarre held her ground, determined not to desert the man she loved, no matter what the danger. The dog wasn't the least bit interested in the quivering Gegs, however. Its attention was centered completely on its master.

"Here!" panted Limbeck, tugging at the god's feet. "You get this end, Jarre. I'll take his head. There, carefully. Carefully. That's got him, I think."

Having braved the dog, Jarre felt equal to anything, even hauling gods around by their feet. Casting a withering glance at her cowardly compatriots, she grasped hold of the god's leather boots and tugged. Limbeck guided the limp body out of the bubble, catching hold of the shoulders when they appeared. Together the Gegs eased the god onto the floor.

"Oh, my," said Jarre softly, her fear forgotten in pity. She touched the gash on his head with a gentle hand. Her fingers came away covered with blood. "He's hurt awfully bad!"

"I know," said Limbeck anxiously. "And I had to handle him kind of roughly, dragging him out of his ship before the dig-claw smashed him to bits."

"His skin's icy cold. His lips are blue. If he were a Geg, I'd say he was dying. But maybe gods are supposed to look like that."

"I don't think so. He didn't look like that when I first saw him, just after his ship crashed. Oh, Jarre, he just *can't* die!"

The dog, hearing the compassion in Jarre's voice and seeing her touch his master soothingly, gave her hand a swipe with his tongue and looked up at her with pleading brown eyes.

Jarre was startled at first at feeling the wet slurp, then relaxed. "Why, there, don't worry. It's going to be all right," she said softly, reaching out and timidly giving the animal a pat on the head. He suffered her to do so, flattening his ears and wagging his bushy tail ever so slightly.

"Do you think it will be?" asked Limbeck in deep concern.

"Of course! Look, his eyelids are moving." Briskly Jarre swung around and began giving orders. "The first thing to do is get him someplace warm and quiet where we can take care of him. It's almost time for scrift change. We don't want anyone to see him—"

"We don't?" interrupted Limbeck.

"No! Not until he's well and we're ready to answer questions. This will be a great moment in the history of our people. We don't want to spoil it by rushing into anything. You and Lof go get a litter—"

"A litter? The god won't fit on a litter," Lof pointed out sulkily. "His legs'll hang over the edge and his feet'll drag the floor!"

"That's true." Jarre wasn't accustomed to dealing with a person whose body was so long and narrow. She paused, frowning, when suddenly a clanging gong sounding very loudly caused her to glance around in alarm. "What's that?"

"They're going to be opening the floor!" Lof gasped.

"What floor?" inquired Limbeck curiously.

"This floor!" Lof pointed at the metal plates beneath their feet.

"Why? Oh, I see." Limbeck looked upward at the dig-claws that had dumped their load and were being readied to descend into the gap to fetch up another.

"We've got to get out of here!" Lof said urgently. Sidling up to Jarre, he whispered, "Let the god stay. When the floor opens, he'll drop back into the air where he came from. His dog too."

But Jarre wasn't paying attention. She was watching the carts trundle along overhead.

"Lof!" she said excitedly, grabbing hold of him by his beard and yanking—a habit she had acquired when dealing with Limbeck and one she found difficult to break. "Those carts! The god will fit inside one of those! Hurry! Hurry!"

The floor was beginning to vibrate ominously, and anything was better than having his beard pulled out by the roots. Lof nodded and ran off with the other Gegs to acquire an empty cart.

Jarre wrapped the god snugly in her own cloak. She and Limbeck dragged him away from the center of the floor, as close to the edge as they could possibly get. By this time, Lof and company had returned with the cart, rolling it down the steep ramp that connected the bottom level with the one above. The gong sounded again. The dog whined and barked. Either the noise hurt its ears or it sensed the danger and was urging the Gegs on. (Lof insisted it was the first. Limbeck argued it was the second. Jarre ordered them both to shut up and work.)

Between them, the Gegs managed to drag the body of the god into the cart. Jarre swaddled the god's injured head in Lof's cloak (Lof seemed inclined to protest, but a smack on the cheek delivered by a nervous and exasperated Jarre brought him around). The gong sounded a third time. Cables creaking and screeching, the dig-claws began to descend. The floor rumbled and started to open. The Gegs, all but losing their footing, lined up in back of the cart and gave a great heave. The cart leapt forward and rolled up the ramp, the Gegs sweating and straining behind it, the dog running around their feet and nipping at their heels.

Gegs are strong, but the cart was made of iron and quite heavy, not to mention that it had the added weight of the god inside. It had never been intended to travel a ramp used mainly by Gegs, and it was far more inclined to roll down the ramp than up it.

Limbeck, noting this, had vague thoughts of weight, inertia, and gravity and would have undoubtedly developed another law of physics had he not been in dire peril of his life. The floor was gaping wide open beneath them, the dig-claws were thundering down into the void, and there came one particularly tense moment when it seemed that the Gegs couldn't hold on and that the cart must win and end up carrying Gegs, god, dog, and all into the gap.

"Now, once more, together!" grunted Jarre. Her stout body was braced against the cart, her face fiery red from the exertion. Limbeck, beside her, wasn't much help, being naturally weak anyway and further weakened by his grueling experience. But he was valiantly doing what he could. Lof was flagging and seemed about to give up.

"Lof," gasped Jarre, "if it starts to roll back, put your foot under the wheel!"

This command from his leader gave Lof, who was naturally flat-footed but saw no reason to carry it to extremes, extra incentive. Strength renewed, he put his shoulder to the cart, gritted his teeth, shut his eyes, and gave a mighty shove. The cart surged forward with such force that Limbeck fell to his knees and slid halfway down the ramp before he could manage to stop himself. The cart popped over the top of the ramp. The Gegs tumbled, exhausted, to the floor of the upper level, and the dog licked Lof's face—much to that Geg's consternation. Limbeck crawled up the ramp on his hands and knees and, reaching the top, sank down in a swoon.

"This is all I need!" Jarre muttered in exasperation.

"I'm not hauling *him* around too!" protested Lof bitterly. He was beginning to think that his father had been right and that he should never have involved himself in politics.

A vicious tug on his beard and a sound smack on the cheek brought Limbeck to semi-consciousness. He began babbling something about inclines and planes, but Jarre told him to keep quiet and make himself useful by picking up the dog and hiding it in the cart with its master.

"And tell it to keep quiet, too!" Jarre commanded.

Limbeck's eyes opened so wide that it seemed they might fall out of his head. "M-me? P-pick up th-that—"

But the dog, seeming to understand, solved the problem by jumping lightly into the cart, where it curled up at its master's feet.

Jarre took a peep at the god and reported that he was still alive and looked somewhat better now that he was wrapped up in the cloaks. The Gegs covered his body with small chunks of coralite and various debris that the Kicksey-winsey let fall from time to time, tossed a gunnysack over the dog, and headed the cart for the nearest exit.

No one stopped them. No one demanded to know *why* they were shoving an ore cart through the tunnels. No one wanted to know *where* they were going or *what* they were going to do once they got there. Jarre, grinning wearily, said it was all for the best. Limbeck, sighing, shook his head and pronounced this lack of curiosity a sad commentary on his people.

CHAPTER ♦ 20

LEK, DREVLIN, LOW REALM

♦

IN THE LABYRINTH, A MAN MUST HONE HIS INSTINCTS TO A FINE, SHARP point, as sharp as any blade of knife or sword, for the instincts, too, are weapons of self-preservation and are oftentimes as valuable as steel. Struggling to regain consciousness, Haplo instinctively kept himself from revealing that he was conscious. Until he could regain complete control of every faculty, he lay perfectly still and unmoving, stifled a groan of pain, and firmly resisted the overwhelming impulse to open his eyes and look at his surroundings.

Play dead. Many times, an enemy will let you alone.

Voices swam in and out of his hearing. Mentally he grasped at them, but it was like snagging fish with bare hands. They darted among his fingers; he could touch them but never quite catch hold. They were loud, deep voices, sounding quite clearly over a roaring thrumming that seemed to be all around him, even inside of him, for he could swear he could feel his body vibrating. The voices were some distance away and sounded as if they were arguing, but they weren't being violent about it. Haplo did not feel threatened and he relaxed.

"I've fallen in with Squatters, seemingly. . . ."

". . . The boy's still alive. Got a nasty crack on the head, but he'll make it."

"The other two? I suppose they're his parents."

"Dead. Runners, by the looks of them. Snogs got them, of course. I guess they thought the kid too little to bother with."

"Naw. Snogs don't care what they kill. I don't think they ever knew the kid was there. He was well-hidden in those bushes. If he hadn't groaned, we never would've heard him. It saved his life this time, but it's a bad habit. We'll have to break him of it. My guess is the parents knew they were in trouble. They clouted the kid a good one to keep him quiet and hid him away, then tried to lead the snogs away from him."

"Lucky thing for the kid it was snogs and not dragons. Dragons would've sniffed him out."

"What's his name?"

The boy felt hands run over his body, which was naked except for a strip of soft leather tied around his loins. The hands traced a pattern of tattoos that began at his heart, extending across his chest, down his stomach and legs to the tops of his feet but not the soles, down his arms to the back of his hands but not the fingers or the palms, up his neck but not on the head or face.

"Haplo," said the man, reading the runes over the heart. "He was born the time the Seventh Gate fell. That would make him about nine."

"Lucky to have lived this long. I can't imagine Runners trying to make it, saddled with a kid. We better be getting out of here. Dragons'll be smelling the blood before long. Come on, boy. Wake up. On your feet. We can't carry you. Here, you, awake now? All right." Grabbing him by the shoulder, the man took Haplo to stand beside the hacked and mangled bodies of his parents. "Look at that. Remember it. And remember this. It wasn't snogs that killed your father and mother. It was those who put us in this prison and left us to die. Who are they, boy? Do you know?" His fingers dug into Haplo's flesh.

"The Sartan," answered Haplo thickly.

"Repeat it."

"The Sartan!" he cried.

"Right, never forget that, boy. Never forget. . . ."

Haplo floated again to the surface of consciousness. The roaring, drumming sound whooshed and thumped around him but he could hear voices over it, the same voices he vaguely remembered hearing earlier, only now there seemed to be fewer of them. He tried to concentrate on their words, but it was impossible. The throbbing pain in his head stamped out every spark of rational thought. He had to end the pain.

Cautiously Haplo opened his eyes a crack and peered out between the lashes. The light of a single candle, placed somewhere near his head, did not illuminate his surroundings. He had no idea where he was, but he could manage to make out that he was alone.

Slowly Haplo lifted his left hand and was bringing it near his head when he saw that it was swathed in strips of cloth. Memory glimmered, shining a feeble ray of light into the darkness of pain that surrounded him.

All the more reason to rid himself of this debilitating injury.

Gritting his teeth, moving with elaborate care so as not to make the slightest sound, Haplo reached across with his right hand and tugged at the cloth covering the left. Wrapped in between the fingers, it did not come completely loose but gave way enough so that the back of the left hand was partially exposed.

The skin was covered with tattoos. The whirls and whorls, curls and curves, were done in colors of red and blue and were seemingly fanciful in nature and design. Yet each sigil had its separate and special meaning, which, when combined with other sigla that they touched, expanded into meaning upon meaning.[1] Prepared to freeze his motion at the barest hint that someone was watching him, Haplo raised his arm and pressed the back of his hand upon the gash in his forehead.

The circle was joined. Warmth streamed from his hand to his head, flowed through his head to his arm, from his arm back to his hand. Sleep would follow, and while his body rested, pain would ease, the wound would close, internal injuries would be healed, complete memory and awareness would be restored on his awaking. With his waning strength, Haplo arranged the cloth so that it covered his hand. His arm fell limply, striking a hard surface beneath him. A cold nose thrust into his palm . . . a soft muzzle rubbed against his fingers. . . .

*   *   *

[1]Much as two words, each with its own definition, can be combined to form a third word with a meaning all its own, yet deriving from the other two. This is a very crude explanation of the rune language of the Patryns, who can create a wide variety of magical effects with the placement of each sigil in relationship to others.

. . . Spear in hand, Haplo faced the two chaodyn. His only emotion was anger—a fiery, raging fury that burned up fear. He was within sight of his goal. The Last Gate was visible on the horizon. To reach it, he had only to cross a vast open prairie that had looked empty when he reconnoitered. He should have known. The Labyrinth would never let him escape. It would hurl every weapon it had in its possession at him. But the Labyrinth was smart. Its malevolent intelligence had fought against the Patryns for a thousand years before a few had been able to gain the skills to conquer it. Twenty-five gates[2] Haplo had lived and fought, only to be defeated in the end. For there was no way he could win. The Labyrinth had allowed him to get well into the empty prairie without so much as a single tree or boulder on which to set his back. And it had pitted him against two chaodyn.

Chaodyn are deadly foes. Bred of the insane magic of the Labyrinth, the intelligent giant insectlike creatures are skilled in the use of all weapons (these two were using broadswords). Tall as a man, with a hard black-shelled body, bulbous eyes, four arms, and two powerful back legs, a chaodyn can be killed—everything in the Labyrinth can be killed. But in order to slay one, you have to hit it directly in the heart, destroying it instantly. For if it lives, even a second, it will cause a drop of its own blood to spring into a copy of itself, and the two of them, whole and undamaged, will continue the fight.

Haplo faced two of these, and he had only one rune-marked spear and his hunting dagger left. If his weapons missed their mark and wounded his opponent he would face four chaodyn. Missing again, he would face eight. No, he could not win.

The two chaodyn were moving, one drifting off to Haplo's right, the other to his left. When he attacked one, the other would strike him from behind. The Patryn's only chance would be to kill the first outright with his spear, then turn and fight the other.

---

[2]Patryns in the Labyrinth measure age in terms of "gates." This probably began in the early days of their imprisonment, when a person's age was determined by the number of gates through which he or she had passed—this passage being the most important symbol in their society.

When the Lord of the Nexus eventually returned to the Labyrinth to gain partial control over it with his magic, he established a standardized system of timekeeping (based on the regular sun cycles in the Nexus) to which the term "gate" now applies.

This strategy in mind, Haplo backed up, feinting first toward one, then the other, forcing them to keep their distance. They did so, toying with him, knowing that they had him, for chaodyn enjoy playing with their victims and will rarely kill outright if there is a chance they can have some sport.

Angered beyond rational thought, no longer caring whether he lived or died, wanting only to strike out at these creatures and, through them, at the Labyrinth, Haplo called on a lifetime of fear and despair and used the strength of his rage and frustration to power his throw. The spear flew from his hand; he shouted after it the rune calls that would send it flying swift and straight to his enemy. His aim was good, the spear tore through the insect's black carapace, and it fell backward, dead before it hit the ground.

A flash of pain shot through Haplo. Gasping in agony, he wrenched his body aside and whirled to face his other foe. He could feel his blood, warm against his chill skin, flow from the wound. The chaodyn cannot use the rune magic, but long experience battling the Patryns has given them the knowledge of where the tattooed body is vulnerable to attack. The head is the best target. This chaodyn, however, had stabbed its sword into Haplo's back. Obviously the insect did not want to kill him, not yet.

Haplo's spear was gone. It was hunting dagger against broadsword. Haplo could either run in under the chaodyn's guard and strike directly for the heart or he could risk a throw. His knife—used for skinning, honing, cutting—did not have runes of flight inscribed upon it. If he missed, he would be weaponless and probably facing two foes. But he had to end the battle soon. He was losing blood and he lacked a shield with which to parry the chaodyn's sword blows.

The chaodyn, realizing Haplo's dilemma, swung its huge blade. Aiming for the left arm, the insect tried to cut it off—disabling its enemy but not yet killing. Haplo saw the blow coming and dodged as best he could, turning to meet it with his shoulder. The blade sank deep, bone crunched. The pain nearly made Haplo black out. He could no longer feel his left hand, let alone use it.

The chaodyn fell back, recovering, getting itself into position for the next strike. Haplo gripped his dagger and fought to see through a red haze that was fast dimming his vision. He didn't care about his life anymore. His hatred had gained control. The last sensation he wanted to feel before his death was satisfaction in knowing he had taken his enemy with him.

The chaodyn lifted the blade again, preparing to launch another torturing blow at its helpless victim. Calm with despair, lost in a stupor that was not entirely feigned, Haplo waited. He had a new strategy. It meant he would die, but so would his foe. The insect arm swung back, and at the same moment, a black shape leapt out from somewhere behind Haplo and launched itself straight at the chaodyn.

Confused by this sudden and unexpected attack, the chaodyn glanced away from Haplo to see what was coming at it, and, in so doing, shifted the angle of its sword thrust to meet this new foe. Haplo heard a pain-filled yelp, a whimper, and had the vague impression of a furry body falling to the ground. He didn't pay any attention to what it had been. The chaodyn, lowering its arms to strike at the new threat, had left its chest exposed. Haplo aimed his dagger straight for the heart.

The chaodyn saw its danger and attempted to recover, but Haplo had come in too close. The insect creature's sword sliced into the Patryn's side, glancing off his ribs. Haplo never felt it. He drove his dagger into the chaodyn's chest with such force that they both toppled over backward and crashed to the ground.

Rolling off the body of his enemy, Haplo did not bother to try to stand. The chaodyn was dead. Now he, too, could die and find peace, like so many others before him. The Labyrinth had won. He had fought it, though. Even to the end.

Haplo lay on the ground and let his life seep out of his body. He could have tried to heal himself, but that would have required effort, movement, more pain. He didn't want to move. He didn't want to hurt anymore. He yawned, feeling sleepy. It was pleasant to lie here and know that soon he wouldn't have to fight ever again.

A low whining sound caused him to open his eyes, not so much in fear as in irritation that he wasn't going to be allowed to die in peace. Turning his head slightly, he saw a dog. So that was the black furry thing that had attacked the chaodyn. Where had it come from? Presumably it had been out in the prairie, perhaps hunting, and had come to his aid.

The dog crouched on its belly, head between its paws. Seeing Haplo looking at it, the dog whined again and, dragging itself forward, made an attempt to lick the man's hand. It was then that Haplo saw the dog was hurt.

Blood flowed from a deep gash in the animal's body. Haplo recalled vaguely hearing its cry and the whimper when it fell. The dog was staring at him hopefully, expecting—as dogs do— that this human would care for it and make the terrible pain it was suffering go away.

"I'm sorry," Haplo mumbled drowsily. "I can't help you. I can't even help myself."

The dog, at the sound of the man's voice, feebly wagged its bushy tail and continued to regard him with complete, trusting faith.

"Go off and die somewhere else!" Haplo made an abrupt, angry gesture. Pain tore through his body, and he cried out in agony. The dog gave a small bark, and Haplo felt a soft muzzle nudge his hand. Hurt as it was, the animal was offering him sympathy.

And then Haplo, glancing over half-irritably, half-comforted, saw that the injured dog was struggling to rise to its feet. Standing unsteadily, the dog fixed its gaze on the line of trees behind them. It licked Haplo's hand once more, then set off, limping feebly, for the forest.

It had misunderstood Haplo's gesture. It was going to try to go for help—help for him.

The dog didn't get very far. Whimpering, it managed to take two or three faltering steps before it collapsed. Pausing a moment to rest, the animal tried again.

"Stop it!" Haplo whispered. "Stop it! It's not worth it!"

The animal, not understanding, turned its head and looked at the man as if to say, "Be patient. I can't go very fast but I won't let you down."

Selflessness, compassion, pity—these are not considered by the Patryns to be virtues. They are faults belonging to lesser races who cover for these inherent weaknesses by exalting them. Haplo was not flawed. Ruthless, defiant, burning with hatred, he'd fought and battled his way through the Labyrinth, solitary and alone. He had never asked for help. He had never offered it. And he had survived, where many others had fallen. Until now.

"You're a coward," he said to himself. "This dumb animal has the courage to fight to live, and you give up. What's more, you will die owing. Die with a debt on your soul, for, like it or not, that dog saved your life."

No tender feeling caused Haplo to reach across with his right hand and grasp his useless left. It was shame and pride that drove him.

"Come here!" he commanded the dog.

The dog, too weak to stand, crawled on its belly, leaving a trail of blood in the grass behind.

Gritting his teeth, gasping, crying out against the pain, Haplo pressed the sigil on the back of his hand against the dog's torn flank. Letting it rest there, he placed his right hand on the dog's head. The healing circle was formed; Haplo saw, with his fading vision, the dog's wound close. . . .

"If he recovers, we'll take him to the high froman and offer him proof that what I said was true! We'll show him and our people that the Welves aren't gods! Our people will see that they've been used and lied to all these years."

"*If* he recovers," murmured a softer female voice. "He's hurt really bad, Limbeck. There's that deep gash on the head, and he may be hurt someplace else too. The dog won't let me get close enough to find out. Not that it matters. Head injuries as bad as that almost always lead to death. You remember when Hal Hammernail missed a step on the pussyfoot and tumbled down—"

"I know. I know," came the discouraged reply. "Oh, Jarre, he just *can't* die! I want you to hear all about his world. It's a beautiful place, like I saw in the books. With clear blue sky and a bright shining light beaming down, and wonderful tall buildings as big as the Kicksey-winsey—"

"Limbeck," said the female voice sternly, "you didn't happen to hit *your* head, did you?"

"No, my dear. I saw them! I truly did! Just like I saw the dead gods. I've brought proof, Jarre! Why won't you believe me?"

"Oh, Limbeck, I don't know what to believe anymore! I used to see everything so clearly—all black and white, with clean, sharp edges. I knew exactly what I wanted for our people— better living conditions, equal share in the Welf's pay. That was all. Stir up a little trouble, put pressure on the high froman, and he'd be forced to give in eventually. Now everything's a muddle, all gray and confusing. You're talking about revolution, Limbeck! Tearing down everything we've believed in for hundreds of years. And what do you have to put in its place?"

"We have the truth, Jarre."

Haplo smiled. He had been awake and listening for about an hour now. He understood the basic language—though these beings called themselves "Gegs," he recognized the tongue as a derivative of one known on the Old World as dwarven. But there were a great many things they said that he didn't understand. For example, what was this Kicksey-winsey that they spoke of with such reverent awe? That was why he'd been sent here. To learn. To keep eyes and ears open, mouth shut, and hands off.

Reaching down on the floor beside his bed, Haplo scratched the dog's head, reassuring the animal that he was well. This journey through Death Gate had not started out exactly as planned. Somewhere, somehow, his liege lord had made serious miscalculations. The runes had been misaligned. Haplo had realized the mistake too late. There had been little he could do to prevent the crash, the resultant destruction of his ship.

The realization that he was now trapped on this world did not unduly worry Haplo. He had been trapped in the Labyrinth and escaped. After that experience, on an ordinary world such as this, he would be—as his lord said—"invincible." Haplo had only to play his part. Somehow, after he'd done what he came to do, he would find a way back.

"I thought I heard something."

Jarre entered the room, bringing with her a flood of soft candlelight. Haplo squinted, blinking up at her. The dog growled and started to jump up, but it lay still at its master's stealthy, commanding touch.

"Limbeck!" Jarre cried.

"He's dead!" The stout Geg came hurrying anxiously into the room.

"No, no, he's not!" Sinking down beside the bed, Jarre reached out a trembling hand toward Haplo's forehead. "Look! The wound's healed! Completely. Not . . . not even a scar! Oh, Limbeck! Maybe you're wrong! Maybe this being truly is a god!"

"No," said Haplo. Propping himself up on one elbow, he gazed intently at the startled Gegs. "I was a slave." He spoke slowly in a low voice, fumbling for words in the thick dwarven tongue. "Once I was as you are now. But my people triumphed over their masters and I have come to help you do the same."

CHAPTER ♦ 21

PITRIN'S EXILE,

MID REALM

♦

THE JOURNEY ACROSS PITRIN'S EXILE WAS EASIER THAN HUGH HAD anticipated. Bane kept up gamely, and when he did tire, he tried very hard not to show it. Alfred watched the boy anxiously, and when the prince began to show signs of being footsore, it was the chamberlain who announced that he himself could not proceed another step. Alfred was, in fact, having a much more difficult time of it than his small charge. The man's feet seemed possessed of a will of their own and were continually going off on some divergent path, stumbling into nonexistent holes or tripping over twigs invisible to the eye.

Consequently, they did not make very good time. Hugh did not push them, did not push himself. They were not far from the wooded inlet on the isle's edge, where he kept his ship moored, and he felt a reluctance to reach it—a reluctance that angered him, but one for which he refused to account.

The walking was pleasant, for Bane and Hugh, at least. The air was cold, but the sun shone and kept the chill from being bitter. There was little wind. They met more than the usual number of travelers on the road, taking advantage of this brief spell of good weather to make whatever pressing journeys had to be made during the winter. The weather was also fine for raiding, and Hugh noted that everyone kept one eye on the road and one on the sky, as the saying went.

They saw three of the dragon-headed, sail-winged elven ships, but they were far distant, traveling to some unknown destination on the kiratrack side. That same day, a flight of fifty dragons passed directly overhead. They could see the dragonknights in their saddles, the bright winter sun gleaming off helm and breast-plate, javelin and arrow tips. This detail had a wizardess with them, flying in the center, surrounded by knights. She carried no visible weapons, only her magic, and that was in her mind. The dragonknights were headed toward the kiratrack as well. The elves weren't the only ones who would take advantage of clear, windless days.

Bane watched the elven ships with wide-eyed, openmouthed, boyish awe. He had never seen one, he said, and was bitterly disappointed that they didn't come closer. A scandalized Alfred had, in fact, been forced to restrain His Highness from pulling off his hood and using it as a flag to wave them this direction. Travelers along the road had not been at all amused by this stunt. Hugh took grim delight in watching the peasants scatter for cover before Alfred managed to put a damper on His High-ness's enthusiasm.

That night, as they gathered around the fire after their frugal meal, Bane went over to sit beside Hugh, instead of his usual place near the chamberlain. Squatting down, he made himself comfortable.

"Will you tell me about the elves, Sir Hugh?"

"How do you know I have anything to tell?" Hugh fished his pipe and the pouch of sterego out of his pack. Leaning back against a tree, his feet stretched out to the flames, he shook the dried fungus out of the leather pouch and into the round, smooth bowl.

Bane gazed not at the assassin but at a point somewhere to Hugh's right, over his shoulder. His blue eyes lost their focus. Hugh thrust a stick into the fire and used it to light his pipe. Puffing on it, he watched the boy with idle curiosity.

"I see a great battle," said Bane dreamily. "I see elves and men fighting and dying. I see defeat and despair, and then I hear men singing and there is joy."

Hugh sat still for so long that his pipe went out. Alfred shifted position uncomfortably and put his palm on a hot coal. Stifling a cry of pain, he wrung his injured hand.

"Your Highness," he said miserably, "I have told you—"

"No, never mind." Casually Hugh knocked the ash out of his pipe, filled it, and lit it again. He puffed on it slowly, his gaze fixed on the boy. "You just described the Battle of Seven Fields."

"You were there," said Bane.

Hugh blew a thin trail of smoke into the air. "Yes, and so was nearly every other human male near my age, including your father, the king." Hugh took a long drag on the pipe. "If this is what you're calling clairvoyance, Alfred, I've seen better acts in a third-rate inn. The boy must have heard the story from his father a hundred times."

Bane's face underwent a swift and startling change—the happiness dissolved into stark, searing pain. Biting his lips, he lowered his head and brushed his hand across his eyes.

Alfred fixed Hugh with an odd look—one that was almost pleading. "I assure you, Sir Hugh, that this gift of His Highness's is quite real and should not be taken lightly. Bane, Sir Hugh does not understand magic, that is all. He is sorry. Now, why don't you get yourself a sweetmelt from the pack."

Bane left Hugh's side, going over to the chamberlain's pack to find his treat. Alfred pitched his voice for Hugh's ears alone. "It's just . . . You see, sir, the king never really talked that much to the boy. King Stephen was never quite . . . uh . . . comfortable in Bane's presence."

No, Hugh mused, Stephen must not have found it pleasant to look into the face of his shame. Perhaps, in the boy's features, the king saw a man he—and his queen—knew all too well.

The glow of the pipe died. Knocking out the ashes, Hugh found a small twig and, splitting the end with his dagger, thrust it into the bowl and attempted to clean out the blockage. He cast a glance at the boy and saw Bane still rummaging through the pack.

"You really believe this kid can do what he claims—sees pictures in the air—don't you?"

"He can!" Alfred assured him earnestly. "I have seen him do it too many times to doubt. And you must believe it too, sir, or else . . ."

Hugh, pausing in his work, looked up at Alfred.

"Or else? That sounds very much like a threat."

Alfred cast his eyes down. His hurt hand nervously plucked the leaves off a cupplant. "I . . . I didn't mean it—"

"Yes, you did." Hugh knocked the pipe on a rock. "It wouldn't have anything to do with that feather he wears, would it? The one given him by a mysteriarch?"

Alfred went livid, becoming so pale Hugh was half-afraid he

might faint again. The chamberlain swallowed several times before he found his voice. "I don't—"

A snapping branch interrupted him. Bane was returning to the fire. Hugh saw Alfred cast the boy the grateful glance of a drowning man who has been tossed a rope.

The prince, absorbed in enjoying his sweetmelt, didn't notice. He threw himself on the ground and, picking up a stick, began to poke at the fire.

"Would you like to hear the story of the Battle of Seven Fields, Your Highness?" Hugh asked quietly.

The prince looked up, eyes shining. "I'll bet you were a hero, weren't you, Sir Hugh!"

"Begging your pardon, sir," interrupted Alfred meekly, "but I don't take you for a patriot. How did you chance to be at the battle to free our homeland?"

Hugh was about to reply when the chamberlain winced and hurriedly jumped up. Reaching down on the ground where he'd been sitting, Alfred picked up a large piece of broken coralite. Its knife-sharp edges sparkled in the firelight. Fortunately, the leather breeches he wore, which they had purchased from a cobbler, had protected him from serious harm.

"You're right. Politics mean nothing to me." A thin trickle of smoke curled up from Hugh's lips. "Let's just say that I was there on business. . . ."

. . . A man entered the inn and stood blinking in the dim light. It was early morning, and the common room was empty except for a slovenly woman scrubbing the floor and a traveler seated at a table in deep shadow.

"Are you Hugh, called the Hand?" the man who had entered asked the traveler.

"I am."

"I want to hire you." The man plunked a bag down in front of Hugh. Opening it and sorting through it, Hugh saw coins, jewelry, and even a few silver spoons. Pausing, he lifted out what was obviously a woman's wedding ring and looked at the man narrowly.

"That comes from a number of us, for none was rich enough to hire you himself. We gave what valuables we had."

"Who's the mark?"

"A certain captain who hires himself out to the gentry to train and lead foot soldiers in battle. He's a bully and a coward and he's sent more than one squad to its doom while he's stayed safe behind and collected his fee. You'll find him with Warren of Kurinandistai, marching with the army of King Stephen. I've heard they're headed for a place called Seven Fields, on the continent."

"And what's the special service you require of me? You and"—Hugh patted the money sack—"all these."

"Widows and kinsmen of those he last led, sir," said the man. His eyes glinted. "We ask this for our money: that he be killed in such a manner that it will be obvious no enemy hand touched him, that he knows who has bought his death, and"—the man carefully held out to Hugh a small scroll—"that this be left on the body. . . ."

"Sir Hugh?" said Bane impatiently. "Go on. Tell me about Seven Fields."

"It was back when the elves ruled us. Over the years, the elves had grown soft in their occupation of our land." Hugh gazed at the smoke curling upward into the darkness. "Elves consider humans to be little better than animals, and so they underrate us. In many ways, of course, they're right, and so you can hardly blame them for continuing to make what seems to be the same mistake over and over.

"The Uylandia Cluster, at the time they ruled it, was divided into bits and pieces, each small bit ruled nominally by a human lord and in actuality by an elven overlord. The elves never had to work to keep the clans from uniting—the clans did that quite well themselves."

"I've often wondered why the elves didn't demand that we destroy our weapons, as was done in centuries past?" interjected Alfred.

Hugh, puffing on the pipe, grinned. "Why bother? It was to their advantage to keep us armed. We used our weapons on each other, saving the elves a lot of trouble.

"The plan worked, so well, in fact, that the elves shut themselves up in their fine castles, never bothering to open a window and take a good look at what was really transpiring around them. I know, for I used to hear their talk."

"You did!" Bane sat forward, blue eyes glittering. "How? How did you come to know so much about elves?"

The ash glowed red in the pipe, then dimmed and faded. Hugh ignored the question.

"When Stephen and Anne managed to unite the clans, the elves finally opened their windows. In flew arrows and spears, and humans with swords scaled their walls. The uprising was swift and well-planned. By the time word reached the Tribus Empire, most of the elven overlords had been killed or driven from their homes. The elves retaliated. They assembled their fleet—the greatest ever seen in this world—and sailed for Uylandia. Hundreds of thousands of trained elven warriors and their sorcerers faced a few thousand humans—without our most powerful wizards, for by then the mysteriarchs had fled. Our people never stood a chance. Hundreds were slaughtered. More taken prisoner. King Stephen was captured alive—"

"It was not his wish!" cried Alfred, stung by the sardonic tone in Hugh's voice.

The pipe gleamed and dimmed. The Hand said nothing; Alfred was goaded by the silence into continuing talking, when he had never meant to speak. "The elven prince Reesh'ahn had marked Stephen out and ordered his men to take the king unharmed. Stephen's lords fell at his side, defending him. And even when he stood alone, he fought on. They say there was a ring of dead around him, for the elves dared not disobey their ruler, and yet none could get close enough to take him without being killed. Finally they rushed him en masse, bore him to the ground, and disarmed him. Stephen fought bravely, as bravely as any of them."

"I wouldn't know about that," said the Hand. "All I know is that the army surrendered—"

Shocked, Bane turned to face him. "You must be mistaken, Sir Hugh! Our army *won* the Battle of Seven Fields!"

"Our army won?" Hugh raised an eyebrow. "No, it wasn't the army who won. It was one woman who beat the elves—a minstrel called Ravenlark, for, they said, her skin was black as a raven's feathers and her voice was like that of a lark singing to welcome the dawn. Her lord had brought her to sing his victory, I suppose, but she ended up chanting his death song. She was captured and taken prisoner like the rest of the humans. They were herded together on a road that ran through the Seven Fields, a road littered with the bodies of the dead, wet with their blood. They were a pitiful lot, for they knew the fate that awaited them—slavery. Envying those who had died, they stood with heads bowed and shoulders slumped.

"And then the minstrel began to sing. It was an old song, one everyone remembers from childhood."

"I know it!" Bane cried eagerly. "I've heard this part."

"Sing it, then," said Alfred, smiling at the boy, pleased to see him happy again.

"It's called 'Hand of Flame.' " The boy's voice rose shrill and slightly off-key but enthusiastic:

The Hand that holds the Arc and Bridge,
The Fire that rails the Temp'red Span,
All Flame as Heart, surmount the Ridge,
All noble Paths are *Ellxman*.[1]
    Fire in Heart guides the Will,
    The Will of Flame, set by Hand,
    The Hand that moves *Ellxman* Song,
    The Song of Fire and Heart and Land:
    The Fire born of Journey's End,
    The Flame a part, a lightened call,
    The sullen walk, the flick'ring aim,
    Fire leads again from futures, all.
    The Arc and Bridge are thoughts and heart,
    The Span a life, the Ridge a part.

"My nurse taught it to me when I was little. But she couldn't tell me what the words meant. Do you know, Sir Hugh?"

"I doubt if anyone does now. The tune stirs the heart. Ravenlark began to sing it, and soon the prisoners lifted their heads proudly, their backs stiffened. They lined up into formation, determined to walk to slavery or death with dignity."

"I've heard it said the song is elvish in origin," murmured Alfred. "And dates back to before the Sundering."

Hugh shrugged, uninterested. "Who knows? All anyone cares about is that it has an effect on elves. From the sound of the first few notes, the elves stood transfixed, staring straight ahead. They looked like men in a dream, except that their eyes moved. Some claimed they were 'seeing pictures.' "

Bane flushed, his hand tightly grasping the feather.

"The prisoners, noticing this, kept on singing. The minstrel knew the words to all the verses. Most of the prisoners were lost after the first, but they kept up the tune and joined in strong on

---

[1]Elven word for "elf." The x is a guttural sound, pronounced "ich."

the chorus. The elves' weapons fell from their hands. Prince Reesh'ahn sank to his knees and began to weep. And, at Stephen's command, the prisoners marched away as fast as their feet could carry them."

"It was to His Majesty's credit that he didn't order a helpless enemy slaughtered," said Alfred.

The Hand snorted. "For all the king knew, a sword in the throat might have broken the spell. Our men were beaten. They wanted only to get out of there. The king had it in his mind, so I've been told, to fall back on one of the nearby castles and regroup and strike again. But it wasn't necessary. When the elves came to their senses, the king's spies reported that they were like men awakened from a beautiful dream who long to go back to sleep. They left their weapons and their dead where they lay and returned to their ships. Once there, they freed their human slaves and limped home."

"The beginning of the elven revolution."

"Supposedly so." Hugh dragged slowly on the pipe. "The elf king proclaimed his son, Prince Reesh'ahn, a disgrace and an outlaw and drove him into exile. Reesh'ahn's now stirring up trouble throughout Aristagon. There've been attempts made to capture him, but each time he's slipped through their fingers."

"And with him, they say, travels the minstrel woman, who—according to legend—was so moved by the prince's sorrow that she chose to follow him," added Alfred softly. "Together they sing the song, and wherever they go, they find more followers." Leaning back, he misjudged the distance between himself and the tree trunk and whanged himself on the head.

Bane giggled, then clapped his hand over his mouth. "I'm sorry, Alfred," he said contritely. "I didn't mean to laugh. Are you hurt?"

"No, Your Highness," Alfred said with a sigh. "Thank you for asking. Now, Your Highness, you should be going to sleep. We have a long day ahead of us tomorrow."

"Yes, Alfred." Bane ran to get his blanket from his pack. "If it's all right, I'm going to sleep here tonight," he said. Looking up at Hugh shyly, he spread his blanket out next to the assassin's.

Hugh rose abruptly to his feet and walked over to the fire. Knocking the bowl of the pipe against his hand, he scattered the ashes. "Rebellion." He stared into the flames, keeping his eyes averted from the child. "Ten years have passed and the Tribus

Empire is as strong as ever. Their prince lives like a hunted wolf in the caves of the Kirikai Outlands."

"The rebellion has at least kept them from crushing us beneath their boot heels," stated Alfred, wrapping himself in blankets. "Are you certain you'll be warm enough that far from the fire, Your Highness?"

"Oh, yes," the boy said happily, "I'll be next to Sir Hugh." Sitting up, clasping his small arms around his knees, he looked up at the Hand questioningly. "What did you do at the battle? . . ."

". . . Where are you off to, captain? It seems to me the battle's being fought behind you."

"Eh?" The captain started in fear at the sound of a voice when he had figured himself to be alone. Drawing his sword, he whirled around, and peered into the brush.

Hugh, his weapon in hand, stepped out from behind a tree. The assassin's sword was red with elven blood; Hugh himself had taken several wounds in the vicious fighting. But he had never for one moment lost sight of his goal.

The captain, seeing a human and not an elf warrior, relaxed and, grinning, lowered his sword, which was still clean and bright. "My lads are back there." He gestured with his thumb. "They'll take care of the bastards."

Hugh, eyes narrowed, stared ahead.

"Your 'lads' are getting cut to ribbons."

The captain shrugged and turned to continue on his way. Hugh caught hold of the man's sword arm, jerked the weapon from his hand, and spun him around. Astounded, the captain swore an oath and lashed out at Hugh with a meaty fist. The captain ceased to fight when he felt the tip of Hugh's dagger at his throat.

"What?" he gabbled, sweating and panting, his eyes bulging from his head.

"My name is Hugh the Hand. And this"—he held up the dagger—"is from Tom Hales, and Henry Goodfellow, and Ned Carpenter, and the Widow Tanner, and the Widow Giles . . ." Hugh recited the names. An elven arrow thudded into a tree nearby. The assassin didn't flinch. The dagger didn't move.

The captain whined and squirmed and shouted for help. But there were many humans who were shouting for help that day, and no one answered. His deathscream mingled with many others.

Work completed, Hugh left. Behind him, he could hear voices raised in song, but he paid scant attention. He was imagining the puzzlement of the Kir monks, who would find the body of the captain far from the field of battle, a dagger in his chest, and in his hand the missive, "No more shall I send brave men to their deaths." . . .

"Sir Hugh!" The small hand was tugging at his sleeve. "What did you do in the battle?"

"I was sent to deliver a message."

CHAPTER ♦ 22

PITRIN'S EXILE,

MID REALM

♦

THE ROAD HUGH FOLLOWED WAS, AT THE BEGINNING OF THE JOURNEY, a broad, clear stretch of highway. They met numerous people on their way, for the interior of the isle was well-traveled. As they neared the shore, however, the road narrowed. It was rough and ill-kept, littered with splintered branches and broken rock. The hargast trees, or crystaltrees as they were sometimes called, grew wild in this region and were far different from the carefully cultivated "civilized" trees grown on the hargast farms.

There is nothing quite so beautiful as an orchard of hargast trees—their silver bark gleaming in the sunlight, the carefully pruned crystalline branches clinking together with musical sounds. The farmers work among them, pruning them, preventing them from growing to the outlandish size that obviates their usefulness. The hargast tree has the natural ability not only to store water but also to produce it in limited quantities. When the trees are kept small—about six to seven feet in height—the water they make is not used to enhance their own growth and can be harvested by driving taps into the trees' bark. A full-grown hargast tree, over a hundred feet tall, uses its water itself. Its bark is too thick to tap. In the wild, the hargast's branches grow to tremendous lengths. Being hard and brittle, they break off easily and shatter when they hit the ground, scattering lethal shards of sharp crystalline bark. A hargast forest is a dangerous place to traverse and consequently Hugh and his companions met fewer and fewer people on the road.

The wind blew strongly, as it always does near the coastline;

currents of air sweeping up from the underside of the isle eddied and swirled among the jagged cliffs. Strong gusts caused the three to lose their footing, trees creaked and shuddered, and more than once they heard the ringing, shattering crack of a falling tree limb. Alfred grew increasingly nervous, scanning the skies for elven ships and the woods for elven warriors, although Hugh amusedly assured him that not even the elves bothered with this worthless part of Pitrin's Exile.

It was a wild and desolate place. Cliffs of coralite jutted into the air. The tall hargast trees crowded close to the road, cutting off the sunlight with their long, thin leathery brown filaments. This foliage remained on the tree during the winter and only fell off in the spring, prior to growing the new filaments, which would suck moisture out of the air. It was nearly noon when Hugh, who had been paying unusual attention to the trunk of every hargast tree growing close to the roadside, suddenly called a halt.

"Hey!" he shouted to Alfred and the prince, who were trudging wearily ahead of him. "This way."

Bane turned to stare at him questioningly. Alfred turned—at least part of Alfred turned. His upper half swung around on Hugh's orders, but his lower half continued acting on previously given instruction. By the time all of Alfred managed to obey, he was lying in the dust of the road.

Hugh waited patiently for the chamberlain to pick himself up.

"We leave the road here." The assassin gestured toward the forest.

"In there?" Alfred peered with dismay into the tangle of underbrush and densely packed hargast trees, standing unmoving, branches clinking together with an ominous musical sound in the swirling winds.

"I'll take care of you, Alfred," said Bane, taking hold of the chamberlain's hand and squeezing it tightly. "There now, you're not scared anymore, are you? I'm not scared, not at all!"

"Thank you, Your Highness," said Alfred gravely. "I feel much better now. However, if I might venture to ask, Sir Hugh, what necessitates our going this way?"

"My airship is hidden in here."

Bane gaped. "An *elven* airship?"

"This way." Hugh gestured. "And be quick about it." He cast a glance up and down the empty road. "Before someone comes along."

"Oh, Alfred! Hurry, hurry!" The prince pulled at the chamberlain's hand.

"Yes, Your Highness," answered Alfred unhappily. He set his foot into the mass of last spring's rotting filaments on the roadside. There was a rustle, the underbrush leapt and quivered, and Alfred did the same. "What . . . what was that?" he gasped, pointing a trembling finger.

"Go!" grunted Hugh, and shoved Alfred ahead.

The chamberlain slid and stumbled. More out of terror at falling headlong into the unknown than out of agility, he managed to stay on his feet in the thick undergrowth. The prince plunged in after him, keeping the poor chamberlain in a constant state of panic by descrying snakes beneath every rock and log. Hugh watched them until the thick foliage had blocked them from his sight—and him from theirs. Reaching down, he picked up a rock and removed from beneath it a sliver of wood, which he thrust back into the notch that had been made in the trunk of a tree.

Entering the forest, he had no trouble finding the two again; a wild boar blundering through the thickets could not have made a greater clamor.

Moving with his accustomed soft-footed tread, Hugh was standing right beside them before either of the two was aware of him. Purposefully he cleared his throat, figuring that if he didn't give some indication of his presence, the chamberlain might drop dead from fright. As it was, Alfred nearly leapt from his skin at the startling sound, and almost wept with relief when he saw it was Hugh.

"Where . . . which way, sir?"

"Keep going straight ahead. You'll strike a cleared path about twenty feet further."

"T-twenty feet!" Alfred stammered. He gestured at the thick brush in which he was entangled. "It will take us an hour to get that far, at least!"

"If something doesn't get us first," teased Bane, round-eyed with excitement.

"Most amusing, Your Highness."

"We're still too close to the road. Get moving," commanded Hugh.

"Yes, sir," muttered the chamberlain.

They reached the path in less than an hour, but it was hard going nonetheless. Though brown and lifeless in the winter, the bramble bushes were like the hands of the undead, reaching out with their sharp nails to tear flesh and rend clothing. This deep in the forest, the three could hear quite plainly the faint crystalline hum caused by the wind rubbing against the hargast branches. It was much like someone running a wet finger over a crystal glass, and had the effect of setting the teeth on edge.

"No one in his right mind would come in this accursed place!" grumbled Alfred, glancing up at the trees with a shudder.

"Exactly," said Hugh, and continued to beat a path through the brush.

Alfred walked ahead of the prince and held back the thorny branches so that Bane could pass through them safely. The brambles were so thick, however, that this was often not possible. Bane endured scratched cheeks and torn hands without complaint, sucking his wounds to alleviate the pain.

How bravely will he face the pain of dying?

Hugh hadn't meant to ask himself the question, and he forced himself to answer it. As bravely as other kids I've seen. Better to die young, after all, as the Kir monks say. Why should a child's life be considered more precious than a man's? Logically, it should be less so, for a man contributes to society and a child is a parasite. It's instinctive, Hugh supposed. Our animallike need to perpetuate our own kind. This is just another job. The fact that he's a child shouldn't, *won't* matter!

The bramble bushes gave way eventually, with a suddenness for which Alfred was evidently unprepared. By the time Hugh reached him, the chamberlain was lying sprawled facefirst on a narrow space of cleared ground.

"Which direction? That's it, isn't it?" cried Bane, dancing around Alfred in excitement. The path led only one direction. Deducing that it must lead to the ship, the prince bolted down it before Hugh could answer his question.

Hugh opened his mouth to command him to come back, then shut it abruptly.

"Oh, sir, shouldn't we stop him?" queried Alfred anxiously as Hugh waited for the chamberlain to drag himself to his feet.

The wind whipped around them, shrieking and moaning, driving fine bits of stinging coralite and hargast bark into their faces. Leaves swirled at their feet and the crystalline tree branches swayed above their heads. Hugh stared through the fine dust to see the boy running headlong down the path.

"He'll be all right. The ship's not far from here. He can't mistake the trail."

"But . . . assassins?"

The child's fleeing his one true danger, Hugh said silently. Let him go. "There's no one in these woods. I would've seen the signs."

"If you don't mind, sir, His Highness *is* my responsibility." Alfred was edging his way down the path. "I'll just hurry after—"

"Go ahead." Hugh waved his hand.

Alfred, smiling and bobbing his head in servile thanks, broke into a run. The Hand half-expected to see the chamberlain break his head at the same time, but Alfred managed to keep his feet under him and pointed the same direction as his nose. His long arms swinging, hands flapping at his sides, he loped down the path after the prince.

Hugh lagged behind, deliberately slowing his steps, pausing, waiting for something uncertain and unknown. He'd felt the same when a storm was approaching—a tension, a prickling of the skin. Yet there was no rain smell in the air, no acrid whiff of lightning. The winds always blew high along the coast—

The sound of the crack splitting the air was so loud that Hugh's first thought was of an explosion, his next that elves had discovered his ship. But the subsequent crash and the shrill, agonized scream, cut off abruptly, informed Hugh of what had really happened.

He felt an overwhelming sense of relief.

"Help, Sir Hugh! Help!" Alfred's voice, blown apart by the wind, was barely heard. "A tree! A tree . . . fallen . . . my prince!"

Not a tree, thought Hugh. A branch. Most likely a big one, from the sound. Sheared off by the wind, it had come crashing down across the path. He'd seen such a thing many times before in this wood, narrowly missed being struck himself.

He did not run. It was as if the black monk at his shoulder laid a restraining hand on his arm and whispered, "There is no need for haste." The shards of broken hargast branch were sharp as arrow points. If Bane was still alive, he wouldn't be for long. There were plants in this forest that would ease the pain, put the boy to sleep, and, though Alfred would never know it, speed the child to an easy death.

Hugh continued walking slowly down the path. Alfred's cries for help had ceased. Perhaps he'd realized how futile it was. Perhaps he'd discovered the prince already dead. They'd take the body to Aristagon and leave it there, as Stephen had wanted. It would appear as if the elves had badly abused the boy before killing him, and that would inflame the humans. King Stephen would have his war, much good it would do him.

But that wasn't Hugh's concern. He'd take the bumbling Alfred along to help, and at the same time worm out of the chamberlain the dark plot he was undoubtedly aiding and abetting. Then, with Alfred in tow, the Hand would communicate with the king from a safe hiding place and demand his fee be doubled. He'd—

Rounding a bend in the path, Hugh saw that Alfred hadn't been far wrong when he said a tree had fallen. A huge limb, big as most trees itself, had cracked in the wind and split the trunk of the ancient hargast in two when it came down. The tree must have been rotten, to have separated like that. Coming nearer, Hugh could see within what was left of the trunk the tunnels of the insects that had been the old tree's true killer.

Though it was lying on the ground, the limb's branches that had remained intact towered above Hugh. The branches that had struck the ground had shattered and cut a wide swath of devastation through the forest; its crystalline remains completely obliterated the path. The dust it had raised still hung in the air. Hugh searched among the branches but could see nothing. He climbed over the split trunk. When he reached the other side, he stopped to stare.

The boy who should have been dead was sitting on the ground rubbing his head, looking dazed and very much alive. His clothing was rumpled and dirty, but it had been rumpled and dirty when he entered the forest. There weren't, Hugh noted, his eyes scanning the boy, any shards of bark or filaments in his hair. He had blood on his chest and on his torn shirt, but nowhere else on his body. The Hand glanced at the split trunk and then turned his measuring gaze on the path. Bane was sitting squarely in the spot where the branch must have fallen. He was surrounded by the sharp, deadly shards.

Yet he wasn't dead.

"Alfred?" Hugh called.

And then he saw the chamberlain, crouched on the ground near the boy, his back to the assassin, intent on doing something that Hugh could not see. At the sound of a voice, Alfred's body twitched in startlement and he jerked to his feet as though someone had yanked him up by a rope attached to his shirt collar. Hugh saw now what the chamberlain had been doing. He was binding a cut on his hand.

"Oh, sir! I'm so thankful you're here—"

"What happened?" Hugh demanded.

"Prince Bane has been extremely fortunate, sir. A terrible tragedy has been averted. The branch came crashing down, just barely missing His Highness."

Hugh, watching Bane closely, saw the puzzled glance the boy gave his chamberlain. Alfred did not notice—his eyes were on his injured hand. He had been attempting, without much success apparently, to wrap a strip of cloth around the wound.

"I heard the boy scream," Hugh said.

"Out of fright, sir," explained Alfred. "I ran—"

"Is he hurt?" Hugh glowered at Bane, pointed to the blood on the child's chest and the front of his shirt.

Bane peered down at himself. "No, I—"

"My blood, sir," interrupted Alfred. "I was running to help His Highness and I fell and cut my hand."

Alfred exhibited the cut. It was deep. Blood was dropping onto the broken remnants of the tree limb. Hugh watched the prince to gauge his reaction to Alfred's statement, saw the boy's frowning gaze fixed intently on his chest. Hugh looked to see what had captured the boy's attention, but saw only a smeared patch of blood.

Or was it? Hugh started to lean down, examine it closer, when Alfred, with a groan, toppled over and collapsed onto the ground. Hugh nudged the chamberlain with the toe of his boot, but got no response. Alfred had, once again, fainted.

Glancing up, Hugh saw Bane trying to wipe the blood off his skin with the tail of his shirt. Well, whatever was there was gone now. Ignoring the comatose Alfred, Hugh faced the prince.

"What really happened, Your Highness?"

Bane gazed up at him with dazzled eyes. "I don't know, Sir Hugh. I remember a cracking sound, and then"—he shrugged—"that's all."

"The branch fell on top of you?"

"I don't remember. Honest."

Scrambling to his feet, moving carefully amidst the shards that were sharp as glass, Bane brushed off his clothes and started over to help Alfred.

Hugh dragged the chamberlain's limp body off the path and

propped him up against a tree trunk. A few slaps on the cheeks and he began to come around, blinking up at Hugh dizzily.

"I'm . . . I'm most sorry, sir," Alfred mumbled, attempting to stand and failing miserably. "It's the sight of blood. I never could stomach—"

"Don't look at it, then!" Hugh snapped, seeing Alfred's horrified gaze go to his hand, his eyes start to roll back in his head.

"No, sir. I . . . won't!" The chamberlain squeezed his eyelids tightly shut.

Kneeling down beside him, Hugh bandaged the hand, taking the opportunity to examine the wound. It was a clean, deep slice.

"What cut you?"

"A piece of bark, I think, sir."

Like hell! That would have made a ragged cut. This was made by a sharp knife—

There came another cracking sound and a crash.

"Blessed Sartan! What was that?" Alfred's eyes flew open, and he shivered so that Hugh had to grasp his hand and hold it steady to wind the bandage around it.

"Nothing," Hugh snapped. He was completely perplexed and he didn't like the feeling, any more than he'd liked the feeling of relief over not having to kill the prince. He didn't like any of this. That tree had fallen on Bane as surely as rain fell from the sky. The prince should be dead.

What in hell was going on?

Hugh gave the cloth a sharp tug. The sooner he got rid of this kid, the better. Any feeling of reluctance he had once experienced at the thought of murdering a child was rapidly freezing over.

"Ouch!" Alfred yelped. "Thank you, sir," he added meekly.

"On your feet. Head for the ship," Hugh ordered.

Silently, none of the three looking at each other, they continued down the path.

CHAPTER ♦ 23

PITRIN'S EXILE,

MID REALM

♦

"Is THAT IT?" THE PRINCE GRASPED HOLD OF HUGH'S ARM AND POINTED at the dragon's head that could be seen floating above the leaves. The main body of the ship was still hidden from their view by the tall hargast trees surrounding it.

"That's it," Hugh answered.

The boy stared, awed. It took a shove from Hugh's hand to start him moving along the path.

It wasn't a real dragon's head, just a carved and painted facsimile. But elven artisans are skilled at their craft and the head looked more real and much more fierce than many live dragons flying the skies. It was about the size of a real dragon's head, for Hugh's was a small one-man ship meant for sailing between the isles and continents of Mid Realm. The figureheads of the gigantic airships the elves flew into battle or used to descend into the Maelstrom were so large that a seven-foot human could walk into one of the snarling mouths without bothering to duck.

The dragon's head was painted black, with flaring red eyes and white teeth, bared in a fighting snarl. It hovered over them, glaring straight ahead with a baleful gaze, looking so threatening that both Alfred and Bane found it difficult to keep from staring at it as they drew nearer. (The third time Alfred stepped in a hole and stumbled to his knees, Hugh ordered him to keep his eyes on the ground.)

The small path they had been following through the woods took them into a natural cut made in a cliff. Emerging on the other side, they came out into a small canyon bowl. The wind could hardly be felt at all in here; the sheer sides of the cliff cut it off. In the center floated the dragonship, its head and tail jutting out over the canyon walls, its body held in place by many stout ropes tied to the trees beneath it. Bane gasped in delight, and Alfred, staring up at the airship, let the prince's pack slip unnoticed from his fingers.

Sleek and graceful, the dragon's neck, topped with a spiky mane that was both functional and decorative, curved back to meet the hull of the ship that was the dragon's body. The sun of late afternoon sparkled off glittering black scales and glinted in the red eyes.

"It looks like a real dragon!" Bane sighed. "Only more powerful."

"It should look like a real dragon, Your Highness," said Alfred, an unusually stern note in his voice. "It is made from the skin of real dragons, and the wings are the wings of real dragons, slaughtered by the elves."

"Wings? Where are the wings?" Bane craned his neck, nearly falling over backward.

"They're folded back along the body. You can't see them now. But you will when we take off." Hugh hurried them forward. "Come on. I want to leave tonight, and there's a lot of work to do first."

"What makes it stay up there, if not the wings?" asked Bane.

"The magic," Hugh grunted. "Now, keep moving!"

The prince surged forward, stopping only once to try to jump up and grab hold of one of the guy ropes. Failing, he scampered down to stand beneath the belly of the ship, staring upward until he grew dizzy.

"So this, sir, is how you come to know so much about the elves," said Alfred in a low voice.

Hugh flicked him a glance, but the chamberlain's face was bland and only slightly troubled-looking.

"Yeah," the assassin answered. "The ship needs its magic renewed once every cycle, plus there are always minor repairs. A torn wing, or sometimes the skin pulls away from the frame."

"Where did you learn to fly one? I've heard it takes enormous skill."

"I was a slave on a watership for three years."

"Blessed Sartan!" Alfred stopped and stared at him.

Hugh cast him an irritated glance, and the chamberlain, recalling himself, stumbled forward.

"Three years! I never heard of anyone surviving that long! And even after that, you can still do business with them? I would think you would hate them all!"

"How would hating benefit me? The elves did what they had to do, and so did I. I learned how to sail their ships. I learned to speak their language fluently. No, as I've discovered, hate generally costs a man more than he can afford."

"And what about love?" Alfred asked softly.

Hugh didn't even bother to reply.

"Why a ship?" The chamberlain thought it wise to change the subject. "Why risk it? The people on Volkaran would tear you apart if they discovered it. Wouldn't a dragon suit your needs just as well?"

"Dragons tire. You have to rest them, feed them. They can be wounded, take sick, drop dead. Then there's always the chance the enchantment will slip and you're left either fending off the beast, or arguing with it, or soothing its hysterics. With this ship, the magic lasts a cycle. If it gets hit, I get it repaired. With this ship, I'm always in control."

"And that's what counts, isn't it?" said Alfred, but he said it well under his breath.

The chamberlain needn't have bothered. Hugh's attention was completely absorbed in his ship. Passing underneath it, he carefully and closely inspected every single part of it from head to tail (prow to stern). Bane trotted along behind, asking questions with every breath.

"What does that cable do? Why? What makes it work? Why don't we hurry up and take off? What are you doing?"

"Because, Your Highness, if we discovered something broken up there"—Hugh pointed at the sky—"it would be of no use fixing it."

"Why?"

"Because we'd be dead."

Bane subsided for a second or two, then began again. "What's its name? I can't read the letters. *Dra . . . Dragon . . .*"

"*Dragon Wing.*"

"How big is it?"

"Fifty feet." Hugh peered up at the dragonskin covering the hull. The blue-black scales glistened with rainbow colors when the sun struck them. Walking beneath them, the length and breadth of the keel, Hugh satisfied himself that no scales were missing.

Coming around to the front, Bane practically tripping at his heels, he gazed intently at two large crystal panes set into what would be the dragon's breast. These panes, designed to look like the breastplates of a dragon's armor, were, in reality, windows. Hugh, seeing scratches across one, frowned. A branch must have fallen and struck it.

"What's behind those?" asked Bane, noting Hugh studying them intently.

"The steerage. That's where the pilot sits."

"Can I go in there? Will you teach me to fly?"

"It takes months and months of study to learn to fly, Your Highness," responded Alfred, seeing that Hugh was too busy to reply. "Not only that, but the pilot has to be physically strong in order to operate the wings."

"Months?" Bane appeared disappointed. "But what's there to learn? You just get up there and"—he waved a hand—"fly."

"You have to know how to get where you're going, Your Highness," said the chamberlain. "In deepsky, so I've been told, there are no landmarks, very few points of reference. It is sometimes difficult to tell up from down. You must know how to use the navigational equipment on board, as well as being familiar with the skyroutes and the airlanes—"

"That stuff's not hard to learn. I'll teach you," said Hugh, seeing the child's face fall.

Bane brightened. Twitching the feather amulet back and forth, he skipped along after Hugh, who was walking the full length of the hull, examining the seams where metal and bone had melded to the epsol[1] keel. There were no cracks. Hugh would have been surprised to find any. He was a skilled and careful pilot. He'd seen, firsthand, what happened to those who weren't, to those who didn't take care of their ships.

He moved on to the stern. The hull arched gracefully upward, forming the afterdeck. A single dragon's wing—the ship's rudder—hung from the back of the hull. Cables attached to the

---

[1]Epsol trees grow in the forests of Aristagon and several of the islands in the Tribus Marches and may reach heights of over three hundred feet. The trees are similar to hargast in that they are of the metallic/organic class of plant life, taking the natural minerals from the soil and using a chemothermal process for their growth. They differ from hargast in that they are supple and their trunks grow straight and round, with a hollow core. This makes them ideal for airship construction.

end of the rudder swung limply in the wind. Grasping the rope, Hugh swung his legs onto the bottom rib of the rudder. Hand over hand, he climbed up the cable.

"Let me come! Please!" On the ground below, Bane jumped for the cable, flapping his arms as though he might fly up without help.

"No, Your Highness!" said a pale-faced Alfred, grasping the prince by the shoulder and firmly holding on to him. "We'll be going up there all too soon, as it is. Let Sir Hugh get on with his work."

"All right," said Bane with cheerful good grace. "Say, Alfred, why don't we go looking for some berries to take with us?"

"Berries, Your Highness?" said Alfred, in some astonishment. "What kind of berries?"

"Just . . . berries. To eat with supper. I know they grow in woods like this. Drogle told me." The child's blue eyes were wide open—as they tended to be when he was proposing something; the blue irises glinted in the midday sun. His hand toyed with the feather amulet.

"A stableboy is hardly a fit companion for Your Highness," Alfred remonstrated. He cast a glance at the tempting stretches of cable, tied to the trees within easy reach and seemingly just made to be climbed by small boys. "Very well, Your Highness, I will take you searching for berries."

"Don't wander far," warned Hugh's voice above them.

"Don't worry, sir," returned Alfred in hollow tones.

The two traipsed off into the woods—the chamberlain sliding down into ravines and careening off trees, the boy dashing into thickets and losing himself among the heavy undergrowth.

"Berries," muttered the Hand.

Thankful they were gone, he concentrated on his ship. Grabbing hold of the deck railing, he pulled himself up and over onto the upper deck. Open planking—one plank placed about every three feet—made walking possible, but not simple. Hugh was used to it and stepped from plank to plank, making a mental note not to let the clumsy Alfred up here. Below the planks ran what appeared to the landlubber's eye to be an overwhelming and confusing number of control cables. Lying down flat on the deck, Hugh inspected the ropes for fraying and wear.

He took his time. Rushing this job might mean a snapped wing cable and resultant loss of control. Soon after he'd completed his task, Bane and Alfred returned. From the sound of the boy's excited chatter, Hugh gathered that the berry picking had been successful.

"Can we come up now?" Bane shouted.

Hugh kicked at a pile of rope lying on the deck with his foot. It tumbled over the side, forming a rope ladder that dangled down almost to the ground. The child swarmed up it eagerly. Alfred cast it one terrified glance and announced his intention of remaining below to guard the packs.

"This is wonderful!" said Bane, tumbling over the rail and nearly falling between the planks. Hugh fished him out.

"Stay here and don't move," the Hand ordered, planting the boy against the bulwarks.

Bane leaned over the rail, looking at the hull. "What's that long piece of wood down there do—? Oh, I know! Those are the wings, aren't they?" he cried in high-pitched excitement.

"That's the mast," explained Hugh, eyeing it critically. "There's two of them, attached to the mainmast there"—he pointed—"at the forecastle."

"Are they like dragon's wings? Do they flap up and down?"

"No, Your Highness. They're more like a bat's wings when they're extended. It's the magic that keeps it afloat. Stand over that way a little more. I'm going to release the mast. You'll see."

The mast swiveled outward, pulling the dragon's wing with it. Hauling on the cable, Hugh didn't allow it to swing out too far for that would activate the magic and they'd take off prematurely. He released the mast on the port side, made certain the center mast that extended the length of the ship—cradled in its support frame—was free to rise properly and that everything functioned smoothly. Then he looked over the side.

"Alfred, I'm going to lower a rope for the packs. Tie them on securely. When you're finished with that, cast off the mooring cables. The ship will rise slightly, but don't worry. It won't take off unless the side wings are extended and the center wing is raised. When all the cables have been cut loose, then you come up."

"Up that!" Alfred gazed, horrified, at the rope ladder swaying in the breeze.

"Unless you can fly," said Hugh, and tossed a length of cable overboard.

The chamberlain attached it to the packs and, giving it a tug, indicated they were ready. Hugh hauled them up on deck. Handing one to Bane, he told the boy to follow him and, hopping from plank to plank, made his way aft. Opening a hatch, he climbed down a sturdy wooden ladder, Bane gleefully coming after.

They entered in a narrow corridor that ran beneath the upper deck, connecting the steerage way with the passengers' quarters, the storage compartments, and the pilot's quarters, located in the afterdeck. The corridor was dark after the brightness of the day outside, and both man and boy stopped to let their eyes adjust.

Hugh felt a small hand fasten onto his.

"I can't believe I'm really going to get to fly in one of these! You know, Sir Hugh," Bane added with a wistful cheerfulness, "once I've flown in a dragonship, I will have done everything in life I ever wanted to do. I really think I could die quite contentedly after this."

A constricting pain in Hugh's chest nearly suffocated him. He couldn't breathe, for long moments he couldn't see, and it wasn't the darkness of the ship's interior that was blinding him. It was fear, he told himself. Fear that the child had found out. Shaking his head to rid his eyes of the shadow that had fallen over them, he turned to look hard at the boy.

But Bane was gazing up at him with innocent affection, not cunning guile. Hugh jerked his hand roughly out of the child's grasp.

"That cabin's where you and Alfred'll sleep," he said. "Stow the packs there." A thud and a muffled groan sounded from above them. "Alfred? Get down here and take care of His Highness. I've got work to do."

"Yes, sir," came the quavering return, and Alfred slid— literally—down the ladder, landing on the deck in a heap.

Turning on his heel, Hugh stalked off toward the steerage way, shoving past Alfred without saying a word.

"Merciful Sartan," said the chamberlain, backing up to avoid being run down. He stared after Hugh, then turned to Bane. "Did you say or do anything to upset him, Your Highness?"

"Why, no, Alfred," the boy said. Reaching out, he took hold of the chamberlain's hand. "Where did you put those berries?"

"Can I come in?"

"No. Stay in the hatchway," Hugh ordered.

Bane peeked inside the steerage way and his eyes widened in astonishment. Then he giggled. "It looks like you're stuck in a big spider's web! What *are* all those ropes hooked to? And why are you wearing that contraption?"

The contraption Hugh was strapping on himself resembled a

leather breastplate, except that it had numerous cables attached
to it. Extending in various directions, the cables ran upward into
a complicated system of pulleys fixed to the ceiling.

"I've never in my life seen so much wood!" Alfred's voice
floated into the steerage way. "Not even in the royal palace. The
wood alone must make this ship worth its weight in barls. Your
Highness, please keep back. Don't touch those cables!"

"Can't I go over and look out the windows? Please, Alfred? I
won't get in the way."

"No, Your Highness," Hugh said. "If one of these cables
wrapped around your neck, it would snap it in a second."

"You can see well enough from where we're standing. Quite
well enough," said Alfred, looking slightly green around the
mouth. The ground was far below them. All that could be seen
were the tops of trees and the side of a coralite cliff.

Harness firmly fastened in place, Hugh settled down on a
high-backed wooden chair that stood on one leg in the center of
the steerage way. The chair swiveled to the left and the right,
allowing the pilot easy maneuvering. Sticking up out of the floor
in front of him was a tall metal lever.

"Why do you have to wear that thing?" Bane asked, staring
at the harness.

"It keeps the cables in easy reach, prevents them from getting tangled, lets me know which cable goes where." Hugh
nudged the lever with his foot. A series of startling bangs resounded through the ship. The cables whirled through the pulleys and snapped taut. Hugh pulled on several of the cables
attached to his chest. There came various creaking and rumbling
sounds, a sharp jerk, and they could feel the ship lift slightly
beneath their feet.

"The wings are unfolding," said Hugh. "The magic is
activating."

A crystal globe sextant, located directly above the pilot's
head, began to gleam with a soft blue light. Symbols appeared
within it. Hugh pulled harder on the cables, and suddenly the
treetops and the cliff side began to drop out of sight. The ship
was rising.

Alfred gasped. Losing his balance, he staggered backward,
clinging to the bulwarks for support. Bane, jumping up and
down, clapped his hands. Suddenly the cliff and the trees vanished, and the vast expanse of clear blue sky stretched endlessly
before them.

"Oh, Sir Hugh, may I go to the upper deck? I want to see where we're going."

"Absolutely not, Your High—" began Alfred.

"Sure," interrupted Hugh. "Take the ladder we used coming down. Keep hold of the rails and you won't get blown off."

Bane scampered away and in another moment they could hear his boots clomp overhead.

"Blown off!" gasped Alfred. "It's not safe!"

"It's safe. The elven wizards put a magical canopy around it. He couldn't even jump off. As long as the wings are extended and the magic's working, he'll be all right." Hugh flicked Alfred an amused glance. "But you might want to go up and keep an eye on him, all the same."

"Yes, sir," said the chamberlain, swallowing. "I . . . I'll do just that."

But he didn't move. Clinging with deathlike grip to the bulwarks, his rigid face white as the clouds sailing past them, Alfred stared fixedly out at the blue sky.

"Alfred?" said Hugh, tugging on one of the cables.

The ship dipped to the left, and a glimpse of treetop sprang suddenly and dizzingly into view.

"I'm going. Right now, sir. I'm going," said the chamberlain, not moving a muscle.

Up on the deck, Bane leaned over the rail, entranced by the sight. He could see Pitrin's Exile sliding away behind him. Below him and before him were blue sky and white clouds; above him sparkled the firmament. The dragon wings extended on either side, their leathery skin barely rippling with the motion of the ship's passage. The center wing stood up straight behind him, swaying slightly back and forth.

Holding the feather in his hands, the boy brushed it idly back and forth across his chin. "The ship is controlled by the harness. Magic keeps it afloat. The wings are like bat's wings. The crystal on the ceiling tells you where you are." Standing on tiptoe, he stared down below him, wondering if he could see the Maelstrom from this high up. "It's easy, really," he remarked, twiddling the feather.

CHAPTER 24

DEEPSKY,

MID REALM

◆

THE DRAGONSHIP SLICED THROUGH THE PEARLY, DOVE-COLORED NIGHT, its wings gliding on the magic and the air currents that swept upward over the floating isle of Djern Hereva. Strapped into the flight harness, snug in the small steerage room, Hugh lit his pipe, leaned back, and relaxed, letting the dragonship almost fly itself. A touch here or there upon the cables attached to the harness tilted the wings to slice through the air currents, sliding effortlessly across the sky, from one swirl to another, gliding trackward toward Aristagon.

The Hand kept a lazy half-watch for other winged transports—either live or mechanical. In his elven ship, he was most vulnerable to attack from his own kind, for human dragonriders would immediately take him for an elf, probably a spy. Hugh was not particularly worried. He knew the flight paths the dragonriders took on their raids of Aristagon or elven shipping. He was flying higher purposefully to avoid these, and figured it unlikely that he'd be annoyed. If he did run into a patrol, he could always dodge it by slipping into a rift of clouds.

The weather was calm, the flying easy, and Hugh had leisure to think. It was then that he decided not to kill the child. The need to make a decision had been in his mind awhile now, but he had put off thinking about it until this time when he was alone and all around him was quiet and conducive to thought. He had never before defaulted on a contract and he needed to satisfy himself that his reasoning was rational and valid and not swayed by sentiment.

Sentiment. Though something within the Hand might have sympathized with a childhood such as Bane's—a childhood unloved, cold, and bleak—the assassin had grown too callous to feel his own pain, much less that of another. He was letting the kid live for the very simple reason that Bane was going to be worth more to the Hand alive than dead.

Hugh did not have his plans quite worked out. He needed time to think, time to wring the truth from Alfred, time to unravel the mysteries that wound around the prince. The Hand had a hideout on Aristagon which he used when he needed his ship repaired. He would go there and wait until he had his information; then he would either return and confront Stephen with his knowledge and demand more money to keep silent, or perhaps contact the queen and discover what she would pay to have her son back. Whatever his decision, Hugh figured his fortune was made.

He was settling into the rhythm of flying the craft, which he could do with his body and part of his mind, letting the other drift free, when the object of his thoughts poked his towhead up through the hatch into the cabin.

"Alfred's sent some dinner."

The boy's eyes were eager and curious, darting here and there at the cables attached to the harness, Hugh's arms resting easily on them.

"Come up," Hugh invited. "Just be careful what you touch and where you step. Keep away from the ropes."

Bane did as he was told, sliding up through the hatch, placing his foot gingerly on the deck. In his hands he carried a bowl of meat and vegetables. It was cold. Alfred had cooked it before they left Pitrin's Exile, then packed it away to be eaten later. But it smelled good to a man accustomed to living on the wayfarer's meal of bread and cheese or the greasy fare of inns.

"Hand it here." Hugh knocked the ashes from his pipe in a crockery mug he carried for this purpose, then held out his hands to take the bowl.

Bane's eyes glistened. "You're supposed to be flying the ship."

"She can fly herself," said Hugh, grasping the bowl and the horn spoon and shoveling the food into his mouth.

"But won't we fall?" Bane peered out the crystal windows.

"The magic keeps us afloat, and even if it didn't, the wings could support us in this calm air. I just have to make certain they stay extended. If I pulled them in, then we'd begin to sink."

Bane nodded thoughtfully, turning his blue-eyed gaze back to Hugh. "What cables draw them in?"

"These." He gestured to two heavy lengths of rope attached to the harness at his breast near his right and left shoulder. "I pull them this way, in front of me, and that draws the wings in. These other cables let me steer by lifting the wings or lowering them. This one controls the mainmast, and this cable's attached to the tail. By flipping it one way or the other, I can control the ship's direction."

"So we could stay afloat like this for how long?"

Hugh shrugged. "Indefinitely, I suppose, or until we came to an isle. Then the wind currents would catch us and might suck us into a cliff or underneath the island, then slam us up against the coralite."

Bane nodded gravely. "I still think I could fly it."

Hugh felt satisfied enough with himself to smile indulgently. "No, you're not strong enough."

The boy gazed at the harness in longing.

"Try it," Hugh invited. "Here, come stand beside me."

Bane did as he was told, moving cautiously, being careful not to accidentally jar one of the ropes. Standing on the deck in front of Hugh, the boy placed his hand on one of the ropes that caused the wing to rise or lower. He pulled at it. The rope moved slightly, enough to cause the wing to shiver, and that was all.

Unaccustomed to having his will thwarted, the prince gritted his teeth and, wrapping both hands around the rope, pulled with all his might. The wooden frame creaked, the wing dipped a fraction of an inch. Grinning in triumph, Bane planted his feet on the deck and pulled even harder. A gust of wind, sweeping upward, caught the wing. The cable slid through his hands. The prince released his grip with a cry, staring at his palms, which were torn and bleeding.

"Still think you can fly it?" the Hand said coolly.

Blinking back tears, Bane mumbled, "No, Sir Hugh," disconsolately. He wrapped his injured hands tightly around the feather amulet, as if seeking some sort of consolation. Perhaps it helped, for he swallowed and lifted shimmering blue eyes to meet Hugh's. "Thank you for letting me try."

"You did well enough, Your Highness," said Hugh. "I've seen men twice your size who didn't do as well."

"Truly?" The tears vanished.

Hugh was rich now. He could afford the lie. "Yeah. Now, go on down and see if Alfred needs any help."

"I'll be back to get the bowl!" Bane said, and ducked through the hatch. Hugh could hear his excited voice calling for Alfred, telling the chamberlain how he had flown the dragonship.

Eating in silence, Hugh idly scanned the skies. He decided that the first thing he would do upon landing on Aristagon would be to take that feather to Kev'am, the elven wizardess, and see what she could make of it. One of the lesser mysteries he had to solve.

Or so he thought at the time.

Three days passed. They flew by the night, hiding during the day on small, uncharted isles. It would take a week, Hugh said, to reach Aristagon.

Bane came every night to sit with Hugh, watch him handle the ship, and ask questions. The Hand answered or not, depending on his mood. Preoccupied with his plans and his flying, Hugh paid no more attention to Bane than he was forced to. Attachments were deadly in this world, bringing nothing but pain and sorrow. The boy was cold hard cash. That was all.

The Hand was, however, puzzled at Alfred. The chamberlain watched the prince nervously, anxiously. It might have been an overreaction to the tree's fall, but Alfred wasn't being protective. Hugh was strongly reminded of the time an elven fire canister had been hurled over a battlement of a castle he'd been caught in during a raid. Rolling about on the stone, the black metal container appeared harmless. But everyone knew that at any moment it could burst into flame. Men regarded that canister in exactly the same way Alfred was regarding Bane.

Noting Alfred's tension, Hugh wondered—not for the first time—what the chamberlain knew that he didn't. The assassin increased his own watchfulness over the boy when they were on the ground, thinking the child might try to run away. Bane meekly obeyed Hugh's command that he not leave the campsite unless escorted by Alfred, and then only to forage in the woods for the berries that he seemed to take such delight in finding.

Hugh never went on these expeditions, considering them foolish. Left to himself to find food, he would have made do with whatever came to hand, so long as it kept life in his body. The chamberlain insisted that His Highness have what he wanted,

however, and each day the clumsy Alfred sallied forth into
the forest to do battle with overhanging limbs, tangled vines,
and treacherous weeds. Hugh stayed behind, resting in a half-
wakeful, half-dozing state that allowed him to hear every snap
and crash.

The fourth night, Bane came up to the steerage way and
stood staring out the crystal windows at the magnificent sight of
cloud and vast empty sky below. "Alfred says dinner will be
ready soon."

Hugh, puffing on his pipe, grunted noncommittally.

"What's that big shadow I can see out there?" Bane pointed.

"Aristagon."

"Is it? Will we be there soon?"

"No. It's farther away than it looks. Another day or two."

"But where will we stay between here and there? I don't see
any more islands."

"There're some, most likely hidden by the mists. Small isles,
used by small ships like us for overnight stays."

Standing on tiptoe, Bane peered down beneath the dragon.
"I can see great dark clouds way, way below us. Whirling round
and round. That's the Maelstrom, isn't it?"

Hugh saw no need to reply to the obvious. Bane stared more
intently.

"Those two things down there. They look like dragons, but
they're bigger than any dragon I ever saw."

Rising from his chair, careful not to disturb the cables, Hugh
glanced out. "Elven corsairs or waterships."

"Elves!" The word was tense, eager. The boy's hand went to
stroke the feather he wore around his neck. When he spoke next,
it was with studied calm. "Shouldn't we run away from them,
then?"

"They're far from us, probably don't even see us. If they did,
they'd think we were one of them. Besides, it looks like they've
got business of their own to tend to."

The prince looked out again, saw two ships and nothing
more. Hugh, however, could tell what was transpiring.

"Rebels, trying to escape an imperial warship."

Bane barely gave them a glance. "I think I heard Alfred
calling. It must be time for supper."

Hugh continued to watch the confrontation with interest.
The warship had caught up with the rebels. Grappling hooks
snaked out from the imperial dragonship and landed on the

rebel's deck. It was to an attack similar to this, made by humans, that Hugh owed his escape from the slavery of the elven waterships.

Several of the rebel elves, in an attempt to boost their level of magic and escape capture, were performing the dangerous maneuver known as "walking the dragon wing." Hugh could see them running swiftly, sure-footedly, out on the wing's mast. In their hands, they carried charms given them by the ship's wizard, that they would touch to the mast.

The move was dangerous, foolhardy, and desperate. That far from the ship's center, the magical canopy could not reach them, could not protect them. A gust or—as was happening now—an enemy arrow could catch them and carry them over the wing's edge, to tumble down into the Maelstrom.

"Walking the dragon wing." It had become a term among elves for any risk-taking adventure worth the price. The saying had always, Hugh felt, held a special meaning for him and his way of life. He had named his ship in its honor.

Bane returned with a bowl.

"Where're the elves?" He handed the bowl to Hugh.

"Back behind us. We've flown out beyond them." Hugh took a mouthful and choked, spitting it out. "Damn! What'd Alfred do, spill the pepper pot into this stuff?"

"I told him it was too spicy. Here, I brought you some wine."

The prince handed Hugh the wineskin. He took a deep drink, swallowed, and took another. Giving it back, he shoved over the bowl of uneaten food with his foot. "Take that gunk back and feed it to Alfred."

Bane picked up the bowl, but he didn't leave the steerage way. Fingers toying with the feather, he stood watching Hugh with a strange, calm expectancy.

"What is it?" the Hand snapped.

But at that very moment, he knew.

He hadn't tasted the poison. The pepper had masked it. But he was feeling the first effects. Cramps clenched his bowels. A burning sensation spread through his body, and his tongue seemed to swell in his mouth. Objects in his sight elongated, then flattened. The boy grew huge, leaning over him with a sweet, charming smile, the feather dangling from his hand.

Rage surged through Hugh, but not as swiftly or strongly as the poison.

Sagging backward, his vision darkening, Hugh saw the feather and heard the boy's awed voice coming from a great distance.

"It worked, father! He's dying!"

Hugh reached out to catch hold and choke the breath out of his murderer, but his arm was too heavy to lift; it hung limp and lifeless at his side. And then the boy was no longer standing over him, but a black monk, with hand outstretched.

"And now, who is master?" asked the monk.

CHAPTER ◆ 25

DEEPSKY,

MID REALM

◆

Hᴜɢʜ ᴄʀᴀsʜᴇᴅ ᴛᴏ ᴛʜᴇ ᴅᴇᴄᴋ, ᴅʀᴀɢɢɪɴɢ ᴛʜᴇ ᴄᴀʙʟᴇs ᴀᴛᴛᴀᴄʜᴇᴅ ᴛᴏ ᴛʜᴇ harness on his body with him. The ship listed sharply, slamming Bane backward into the bulkhead. The bowl of food fell from the child's hand with a clatter. From the cabin below, there was a resounding crash, followed by a pained and panicked yell.

Staggering to his feet, clinging to the ship's side, the prince looked around dazedly. The deck slanted at a precarious angle. Hugh lay on his back, entangled in the cables. Bane glanced hastily outside, saw the nose of the dragon pointing straight down, and realized what had happened. Hugh's fall had pulled the wings in, the magic was not working, and now they were plunging out of control through the sky, plummeting down toward the Maelstrom.

It had not occurred to Bane that this would happen. Nor had it, apparently, occurred to his father. That was not surprising. A human mysteriarch of the Seventh House, living in realms far above the strife and turmoil of the rest of the world, could have no knowledge of things mechanical. Sinistrad had probably never even seen an elven dragonship. And, after all, Hugh had assured the boy the ship could fly itself.

Bane scrambled among the tangle of cables. Reaching Hugh's body, he pulled and tugged with all his might at the ropes. But he couldn't move them. The wings would not budge.

"Alfred!" the prince yelled. "Alfred, come quickly!"

There was another crash and a scuffling below; then Alfred's face—deathly white—poked up through the hatch.

"Sir Hugh! What's happening! We're falling—" His gaze rested on the man's body. "Blessed Sartan!" With a swiftness and ease unusual in such a clumsy, ungainly body, Alfred dashed in through the hatch, made his way over the coils of rope, and knelt beside Hugh.

"Oh, never mind him! He's dead!" cried the prince. Grabbing hold of Alfred's coat, he jerked him around to face the front of the ship. "Look! You've got to stop us! Take the harness off him and fly this thing!"

"Your Majesty!" Alfred was livid. "I can't fly a ship! It takes skill, years of practice!" The chamberlain's eyes narrowed. "What do you mean, he's dead?"

Bane glared at him defiantly, but his gaze dropped before Alfred's. The chamberlain was no longer the buffoon; his eyes were suddenly strangely compelling and intense, and the boy found their penetrating stare highly uncomfortable.

"He got what he deserved," Bane said sullenly. "He was an assassin, hired by King Stephen to kill me. I've killed him first, that's all."

"You?" Alfred's gaze went to the feather. "Or your father?"

Bane looked confused. His lips opened, then clamped shut. His hand clenched around the amulet as if to hide it, and he began to stammer.

"No need to lie," Alfred said, sighing. "I've known for a long time. Longer than your father and mother, or should I say your *adopted* father and mother, although adoption implies a choice, and they never had one. What kind of poison did you give him, Bane?"

"Him? Why are you worried about him? Are you just going to let us crash?" the prince screeched shrilly.

"He's the only one who can save us! What did you use on him?" Alfred demanded, reaching out his hand to grasp hold of the boy and shake the information out of him if need be.

The prince darted backward, slipping and sliding across the slanting deck until he was brought to a halt by the bulkhead. Turning, he stared through the window. The prince let out a whoop.

"The elven ships! We're heading straight for them! We don't need that filthy murderer. The elves will save us!"

"No! Wait! Bane! It was the berries, wasn't it?"

The boy dashed out of the steerage way. Behind him, Bane

heard Alfred shouting that elves were dangerous, but he paid no attention.

"I'm prince of Uylandia," he said to himself, climbing the ladder to the top deck. There, clinging with his hands to the rails, he entwined his legs through them to hold on securely. "They won't dare lay a hand on me. I've still got the enchantment. Trian thinks he broke it, but that's only because it was what I wanted him to think. Father says we mustn't take a chance, and so we had to kill the assassin to get his ship. But I know the enchantment's still with me! Now I'll have an elf ship. I'll make them fly me to my father, and he and I will rule them. We'll rule them all! Just as we planned.

"Hey!" Bane shouted. Holding on to the rail with his legs, he let loose long enough to wave his arms. "Hey, there! Help! Help us!"

The elves were far below, too far away to hear the boy's cry. Besides, they had other, more important things on their minds— such as staying alive. Looking down from his perch, Bane could see the rebel ship and the imperial warship locked together, and he wondered what was going on. He was too high to see the blood spilling over the deck. He could not hear the screams of the cable-haulers, trapped in their harnesses, being dragged through the splintered hulls, nor could he hear the song of the rebel elves who attempted, even as they defended themselves, to turn the hearts of their brothers.

Bright-colored dragonwings beat the air frantically or swung, broken, from snapped cables. Long grappling hooks attached to ropes held one ship firmly to the other. Elven warriors swung, hand over hand, along the cables to board the ship or leapt through the air to land on the deck. Far beneath them, the Maelstrom swirled and boiled, its black clouds with frothy white fringes lit purple by the incessantly flaring lightning.

Bane stared down at the elves eagerly. He felt no fear, only a heady exhilaration caused by the rushing of the wind in his face, the novelty of his situation, and the excitement of his father's plans coming to fulfillment. The dragonship's fall had slowed somewhat. Alfred had managed to pull the wings out far enough so that the ship was no longer tumbling headfirst into the Maelstrom. But it was out of control and falling still, drifting downward in a lazy spiral.

Alfred's voice came to him from below. It was indistinct, he couldn't understand the man's words, yet something about the

tone or the rhythm brought back to his mind the hazy memory of
when the tree had crashed down on top of him. Bane didn't pay
much attention to it. They were nearing the elves, coming closer
by the moment. He could see faces upturned, looking at him and
pointing. He started to shout again, when suddenly both the
elven ships broke apart, disintegrating before his eyes.

Slender figures toppled into the nothingness around them,
and Bane was close enough now to hear the screams that would
end when they were swallowed up in the Maelstrom. Here and
there fragments of the two ships, held aloft by their own enchantment, floated in the air, and he could see elves clinging to
them or, on the larger pieces, some still battling.

And Bane and his small ship were plunging down right into
the center of the chaos.

Kir monks do not laugh. They see nothing funny in life, and like
to point out that when humans laugh, it is often at the misfortune of others. Laughing is not prohibited in a Kir monastery. It
simply isn't done. A child, when first taken into the halls of the
black monks, may laugh for a day or two, but not longer.

The black monk holding Hugh by the hand did not smile, but
Hugh saw laughter in the eyes. Furious, he fought and struggled
more fiercely against this one opponent than he had fought
against any in his life. This opponent was not flesh and blood.
No wound left its mark on it. No jab slowed it down. It was
eternal and it held him fast.

"You hated us," said the black monk, laughing at him soundlessly, "yet you served us. All your life you served us."

"I serve no man!" shouted Hugh. His struggles were lessening. He was growing weak, tired. He wanted to rest. Only
shame and anger kept him from slipping into welcome oblivion.
Shame because he knew the monk was right. Anger that he had
so long been their dupe.

Bitter, frustrated, he summoned all his waning strength and
made one final attempt to free himself. It was a weak and pitiful
blow that wouldn't have made tears come to the eyes of a child.
But the monk let loose.

Astounded, bereft of the support, Hugh fell. There was no
terror in his heart, for he had the strangest impression that he
was not falling down, but up. He was not plunging into darkness.

He was plunging into light.

*   *   *

"Sir Hugh?" Alfred's face, fearful and anxious, floated above him. "Sir Hugh? Oh, praise the Sartan! You're all right! How do you feel, sir?"

With Alfred's help, Hugh sat up. He glanced swiftly around him, searching for the monk. He saw no one other than the chamberlain, nothing except a tangle of ropes and his harness.

"What happened?" Hugh shook his head to clear it. He felt no pain, only a kind of grogginess. His brain seemed too large for his skull, his tongue too big for his mouth. He'd awakened in an inn, on occasion, with exactly this same feeling, an empty wineskin at his side.

"The boy drugged you. It's wearing off now. I know you're not feeling too well, Sir Hugh, but we're in trouble. The ship is falling—"

"Drugged?" Hugh looked at Alfred, trying to bring him into focus through the fog. "He didn't drug me! It was poison." His eyes narrowed. "I was dying."

"No, no, Sir Hugh. I know it might feel that way, but—"

Hugh leaned forward. Catching hold of Alfred by the collar, he dragged the man near him, staring into the light-colored eyes in an effort to see into his very soul. "I was *dead*." Hugh tightened his grip. "*You* brought me back to life!"

Alfred returned Hugh's gaze calmly. He smiled, somewhat sadly, and shook his head. "You are mistaken. It was a drug. I have done nothing."

Bumbling, oafish, how could this man lie and Hugh not know it? More important, how could Alfred have saved his life? The face was guileless; the eyes looked at him with pity and sadness, nothing more. Alfred seemed incapable of hiding anything. Had Hugh been anyone else, he must have believed him.

But the assassin knew that poison. He had given it to others. He had seen them die as he had. None of them had ever come back.

"Sir Hugh, the ship!" Alfred persisted. "We're falling! The wings . . . pulled inward. I tried, but I couldn't get them out again."

Now that his attention was called to it, Hugh could feel the ship rolling. He stared at Alfred, then let loose his grip on the man. Another mystery, but it wouldn't be solved by tumbling into the Maelstrom. Hugh staggered to his feet, his hands clutching his pounding head. It was too heavy. He had the dazed feeling that if he let go, his skull might snap loose and roll off his neck.

A glance out the window showed him that they were in no immediate danger—at least not from falling. Alfred had managed to bring the ship into some semblance of control, and Hugh could regain it completely easily enough, despite the fact that some of the cables had snapped.

"Falling into the Maelstrom's the least of our worries."

"What do you mean, sir?" Alfred hurried to his side and looked out.

Gazing up at them, so near that they could see every detail of their torn and bloodied clothing, were three elven warriors, grappling hooks in their hands.

"Here, toss them up! I'll make them fast!" It was Bane's voice, coming from the deck above.

Alfred gasped. "His Majesty said something about seeking help from the elves—"

"Help!" Hugh's lips twisted into a mocking grin. It seemed he had come back to life only to die again.

The grappling hooks snaked through the air. He heard the thuds when they landed on the deck, the scraping sound of the iron claws sliding over the wood. There was a tug and a jerk that knocked him—unsteady as he was—off his feet. The hooks had caught hold. He put his hand to his side. His sword was gone.

"Where . . . ?"

Alfred had seen his gesture and was slipping and sliding across the unsteady deck. "Here, sir. I had to use it to cut you free."

Hugh grabbed hold of the weapon and nearly dropped it. If Alfred had handed him an anvil, it could have seemed no heavier than his sword in his weak and shaking hand. The hooks were dragging the ship to a stop, keeping it floating in the air next to the disabled elven vessel. There was a sharp pull and the ship sagged downward—the elves were scaling the ropes, coming aboard. Up above, Hugh could hear Bane chattering excitedly.

Gripping the sword, Hugh left the steerage way, padded soft-footed into the corridor to stand beneath the hatch. Alfred stumbled behind, the man's loud, clumsy footfalls making Hugh cringe. He cast the chamberlain a baleful glance, warning him to be silent. Then, slipping his dagger from the top of his boot, the assassin held it out.

Alfred blenched, shook his head, and put his hands behind his back. "No," he said through trembling lips. "I couldn't! I can't . . . take a life!"

Hugh looked up above, where booted feet could be heard walking across the deck.

"Not even to save your own?" he hissed.

Alfred lowered his eyes. "I'm sorry."

"If you're not now, you're soon going to be," muttered Hugh, and began to silently climb the ladder.

CHAPTER ♦ 26

DEEPSKY,

DESCENDING

♦

Bane watched the three elves propel themselves hand over hand across the ropes, their thin, shapely legs grasping it with heels and knees. Beneath them was nothing but empty air and, far below, the dark and awesome, perpetually raging storm. The elves were expert at boarding, however, and did not pause or look down. Reaching the deck of the small dragonship, they swung their legs over the sides and landed lightly on their feet.

Having never seen elves before, the prince studied them as intently as they were ignoring him. The elves were nearly the same height as average humans, but their slender bodies made them appear taller. Their features were delicate, yet hard and cold, as if they had been carved out of marble. Smooth-muscled, they were extremely well-coordinated and walked with ease and grace even on the listing ship. Their skin was nut-brown, their hair and eyebrows white, tinted with silver that glistened in the sun. They wore what appeared to be vests and short skirts made like finely stitched tapestries, decorated with fanciful pictures of birds and flowers and animals. Humans often made fun of the elves' bright-colored garb—to their regret, most discovering too late that it was, in reality, elven armor. Elven wizards possess the power to magically enhance ordinary silken thread, making it as hard and tough as steel.

The elf who appeared to be the leader motioned the other two to look around the ship. One ran aft, staring over the side at the wings, possibly to assess the damage that had caused this ship to tumble out of control. The other ran back to the stern.

The elves were armed, but they didn't carry their weapons in hand. They were, after all, on a ship made by their own kind.

Seeing his men deployed, the elven commander finally deigned to notice the child.

"What is a human brat doing on board a ship of my people?" The commander stared down his long aquiline nose at the boy. "And where is the captain of this vessel?"

He spoke human well, but with a twist to his mouth, as if the words tasted bad and he was glad to be rid of them. His voice was lilting and musical, his tone imperious and condescending. Bane was angry, but knew how to hide it.

"I am crown prince of Volkaran and Uylandia. King Stephen is my father." Bane thought it best to begin this way, at least until he had the elves convinced that he was someone important. Then he would tell them the truth, tell them that he was of truly great importance—greater than they could imagine.

The elf captain was keeping one eye on his men, giving Bane half his attention. "So, my people have captured a human princeling, have they? I don't know what they think they'll get for you."

"An evil man captured me," Bane said, tears coming readily to his eyes. "He was going to murder me. But you've rescued me! You'll be heroes. Take me to your king, that I may extend my thanks. This could be the beginning of the peace between our people."

The elf who had been inspecting the wings returned, his report on his lips. Overhearing the boy's speech, he looked at his captain. Both laughed simultaneously.

Bane sucked in his breath. Never in his life had anyone laughed at him! What was happening? The enchantment should be working. He was positive Trian hadn't been able to break the spell. Why wasn't his enchantment working on the elves?

And then Bane saw the talismans. Worn around the elves' necks, the talismans were created by the elven wizards to protect their people against human war magic. Bane didn't understand this, but he knew a warding talisman when he saw it and knew that, inadvertently, it was shielding the elves from the enchantment.

Before he could react, the captain grabbed hold of him and tossed him through the air like a bag of garbage. He was caught by the other elf, whose strength belied the slender body. The elf captain gave a careless command, and the elf, holding the boy at arm's length as if he were a skunk, walked over to the ship's rail.

Bane did not speak elven, but he understood the command given by the elf captain's gesture.

He was to be tossed overboard.

Bane tried to scream, fear choked off his breath. He fought and struggled. The elf held him by the scruff of the neck and seemed to be highly amused at the child's frantic efforts to free himself. Bane possessed the power of magic, but he was untrained, not having been brought up in his father's house. He could feel magic run through him like adrenaline, he lacked the knowledge to make it work.

There was someone who could tell him, however.

Bane grasped hold of the feather amulet. "Father!"

"He can't help you now," laughed the elf.

"Father!" Bane cried again.

"I was right," said the elf captain to his cohort. "There *is* someone else aboard—the brat's father. Go search." He gestured to the third elf, who came running back from the stern.

"Go ahead, get rid of the little bastard," the captain grunted.

The elf holding Bane held the boy over the rail and then dropped him.

Bane tumbled through the air. He sucked in his breath to let it out in a howl of terror, when a voice commanded him abruptly to be silent. The voice came as it always did to the child, speaking words that he heard in his mind, words audible only to himself.

"You have the ability to save yourself, Bane. But first you must conquer fear."

Falling rapidly, seeing below him floating pieces of debris from the elven ship and below that the black clouds of the Maelstrom, Bane went stiff and rigid with fright.

"I . . . I can't, father," he whimpered.

"If you can't, then you will die, which will be all to the best. I have no use for a son who is a coward."

All his short life, Bane had striven to please the man who spoke to him through the amulet, the man who was his true father. To win the powerful wizard's approval was his dearest wish.

"Shut your eyes," was Sinistrad's next command.

Bane did so.

"Now we are going to work the magic. Think to yourself that you are lighter than the air. Your body is not solid flesh, but airy, buoyant. Your bones are hollow, like a bird's."

The prince wanted to laugh, but something inside told him if he did so he would never be able to control it and would drop to his death. Swallowing the wild, hysterical giggling, he tried to do as his father commanded. It seemed ludicrous. His eyes wouldn't stay shut, but kept flying open to watch in panic-stricken desperation for a bit of debris to cling to until he could be rescued. The wind rushing past made his eyes tear, however, and he couldn't see clearly. A sob welled up in his throat.

"Bane!" Sinistrad's voice flicked through the child's mind like a whip.

Gulping, Bane squinched his eyes tightly shut and tried to picture himself a bird.

At first it was difficult and seemed impossible. Generations of wizards long dead plus the boy's own inherent skill and intelligence came to Bane's aid. The trick was to banish reality, to convince the mind that its body did not weigh sixty-some rock, that it weighed nothing or less than nothing. It was a skill most young human wizards must study years to attain, yet Bane was having to learn it in seconds. Mother birds teach the young to fly by tossing them out of the nest. Bane was acquiring the art of magic in the same way. Shock and sheer terror jolted his natural talent into taking over and saving him.

My flesh is made of cloud. My blood is fine mist. My bones are hollow and filled with air.

A tingling sensation spread through the prince's body. It seemed as if the magic was changing him into a cloud, for he felt weightless and airy. As this feeling increased, so did his confidence in the illusion he was spinning around himself, and the magic in turn increased, growing stronger and more powerful. Opening his eyes, Bane saw to his delight that he was no longer falling. Lighter than a snowflake, he was drifting in the sky.

"I've done it! I've done it!" He laughed gleefully, flapping his arms like a bird.

"Concentrate!" Sinistrad snapped. "This is not play! Break the concentration and you lose the power!"

Bane sobered. His father's words had not affected him so much as the sudden frightening sensation he'd experienced of growing heavier again. Resolutely he set his mind to its task of keeping him afloat among the wispy clouds.

"What do I do now, father?" he asked, more subdued.

"Remain where you are for the moment. The elves will rescue you."

"But they tried to kill me!"

"Yes, but now they will see that you possess the power and they will want to take you to their wizards. That will lead you to their court. You may as well spend some time there before you return to me. You might gather useful information."

Bane gazed upward, trying to see what was happening on the ship. All that was visible to him from his angle was the underside of the hull and the half-spread wings. The dragonship was still falling, however.

Bane relaxed, floating in the air, and waited for it to come to him.

CHAPTER ♦ 27

DEEPSKY,

DESCENDING

♦

Hugh and Alfred crouched at the foot of the stairs. They could hear the elves searching the ship; they heard the elf captain's conversation with Bane.

"Little bastard," Hugh muttered beneath his breath.

Then they heard Bane scream.

Alfred paled.

"You want him, you better help rescue him," Hugh said to the chamberlain. "Keep close behind me."

Clambering up the ladder, Hugh threw open the hatch. Sword in hand, he surged out onto the deck with Alfred right behind him. The first thing he saw was the elf hurling Bane over the side of the ship. Alfred cried out in horror.

"Never mind!" shouted Hugh, looking about swiftly for something to use as a weapon. "Cover my back— By the ancestors! No you don't!"

Alfred's eyes were rolling up into his head. His face was ashen as he swayed on his feet. Hugh reached out a hand, grabbed him to shake him furiously, but it was too late. The chamberlain keeled over and landed on the deck in a pathetic heap.

"Damn!" Hugh swore viciously.

The elves were stiff and weary from their fight with the rebels. They had not expected to find humans on board a dragonship and they were slow to react. Hugh grabbed for the spar, just as one of the elf fighters attempted to reach it first. The Hand was quicker. Lifting it, he snatched it up with all the force he could manage and thwacked the elf across the face. The fighter toppled, striking his head against the hatch when he fell. Presumably he would be out for a while. Hugh dared not finish him off, for he had two other elves in front of him.

Elves are not particularly skilled swordsmen. They prefer the bow and arrow, which demonstrates skill and judgment, not merely brute strength—all they consider swordplay. The short blades elves carry at their sides are generally used for close fighting or to dispatch victims already wounded by arrows.

Knowing the elves' dislike for the blade, Hugh swung his sword wildly, forcing them to keep out of his reach. He edged backward—hopping from plank to plank—until he ran into the bulwarks, the elves pressing him, but not moving in to attack. Not yet. Whatever they lack in technique, elves make up for in patience and wariness. It was taking all Hugh's waning strength just to keep the blade in his hand. The elves could see that he was sick and weak. Feinting, jabbing, they drained his energy. They could afford to wait until weariness forced him to drop his guard.

Hugh's arms ached, his head throbbed. He knew that he could not hold out long. Somehow, this must end. Movement caught his eye.

"Alfred!" Hugh bellowed. "That's it! Take them from behind!"

It was an old trick, and no human fighter worth his codpiece would have fallen for it. As it was, the elven captain kept his eyes fixed on Hugh, but the other warrior lost his nerve and turned his head. What he saw was not a menacing human bearing down on him, but Alfred sitting up and looking about him dazedly.

Hugh was on the elf in a flash, slashing the sword out of his hand and bashing the warrior in the face with his fist. This move left him open to attack from the captain, but he couldn't help that. The elf captain leapt forward to strike. His feet slipped on the slanting deck; the clumsy stroke missed Hugh's heart and tore through the muscles of his sword arm. Hugh spun on his heel, caught the captain across the jaw with the hilt of the blade and sent the elf sprawling on his back on the deck, his weapon flying from his hand.

Hugh sank to his knees, fighting dizziness and nausea.

"Sir Hugh! You're injured! Let me help—" Hands touched his arm, but Hugh jerked away.

"I'm all right," he snapped. Staggering to his feet, he glared at the chamberlain, who flushed and hung his head.

"I . . . I'm sorry I let you down," he stammered. "I don't know what comes over me—"

Hugh cut him off, gesturing at the elves. "Toss this scum overboard before they come to."

Alfred went so pale that Hugh thought he was going to faint again. "I can't do that, sir. Throw a helpless man . . . to his death."

"They threw that kid of yours to his death!" Hugh raised his sword, holding it above the neck of the unconscious elf. "Then I'll have to get rid of them here. I can't take a chance on them coming around."

He started to cut the slender neck, but a strange reluctance halted him. A voice came to him from out of a vast and horrifying darkness.

All your life you served us.

"Please, sir!" Alfred caught hold of his arm. "Their ship is still attached to ours." He pointed to where the remnants of the elven vessel nosed alongside the dragonship, the grappling hooks holding it fast. "I could transfer them back there. At least they'd have a chance of being rescued."

"Very well." Too sick and tired to argue, Hugh gave in with an ill grace. "Do what you want. Just get rid of them. What do you care about elves anyway? They murdered your precious prince."

"All life is sacred," said Alfred softly, leaning down to lift the unconscious elf captain by the shoulders. "We learned that. Too late. Too late."

At least that's what Hugh thought he said. The wind was whistling through the rigging, he was sick and in pain, and who cared anyway?

Alfred performed the task in his usual bumbling fashion— tripping over the planks, dropping the bodies, once nearly hanging himself when he became entangled in one of the wing cables. Eventually he managed to haul the unconscious elves to the ship's rail and heaved them onto their own ship with a strength the Hand found difficult to credit in the tall, gangling man.

But then, there was a lot about Alfred that was inexplicable. Was I really dead? Did Alfred bring me back to life? And, if so, how? Not even the mysteriarchs have the ability to restore the dead.

"All life is sacred. . . . Too late. Too late."

Hugh shook his head and was immediately sorry. He thought his eyeballs must burst out of their sockets.

Alfred returned to find Hugh trying to knot a clumsy bandage around his arm.

"Sir Hugh?" Alfred began timidly.

Hugh did not look up from his work. Gently the chamberlain took over, tying the bandage deftly.

"I think you should come and see something, sir."

"I know. We're still falling. But I can pull us out. How close are we to the Maelstrom?"

"It's not just that, sir. It's the prince. He's safe!"

"Safe?" Hugh stared at him, thinking the man had gone mad.

"It's very peculiar, sir. Although not so peculiar, I suppose, considering who he is and who his father is."

Who the hell is he? Hugh wanted to ask, but now was not the time. Sick and hurting, he made his way across the deck, whose movements were becoming more and more erratic as they drew nearer the storm. Looking down below, he could not repress a low whistle of amazement.

"His father is a mysteriarch of the High Realm," said Alfred. "I suppose he taught the boy to do that."

"They communicate through the amulet," said the Hand, recalling his failing vision focusing on the boy clasping the feather in his hand.

"Yes."

Hugh could see the boy's upturned face, looking at them triumphantly, evidently quite pleased with himself.

"I'm supposed to rescue him, I suppose. A kid who tried to poison me. A kid who wrecked my ship. A kid who tried to turn us all over to the elves!"

"After all, sir," replied Alfred, gazing at Hugh steadily, "you did agree to murder him—for money."

Hugh glanced back down at Bane. They were nearing the Maelstrom. He could see the stinging clouds of dust and debris floating above it and hear the dull booming of the thunder. A cool, moist wind smelling of rain was causing the tail rudder to flap wildly. Right now, Hugh should be examining the snapped cables, trying to rig them so that he could extend the wings and regain the upper air before the ship drifted too close, before the winds of the storm could prevent them from rising. And the pounding in his head was making him sick.

Turning, Hugh left the rail.

"I don't blame you," said Alfred. "He is a difficult child—"

"Difficult!" Hugh laughed, then paused, eyes closed, as the deck canted away beneath his feet. When he was himself again, he drew a deep breath. "Take that spar and hold it out to him. I'll try to maneuver the ship closer. We're risking our own lives doing this. Chances are we'll get caught by the winds and sucked into the storm."

"Yes, Sir Hugh." Alfred ran to get the spar—for once, his feet and his body all going the same direction.

The Hand dropped through the hatch into the steerage way and stood staring at the mess. Why am I doing this? he asked himself. It's simple, was the response. You've got a father who will pay to have his son *not* come back and another father who will pay to get hold of the kid.

That makes sense, Hugh admitted. All, of course, provided we don't wind up in the Maelstrom. Looking out the crystal window, he could see the boy floating among the clouds. The dragonship was falling down to meet him, but unless Hugh could alter their course, they would miss him by over a wing's length.

Gloomily the Hand surveyed the wreckage, prodding his aching mind to function and delineate between the various ropes that were twisting and slithering across the deck like snakes. Finding those he needed, he untangled them and laid them out straight so that they could run easily through the hawseholes. Once the cables were arranged, he cut them loose from the harness with his sword and wound them around his arms. He had seen men suffer broken bones from doing this. If he lost control, the heavy wing would fly out suddenly, jerk the rope, and snap his arms like a twig.

Seating himself, his feet braced against the deck, Hugh began to pay out the line slowly. One length of cable ran swiftly and smoothly through the hawsehole. The wing began to lift and the magic to activate. But the cable on Hugh's right arm remained limp and lifeless, straggling across the deck. He wiped sweat from his brow with the back of his hand. The wing was stuck, jammed.

Hugh hauled back on the cable with all his might, hoping to jolt it free. It did no good, and he realized that one of the exterior cables attached to his guide rope must have snapped. Swearing to himself beneath his breath, the Hand abandoned the broken cable and concentrated on flying the ship with one wing.

"Nearer!" Alfred shouted. "A little more to the left—or is that starboard? I can never remember. Port? Perhaps port? There, I've almost got him . . . Now! Hang on tightly, Your Highness!"

Hugh heard the prince's shrill voice, yammering excitedly about something, the sound of small boots hitting the deck.

Then he heard Alfred's voice, low and rebuking, and Bane's defensive whine.

Hugh pulled back on the cable, felt the wing lift, and the dragonship, aided by its magic, began to float upward. The clouds of the Maelstrom swirled below, seemingly angry to see the prey escaping. Hugh held his breath, concentrating all his energy on holding the wing steady as they continued slowly rising.

It was as if a giant hand reached out to slap them like an irritating mosquito. The ship dropped suddenly and sickeningly, plunging downward so fast that it seemed their bodies went with it but their stomaches and bowels stayed up above. Hugh heard a frightened shriek and a heavy bump and knew someone must have been thrown to the deck. The Hand hoped both Alfred and the kid had found something to hang on to, but there was nothing he could do about it if they hadn't.

Grimly he held on to the cables, fighting to keep the wing up to slow their descent. Then he heard an ominous ripping sound and the eerie whistle that stops the hearts of all dragonship pilots. The wing had torn, the wind was rushing through it. Hugh paid out the line as far as it would go, opening the wing all the way. Although he couldn't use it to steer, at least its magic would help cushion their fall when they hit the ground—*if* they hit the ground and *if* the Maelstrom didn't rip them apart first.

Unwinding the rope from around his arm, Hugh threw it onto the deck. They hadn't reached the Maelstrom yet, and already the wind was whipping the ship around. He couldn't stand up and was forced to crawl across the planking, clinging to the cables and using them to pull himself into the corridor. Once there, he dragged himself up the ladder and peered out. Alfred and Bane were lying flat on the top deck, the chamberlain with his arm wrapped tightly around the boy.

"Down here!" Hugh yelled above the buffeting of the wind. "The wing's split. We're sinking into the storm!"

Alfred slithered on his stomach across the deck, hauling Bane with him. Hugh took a certain grim pleasure in noting that the child appeared to be stricken dumb with terror. Reaching the hatch, the chamberlain shoved the prince ahead of him. Hugh grasped hold of the boy none too gently, pulled him inside, and dropped him onto the deck.

Bane let out a howl of pain that was cut short when the ship flipped over, slamming him into the bulwarks and knocking the breath from his body. The motion sent Alfred plunging through the hatch headfirst, causing Hugh to lose his footing. He crashed down the ladder onto the deck below.

The Hand staggered to his feet and made his way back up the ladder—or perhaps it was down the ladder. The ship was rolling over and over, and he had lost all sense of direction. He grabbed hold of the hatch cover. A rain squall hit the ship; water lashed down with the force of elven spears. A jagged bolt of lightning split the air near enough that the smell made him wrinkle his nose; the concussion of the air rushing back together nearly deafened him. He fumbled at the hatch cover—it was slippery and wet—and finally managed to yank it shut. Wearily he slid back down the ladder and collapsed onto the deck.

"You . . . you're alive!" Bane stared at him in blank astonishment. Then his expression changed to one of joy. Running over to Hugh, the child threw his arms around him and hugged him close. "Oh, I'm so glad! I was so frightened! You saved my life!"

Detaching the clinging hands, Hugh held the prince at arm's length. There was no doubting the sincerity either in the tear-choked voice or on the innocent face. There was no guile or deceit in the blue eyes. The Hand could have almost imagined that he had dreamed everything.

Almost, but not quite.

This Bane, so aptly named, had tried to poison him. Hugh put his hand around the boy's white throat. It would be a simple matter. One twist. Snap the neck. Contract fulfilled.

The ship pitched and tossed in the storm. The hull creaked and groaned and seemed likely to fly apart at any moment. Lightning flashed around them; thunder boomed in their ears.

All your life you served us.

Hugh tightened his grasp. Bane gazed up at him; the child was trusting, shyly smiling. The assassin might have been soothing the prince with a loving caress.

Angrily the Hand hurled the boy away from him, sent him stumbling into Alfred, who caught him reflexively.

Stumbling past the two, heading for the steerage way, Hugh dropped to his hands and knees and heaved up his guts.

CHAPTER ♦ 28

DREVLIN,

LOW REALM

♦

BANE WAS THE FIRST TO REGAIN CONSCIOUSNESS. OPENING HIS EYES, HE stared around at his surroundings, at the dragonship and its other two occupants. He could hear a low rumble of thunder, and for a moment his terror returned; then he realized the storm was some distance away. Looking outside, he could see it was calm, with only a spatter of rain hitting the ship. The horrid motion had ended. Everything was still, nothing moved.

Hugh lay on the deck amidst the cables, his eyes closed, blood on his head and arm, his hand hanging on to one of the ropes as though his last effort had been to make some attempt to save them. Alfred lay sprawled on his back. The chamberlain did not appear to be injured. Bane remembered little about the terrifying descent through the storm, but he had the impression from somewhere that Alfred had fainted.

Bane, too, had been afraid, more afraid even than when the elf captain had tossed him over the side of the ship. That had happened swiftly, so there had been only a short time for fear. The fall into the storm had seemed to take forever, with terror growing stronger every second. Bane had really thought he might die of it. He recalled, then, his father's voice whispering words that lulled him into sleep.

The prince attempted to sit up. He felt peculiar—not hurt, just peculiar. His body seemed too heavy, a tremendous force was weighing him down, yet there was nothing on top of him. Bane whimpered a little in fright and at the feeling of being alone. He didn't like these strange sensations and he crawled over to shake Alfred, to try to wake him. Then Bane saw Hugh's sword, lying on the deck beneath him, and the child had a thought.

"I could kill them both now," he said, gripping the feather amulet tightly. "We could be rid of them, father."

"No!" The word was stern and sharp and startled him.

"Why not?"

"Because you need them to get you away from this place and bring you to me. But first, there is a task I want you to perform. You have landed on the isle of Drevlin in the Low Realm. A people known as Gegs inhabit this land. Actually, I am quite pleased that chance has brought you here. I was planning to come myself, when I acquired a ship.

"There is a great machine on this isle that very much intrigues me. It was built long ago by the Sartan, but for what purpose, no one has ever been able to discover. I want you to investigate it while you are there. Do this and find out what you can about these Gegs. Though I doubt if they can be of much use to me in my conquest of the world, it is wise to know as much as I can about those I intend to conquer. I might even be able to make use of them. You must watch, my son, for the opportunity."

The voice faded. Bane scowled. If only Sinistrad would stop his irritating habit of saying "When *I* conquer, when *I* rule." It was to be "we." Bane had determined this.

"Of course, my father can't know much about me yet; that's why he's never included me in his plans. When we meet, he'll get to know me. He'll be proud of me and he'll be glad to share his power with me. He'll teach me all his magic. We'll do everything together. I won't be lonely anymore."

Hugh began to groan and stir. Bane hurriedly lay back down on the deck and shut his eyes.

Hugh eased himself up painfully, propping his body with his arms. His first thought was one of absolute astonishment to discover he was alive. His next was that he would pay that elven wizard who cast the spell on his ship double what he charged for magic and feel that it was cheap. His next was for his pipe. Reaching into the soiled and sodden velvet tunic, Hugh discovered it safe, unbroken.

The Hand glanced at his companions. Alfred was out cold. Hugh had never in his life known anyone to pass out from sheer terror. Marvelous person to have around in a crisis. The boy was also unconscious, but he was breathing steadily, his color was good. He hadn't been hurt. Hugh's future security was alive and well.

"But first," muttered the Hand, edging across the deck to the boy, "we need to get rid of daddy, if that's who this really is."

Moving slowly and cautiously, careful not to wake the child, Hugh slid his fingers beneath the silver chain from which the feather amulet was suspended and started to lift it from around the boy's neck.

The chain slid through his fingers.

Hugh stared at it incredulously. The chain had not slipped *off* his fingers but *through* them—literally! He had seen it pass right through solid flesh and bone with as much ease as if his hand had been as insubstantial as that of a ghost's.

"I'm imagining things. The bump on the head," he said, and grasped the chain, this time firmly.

He held nothing in his hand but air.

Hugh realized then that Bane's eyes had opened, the boy was watching him, not angrily or suspiciously, but with sadness.

"It won't come off," he said. "I've tried." The prince sat up. "What happened? Where are we?"

"We're safe," Hugh said, sitting back and drawing forth his pipe. He'd smoked the last of the sterego, not that he had any way to light it even if he hadn't. He clamped the stem in his teeth and sucked on the empty bowl.

"You saved our lives," Bane told him. "And after I tried to kill you. I'm sorry. I truly am!" The limpid blue eyes lifted to gaze at Hugh. "It was only that I was afraid of you."

Hugh sucked on the pipe and said nothing.

"I feel so strange," continued the prince in easy conversation, that one small matter between them having now finally been cleared up. "Like I'm too heavy for my body."

"It's the pressure down here, the weight of the air. You'll get used to it. Just sit still and don't move."

Bane sat, fidgeting. His gaze went to Hugh's sword. "You're a warrior. You can defend yourself the honorable way. But I'm weak. What else could I do? You *are* an assassin, aren't you? You *were* hired to kill me?"

"And you're *not* Stephen's son," Hugh countered.

"No, sir, he is not."

The voice was Alfred's. The chamberlain sat up, looking around him in confusion. "Where are we?"

"My guess is we're in the Low Realm. With luck, we're on Drevlin."

"Why luck?"

"Because Drevlin's the only continent down here that's inhabited. The Gegs will help us if we can make it to one of their cities. This Low Realm is swept constantly by terrible storms," he added in explanation. "If we're caught in one out in the open . . ." Hugh finished his sentence with a shrug.

Alfred blanched and cast a worried glance outside. Bane squirmed and twisted to see. "It's not storming now. Shouldn't we leave?"

"Wait until your body's gotten used to the change in pressure. We'll need to move fast when we go."

"And you think we're on this Drevlin?" Alfred asked.

"Judging from our location when we fell, I'd say so. We were blown around some by the storm, but Drevlin's the largest landmass down here, and it'd be hard to miss. If we'd been blown off course too far, we wouldn't be anywhere."

"You've been here before." Bane sat up straight, staring at Hugh.

"Yes."

"What's it like?" he questioned eagerly.

Hugh did not immediately reply. His eyes shifted to Alfred, who had lifted his hand and was examining it in puzzlement, as if certain it must belong to someone else.

"Go outside and see for yourself, Your Highness."

"You mean it?" Bane scrambled to his feet. "I can go outside?"

"See if you can find any signs of a Geg settlement. There's a big machine on this continent. If you can see parts of it, there'll be Gegs living nearby. Keep close to the ship. You get caught by a storm with nowhere to go for shelter, and you're finished."

"Is that wise, sir?" Alfred looked anxiously after the boy, who was squeezing his small body out of a hole smashed in the hull.

"He won't go far. He'll get tired sooner than he realizes. Now, while he's gone, tell me the truth."

Alfred became very pale. Shifting uncomfortably, he lowered his eyes and stared at his too-large hands. "You were right, sir, when you said that Bane was not Stephen's child. I will tell you what I know—what any of us knows for certain, as far as that goes, although I believe Trian has conjectured some theories to explain what happened. I must say that they didn't seem to completely cover all the circumstances—" He saw Hugh's face darken, the brows draw together with impatience.

"Ten cycles ago, a child was born to Stephen and Anne. It was a boy, a beautiful baby, with his father's dark hair and his mother's eyes and ears. You think that is odd, that I mention the ears, but it will become important later on. Anne, you see, has a nick in her left ear, right here, at the outer curve. It is a trait in her family. The story goes that long ago, when the Sartan still walked the world, one of their kind was saved from harm when a spear thrown at him was deflected by Anne's ancestor. The point sliced off a part of the man's left ear. All children born since have been marked with that notch as a symbol of the family's honor.

"Anne's child had the notch. I saw it myself when they brought the babe out for the showing." Alfred's voice lowered. "The child found in the cradle the next morning did not."

"A changeling," commented Hugh. "Surely they knew?"

"Yes, they knew. We all knew. The baby appeared to be the same age as the prince, only a day or two old. But this baby was fair-haired with bright blue eyes, not the milky kind of blue that will turn brown. And the child's ears were both perfectly shaped. We questioned everyone in the palace, but no one knew how the switch was made. The guards swore no one had slipped past them. They were good men. Stephen did not doubt their word. The nurse slept in the room with the baby all night and woke to take him to the wet nurse, who said that she put to her breast Anne's dark-haired boy. By this and by other tokens, Trian judged that the child had been placed there by magic."

"Other tokens?"

Alfred sighed. His gaze strayed outside. Bane was standing on a rock, peering intently into the distance. On the horizon, black clouds flecked with lightning were massing. The wind was beginning to rise.

"The baby had a powerful enchantment woven round him. Anyone who looked at him must immediately love him. No, 'love' isn't the right word." The chamberlain considered the matter. " 'Dote on,' perhaps, or 'become obsessed by.' We couldn't bear to see him unhappy. A tear falling from his eye made us feel wretched for days. We would have parted with our lives before we parted with that child." Alfred's voice fell silent and he ran his hand over his bald pate. "Stephen and Anne knew the danger of taking this child as their own, but they—all of us—were helpless to prevent it. That's why they named him Bane."

"And what was the danger?"

"A year after the changeling was delivered to us, on the birthday of Anne's true child, a mysteriarch from the High Realm came among us. At first we were honored, for such a thing had not happened in years—that one of the powerful magi of the Seventh House should so humble himself that he would deign to leave his glorious realm above and visit with us below. But our pride and our gladness changed to ashes in our mouths. Sinistrad is an evil man. He took care that we should know him and fear him. He came, he said, to do honor to the little prince. He had brought him a present. When Sinistrad lifted the babe in his arms, we knew—every one of us—whose child Bane truly was.

"No one could do a thing, of course—not against a powerful wizard of the Seventh House. Trian himself is one of the most skilled wizards in the kingdom, and he is only Third House. No, we had to watch with smiles plastered on our faces as the mysteriarch slipped that feather amulet around the baby's neck. Sinistrad congratulated Stephen on his *heir* and left. His emphasis on that word sent shivers of horror through all of us. But Stephen was helpless to do anything except dote on the child more fiercely than ever, even though he began to loathe the sight of him."

Hugh tugged at his beard, frowning. "But why would a wizard of the High Realm want a kingdom in the Middle? They left us cycles ago of their own free will. Their own kingdom is wealthy beyond anything we can imagine, or so we've heard.

"As I've said, we do not know. Trian has theories—conquest is the most obvious, of course. But if they wanted to rule us, they could bring an army of mysteriarchs down and defeat us easily. No, as I said, it doesn't make sense. Stephen knew that Sinistrad was in communication with his son. Bane is a cunning spy. The boy has learned every secret in the kingdom and has passed it all on, of that we are certain. We might have lived with that, for ten cycles have passed and our strength grows. If the mysteriarchs wanted to take over, they could have done it before this. But something has happened that made it urgent for Stephen to rid himself of the changeling." Alfred glanced outside to see the boy still occupied in scouting out a city, though he was obviously tired and now sitting on the rock instead of standing. The chamberlain motioned Hugh near, whispering in his ear. "Anne is with child!"

"Ah!" Hugh nodded in sudden understanding. "And so they decide to get rid of one heir, now that there's another on the way. What about the enchantment?"

"Trian broke it. Ten years of study it took him, but he managed at last. Now Stephen was able to"—Alfred halted, stammering in confusion—"to . . ."

". . . hire an assassin to kill him. How long have you known?"

"From the first." Alfred flushed. "It was why I followed you."

"And you would have tried to stop me?"

"I'm not certain." Alfred's brow furrowed, and he shook his head confusedly. "I . . . don't know."

A dark seed fell into Hugh's mind and took root. It grew fast, twisting around his brain, flowering and bearing a noxious fruit. *I decided to break the contract. Why? Because the boy is more valuable alive than dead. But so were a number of men I contracted to kill. I never before broke faith. I never before broke a contract, though sometimes I could have made ten times the fee paid me. Why now? I risked my own life to rescue the bastard! I couldn't kill him after he tried to kill me!*

What if the enchantment isn't *broken? What if Bane is still manipulating all of us, beginning with King Stephen?*

Hugh looked intently at Alfred. "And what's the truth about you, chamberlain?"

"You see it before you, sir, I am afraid," said Alfred humbly, spreading his hands. "I have been in service all my life. I was with Her Royal Highness's family at their castle in Uylandia. When Her Majesty became queen, she was kind enough to bring me with her." A slow flush spread over Alfred's face. His eyes sought the deck. He plucked nervously at the shabby clothing with his clumsy fingers.

Lying does not come easily for this man, not like it does for the child, thought Hugh. *Yet, like the child, Alfred is, seemingly, living a lie.*

The assassin let it drop, closing his eyes. His shoulder pained him, he felt queasy and lethargic, effects of both the poison and the heavy air pressure. Thinking of all that had passed, he twisted his lips into a bitter smile. Worst of all, his hands smeared red with the blood of countless men, he who had proudly believed himself to be masterless had been mastered—by a child.

Prince Bane poked his head back through the shattered side of the ship. "I think I see it. The great machine! It's off in the distance, that direction. You can't see it now, because the clouds have covered it. But I remember the way. Let's go there now! After all, how can it be dangerous? It's only rain—"

A bolt of lightning sizzled from sky to ground, blasting a hole in the coralite. The thunderclap shook the ground and nearly knocked the boy over.

"That's why," said Hugh.

Another lightning bolt struck with shattering force. Bane shot across the deck and crouched down beside Alfred. Rain pounded on the hull. Hail beat on it with deafening ferocity. Soon, water began pouring in through the cracks in the smashed timber. Bane's eyes were wide, his face pale, but he didn't cry out. When he saw his hands were trembling, he clasped them together tightly. Looking at the boy, Hugh saw himself long ago, battling fear with pride—the only weapon in his arsenal.

And it occurred to him that perhaps this was just what Bane wanted him to see.

The assassin fingered the hilt of his sword. It would take only a few seconds. Grasp it, wield it, thrust it deep into the boy's body. If he was going to be stopped by magic, then he wanted to see it act, know for certain.

Or perhaps he had seen it already.

Hugh moved his hand away from the sword. Lifting his pipe, he saw Bane watching him. The boy's lips curved in a sweet, charming smile.

CHAPTER 29

WOMBE, DREVLIN,

LOW REALM

♦

THE HIGH FROMAN WAS HAVING A SAD TIME OF IT. HE WAS BEING plagued by gods. Literally dropping from the skies, gods rained down on his defenseless head. Nothing was going right. His once-peaceful realm that had not known a whisper of trouble in the last several centuries was now running amok.

Trudging across the coralite, his band of coppers marching along reluctantly behind him, the head clark marching righteously at his side, the froman thought long and hard about gods and decided that he hadn't much use for them. First, instead of neatly getting rid of Mad Limbeck, the gods had actually had the audacity to send him back alive. Not only that, but they came with him! Well, one of them did—a god who called himself Haplo. And though confused reports had reached the ears of the high froman that the god didn't consider himself a god, Darral Longshoreman didn't believe it for a flicker.

Unfortunately, whether this Haplo was or he wasn't, he was stirring up trouble wherever he went—and that was pretty nearly everywhere, including, now, the Gegs' capital city of Wombe. Mad Limbeck and his wild WUPP's were dragging the god across the countryside, making speeches, telling the people that they were being misused, ill-treated, enslaved, and the Mangers knew what else. Of course, Mad Limbeck had been ranting and raving about this for some considerable length of time, but now, with the god standing at his side, the Gegs were beginning to listen to him!

Half the clarks had been completely won over. The head clark, seeing his church falling apart around him, was demanding that the high froman do something.

"And what am I supposed to do?" Darral asked sourly.
"Arrest this Haplo, this god who says he isn't a god? That won't
do anything except convince the people who do believe in him
that they've been right all along and convince the rest who don't
that they should!"

"Bosh!" sniffed the head clark, who hadn't understood a
thing the high froman said but who knew he didn't agree with it.

"Bosh! That's all you've got to say! It's all your fault, anyhow!" the high froman shouted, working himself into a rage.
"Let the Mangers take care of Mad Limbeck, you said. Well, they
took care of him, all right! Sent him back to destroy us!"

The head clark had stormed off in a huff. But he'd been back
quick enough when the ship was sighted.

Plummeting out of the skies where it had no business being,
since it wasn't time for the monthly festival yet, the dragonship
had landed in the Outland some distance away from an outer
sector of Wombe known as Stomak. The high froman had seen it
from his bedroom window and his heart had sunk. More gods—
just what he needed!

At first Darral thought he might have been the only one to
see it and that he could pretend he hadn't. No such luck. A
number of other Gegs saw it, including the head clark. Worse
still, one of his sharp-eyed, no-brains coppers had reported seeing
Something Alive come out of it. The copper, as punishment, was
now stumbling along after his chief on their way to investigate.

"I guess this'll teach you!" Darral rounded on the unfortunate copper. "It's because of you we're being forced to come out
here. If you'd kept your lips from flapping! But, no! You have to
go and see one of 'em! Not only that, but you have to shout it
out to half the realm!"

"I only said it to the head clark," protested the copper.

"It's the same thing," Darral muttered.

"Well, but I think it's only right that we have our own god
now, High Froman," persisted the copper. " 'Tisn't fair, to my
mind, those clods in Het having a god and us going without. I
reckon this'll show 'em!"

The head clark raised an eyebrow. Anger forgotten, he sidled
over to the high froman. "He *does* have a point," murmured the
clark in Darral's ear. "If we have our own god, we can use him to
counter Limbeck's god."

Stumbling along over the cracked and gouged coralite, the
high froman had to admit that his brother-in-law had, for once in

his life, come up with something that sounded halfway intelligent. *My own god,* mused Darral Longshoreman, squelching through the puddles, heading for the dragonship. *There's got to be some way to work this to my advantage.*

Seeing that they were nearing the wrecked dragonship, the High Froman slowed his march, raising his hand to warn those behind him to slow theirs—something that was not necessary. The coppers had already come to a standstill about ten feet behind their leader.

The high froman glared at his men in exasperation and started to curse them all for cowards, but on second thought, he considered that it was probably just as well his men remained behind. It would look better if he treated with the gods alone. He cast a sidelong glance at the head clark.

"I think you should stay here," said Darral. "It might be dangerous."

Since Darral Longshoreman had never in his entire life been concerned about his welfare, the head clark was very rightly suspicious at this sudden consideration and promptly and unequivocally refused. "It's only proper that a churchman greet these immortal beings," said the head clark loftily. "I suggest, in fact, that you allow me to do the talking."

The storm had cleared, but there was another coming (on Drevlin there was *always* another coming!), and Darral didn't have time to argue. Contenting himself with muttering that the head clark could talk all he wanted through a split lip, the high froman and his cohort turned and marched—with a remarkable courage that would later be celebrated in story and song—right up to the battered hull of the downed ship. (The courage exhibited by the two Gegs should not, after all, be considered that remarkable, the copper having reported that the Creature he had seen emerge from the ship was small and puny-looking. Their true courage would be tested shortly.)

Standing next to the damaged hull, the high froman was momentarily at a loss. He'd never spoken to a god before. At the monthly sacred docking ceremonies, the Welves appeared in their huge winged ships, sucked up the water, threw down their reward, and departed. Not a bad way of doing things, the high froman thought regretfully. He was just opening his mouth to announce to the small, puny-looking god inside the ship that his servants were here when there emerged a god who was anything but small and puny-looking.

The god was tall and dark, with a black beard that hung in two braids from his chin and long black hair that flowed over his shoulders. His face was hard, his eyes as sharp and cold as the coralite on which the Geg stood. The god carried in his hand a weapon of bright, glittering steel.

At the sight of this formidable, frightening creature, the head clark, forgetting completely about church protocol, turned and fled. Most of the coppers, seeing the church abandoning the field, figured doom had descended and took to their heels. Only one stalwart copper remained—the one who had sighted the god and had reported it to be small and puny. Perhaps he thought he had nothing to lose.

"Humpf! Good riddance," muttered Darral. Turning to the god, he bowed so low his long beard dragged the wet ground. "Your Wurship," said the high froman humbly, "we welcome you to our realm. Have you come for the Judgment?"

The god stared at him, then turned to another god (the froman inwardly groaned—how many of these were there?) and spoke something to this second god in words that were a meaningless babble to the high froman. The second god—a bald, weak, soft-looking god, if you asked Darral Longshoreman—shook his head, a blank expression on his face.

And it occurred to the high froman that these gods hadn't understood a word he'd said.

In that instant, Darral Longshoreman realized that Mad Limbeck wasn't mad after all. These weren't gods. Gods would have understood him. These were mortal men. They had come in a dragonship, which meant that the Welves in their dragonships were most likely mortal. If the Kicksey-winsey had suddenly ceased to function, if every whirly had stopped whirling, every gear stopped grinding, every whistle stopped tooting, the high froman could not have been more appalled. Mad Limbeck was right! There would be no Judgment! They would never be lifted up to Geg's Hope. Glowering at the gods and at their wrecked ship, Darral realized that the gods themselves couldn't even get off Drevlin!

A low rumble of thunder warned the high froman that he and these "gods" didn't have time to stand around and stare at one another. Disillusioned, angry, needing time to think, the high froman turned his back on the "gods" and started to head for his city.

"Wait!" came a voice. "Where are you going?"

Startled, Darral whirled around. A third god had appeared.

This must have been the one the copper had seen, for this god was small and frail-looking. This god was a child! And had Darral only imagined it, or had the child spoken to him in words he understood?

"Greetings. I am Prince Bane," said the child in excellent but halting Geg, sounding almost as if he were being prompted. One hand was clasped tightly around a feather amulet he wore on his breast. He held out his other hand, palm open, in the ritual Geg gesture of friendship. "My father is Sinistrad, Mysteriarch of the Seventh House, Ruler of the High Realm."

Darral Longshoreman drew in a deep, shivering breath. Never in his life had he seen such a beautiful being as this. Bright golden hair, bright blue eyes—the child glistened like the shining metal of the Kicksey-winsey.

Perhaps I've been mistaken. Mad Limbeck is wrong, after all. Surely this being is immortal! Somewhere from deep within the Geg, buried beneath centuries of Sundering, holocaust, and rupture, came a phrase to Darral's mind, "And a little child shall lead them."

"Greetings, Prince B-Bane," returned the high froman, stumbling over the name that held, in his language, no meaning. "Have you come to pass Judgment on us at last?"

The child's eyelids flickered; then he said coolly, "Yes, I have come to judge you. Where is your king?"

"I am the high froman, Your Wurship, ruler of my people. It would be a great honor if you would deign to visit our city, Your Wurship." The high froman's gaze strayed nervously to the approaching storm. Gods probably weren't bothered by bolts of lightning sizzling down from the heavens, and Darral found it somewhat embarrassing to hint that high fromen were. However, the child appeared to be cognizant of the Geg's plight and to take pity on it. Casting a glance back at his two companions, whom Darral now took for the god's servants or guards, Prince Bane indicated he was ready to travel and glanced about for the conveyance.

"I'm sorry, Your Wurship," muttered the high froman, flushing warmly, "but we have to . . . er . . . walk."

"Oh, that's all right," said the god, and jumped gleefully into a puddle.

CHAPTER ♦ 30

WOMBE, DREVLIN,

LOW REALM

♦

LIMBECK WAS SITTING IN THE DRAFTY HEADQUARTERS OF WUPP WRITING the speech he would deliver at the rally tonight. His spectacles perched precariously on his head, the Geg scribbled his words onto the paper, happily spattering ink over everything and completely oblivious of the chaos erupting around him. Haplo sat near him, the dog at his feet.

Quiet, taciturn, unobtrusive—indeed, going almost unnoticed— the Patryn lounged in a Geg chair that was too short for him. His long legs extending out in front of him, he idly watched the organized confusion. His cloth-wound hand dropped occasionally to scratch the dog on the head or to pat it reassuringly in the event that something startled it.

WUPP Headquarters in the Geg capital city of Wombe was— literally—a hole in the wall. The Kicksey-winsey had once decided it needed to expand in a certain direction, knocked a hole in the wall of a Geg dwelling, then had apparently decided, for some unknown reason, that it didn't want to go that way after all. The hole in the wall remained and the twenty or so Geg families who had occupied the dwelling had moved, since one could never be certain but that the Kicksey-winsey might change its mind again.

Beyond a few minor inconveniences—such as the perpetual draft—it was, however, ideal for the establishment of WUPP Headquarters. There had been no WUPP Headquarters in the capital of Drevlin. The high froman and the church both held crushing power here. But after Limbeck's triumphant return from the dead—bringing with him a god who claimed he wasn't a god—reached Wombe via the newssingers, the Gegs clamored to know more about WUPP and its leader. Jarre herself traveled to Wombe to establish the Union, distribute pamphlets, and find a suitable building to serve both as center of operations and a place to live. Her primary, secret goal, however, was to discover if the high froman and/or the church was going to give them trouble.

Jarre hoped they would. She could almost hear the newssingers across the land warbling, "Coppers Crush Converts!" Nothing of the sort had occurred, much to Jarre's disappointment, and Limbeck and Haplo (and the dog) were met by cheering crowds when they entered the city. Jarre hinted that this was undoubtedly a dark and subtle plot by the high froman to ensnare them all, but Limbeck said it simply proved that Darral Longshoreman was fair and open-minded.

Now crowds of Gegs stood outside the hole in the wall, craning their necks to catch a glimpse of the famous Limbeck or of his god-who-wasn't. WUPP members rushed importantly in and out, bearing messages to or from Jarre, who was so busy running things that she didn't have time to make speeches anymore.

Jarre was in her element. She led WUPP with ruthless efficiency. Her skills in organization, her inherent knowledge of the Gegs, and her management of Limbeck had been responsible for setting the Gegs' world aflame with anger and the call for revolution. She poked, prodded, and pummeled Limbeck into shape, shoved him forth to issue words of genius, and hauled him back when it was time to quit. Her awe of Haplo soon faded and she began to treat him the same way she treated Limbeck, telling him what to say and how long to say it.

Haplo submitted to her in everything with easy, casual pliability. He was, Jarre discovered, a man of few words, but those words had a way of searing into the heart, leaving a mark that burned long after the iron had grown cool.

"Is your speech ready for tonight, Haplo?" She paused in the act of drafting a reply to an attack that the church had made on them—an attack so simpleminded that to answer it was to give it more credence than it deserved.

"I will say what I always say, if that is agreeable to you, madam," he replied with the quiet respect that marked all his dealings with the Gegs.

"Yes," said Jarre, brushing her chin with the end of the feather quill. "I think that will be most satisfactory. You know that we are likely to draw our biggest crowd yet. They say that some scrifts are even talking of walking off the job—a thing absolutely unprecedented in the history of Drevlin!"

Limbeck was startled enough by the tone of her voice to lift his myopic gaze from his paper and stare vaguely in her general direction. In reality, all he could see of her was a squarish blur surmounted by a lump that was her head. He couldn't see her eyes but he knew her well enough to envision them sparkling with pleasure.

"My dear, is that wise?" he said, holding his pen poised above the paper and unconsciously allowing a large drop of ink to splat right in the center of his text. "It's certain to anger the high froman and the clarks—"

"I hope it does!" Jarre stated emphatically, much to Limbeck's consternation. Nervously he set his elbow in the ink splot.

"Let him send his coppers to break up our meeting," Jarre continued. "We'll gain hundreds more followers!"

"But there could be trouble!" Limbeck was aghast. "Someone could get hurt!"

"All in the name of the cause." Jarre shrugged and returned to her work.

Limbeck dropped another ink blot. "But my cause has always been peace. I never meant for people to get hurt!"

Rising to her feet, Jarre cast a swift meaningful glance at Haplo, reminding Limbeck that the god-who-wasn't was listening. Limbeck flushed and bit his lip, but shook his head stubbornly, and Jarre moved over to his side. Lifting up a rag, she wiped away a particularly large ink spot on the end of his nose.

"My dear," she said, not unkindly, "you've always talked about the need for change. How did you think it would happen?"

"Gradually," said Limbeck. "Gradually and slowly, so that everyone has time to get used to it and comes to see that it is for the best."

"That is so like you!" sighed Jarre.

A WUPPer stuck his head through the hole in the wall, seeking to attract Jarre's attention. She frowned at him severely and the Geg appeared slightly daunted but held his ground, waiting. Turning her back on the WUPPer, Jarre smoothed Limbeck's wrinkled brow with a hand rough and callused from hard work.

"You want change to come about nicely and pleasantly. You want to see it just sort of slip up on people so that they don't notice it until they wake up one morning and realize that they're happier than they were before. Isn't that true, Limbeck?"

Jarre answered her own question. "Of course it is. And it's very wonderful and very thoughtful of you and it's also very naive and very stupid." Leaning down, she kissed him on the crown of the head, to rob her words of their sting. "And it's just what I love about you, my dear. But haven't you been listening to Haplo, Limbeck? Give part of your speech now, Haplo."

The WUPPer who had been waiting to see Jarre turned to shout to the crowd, "Haplo's going to give his speech!"

The Gegs standing in the street broke into rousing cheers and as many as could possibly fit squeezed heads, arms, legs, and other body parts in through the hole in the wall. This somewhat alarming sight caused the dog to leap to its feet. Haplo patted the dog down and obligingly began to orate, speaking loudly in order to be heard above the crunch, whiz, bang of the Kicksey-winsey.

"You Gegs know your history. You were brought here by those you call the 'Mangers.' In my world, they are known as the Sartan and they treated us as they did you. They enslaved you, forced you to work on this thing that you know as the Kicksey-winsey. You consider it to be a living entity, but I tell you that it's a machine! Nothing more! A machine kept running by your brains, your brawn, your blood!

"And where are the Sartan? Where are these so-called gods who claimed that they brought you—a gentle, peaceful people—here to protect you from the Welves? They brought you here because they knew they could take advantage of you!

"Where are the Sartan? Where are the Mangers? That is the question we must ask! No one, it seems, knows the answer. They were here and now they're gone and they've left you to the mercy of the minions of the Sartan, those Welves you were taught to believe were gods! But they're not gods, either, any more than I am a god—except for the fact that they live like gods. Live like gods because you are their slaves! And that's how the Welves think of you!

"It's time to rise up, throw off your chains, and take what is rightfully yours! Take what has been denied you for centuries!"

Wild applause from the Gegs peering through the hole cut him off. Jarre, eyes shining, stood with clasped hands, her lips moving to the sound of the words, which she had memorized. Limbeck listened, but his eyes were downcast, his expression troubled. Though he, too, had heard Haplo's speech often, it seemed that only now was he really hearing it for the first time. Words such as "blood," "rise up," "throw off," "take," leapt up, growling, like the dog at Haplo's feet. He had heard them, perhaps even said them himself, but they had been only words. Now he saw them as sticks and clubs and rocks, he saw Gegs lying in the streets or being herded off to prison or being made to walk the Steps of Terrel Fen.

"I never meant this!" he cried. "Any of this!"

Jarre, her lips pressed tightly together, strode over and, with a vicious jerk, flung down the blanket that had been hung up over the hole in the wall. There were disappointed murmurings from the crowd whose view inside was cut off.

"Whether you did or you didn't, Limbeck, it's gone too far now for you to stop it!" she snapped. Seeing the harried expression on her beloved's face, she softened her voice. "There are pain and blood and tears at every birth, my dear. The baby always cries when it leaves its safe, quiet prison. Yet if it stayed in the womb, it would never grow, never mature. It would be a parasite, feeding off another body. That's what we are. That's what we've become! Don't you see? Can't you understand?"

"No, my dear," said Limbeck. The hand holding the pen was shaking. Ink drops were flying everywhere. He laid it down across the paper on which he'd been writing and slowly rose to his feet. "I think I'll go out for a walk."

"I wouldn't," said Jarre. "The crowds—"

Limbeck blinked. "Oh, yes. Of course. You're right."

"You're exhausted. All this traveling and excitement. Go lie down and take a nap. I'll finish your speech. Here are your spectacles," Jarre said briskly, plucking them from the top of Limbeck's head and popping them onto his nose. "Up the stairs and into bed with you."

"Yes, my dear," said Limbeck, adjusting the spectacles that Jarre had, with well-meaning kindness, stuck on lopsided. Looking through them that way—with one eyeglass up and the other down—made him nauseous. "I . . . think that would be a good idea. I do feel . . . tired." He sighed and hung his head. "Very tired."

Walking to the ramshackle stairs, Limbeck was startled to feel a wet tongue lick across his knuckles. It was Haplo's dog, looking up at him, wagging its tail.

"I understand," the animal seemed to say, its unspoken words startlingly clear in Limbeck's mind. "I'm sorry."

"Dog!" Haplo spoke to it sharply, calling it back.

"No, that's all right," said Limbeck, reaching down to give the animal's sleek head a gingerly pat. "I don't mind."

"Dog! Come!" Haplo's voice had an almost angry edge to it. The dog hurried back to its master's side, and Limbeck retired up the stairs.

"He's so very idealistic!" said Jarre, gazing after Limbeck in admiration mixed with exasperation. "And not at all practical. I just don't know what to do."

"Keep him around," suggested Haplo. He stroked the dog's long nose to indicate that all was forgiven and forgotten. The animal lay down, rolled over on its side, and closed its eyes. "He gives your revolution a high moral tone. You'll need that, when blood starts to flow."

Jarre looked worried. "You think it will come to that?"

"Inevitable," he said, shrugging. "You said as much yourself, to Limbeck."

"I know. It seems, as you say, that it is inevitable, that this is the natural end of what we began long ago. Yet it has seemed to me lately"—she turned her eyes to Haplo—"that we never seriously turned our thoughts to violence until you came. Sometimes I wonder if you aren't really a god."

"Why is that?" Haplo smiled.

"Your words have a strange power over us. I hear them and I keep hearing them, not in my head, but in my heart." She placed her hand on her breast, pressing it as if it pained her. "And because they're in my heart, I can't seem to think about them rationally. I just want to react, to go out and do . . . something! Make somebody pay for what we've suffered, what we've endured."

Haplo rose from the chair and came over to Jarre, kneeling down so that he put himself at eye level with the short, stocky Geg. "And why shouldn't you?" he said softly, so softly that she couldn't hear over the whumping, whooshing of the Kicksey-winsey. Yet she knew what he said, and the pain in her heart increased. "Why shouldn't you make them pay? How many of your people have lived and died down here, and all for what? To serve a machine that eats up your land, that destroys your homes, that takes your lives and gives nothing to you in return! You've been used, betrayed! It's your right, your duty to strike back!"

"I will!" Jarre was caught, mesmerized by the man's crystal blue eyes. Slowly the hand over her heart clenched into a fist.

Haplo, smiling his quiet smile, rose and stretched. "I think I'll join our friend in a nap. It's liable to be a long night."

"Haplo," called Jarre, "you said you come from below us, from a realm that we . . . that no one knows is down there."

He did not reply, merely looked at her.

"You were slaves. You told us that. But what you haven't told us is how you came to crash on our isle. You weren't"—she paused and licked her lips, as if to make the words come more easily—"running away?"

One corner of the man's mouth twitched. "No, I wasn't running. You see, Jarre, we won our fight. We are slaves no longer. I've been sent to free others."

The dog raised its head, turning to stare sleepily at Haplo. Seeing him leaving, the dog yawned and got up, hind end first, stretching out its front legs luxuriously. Yawning again, it rocked forward, stretching the back legs, then lazily accompanied its master up the stairs.

Jarre watched, then shook her head, and was sitting down to finish Limbeck's speech when a thumping against the curtain recalled her to her duties. There were people to meet, pamphlets to be delivered, the hall to be inspected, parades to be organized.

The revolution just wasn't much fun anymore.

Haplo mounted the stairs carefully, keeping to the inside against the wall. The knobwood boards were cracked and rotting. Large snaggletoothed gaps waited to snare the unwary and send them crashing down to the floor below. Once inside his room, he lay down on the bed, but not to sleep. The dog jumped up on the bed next to him and rested its head on the man's chest, bright eyes fixed on his face.

"The woman is good, but she won't serve our purpose. She thinks too much, as my lord would say, and that makes her dangerous. What we need in this realm to foment chaos is a fanatic. Limbeck would be ideal, but he must have that idealistic bubble of his burst. And I've got to leave this place, to carry on with my mission—investigate the upper realms and do what I can to prepare the way for the coming of my lord. My ship is destroyed. I have to find another. But how . . . how?"

Musing, he fondled the dog's soft ears. The animal, sensing the man's tension, remained awake, lending its small support, and slowly Haplo relaxed. Opportunity would come. He knew it. He had only to watch for it and take advantage of it. The dog closed its eyes with a contented sigh and slept, and after a few moments, so did Haplo.

CHAPTER 31

WOMBE, DREVLIN,

LOW REALM

♦

"Alfred."

"Sir?"

"Do you understand what they're saying?"

Hugh motioned to Bane, chatting with the Geg, the two of them scrambling across the coralite. Storm clouds gathered at their backs and the wind was rising and keened eerily among the bits and pieces of lightning-blasted coralite. Ahead of them was the city Bane had seen. Or rather, not a city but a machine. Or perhaps a machine that was a city.

"No, sir," said Alfred, looking directly at Bane's back and speaking more loudly than was usual for him. "I do not speak the language of these people. I do not believe that there are many of our race, or the elves either, for that matter, who do."

"A few of the elves speak it—those who captain the waterships. But if you don't speak it, and I assume that Stephen didn't, then where did His Highness learn it?"

"How can you ask, sir?" said Alfred, glancing significantly toward the heavens.

He wasn't referring to the storm clouds. Up there, far above the Maelstrom, was the High Realm, where dwelt the mysteriarchs in their self-imposed exile, living in a world said by legend to be wealthy beyond the dreams of the greediest man and beautiful beyond the imagining of the most fanciful.

"Understanding the language of a different race or culture is one of the simpler of the magical spells. I wouldn't be surprised if that amulet he wears— Oh!"

Alfred's feet decided to take a side trip down a hole and took the rest of Alfred with them. The Geg stopped and looked around in alarm at the man's cry. Bane said something, laughing, and he and the Geg continued on their way. Hugh extricated Alfred and, keeping his hand on his arm, guided him rapidly over the rough ground. The first raindrops were falling out of the sky, hitting the coralite with loud splatters.

Alfred cast an uneasy sidelong glance at Hugh, and the Hand read the unspoken appeal to keep his mouth shut. In that appeal, Hugh had his answer, and it wasn't the one Alfred had given for Bane's benefit. Of course Alfred spoke the Gegs' language. No one listened intently to a conversation he couldn't understand. And Alfred had been listening intently to Bane and the Geg. What was more interesting—to Hugh's mind—was that Alfred was keeping his knowledge secret from the prince.

Hugh thoroughly approved spying on His Highness, but that opened the other nagging question. Where—and why—had a chamberlain learned to speak Geg? Who—or what—was Alfred Montbank?

The storm broke in all its deadly fury and the humans and the Gegs made for the city of Wombe at a dead run. Rain fell in a gray wall in front of them, partially obscuring their vision. But the noise made by the machine was, fortunately, so loud that they could hear it over the storm, feel its vibrations underfoot, and knew they were headed in the right direction.

A crowd of Gegs were waiting by an open doorway for them and hustled them all inside the machine. The sounds of the storm ceased, but the sounds of the machine were louder, clanking and banging above, around, below, and beyond. Several Gegs, who appeared to be armed guards of some sort, plus a Geg dressed up to look like an elflord's footman, were waiting—somewhat nervously—to greet them.

"Bane, what's going on?" Hugh demanded loudly, shouting to be heard above the racket made by the machine. "Who is this guy and what does he want?"

Bane looked up at Hugh with an ingenuous grin, obviously highly pleased with himself and his newfound power. "He's the king of his people!" shouted Bane.

"What?"

"King! He's going to take us to some sort of judgment hall."

"Can't he take us somewhere quiet?" Hugh's head was beginning to throb.

Bane turned to the king with the question. To Hugh's amazement, all the Gegs stared at him in horror, shaking their heads emphatically.

"What the hell is the matter with them?"

The prince began to giggle.

"They think you've asked for a place to go to die!"

At this juncture, the Geg dressed in silk hose, knee breeches, and a worn velvet doublet was introduced to Bane by the Geg king. The velvet-clad Geg threw himself to his knees. Taking Bane's hand, he pressed it against his forehead.

"Who do they think you are, kid?" Hugh asked.

"A god," Bane answered airily. "One they've been looking for, it seems. I'm going to pass judgment on them."

The Gegs led their newly discovered gods through the streets of Wombe—streets that ran up, under, and straight through the Kicksey-winsey. Hugh the Hand was not awed by many things in this world—not even death impressed him much—but he was awed by the great machine. It flashed, it glittered, it sparkled. It whumped and thwanged and hissed. It pumped and whirled and shot out blasts of searing hot steam. It created arcs of sizzling blue lightning. It soared higher than he could see, delved deeper than he could imagine. Huge gears engaged, huge wheels revolved, huge boilers boiled. It had arms and hands and legs and feet, all made of shining metal, all busily engaged in going somewhere other than where they were. It had eyes that shed a blinding light and mouths that screeched and hooted. Gegs crawled over it, climbed up it, clambered down into it, turned it, tapped it, and tended it with obvious loving care and devotion.

Bane, too, was overwhelmed. He gazed with wide-open eyes, his mouth gaping in ungodlike wonder.

"This is amazing!" breathed the boy. "I've never seen anything like this!"

"You haven't, Your Wurship?" exclaimed the high froman, looking at the child-god in astonishment. "But you gods built it!"

"Oh, er, yes," Bane stammered. "It's just that I meant I'd never seen . . . anything like the way you're taking care of it!" he finished with a rush, exhaling the words in relief.

"Yes," said the high clark with dignity, his face glowing with pride. "We take excellent care of it."

The prince bit his tongue. He wanted very much to ask what this wondrous machine did, but it was obvious that this little king fellow expected him to know everything—not an unreasonable assumption in a god. Bane was on his own in this too, his father having imparted to him all the information he had on the great machine of the Low Realm. This being a god wasn't as easy as it had first appeared, and the prince began regretting he'd agreed to it so fast. There was this judgment thing. Who was he judging, and why? Would he be sending anyone to the dungeons? He really needed to find out, but how?

The little king fellow was, Bane decided, just a bit too shrewd. He was very respectful and polite, but the boy saw that when he wasn't looking, the Geg was scrutinizing him with a gaze that was sharp and penetrating. Walking along on the prince's right, however, was another Geg who reminded the child of a performing monkey he'd seen once at court. Bane guessed from what he'd heard that the beruffled, beribboned, velvet-lined Geg had something to do with the religion in which the boy had suddenly found himself so intimately involved. This Geg didn't appear to be all that bright, and the prince decided to turn to him for answers.

"Pardon me," said the boy with a charming smile for the head clark, "but I didn't catch your name."

"Wes Wrenchwranger, Your Wurship," said the Geg, bowing as best he could for his stoutness, and nearly tripping on his long beard. "I have the honor to be Your Wurship's head clark."

Whatever that is, Bane muttered to himself. Outwardly he smiled and nodded and gave every indication that nowhere else on Drevlin could he have found a Geg more suited for that position.

Sidling close to the head clark, Bane slipped his hand into the Geg's hand—a proceeding which caused the head clark to swell rather alarmingly and cast a glance of supreme self-satisfaction at his brother-in-law, the high froman.

Darral paid little attention. The crowds lining the streets to see them were getting unruly. He was glad to see the coppers reacting to it. For the moment they appeared to have matters under control, but he knew he would need to keep a watchful eye on things. He only hoped the child-god couldn't understand what some of the Gegs were shouting. Damn that Limbeck anyway!

Fortunately for Darral, the child-god was completely absorbed in his own problems.

"Perhaps you could help me, Head Clark," said Bane, flushing shyly and very prettily.

"I would be honored, Your Wurship!"

"You know, it's been an awfully long time since we—your gods . . . Uh, what did you call us?"

"The Mangers, Your Wurship. That is what you call yourselves, isn't it?"

"Yes, oh, yes! Mangers. It's just that, well, as I was saying, we Mangers have been away an awfully long time—"

"—many centuries, Your Wurship," said the head clark.

"Yes, many centuries, and we've noticed that quite a few things have changed since we were away." Bane drew a deep breath. This was coming easier all the time. "Therefore we've decided that this judgment-thing should be changed as well."

The head clark felt some of his smugness begin to drain from him. He glanced uneasily at the high froman. If he, the head clark, screwed up the Judgment, it would be the last screw he ever turned.

"I'm not quite certain what you mean, Your Wurship."

"Modernize it, bring it up-to-date," suggested Bane.

The head clark appeared terribly confused. How could you change something that had never before happened? Still, he supposed that the gods must have had it planned out. "I guess it would be all right—"

"Never mind. I can see you're uncomfortable with the idea," said the prince, patting the head clark on his velvet-covered arm. "I've got a suggestion. You tell me the way you want me to handle it and I'll do it just like you say."

The head clark's face brightened. "You can't believe how wonderful this moment is for me, Your Wurship! I've dreamed of it for so long. And now, to have the Judgment go just as I've always imagined . . ." He wiped tears from his eyes.

"Yes, yes," said Bane. He noted that the high froman was watching them with narrowed eyes and edging nearer all the time. He might have stopped their conversation before this except that it was undoubtedly considered bad manners to interrupt a god in confidential conference. "Go on."

"Well, I always pictured all the Gegs—or at least as many as we could get in there—dressed in their very best clothes, standing in the Factree. You would be there, seated in the Manger's Chair, of course."

"Of course, and—"

"And I would be there, standing before the crowd in my new head-clark suit that I would have made specially for the occasion. White, I think, would be proper, with black bows at the knees, nothing too overdone—"

"Very tasteful. And then—"

"The high froman would be standing there with us too, I suppose, Your Wurship? That is, unless we could find something else for him to do. You see, Your Wurship, what he'll find fit to wear is going to be a problem. Perhaps, with this modernization you were discussing, we might dispense with him."

"I'll think about it." Bane gripped the feather amulet and tried very hard to be patient. "Go on. We're all up in front of the crowd. I stand up and I . . ." He looked expectantly at the head clark.

"Why, you judge us, Your Wurship."

The prince had the sudden satisfying vision of sinking his teeth into the Geg's velvet arm. Reluctantly banishing the thought, he drew a deep breath. "Fine. I judge you. And then what happens? I know! We'll declare a holiday!"

"I don't really think there'll be time for that, do you, Your Wurship?" said the Geg, looking at Bane with a puzzled expression.

"P-perhaps not," stammered the prince. "I forgot about . . . the other. When we're all . . ." Slipping his hand from the hand of the head clark, the boy wiped his sweating forehead. It was certainly hot inside the machine. Hot and noisy. His throat was getting sore from shouting. "What is it we're all doing now, after I've judged you?"

"Why, that depends on whether or not you've found us worthy, Your Wurship."

"Let's say I find you worthy," Bane said, gritting his teeth. "Then what?"

"Then we ascend, Your Wurship."

"Ascend?" The prince looked at the catwalks running hither and thither above him.

The head clark, misunderstanding his gaze, sighed with happiness. His face glowing beatifically, he lifted his hands.

"Yes, Your Wurship. Right straight up into heaven!"

Marching along behind Bane and his adoring Gegs, Hugh devoted one eye to his surroundings and the other to the prince. He soon ceased to try to keep track of where they were, admit-

ting to himself that he could never find his way out of the insides
of the machine without help. News of their coming had apparently rushed on ahead of them. Thousands of Gegs lined the
halls and corridors of the machine, staring, shouting, and pointing. Gegs busy with their work actually turned their heads,
bestowing on Hugh and his companions—had they known it—a
high honor by forgetting their tasks for a few seconds. The
reaction of the Gegs, however, was mixed. Some were cheering
with enthusiasm, but others appeared to be angry.

Hugh was more interested in Prince Bane and what he was
doing in such close confab with the ruffled Geg. Silently cursing
himself for never having bothered to learn any of the Geg language when he was with the elves, Hugh felt a tug on his sleeve
and turned his attention to Alfred.

"Sir," said Alfred, "have you noticed what the crowd is
yelling?"

"Gibberish, as far as I'm concerned. But you understand it,
don't you, Alfred?"

Alfred flushed deeply. "I am sorry I had to conceal my
knowledge from you, Sir Hugh. But I believed it important that I
conceal it from another." He glanced at the prince. "When you
asked me that question, it was just possible that he could have
heard my answer, and so I felt I had no choice—"

Hugh made a deprecating motion with his hand. Alfred had
a point. It had been the Hand who had made the mistake. He
should have realized what Alfred was doing and never spoken up.
It was just that never in Hugh's life had he felt so damn helpless!

"Where did you learn to speak Geg?"

"The study of the Gegs and the Low Realm has been a hobby
of mine, sir," answered Alfred with the shy, proud consciousness of a true enthusiast. "I daresay I have one of the finest
collections of books written about their culture in the Mid Realm.
If you would be interested, when we return, I'll be happy to
show you—"

"If you left those books in the palace, you can forget them.
Unless you plan on asking Stephen to give you leave to run back
in and pick up your things."

"You're right, sir, of course. How stupid of me." Alfred's
shoulders sagged. "All my books . . . I don't suppose I'll ever
see them again."

"What were you saying about the crowd?"

"Oh, yes." The chamberlain glanced around at the cheering

and occasionally jeering Gegs. "Some are calling out, 'Down with the froman's god!' and 'We want Limbeck's god!' "

"Limbeck? What does that mean?"

"It's a Geg name, I believe, sir. It means 'to distill or extract.' If I might make a suggestion? I think . . ." Instinctively he lowered his voice, and in the noise and commotion, Hugh lost his words.

"Talk louder. No one can understand *us*, can they?"

"Oh, I suppose not," said Alfred, light dawning. "That hadn't occurred to me. I was saying, sir, that there might be another human such as ourselves down here."

"Or an elf. That's more likely. Either way, odds are they've got a ship we can use to get out of here!"

"Yes, sir. I thought that might be the case."

"We've got to see this Limbeck and his god or whatever."

"That shouldn't be difficult, sir. Not if our little 'god' commands it."

"Our little 'god' seems to have gotten himself in some sort of trouble," said Hugh, his gaze going to the prince. "Look at his face."

"Oh, dear," murmured Alfred.

Bane had twisted his head back to search for his companions. His cheeks were pale, his blue eyes wide. Biting his lip, he made a hurried motion for them to come up to him.

An entire squadron of armed Gegs marched between them and the prince. Hugh shook his head. Bane gazed at him pleadingly. Alfred, looking sympathetic, gestured at the crowd. Bane was a prince. He knew what was due an audience. Sighing, he turned around and began to wave his small hand feebly and without enthusiasm.

"I was afraid of this," said Alfred.

"What do you think's happened?"

"The boy said something about the Gegs thinking he was the god who had come to 'judge' them. He spoke about it glibly, but it is very serious to the Gegs. According to their legends, it was the Mangers who built the great machine. The Gegs were to serve it until the Day of Judgment, when they would be rewarded and carried up into the higher realms. That was how the isle Geg's Hope came by its name."

"Mangers. Who are these Mangers?"

"The Sartan."

"Devil take us!" the Hand swore. "You mean they think the kid is one of the Sartan?"

"It would seem so, sir."

"I don't suppose he could fake it, with help from daddy?"

"No, sir. Not even a mysteriarch of the Seventh House, such as his father, possesses magical powers compared to those of the Sartan. After all," said Alfred, gesturing, "they built all this."

Hugh cared little about that now. "Great! Just great! And what do you think they'll do when they find out we're impostors?"

"I couldn't say, sir. Ordinarily, the Gegs are peaceful, gentle people. But then, I don't suppose they've ever had anyone pretend to be one of their gods before. In addition, they seem to be in a turmoil over something." Alfred, looking at the crowds growing increasingly hostile, shook his head. "I would say, sir, that we've come at rather a bad time."

CHAPTER ♦ 32

WOMBE, DREVLIN,

LOW REALM

♦

THE GEGS TOOK THE "GODS" TO THE FACTREE—THE SAME PLACE WHERE Limbeck had been given his trial. They had some difficulty entering, due to the crowds of milling Gegs massed outside. Hugh couldn't understand a word they were shouting; despite that, it was obvious to him that the populace was divided into two distinct and highly vocal factions, with a large segment who seemed unable to make up their minds. The two factions appeared to feel strongly about their beliefs, because Hugh saw fights break out on several occasions. He remembered what Alfred had said about the Gegs being ordinarily peaceful and gentle.

We've come at rather a bad time. No kidding. It looked to be in the middle of a revolution of some sort!

The coppers kept back the crowd, and the prince and his companions managed to squeeze through the stout bodies into the relative quiet of the Factree—relative to the fact that the whanging and banging of the Kicksey-winsey was constantly in the background.

Once inside, the high froman held a hasty meeting with the coppers. The little king's face was grave and Hugh observed several times that he shook his head. The Hand didn't give a half-barl for the Gegs, but he had lived long enough to know that being caught in a country undergoing political upheaval was not conducive to a long and healthy life.

"Excuse us." He approached the head clark, who bowed and stared at him with the blank, bright smile of one who doesn't understand a word that is being said to him but who is trying to appear as if he did, in order not to be rude. "We have to have a little talk with your god."

Gripping Bane firmly by the shoulder, ignoring the boy's yelps and squirming, Hugh marched the prince across the vast empty floor, over to where Alfred stood gazing up at a statue of a hooded man holding what appeared to be an eyeball in his hand.

"Do you know what they expect me to do?" Bane demanded of Alfred as soon as they neared him. "They expect me to transport them up into heaven!"

"May I remind His Highness that he brought this on himself by telling them he was a god?"

The child's head drooped. He stole up to Alfred's side and slipped a hand in the chamberlain's. Lower lip quivering, Bane said softly, "I'm sorry, Alfred. I was afraid they were going to hurt you and Sir Hugh, and it was the only thing I could think of to do."

Strong hands jerked Bane around, rough fingers bit into his shoulders. Hugh knelt down and looked straight into the child's eyes, behind which he wanted to see cunning and malevolent purpose. All he saw were the eyes of a frightened kid. It angered him.

"All right, Your Highness, you go on fooling the Gegs as long as you can—anything to get us out of here. But we just want to make it plain that you don't fool us one bit, not anymore. Those phony tears better dry up and you better listen—you and daddy both." He glanced at the feather as he spoke, and the boy's hand closed over it protectively. "Unless you can hoist these dwarves into the skies, you better be prepared to do some fast thinking. I don't suppose these people will take kindly to being hoodwinked."

"Sir Hugh," warned Alfred, "we're being watched."

The Hand looked over to the high froman, who was observing the proceedings with interest. Releasing the boy, patting him on the shoulders, Hugh smiled.

"What is it you plan to do, Your Highness?" he muttered in an undertone.

Bane gulped back his tears. Fortunately there was no need to keep their voices lowered. The rhythmic pounding and thumping of the machine muffled everything, including thought.

"I've decided I'll tell them I've judged them and found them
wanting. They haven't earned the right to go up to heaven."

Hugh glanced at Alfred. The man shook his head. "It would
be very dangerous, Your Highness. If you said such a thing, in
the state of turmoil that seems to have gripped the realm, the
Gegs might well turn on us."

The child's eyes blinked rapidly, their gaze shifting quickly
from Alfred to Hugh and back again. Bane was obviously frightened. He had plunged in over his head and felt himself sinking.
Worse still, he must know that the only two who could save him
had very good reasons for letting him drown.

"What do we do?"

We! Hugh would have liked nothing better than to leave the
changeling on this storm-swept patch of rock. He knew he
wouldn't, however. Enchantment? Or did he just feel sorry for
the brat? Neither, he assured himself, still planning to use the
kid to make his fortune.

"There's talk of another god down here. 'Limbeck's god,' "
said Alfred.

"How did you know that?" Bane flared. "You can't understand what they're saying!"

"Yes, I can, Your Highness. I speak some Geg—"

"You lied!" The child gazed at him in shock. "How could
you, Alfred? I trusted you!"

The chamberlain shook his head. "I think it best for all of us
to admit that none of us trusts the others."

"Who can blame me?" cried Bane with glittering innocence.
"This man tried to kill me, and for all I know, Alfred, you were
helping him!"

"That is not true, Your Highness, yet I can understand how
you might come to think so. But I had not meant to make
accusations. I think it behooves us to realize that, though we do
not trust each other, our lives in total now depend on each other
individually. I think—"

"—too much!" Hugh broke in. "The kid understands, don't
you, Bane? And drop the babe-lost-in-the-woods act. We both
know who and what you are. I presume that you want to get out
of here, go up and pay dad a visit. The only way you're going to
get off this rock is with a ship, and I'm the only pilot you've got.
Alfred, here, knows something about these people and how they
think—at least he claims he does. He's right when he says we're

each other's only chance in this game, so I suggest that you and daddy there play along nicely."

Bane stared at him. His eyes were no longer the eyes of a child who is eagerly studying the world; they were the eyes of one who knows all about it. Hugh saw himself reflected in those eyes; saw a chill, unloved childhood; saw a child who had unwrapped all of life's pretty presents and discovered the boxes contained filth.

Like me, Hugh thought, he no longer believes in the bright, the shining, the beautiful. He knows what's underneath.

"You're not treating me like a kid," said Bane, wary and cautious.

"Are you one?" Hugh asked bluntly.

"No." Bane clasped the feather tightly as he spoke, and repeated more loudly, "No, I'm not! I'll work with you. I promise, so long as you don't betray me. If you do, either of you, then I'll make you regret it." The blue eyes gleamed with a most unchildlike shrewdness.

"Fair enough. I give you each the same promise. Alfred?"

The chamberlain looked at them in despair and sighed. "Must it be like this? Trusting only because each of us holds a knife in the other's back?"

"You lied about speaking Geg. You didn't tell me the truth about the kid until it was almost too late. What else have you lied about, Alfred?" Hugh demanded.

The chamberlain went white. His mouth worked, but he couldn't answer. Finally he managed to squeeze out, "I promise."

"All right. That's done. Now, we've got to find out about this other god. He could be our way off this rock. Chances are, it's an elf whose ship got caught in the storm and sucked down."

"I could tell the high froman that I want to meet this god." Bane was swift to see and understand the possibilities. "I'll tell him that I can't judge the Gegs until I find out what this fellow 'god' of mine thinks about the matter." The boy smiled sweetly. "Who knows, it could take us days to come up with the answer! But would an elf help us?"

"If he's in as much trouble down here as we are, he would. My ship's wrecked. His probably is too. But we might be able to use parts of one to fix the other. Shhh. We've got company."

The high froman joined them, the head clark bustling importantly along behind. "When would Your Wurship like to commence the Judgment?"

Bane drew himself up to his full height and managed to look offended. "I heard the people shouting something about another god being present in your land. Why wasn't I informed of this?"

"Because, Your Wurship," said the high froman, casting a reproachful glance at the head clark, "this is a god who claims he isn't a god. He claims that none of you are gods, but says you are mortals who have enslaved us."

Hugh contained himself patiently during this conversation that he couldn't understand. Alfred was listening to the Gegs with close attention, and the Hand kept close watch on Alfred's face. He did not miss the man's dismayed reaction over what was being said. The assassin ground his teeth, frustrated nearly to the point of madness. Their lives were dependent on a ten-cycle kid who, at this point, looked like he might very well burst into tears!

Prince Bane got a grip on himself, however. Pointed chin in the air, he made some answer that apparently eased the situation, for Hugh saw Alfred's face relax. The chamberlain even nodded slightly, before he caught himself, aware that he shouldn't be reacting.

The kid has nerve, he's quick-thinking. Hugh twisted his beard. And perhaps I'm "enthralled," he reminded himself.

"Bring this god to me," said Bane with an imperious air that made him, for a brief moment, resemble King Stephen.

"If Your Wurship wishes to see him, he and the Geg who brought him here are speaking at a rally tonight. You could confront him publicly."

"Very well," said Bane, not liking it but not knowing what other response to make.

"Now, perhaps Your Wurship would care to rest. I notice that one member of your party is injured." The Geg's glance went to Hugh's torn and bloodstained shirt sleeve. "I could send for a healer."

Hugh saw the glance, understood, and made a negating gesture.

"Thank you, his injury isn't serious," said Bane, "but you could send us food and water."

The high froman bowed. "Is that all I can do for Your Wurship?"

"Yes, thank you. That will be all," said Bane, failing to conceal the relief in his voice.

*   *   *

The gods were shown to chairs placed at the feet of the Manger, possibly to provide inspiration. The head clark would have liked very much to stay and visit, but Darral nabbed his brother-in-law by the velvet sleeve and dragged him—protesting volubly—away.

"What are you doing?" raved the head clark. "How could you risk insulting His Wurship by saying such a thing? Implying that he isn't a god! And that talk about slaves!"

"Shut up and listen to me," snapped Darral Longshoreman. He'd had his fill of gods. One more "Your Wurship" and he thought he'd gag. "Either these folk are gods or they're not. If they're not, and this Limbeck turns out to be right, what do you think will happen to us, who've spent our lives telling our people that we were serving gods?"

The head clark stared at his brother-in-law. Slowly his face drained of all its ruddy color. He gulped.

"Exactly." Darral nodded emphatically, his beard wagging. "Now, suppose they are gods, do you really want to be judged and taken up into heaven? Or do you like it down here, the way things used to be before all this hullabaloo started?"

The head clark considered. He was very fond of being head clark. He lived well. Gegs respected him, bowed and took off their hats when he walked down the street. He didn't have to serve the Kicksey-winsey, except when and where he chose to put in an appearance. He got invited to all the best parties. When you came right down to it, what more did heaven have to offer?

"You're right," he was forced to admit, though it galled him to do so. "What do we do?"

"I'm working on it," said the high froman. "Just leave it to me."

"I'd give a hundred barls to know what those two are talking about." Hugh watched the two Gegs walk off in close conversation.

"I don't like this at all," said Alfred. "This other god, whoever it is, is fomenting rebellion and chaos down here. I wonder why. The elves wouldn't have any reason to upset things in the Low Realm, would they?"

"No. It's to their advantage to keep the Gegs quiet and hard at work. But there's nothing we can do, I guess, except to go to this rally tonight and hear what this god has to say."

"Yes," said Alfred absently.

Hugh glanced at the man. The high domed forehead glistened with sweat, and his eyes had acquired a fevered luster. His skin was ashen, his lips gray. He hadn't, it occurred to Hugh suddenly, fallen over anything in the last hour.

"You don't look good. Are you all right?"

"I . . . I'm not feeling very well, Sir Hugh. Nothing serious. Just a reaction from the crash. I'll be fine. Please don't worry about me. Your Highness understands the serious nature of tonight's encounter?"

Bane gave Alfred a thoughtful, considering look. "Yes, I understand. I'll do my best to help, although I'm not certain what it is I'm supposed to do."

The boy appeared to be sincere, but Hugh could still see that innocent smile as the child fed him poison. Was Bane, in truth, playing the game with them? Or was he merely moving them ahead one more square?

CHAPTER ♦ 33

WOMBE, DREVLIN,

LOW REALM

♦

A COMMOTION OUTSIDE THE HOLE IN THE WALL ATTRACTED JARRE'S attention. She had just put the finishing touches on Limbeck's speech. Laying it down, she went to what served as the door and peered out the curtain. The crowds in the street had grown larger, she saw with satisfaction. But the WUPP's assigned to guard the door were arguing loudly with several other Gegs attempting to enter.

At the sight of Jarre, their clamor increased.

"What is it?" she asked.

The Gegs began shouting at once, and it took her some time to quiet them down. When she had done so and had heard what they had to say, she gave instructions and reentered WUPP Headquarters.

"What's going on?" Haplo was standing on the stairs, the dog at his side.

"I'm sorry the commotion woke you," Jarre apologized. "It's nothing, really."

"I wasn't asleep. What is it?"

Jarre shrugged. "The high froman's come up with his own god. I might have expected something like this of Darral Long-shoreman. Well, it won't work, that's all."

"His own god?" Haplo descended the stairs with a step swift and light as a cat's. "Tell me."

"Surely you can't take this seriously? You know there are no such things as gods. Darral probably told the Welves we were threatening them, and they've sent someone down here to try to convince my people that, 'Yes, we Welves really are gods.' "

"*Is* this god an el . . . a Welf?"

"I don't know. Most of our people have never seen a Welf. I don't suppose anyone knows what they look like. All I know is that it seems this god is a child and he's been telling everyone he's come to judge us and he's going to do so at the rally tonight and prove that we're wrong. Of course, you can deal with him."

"Of course," murmured Haplo.

Jarre was bustling about. "I've got to go make certain everything's arranged at the Together Hall." She threw a shawl around her shoulders. On her way out the hole in the wall, she paused and looked back. "Don't tell Limbeck about this. He'll get himself all worked up. It'll be better to take him completely by surprise. That way, he won't have time to think."

Thrusting aside the curtain, she stepped outside, to the sound of loud cheers.

Left alone, Haplo threw himself in a chair. The dog, sensing his master's mood, thrust his muzzle comfortingly into the man's hand.

"The Sartan, do you think, boy?" mused Haplo, absently scratching the dog beneath the chin. "They're as close to a god as these people are likely to find in a godless universe. And what do I do if it is? I can't challenge this 'god' and reveal to him my own powers. The Sartan must *not* be alerted to our escape from their prison. Not yet, not until my lord is fully prepared."

He sat in thoughtful, brooding silence. The hand stroking the animal slowed in its caress and soon ceased altogether. The dog, knowing itself no longer needed, settled down at the man's feet, chin on its paws, its liquid eyes reflecting the concern in the eyes of its master.

"Ironic, isn't it?" said Haplo, and at the voice the dog's ears pricked and it glanced up at him, one white eyebrow slightly raised. "Me with the powers of a god and unable to use them." Drawing back the bandage that swathed his hand, he ran a finger over the blue-and-red spiderweb lines of the sigla whose fantastic whorls and patterns decorated his skin. "I could build a ship in a day. Fly out of here tomorrow if I so chose. I could show these dwarves power they've never imagined. I could become a god for them. Lead them to war against the humans and the 'Welves.' " Haplo smiled, but his face grew immediately sober. "Why not? What would it matter?"

A strong desire to use his power came over him. Not only to use the magic, but to use it to conquer, to control, to lead. The Gegs were peaceful, but Haplo knew that wasn't the true nature of dwarves. Somehow the Sartan had managed to beat it out of them, reduce them to the mindless machine-serving "Gegs" that they had become. It should be easy to uncover the fierce pride, the legendary courage of the dwarves. The ashes appeared cold, but surely a flame must flicker somewhere!

"I could raise an army, build ships. No! What has gotten into me!" Haplo angrily jerked the cloth back over his hand. The dog, cringing at the sharp tone, looked up apologetically, thinking, perhaps, that it had been at fault. "It's my true nature, the nature of the Patryns, and it will lead me into disaster! My lord warned me of this. I must move slowly. The Gegs are not ready. And I'm not the one who should lead them. Their own. Limbeck. Somehow, I must blow on the spark that is Limbeck.

"As for this child-god, there's nothing to be done but wait and see and trust in myself. If it is a Sartan, then that might be all for the better. Right, boy?" Leaning down, Haplo thumped the animal on its flank. The dog, pleased at the return of its master's good humor, closed its eyes and sighed deeply.

"And if it is a Sartan," muttered Haplo beneath his breath, leaning back in the small uncomfortable chair and stretching his legs, "may my lord keep me from ripping out the bastard's heart!"

By the time Jarre had come back, Limbeck was awake and anxiously perusing his speech, and Haplo had made a decision.

"Well," said Jarre brightly, unwinding her shawl from around her ample shoulders, "everything is all ready for tonight. I think, my dear, that this will be the biggest rally yet—"

"We need to talk to the god," interrupted Haplo in his quiet voice.

Jarre flashed him a look, reminding him that this subject was not to be mentioned in front of Limbeck.

"God?" Limbeck peered at them from behind the spectacles perched precariously on his nose. "What god? What's going on?"

"He had to know," Haplo mollified an angry Jarre. "It's best to always know as much as you can about the enemy."

"Enemy! What enemy!" Limbeck, pale but calm, had risen to his feet.

"You don't seriously believe that they are what they claim—Mangers—do you?" demanded Jarre, staring at Haplo with narrowed eyes, arms akimbo.

"No, and that is what we must prove. You said yourself this was undoubtedly a plot by the high froman to discredit your movement. If we can capture this being who calls himself a god and can prove publicly that he's not—"

"—then we can cast down the high froman!" cried Jarre, clapping her hands together eagerly.

Haplo, pretending to scratch the dog, lowered his head to hide his smile. The animal gazed up at his master with a wistful, uneasy aspect.

"Certainly there's that possibility, but we must take this one step at a time," said Haplo after a pause, seeming to give the matter grave consideration. "First, it's essential that we find out who this god really is and why he's here."

"Who who is? Why who is here?" Limbeck's spectacles slid down his nose. He pushed them back and raised his voice. "Tell me—"

"I'm sorry, my dear. It all happened while you were asleep." Jarre informed him of the arrival of the high froman's god and how he had paraded the child through the city streets and what the people were saying and doing and how some of them believed the child was a god and some believed he wasn't and—

"—and there's going to be trouble, that's what you mean, don't you?" concluded Limbeck. Sinking down into his chair, he stared bleakly at her. "What if they really are the Mangers! What if I've been wrong and they've come to . . . to pass judgment on the people? They'll be offended and they might abandon us again!" He twisted the speech in his hands. "I might have brought great harm to all our people!"

Jarre, looking exasperated, opened her mouth, but Haplo shook his head at her.

"Limbeck, that is why we need to talk to them. If they are the Sar . . . Mangers," he corrected himself, "then we can explain and they'll understand, I'm sure."

"I was so certain!" Limbeck cried woefully.

"And you *are* right, my dear!" Jarre knelt beside him and, putting her hands on his face, turned it so that he was forced to look at her. "Believe in yourself! This is an impostor, brought by the high froman! We'll prove that and we'll prove that he and the clarks have been in league with those who have enslaved us! This could be our great chance, our chance to change our world!"

Limbeck did not reply. Gently removing Jarre's hands, he held them fast, thanking her silently for her comfort. But he lifted his head and fixed a troubled gaze on Haplo.

"You've gone too far to back out now, my friend," said the Patryn. "Your people trust you, believe in you. You can't let them down."

"But what if I'm wrong?"

"You're not," said Haplo with conviction. "Even if this is a Manger, the Mangers are not gods and never were. They are human, like myself. They were endowed with great magical power, but they were mortal. If the high froman claims the Manger is a god, just ask the Manger. If he really is one, he will tell you the truth."

The Mangers always told the truth. They had gone throughout the world protesting that they were not divine, yet taking upon themselves the responsibilities of the divine. False humility to mask pride and ambition. If this was a true Sartan, he would refute his own godhood. If not, Haplo would know he was lying, and exposing him would be easy.

"Can we get in to see them?" he asked Jarre.

"They're being held in the Factree," she said, pondering. "I don't know much about it, but we have those in our group who do. I'll ask them."

"We should hurry. It's almost dark and the meeting is supposed to commence in two hours' time. We should see them before that."

Jarre was on her feet and heading for the hole in the wall. Limbeck, sighing, leaned his head on his hand. His spectacles slid down his nose and dropped into his lap, where they lay unnoticed.

The woman has the energy and determination, mused Haplo. Jarre knows her limitations. She can make the vision reality, but it is Limbeck who has the eyes—half-blind that they are—to see. I must show him the vision.

Jarre returned with several eager, grim-looking Gegs. "There's a way in. Tunnels run underneath the floor and come up near the statue of the Manger."

Haplo nodded his head toward Limbeck. Jarre understood.

"Did you hear me, my dear? We can get inside the Factree and talk to this so-called god. Do we go?"

Limbeck raised his head. His face beneath the beard was pale, but there was an expression of determination. "Yes." He raised a hand, stopping her from interrupting. "I've realized it doesn't matter if I'm right or if I'm wrong. All that matters is to discover the truth."

CHAPTER ◆ 34

WOMBE, DREVLIN,

LOW REALM

◆

TWO GUIDE GEGS, LIMBECK, JARRE, HAPLO, AND, OF COURSE, THE DOG
navigated a series of twisting, winding tunnels that intersected,
bisected, and dissected the ground below the Kicksey-winsey.
The tunnels were old and marvelous in their construction, lined
with stone that appeared, from its regular shape, to have been
made either by the hand of man or the metal hands of the
Kicksey-winsey. Here and there, carved into the stones, were
curious symbols. Limbeck was absolutely fascinated with these,
and it was with some difficulty and a few tugs on his beard that
Jarre managed to persuade him that there was a need for hurry.

Haplo could have told him much about these symbols. He
could have told him they were in reality sigla—the runes of the
Sartan—and that it was the sigla carved upon the stones that
kept the tunnels dry despite the almost constant flow of rainwa-
ter dripping through the porous coralite. It was the sigla that
maintained the tunnels centuries after those who built them had
left them.

The Patryn was nearly as interested in the tunnels as Limbeck. It was becoming increasingly obvious to him that the Sartan
had abandoned their work. Not only that, but they had left it
unfinished . . . and that was not at all like these humans who
had attained the power and the status of demigods. The great
machine, which, even far below ground, they could still feel
throbbing and pulsing and pounding, was, Haplo had observed,
running on its own, at its own whim, by its own design.

And it was doing nothing. Nothing creative, that Haplo could see. He had traveled the length and breadth of Drevlin with Limbeck and the WUPPers, and everywhere he had gone he had inspected the great machine. It knocked over buildings, it dug holes, it built new buildings, it filled in holes, it roared and steamed and tooted and hummed and did what it did with a wondrous amount of energy. But what it was doing was nothing.

Once a month, so Haplo had heard, the "Welves" came down from above in their iron suits and their flying ships and picked up the precious substance—water. The Welves had been doing this for centuries and the Gegs had come to believe that this was the ultimate purpose of their beloved and sacred machine—to produce water for these godlike Welves. But Haplo saw that the water was merely a by-product of the Kicksey-winsey, perhaps even a waste product. The function of the fabulous machine was something grander, something far more magnificent than spitting out water to slake the thirst of the elven nation. But what that purpose was, and why the Sartan had left before it could be accomplished, was something Haplo could not begin to fathom.

There was no answer for him in the tunnels. Possibly it lay ahead. He had learned, as had all the Patryns, that impatience— any slip from the tightly held reins of control imposed upon themselves—could lead to disaster. The Labyrinth was not kind to those with flaws. Patience, endless patience—that was one of the gifts the Patryns had received from the Labyrinth, though it came to them covered with their own blood.

The Gegs were excited, noisy, and eager. Haplo walked through the tunnels after them, making no more noise than did his shadow cast by the light of Geg glimmerglamps. The dog trotted along behind, silent and watchful as his master.

"Are you certain this is the right way?" Jarre asked more than once, when it seemed that they must be walking in endless circles.

The guide Gegs assured her it was. It seemed that several years ago, the Kicksey-winsey had taken it into its mechanical head that it should open the tunnels. It had done so, punching through the ground with its iron fists and feet. Gegs swarmed below, shoring up the walls and providing the machine support. Then, just as suddenly, the Kicksey-winsey changed its mind and launched off in a completely new direction. These particular Gegs had been part of the tunnel scrift and knew them as well as they knew their own houses.

Unfortunately, the tunnels were not deserted, as Haplo had hoped. The Gegs now used them to get from one place to another, and the WUPPers on their way to the Factree ran into large numbers of Gegs. The sight of Haplo created excitement, the guide Gegs felt called upon to tell everyone who he was and who Limbeck was, and almost all the Gegs that didn't have other, more pressing business, decided to follow along.

Soon there was a parade of Gegs tromping through the tunnels, heading for the Factree. So much for secrecy and surprise. Haplo comforted himself with the knowledge that an army of Gegs mounted on shrieking dragons could have flown through the tunnel and, due to the noise of the machine, no one topside would be the wiser.

"Here we are," shouted one Geg in a booming voice, pointing to a metal ladder leading up a shaft and into darkness. Glancing further down the tunnel, Haplo could see numerous other ladders, placed at intervals—the first time they had come across such a phenomenon—and he calculated that the Geg was correct. These ladders obviously led somewhere. He just hoped it was the Factree.

Haplo motioned the guide Gegs, Jarre, and Limbeck to draw near him. Jarre kept the numerous other Gegs back with a wave of her hand.

"What's up the ladder? How do we get into the Factree?"

There was a hole in the floor, explained the Gegs, covered with a metal plate. Moving the plate allowed access to the main floor of the Factree.

"This Factree is a huge place," said Haplo. "What part of it will I come up in? What part have they given over to the god?"

There was some lengthy discussion and argument over this. One Geg had heard that the god was in the Manger's room two floors up over the main floor of the Factree. The other Geg had heard that the god was, by orders of the high froman, being kept in the Bored Room.

"What's that?" Haplo asked patiently.

"It's where my trial was held," said Limbeck, his face brightening at the memory of his moment of supreme importance. "There's a statue of a Manger there, and the chair where the high froman sits in judgment."

"Where is this place from here?"

The Gegs thought it was about two more ladders down, and they all trooped in that direction, the two guide Gegs arguing among themselves until Jarre, with an embarrassed glance at Haplo, ordered them sharply to hold their tongues.

"They think this is it," she said, placing her hand upon the ladder's steel rungs.

Haplo nodded. "I'll go up first," he said as softly as he could and still make himself heard above the roar of the machine.

The guide Gegs protested. This was their adventure, they were leading, they should get to go up first.

"There might be guards of the high froman up there," said Haplo. "Or this so-called god might be dangerous."

The Gegs looked at each other, looked at Haplo, and backed away from the ladder. There was no further discussion.

"But I want to see them!" protested Limbeck, who was beginning to feel they'd come all this way for nothing.

"Shhh!" remonstrated Haplo. "You will. I'm just going up to . . . scout around. Reconnoiter. I'll come back and get you when it is safe."

"He's right, Limbeck, so be quiet," scolded Jarre. "You'll have your chance soon enough. It would never do for the high froman to arrest us before tonight's rally!"

Cautioning the need for quiet—at which all the Gegs stared at him as if he were absolutely insane—Haplo turned to the ladder.

"What should we do with the dog?" asked Jarre. "He can't climb the ladder, and you can't carry him."

Haplo shrugged, unconcerned. "He'll be all right, won't you, dog?" Leaning down, he patted the animal on the head. "You stay, dog, all right? Stay."

The dog, mouth open and tongue lolling, plopped itself down on the floor and, ears cocked, looked around with interest.

Haplo began his ascent, climbing the ladder slowly and carefully, allowing his eyes time to adjust to the increasing darkness as he moved out of the bright light of the glimmerglamps. The climb was not long. Soon he was able to see pinpoints of the glimmerglamp light below him, reflecting off a metal surface above.

Reaching the plate, he put his hand on it and cautiously and gently pushed. It gave way smoothly and easily and, he was thankful to note, quietly. Not that he was anticipating trouble. He wanted this chance to observe these "gods" without them observing him. Thinking regretfully that, in the old days, the threat—or the promise—of danger would have caused the dwarves to clamor up the ladders in droves, Haplo cursed the Sartan beneath his breath, silently lifted the plate, and peered out.

The glimmerglamps lit the Factree brighter than a Geg day. Haplo could see clearly and he was pleased to note his guides had judged correctly. Directly in his line of vision stood a tall statue of a robed and hooded figure. Lounging around the statue were three people. They were human—two men and a child. That much Haplo could tell at a glance. But the Sartan were also of human derivation.

He inspected each one closely, though he was forced to admit to himself that he would not be able to tell, simply by looking, if these humans were Sartan or not. One man sat beneath the statue, in its shadow. Clad in plain clothing, he appeared to be of middle age, with thinning, receding hair that emphasized a domed, protruding forehead, and a lined, careworn face. This man shifted restlessly, his gaze going worriedly to the child, and when he did so, Haplo saw that his movements, particularly of his hands and feet, were ungainly and awkward.

By sharp contrast, the other adult human male present was one Haplo might have mistaken for a fellow survivor of the Labyrinth. Lithe, well-muscled, there was an alert watchfulness about the man that—though he was lying relaxed, stretched out on the floor, smoking a pipe—indicated he kept instinctive, watchful vigil. The face, with its dark, deep crevices and twisted black beard, reflected a soul of cold, hard iron.

The kid was a kid, nothing more, unless you counted a remarkable beauty. An odd trio. What brought them together? What brought them here?

Down below, one of the overly excited Gegs forgot the injunction to maintain silence and shouted in what he apparently thought was a whisper to ask if Haplo could see anything.

The man with the twisted beard reacted instantly, his body coiling swiftly to a standing position, his black eyes darting to the shadows, his hand closing over the hilt of a sword. Beneath him, Haplo heard a resounding smack and knew that Jarre had effectively punished the offender.

"What is it, Hugh?" asked the man sitting in the shadow of the statue. The voice spoke human and it quavered with nervousness.

The man addressed as Hugh put his fingers to his lips and crept several steps in the direction of Haplo. He did not look down or he must have seen the plate, but was staring into the shadows.

"I thought I heard something."

"I don't know how you can hear anything over that racket that damn machine's making," stated the child. The boy was eating bread and staring up at the statue.

"Do not use such language, Your Highness," rebuked the nervous man. He had risen to his feet and seemed to have some idea of joining this Hugh in his search, but he tripped and only saved himself from a headlong fall by bracing himself against the statue. "Do you see anything, sir?"

The Gegs, undoubtedly under threat of bodily harm from Jarre, actually managed to keep quiet. Haplo froze, hardly daring to breathe, watching and listening intently.

"No," said Hugh. "Sit down, Alfred, before you kill yourself."

"It probably *was* the machine," said Alfred, looking as though he wanted very much to convince himself.

The boy, bored, tossed his bread to the floor and walked over to stand directly in front of the statue of the Manger. He reached out to touch it.

"Don't!" Alfred cried in alarm.

The child, jumping, snatched his hand back.

"You frightened me!" he said accusingly.

"I'm sorry, Your Highness. Just . . . move away from the statue."

"Why? Will it hurt me?"

"No, Your Highness. It's just that the statue of the Manager is . . . well, sacred to the Gegs. They wouldn't like you bothering it."

"Pooh!" said the child, glancing around the Factree. "They're all gone anyway. Besides, it seems like he wants to shake hands or something." The boy giggled. "The way he has his hand stuck out like that. He *wants* me to take it—"

"No! Your Highness!" But the stumble-footed man was too late to prevent the boy reaching out and grasping hold of the Manger's mechanical hand. To the child's delight, the eyeball flickered with a bright light.

"Look!" Bane shoved aside Alfred's frantic grasping hand. "Don't stop it! It's showing pictures! I want to see!"

"Your Highness, I must insist! I know I heard something! The Gegs—"

"I think we could handle the Gegs," said Hugh, coming over to look at the pictures. "Don't stop it, Alfred. I want to see what it's showing."

Taking advantage of the trio's preoccupation and feeling an

intense interest in this statue himself, Haplo crept up out of the hole.

"Look, it's a map!" cried the child, much excited.

The three were intent on the eyeball. Haplo, coming up silently behind, recognized the images flitting across the eye's surface as a map of the Realm of the Sky, a map remarkably like one his lord had discovered in the Halls of the Sartan in the Nexus. At the very top were the isles known as Lords of Night. Beneath them the firmament, and near them floated the isle of the High Realm. Then came the Mid Realm. Further down were the Maelstrom and the land of the Gegs.

Most remarkable, the map moved! The isles drifted around in their oblique orbits, the storm clouds swirled, the sun was periodically hidden by the Lords of Night.

Then, suddenly, the images changed. The isles and continents ceased to orbit at random and all lined up neatly in a row—each realm positioning itself directly beneath the one above. Then the segment flickered, faltered, and went out.

The man known as Hugh was not impressed.

"A magic lantern. I've seen them in the elven kingdom."

"But what does it mean?" asked the boy, staring, fascinated. "Why does everything go around, then stop?"

Haplo was asking himself the same question. He had seen a magic lantern before. He had something similar to it on his ship, projecting images of the Nexus, only it had been devised by his lord and was much more sophisticated. It seemed to Haplo that there might be more pictures than what they were seeing, for the images stopped with an abrupt jerk in what looked to be mid-frame.

There came a low whirring sound and, suddenly, the pictures started over again. Alfred, whom Haplo took to be some sort of servant, started to reach out and grab the statue's hand, probably with the design of stopping the pictures.

"Please don't do that," said Haplo in his quiet voice.

Hugh whirled, sword drawn, and faced the intruder with an agility and skill that Haplo inwardly applauded. The nervous man crumpled to the floor, and the boy, turning, stared at the Patryn with blue eyes that were not frightened so much as shrewdly curious.

Haplo stood with his hands up, palms outward. "I'm not armed," he said to Hugh. The Patryn wasn't the least afraid of the man's sword. There were no weapons in this world that could harm him, guarded as he was by the runes upon his body, but he must avoid the fight, for by that very act of protecting himself he would reveal to knowing eyes who and what he truly was. "I don't mean anyone any harm." He smiled and shrugged, keeping his hands in the air and plainly visible. "I'm like the boy, here. I only want to see the pictures."

Of all of them, it was the child who intrigued Haplo. The cowardly servant, lying in a pathetic heap on the floor, did not merit his interest. The man he assumed to be a bodyguard he could dismiss now that he had noted his strength and agility. But when Haplo looked at the child, he felt a stinging sensation of the runes upon his chest and knew by that sensation that some sort of enchantment was being cast at him. His own magic was instinctively acting to repel it, but Haplo was amused to note that whatever spell the child was casting wouldn't have worked anyway. His magic—whatever its source—had been disrupted.

"Where did you come from? Who are you?" demanded Hugh.

"My name is Haplo. My friends, the Gegs"—he gestured to the hole out of which he'd come. Hearing a commotion behind him, he assumed that the ever-curious Limbeck was following— "and I heard of your coming and decided that we should meet and talk to you in private, if that's possible. Are the high froman's guards around?"

Hugh lowered the sword slightly, though his dark eyes continued to follow Haplo's every move. "No, they left. But we're probably being watched."

"No doubt. Then we haven't much time before someone returns."

Limbeck, puffing and panting from his scramble up the ladder, trotted up behind Haplo. The Geg glanced askance at Hugh's sword, but his curiosity was stronger than his fear.

"Are you Mangers?" he asked, his gaze going from Haplo to the boy.

Haplo, watching Limbeck closely, saw an awed expression smooth out his face. The Geg's myopic eyes, magnified behind the spectacles, grew wide. "You *are* a god, aren't you?"

"Yes," answered the child, speaking Geg. "I am a god."

"Do these speak human?" asked Hugh, pointing to Limbeck, Jarre, and the other two Gegs, who were cautiously poking their heads up out of the hole.

Haplo shook his head.

"Then I can tell you the truth," said Hugh. "The kid's no more a god than you are." To judge by the expression in Hugh's dark eyes, he had apparently reached the same decision about Haplo that Haplo had reached about Hugh. He was wary, cautious, suspicious still, but crowded inns force people to sleep with odd bedfellows or spend the night out in the cold. "Our ship got caught in the Maelstrom and crashed on Drevlin, not far from here. The Gegs found us and thought we were gods, and we had to play along."

"Like me," said Haplo, nodding. He glanced down at the servant, who had opened his eyes and was staring around him with a bemused look. "Who's that?"

"The kid's chamberlain. I'm called Hugh the Hand. That's Alfred, and the kid's name is Bane, son of King Stephen of Volkaran and Uylandia."

Haplo turned to Limbeck and Jarre—who was staring at the three with deep suspicion—and made introductions. Alfred staggered to his feet and gazed at Haplo with a curiosity that deepened when he saw the man's wrapped hands.

Haplo, becoming aware of Alfred's stare, self-consciously tugged at the cloth.

"Are you injured, sir?" questioned the servant in respectful tones. "Forgive me for asking, but I notice the bandages you wear. I am somewhat skilled in healing—"

"Thank you, no. I'm not wounded. It's a skin disease, common to my people. It's not contagious and it doesn't cause me any pain, but the pustules it creates aren't pleasant to look at."

Disgust twisted Hugh's features. Alfred's face paled slightly, and it was a struggle for the servant to express the proper sympathy. Haplo watched with inward satisfaction and did not believe he would encounter any further questions about his hands.

Hugh sheathed his sword and drew near. "Your ship crashed?" he asked Haplo in low tones.

"Yes."

"Destroyed?"

"Completely."

"Where are you from?"

"Down below, on one of the lower isles. You've probably never heard of it. Not many have. I was fighting a battle in my own lands when my ship was hit and I lost control—"

Hugh walked toward the statue. Apparently deeply engrossed

in the conversation, Haplo joined him, but managed to cast a casual glance back at the servant. Alfred's skin was a deathly hue, his eyes still staring intently at the Patryn's hands, as if the man wished desperately his look could pierce through the cloth.

"You're stranded down here, then?" asked Hugh.

Haplo nodded.

"And you want . . ." Hugh hesitated, certain, perhaps, that he knew the answer but wanting the other to say it.

". . . to get out." Haplo was emphatic.

Now it was Hugh who nodded. The two men understood each other completely. There was no trust between them, but that wasn't necessary, not as long as each was able to use the other to achieve a common goal. Bedfellows, it seemed, who wouldn't fight over the blankets. They continued to converse in low tones, considering their problem.

Alfred stood staring at the man's hands. Bane, frowning, gazed after Haplo; the boy's fingers stroked the feather amulet. His thoughts were interrupted by the Geg.

"You're not a god, then?" Drawn by an irresistible force, Limbeck had moved nearer to talk to the child.

"No," answered Bane, wrenching his gaze from Haplo. Turning to the Geg, the prince carefully and quickly smoothed his dour expression. "I'm not, but they told me to tell that man, your king, that I was so that he wouldn't hurt us."

"Hurt you?" Limbeck appeared amazed. The concept was beyond him.

"I'm really a prince of the High Realm," continued the child. "My father is a powerful wizard. We were going to see him when our ship crashed."

"I'd dearly love to see the High Realm!" exclaimed Limbeck. "What's it like?"

"I'm not sure. You see, I've never been there before. I've lived all my life in the Mid Realm with my adopted father. It's a long story."

"I've never been to the Mid Realm either. But I've seen pictures of it in a book I found in a Welf ship. I'll tell you how I found it." Limbeck began to recite his favorite tale—that of stumbling across the elven vessel.

Bane, fidgeting, craned his head to look back at Haplo and Hugh, standing together before the statue of the Manger. Alfred was muttering to himself. None of them was paying any attention to Jarre.

She didn't like this, any of it. She didn't like the two tall, strong gods putting their heads together and talking in a language she couldn't understand. She didn't like the way Limbeck was looking at the child-god, she didn't like the way the child-god was looking at anyone. She didn't even like the way the tall, gawky god had tumbled down onto the floor. Jarre had the feeling that, like poor relatives coming to visit, these gods were going to devour all the food and, when that was gone, leave the Gegs with nothing but an empty cupboard.

Jarre slipped over to where the two Gegs were standing nervously beside the hole.

"Bring up everybody," she said in as soft a voice as is possible for a Geg. "The high froman's tried to fool us with sham gods. We're going to capture them and take them before the people and prove that the high froman is a fraud!"

The Gegs looked at the so-called gods, then at each other. These gods didn't appear very impressive. Tall, maybe, but skinny. One of them carried a formidable-looking weapon. If he were mobbed, he wouldn't get a chance to use it. Haplo had mourned the extinction of Geg courage. It hadn't completely died out. It had just been buried under centuries of submission and toil. Now the coals had been stirred up. Here and there, flames were flickering.

The excited Gegs backed down the ladder. Jarre leaned over and looked down after them. Her square face, dimly illuminated by the glimmerglamps, was awesome, almost ethereal, when viewed from below. More than one Geg had a sudden image of ancient days when the clan priestesses would have summoned them to war.

Noisily, but in the disciplined manner the Gegs had learned serving the great machine, they clambered up the ladder. What with the whumping and the thumping going on all around, no one heard them.

Forgotten in the confusion, Haplo's dog lay at the foot of the ladder. Nose on paws, it watched and listened and seemed to ponder whether its master had really been serious about that word "stay."

CHAPTER ✦ 35

WOMBE, DREVLIN,

LOW REALM

✦

HAPLO HEARD A WHINE, FELT A PAWING AT HIS LEG. HE TURNED HIS attention from examining the Manger pictures to look down at his feet.

"What is it, boy? I thought I told you to . . . Oh." The Patryn glanced over and saw the Gegs streaming up out of the hole. The Hand, hearing a sound at his back, looked in the opposite direction—toward the main entrance of the Factree.

"Company," said Hugh. "The high froman and his guards."

"And over there."

Hugh glanced swiftly toward the hole, his hand going to his sword. Haplo shook his head. "No, we can't fight. There are too many. Besides, they don't want to harm us. They want to claim us. We're the prize. There's no time to explain. It looks as if we're going to be caught in the middle of a riot. You better go take care of that prince of yours."

"He's an investment—" began Hugh.

"The coppers!" Jarre shrieked, catching sight of the high froman. "Quick, grab the gods before they stop us!"

"Then you better go guard your investment," suggested Haplo.

"What is it, sir?" gasped Alfred, seeing Hugh running toward them, sword in hand.

The two groups of Gegs were yelling and shaking their fists and snatching up makeshift weapons off the Factree floor.

"Trouble. Take the kid and go with . . ." Hugh began. "No, dammit, don't faint . . ."

Alfred's eyes rolled back in his head. Hugh reached out to

shake him or slap him or something, but it was too late. The chamberlain's limp body slid down and flopped gracelessly across the feet of the Manger's statue.

The Gegs rushed toward the gods. The high froman, instantly recognizing his danger, ordered the coppers to rush the Gegs. Shouting wildly—some for the WUPPers and some for the froman—the two groups came together. For the first time in the history of Drevlin, blows were struck, blood was shed. Haplo, gathering up his dog in his arms, melted back into the shadows and watched quietly, smiling.

Jarre stood near the hole, helping Gegs climb out, rallying her people to attack. When the last Geg was up out of the tunnels, she looked around and discovered that the battle had surged ahead of her. Worse, she had completely lost sight of Limbeck, Haplo, and the three strange beings. Leaping onto the top of a crate, Jarre peered over the heads of the milling, fighting press of Gegs and saw, to her horror, the high froman and the head clark standing near the statue of the Manger, taking advantage of the confusion to spirit away not only the gods but also the august leader of WUPP!

Furious, Jarre jumped from her crate and ran toward them, but got caught up in the midst of the battle. Pushing and shoving and lashing out with her fists at the Gegs blocking her path, she struggled to get near the statue. She was flushed and panting, her trousers were torn, her hair had fallen down over her face, and one eye was swelling shut when she finally reached her destination.

The gods were gone. Limbeck was gone. The high froman had won.

Her fist doubled, Jarre was prepared to punch the head of the first copper who came near her when she heard a moan and, looking down, saw two large feet sticking up in the air. They weren't Geg feet. They were god feet!

Hurrying around to the front of the Manger, Jarre was amazed to see the base of the statue standing wide open! One of the froman's gods—the tall, gawky one—had apparently fallen into this opening and was lying half in and half out of it.

"I'm in luck!" said Jarre. "I've got this one, at least!"

She glanced fearfully behind her, expecting to see the froman's coppers, but in the confusion and turmoil, no one was paying any attention to her. The froman would be intent on getting his gods out of danger and, undoubtedly, no one had missed this one yet.

"But they will. We have to get you away from here," muttered Jarre. Hurrying over to the god, she saw that he was lying on a staircase that led inside the statue. Descending below the floor level, the stairs provided a quick and easy means of escape.

Jarre hesitated. She was violating the statue—the Gegs' most Holy of Holies. She had no idea why this opening was here or where it might lead. It didn't matter. This was only going to be a hiding place. She'd wait inside here until everyone was gone. Jarre bounded over the comatose god and stumbled down the stairs. Turning, she grabbed the god's shoulders and dragged him, bumping and sliding and groaning, inside the statue.

Jarre had no clear plan in mind. She only hoped that by the time the high froman came looking for this god and discovered the opening in the statue, she would have been able to smuggle him back to WUPP Headquarters. But when Jarre drew the god's feet over the base, the opening suddenly and silently slid shut. The Geg found herself in darkness.

Jarre held perfectly still and tried to tell herself everything was all right. But panic was swelling up inside her until it seemed she must split apart. Her terror wasn't caused by fear of the dark. Living nearly all of their lives inside the Kickseywinsey, the Gegs were used to the darkness. Jarre shook all over. Her hands were sweating, her breath came fast, her heart pounded, and she didn't know why. And then it came to her.

It was quiet.

She couldn't hear the machine, couldn't hear the comforting whistles and bangs and hammerings that had lulled her to sleep as a babe. Now there was nothing but awful, terrible silence. Sight is a sense outside and apart from the body, an image on the surface of the eye. But sound enters the ears, the head, it lives inside. In sound's absence, silence echoes.

Abandoning the god on the staircase, heedless of pain, forgetting her fear of the coppers, Jarre flung herself against the statue. "Help!" she screamed. "Help me!"

Alfred regained consciousness. Sitting up, he accidentally began to slide down the stairs, and only saved himself by reflexively grabbing and hanging on to the steps beneath. Thoroughly confused, surrounded by pitch-black night with a Geg screaming like a steam whistle in his ears, Alfred endeavored to ask several times what was going on. The Geg paid no attention to him.

Finally, crawling on hands and knees in the darkness back up the stairs, he reached out a hand in the direction of the nearly hysterical Jarre.

"Where are we?"

She pounded and shrieked and ignored him.

"Where are we?" Alfred caught hold of the Geg in his large hands—uncertain, in the darkness, just what part he'd grabbed—and began to shake her. "Stop this! It isn't helping! Tell me where we are and maybe I can get us out of here!"

Not clearly understanding Alfred's words, but angered at his rough handling, Jarre came to herself with a gulp and shoved the chamberlain away with a heave of her strong arms. He slid and slithered and nearly tumbled back down the stairs, but managed to stop his fall.

"Now, listen to me!" Alfred said, separating each word and speaking it slowly and distinctly. "Tell me where we are and maybe I can help get us out!"

"I don't know how!" Breathing hard, shivering, Jarre huddled as far away from Alfred as possible on the opposite side of the staircase. "You're a stranger here. What could you know?"

"Just tell me!" pleaded Alfred. "I can't explain. After all, what will it hurt?"

"Well . . ." Jarre considered. "We're inside the statue."

"Ah!" breathed Alfred.

"What does 'ah' mean?"

"It means . . . uh . . . I thought that might be the case."

"Can you open it back up?"

No, I can't. No one can. Not from the inside. But how would I know that if I've never been here before? What do I tell her? Alfred was thankful for the darkness. He was a terrible liar and it made it easier that he couldn't see her face and that she couldn't see his.

"I'm . . . not certain, but I doubt it. You see, uh . . . What is your name?"

"It doesn't matter."

"Yes, it does. We're here together in the dark and we should know each other's names. Mine is Alfred. And yours?"

"Jarre. Go on. You opened it once, why can't you open it again?"

"I . . . I didn't open it," stammered Alfred. "It opened by accident, I guess. You see, I have this terrible habit. Whenever I'm frightened, I faint. It's something I can't control. I saw the fighting, you see, and some of your people were rushing toward us, and I . . . just passed out." That much was true. What followed wasn't. "I guess that when I fell I must have tripped something on the statue that caused it to open."

I regained consciousness. I looked up to see the statue, and I felt, for the first time in a long, long while, safe and secure and deeply, fervently at peace. The suspicion that had been awakened in my mind, the responsibility, the decisions I will be forced to make if that suspicion is true, overwhelmed me. I longed to escape, to disappear, and my hand moved of its own volition, without my prompting, and touched the statue's robe in a certain place, in a certain way.

The base slid open, but then the enormity of my action must have been too much for me. I suppose I fainted again. The Geg came upon me and, seeking a haven from the melee raging outside, dragged me in here. The base closed automatically and it will stay closed. Only those who know the way in know the way out. Anyone stumbling across an entrance by mistake would never return to tell of it. Oh, they wouldn't die. The magic, the machine, would care for them, and care for them very well. But they would be prisoners for the rest of their lives.

Fortunately, I know the way in, I know the way out. But how can I explain this to the Geg?

A terrible thought occurred to Alfred. By law, he should leave her here. It was her own fault, after all. She shouldn't have entered the sacred statue. But then Alfred considered, with a pang of conscience, that perhaps she had endangered herself for him—trying to save his life. He couldn't just abandon her. He knew he couldn't, no matter what the law said. But right now it was all so confusing. If only he hadn't given way to his weakness!

"Don't stop!" Jarre clutched at him.

"Stop what?"

"Talking! It's the quiet! I can't stand listening to it! Why can't we hear anything in here?"

"It was made that way purposely," said Alfred with a sigh. "Designed to offer rest and sanctuary." He had reached a decision. It probably wasn't the right one, but then, he'd made few right decisions in his lifetime. "I am going to lead us out of here, Jarre."

"You know the way?"

"Yes."

"How?" She was deeply suspicious.

"I can't explain it. In fact, you will see many things that you won't understand and that I can't explain. I can't even ask you to trust me, because, of course, you don't, and I can't expect you to." Pausing, Alfred considered his next words. "Let's look at it like this: you can't get out this way. You've tried. You can either stay here or you can come with me and I'll show you the way out."

Alfred heard the Geg draw breath to speak, but he forestalled her.

"There's one more thing you should consider. I want to return to my people just as desperately as you want to go back to yours. The child you saw is in my care. And the dark man with him needs me, although he doesn't know it." Alfred was silent a moment, thinking of the other man, the one who called himself Haplo, and it occurred to him that the silence was loud in here, louder than he'd remembered.

"I'll go with you," said Jarre. "What you say makes sense."

"Thank you," answered Alfred gravely. "Now, hold still one moment. This stairway is steep and dangerous without light."

Alfred reached out his hand and felt the wall behind him. It was made of stone, like the tunnels, and was smooth and even. Running his hand along the surface, he had nearly reached the juncture where the wall met the stairs when his fingers brushed over lines and whorls and notches carved in the stone. They formed a distinct pattern, one that he knew. Tracing his finger over the rough edges of the carving, following the lines of the pattern he could see clearly in his mind, he spoke the rune.

The sigil beneath his fingers began to glow with a soft, radiant blue light. Jarre, seeing it, caught her breath and sank backward, pressing herself against the wall. Alfred gave her a soothing, reassuring pat on the arm and repeated the rune. A sigil carved beside and touching the first caught the magical fire and began to glow. Soon, one after the other, a line of runes appeared out of the darkness, running the length of the steep staircase. At the bottom, they curved around a corner leading to the right.

"Now it's safe for us to go down," said Alfred, rising and brushing the dust of ages from his clothes. Keeping his words and actions purposefully brisk, his tone matter-of-fact, he held out his hand to Jarre. "If I might be of assistance?"

Jarre hesitated, gulped, and hugged her shawl closely around her. Then, pressing her lips together, her face grim, she rested her small work-worn hand in Alfred's. The blue-glowing runes glittered brightly in her fearful eyes.

They descended the stairs swiftly, the runes making it easy to see the way. Hugh would not have recognized the bumbling, stumble-footed chamberlain. Alfred's movements were surefooted, his stance erect. He hurried ahead with an anticipation that was eager, yet wistful and tinged with melancholy.

Reaching the bottom of the steep staircase, they found that it opened into a small narrow corridor; a veritable honeycomb of doorways and tunnels branched off it in countless directions. The blue runes led them out of the corridor and into a tunnel— third from their right. Alfred followed the sigla unhesitatingly, bringing with him a wide-eyed and awestruck Jarre.

At first the Geg had doubted the man's words. She had lived among the delvings and burrowings of the Kicksey-winsey all her life. Gegs have a keen eye for minute detail and excellent memories. What looks to be a blank wall to a human or an elf holds a myriad of individual characteristics—cracks, crevices, chipped paint—for a Geg, and once seen, is not soon forgotten. Consequently, Gegs do not easily lose themselves, either above ground or below. But Jarre was almost instantly lost in these tunnels. The walls were flawless, perfect and completely devoid of the life that a Geg can find, even in stone. And though the tunnels branched out in all directions, they did not turn and twist or ramble. There was no indication anywhere that a tunnel had been built just for the hell of it, out of a sense of adventure. The corridors ran straight and smooth and gave the impression that wherever you were going, they'd get you there the quickest route possible, and no nonsense. Jarre recognized in the design a sense of strong purpose, a calculated intent that frightened her by its sterility. Yet her strange companion seemed to find it comforting, and his confidence eased her fear.

The runes led them in a gentle curve that kept taking them to their right. Jarre had no idea how far they traveled, for there was no feeling of time down here. The blue sigla ran on before them, lighting their path, each flaming to life out of the darkness as they neared it. Jarre became mesmerized by them; it seemed as if she walked in a dream and might have kept walking forever as long as the runes led the way. The man's voice added to this eerie impression, for—as she had asked—he talked the entire time.

Then, suddenly, they rounded a corner and Jarre saw the sigla climb into the air, form a glowing archway that burned and glistened in the darkness, inviting them to enter. Alfred paused.

"What is it?" Jarre asked, starting out of her trance, blinking, and tightening her grip on Alfred's hand. "I don't want to go in there!"

"We have no choice. It's all right," said Alfred, and there was that note of wistful melancholy in his voice. "I'm sorry I frightened you. I'm not stopping because I'm afraid. I know what's in there, you see, and . . . and it only makes me sad, that's all."

"We'll go back," said Jarre suddenly, fiercely. She turned and took a step, but almost immediately the runes that had showed the way behind them flared a bright blue, then slowly began to fade. Soon the two were surrounded by darkness, the only light coming from flickering blue sigla outlining the archway.

"We can go in now," said Alfred, drawing a deep breath. "I'm ready. Don't be frightened, Jarre," he added, patting her hand. "Don't be frightened by anything you see. Nothing can harm you."

But Jarre was frightened, though she couldn't say of what. Whatever lay beyond was hidden in darkness, yet what frightened her wasn't a fear of bodily harm or the terror of the unknown. It was the sadness, as Alfred had said. Perhaps it had come from the words he'd been speaking during their long walk, although she was so disoriented and confused that she could recall nothing of what he'd said. But she experienced a feeling of despair, of overwhelming regret, of something lost and never found, never even sought. The sorrow made her ache with loneliness, as if everything and everyone she had ever known was suddenly gone. Tears came to her eyes, and she wept, and she had no idea for whom she was crying.

"It's all right," repeated Alfred. "It's all right. Shall we go in now? Do you feel up to it?"

Jarre couldn't answer, couldn't stop crying. But she nodded, and, weeping, clinging closely to Alfred, walked with him through the archway. And then Jarre understood, in part, the reason for her fear and her sadness.

She stood in a mausoleum.

CHAPTER ♦ 36

WOMBE, DREVLIN,

LOW REALM

♦

"THIS IS DREADFUL! SIMPLY DREADFUL! UNHEARD-OF! *WHAT* ARE YOU going to do? What *are* you going to do?"

The head clerk was clearly becoming hysterical. Darral Long-shoreman felt a tingling in his hands and was hard pressed to resist the temptation to administer a right to the jaw.

"There's been enough bloodshed already," he muttered, grasping hold of his hands firmly behind his back in case they took it upon themselves to act on their own. And he managed to ignore the voice that whispered, "A little more blood wouldn't hurt, then, would it?"

Decking his brother-in-law, though undoubtedly very satisfying, wasn't going to solve his problems.

"Get hold of yourself!" Darral snapped. "Haven't I got trouble enough?"

"Never has blood been spilled in Drevlin!" cried the head clerk in an awful tone. "It's all the fault of this evil genius Limbeck! He must be cast forth! Made to walk the Steps of Terrel Fen. The Mangers must judge him—"

"Oh, shut up! That's what brought on all this trouble in the first place! We gave him to the Mangers, and what did they do? Gave him right back to us! And threw in a god! Sure, we'll send Limbeck down the Steps!" Darral waved his arms wildly. "Maybe this time he'll come up with a whole army of gods and destroy us all!"

"But that god of Limbeck's isn't a god!" protested the head clerk.

"They're none of them gods, if you ask me," stated Darral Longshoreman.

"Not even the child?"

This question, asked in wistful tones by the head clark, posed a problem for Darral. When he was in Bane's presence, he felt that, yes, indeed, he had at last discovered a god. But the moment he could no longer see the blue eyes and the pretty face and the sweetly curved lips of the little boy, the high froman seemed to waken from a dream. The kid was a kid, and he, Darral Longshoreman, was a sap for ever thinking otherwise.

"No," said the high froman, "not even the child."

The two rulers of Drevlin were alone in the Factree, standing beneath the statue of the Manger, gloomily surveying the battlefield.

It hadn't, in reality, been much of a battle. One might hardly even term it a skirmish. The aforesaid blood had flowed, not from the heart, but from several cracked heads, gushed out a few smashed noses. The head clark had sustained a bump, the high froman a jammed thumb that had swelled up and was now turning several quite remarkable colors. No one had been killed. No one had even been seriously injured. The habit of living peacefully over numerous centuries is a hard one to break. But Darral Longshoreman, high froman of his people, was wise enough to know that this was only the beginning. A poison had entered the collective body of the Gegs, and though the body might survive, it would never be healthy again.

"Besides," said Darral, his heavy brows creased in a scowl, "if these gods aren't gods, like Limbeck said they weren't, how can we punish him for being right?"

Unaccustomed to wading in such deep philosophical waters, the head clark ignored the question and struck out for high ground. "We wouldn't be punishing him for being right, we'd be punishing him for spreading it around."

There was certainly some logic to that, Darral had to admit. He wondered sourly how his brother-in-law had come up with such a good idea and concluded it must have been the bump on the head. Wringing his wounded thumb and wishing he was back home in his holding tank with Mrs. High Froman clucking over him and bringing him a soothing cup of barkwarm,[1] Darral

---

[1] A hot drink concocted by boiling the bark from a ferben bush in water for about half an hour. To elves, the drink is mildly narcotic, acting as a sedative, but to humans and dwarves it merely brings on a feeling of restful relaxation.

pondered the idea, born of desperation, that was lurking about in the dark alleys of his mind.

"Maybe this time, when we throw him off the Steps of Terrel Fen, we can leave off the kite," suggested the head clark. "I always did think that was an unfair advantage."

"No," said Darral, the rattle-brained ideas of his brother-in-law making his decision for him. "I'm not sending him or anyone else Down anymore. Down isn't safe, seemingly. This god-that-isn't-a-god of Limbeck's says he comes from Down. And therefore"—the high froman paused during a particularly loud spate of banging and whanging from the Kicksey-winsey—"I'm going to send him Up."

"Up?" The bump on the head was not going to come to the aid of the head clark on this one. He was absolutely and categorically lost.

"I'm going to turn the gods over to the Welves," said Darral Longshoreman with dark satisfaction.

The high froman paid a visit to the prison vat to announce the captives' punishment—an announcement he reckoned must strike terror into their guilty hearts.

If it did, the prisoners gave no outward sign. Hugh appeared disdainful, Bane bored, and Haplo impassive, while Limbeck was in such misery that it was doubtful if he heard the high froman at all. Getting nothing from his prisoners but fixed cold stares and, in Bane's case, a yawn and a sleepy smile, the high froman marched out in high dudgeon.

"I presume you know what he's talking about?" inquired Haplo. "This being given to the 'Welves'?"

"Elves," corrected the Hand. "Once a month, the elves come down in a transport ship and pick up a supply of water. This time, they'll pick us up with it. And we *don't* want to end up prisoners of the elves. Not if they catch us down here with their precious water supply. Those bastards can make dying very unpleasant."

The captives were locked up in the local prison—a grouping of storage vats that the Kicksey-winsey had abandoned and which, when fitted with locks on the doors, made excellent cells. Generally the cells were little used—perhaps the occasional thief or a Geg who had been lax in his service to the great machine. Due to the current civil unrest, however, the vats were filled to capacity with disturbers of the peace. One vat had to be emptied of its inhabitants in order to make room for the gods. The Geg prisoners were crowded into another vat so as to avoid being placed into contact with Mad Limbeck.

The vat was steep-walled and solid. Several openings covered with iron grilles dotted the sides. Hugh and Haplo investigated these grilles and discovered that fresh air, smelling damply of rain, was flowing in through them, leading the men to assume the grilles covered shafts that must eventually connect with the outside. The shafts might have offered a means of escape except for two drawbacks: first, the grilles were bolted to the metal sides of the vat, and second, no one in his right mind wanted to go Outside.

"So you're suggesting we fight?" inquired Haplo. "I presume these elven ships are well-manned. We're four, counting the chamberlain, plus a child, and one sword between us. A sword that's currently in the possession of the guards."

"The chamberlain's worthless," grunted Hugh. Leaning back comfortably against the brick wall of their prison, he drew out his pipe and stuck the stem between his teeth. "The first sign of danger, and he faints dead away. You saw him back there during the riot."

"That's odd, isn't it?"

"*He's* odd!" stated Hugh.

Haplo could remember Alfred's eyes trying desperately to pierce the cloth covering the Patryn's hands, almost as if the chamberlain knew what was beneath. "I wonder where he got to? Did you see?"

Hugh shook his head. "All I saw was Gegs. I had the kid. But the chamberlain's bound to turn up. Or rather stumble up. He won't leave His Highness." The Hand nodded at Bane, who was talking away at the misery-stricken Limbeck.

Haplo followed Hugh's gaze and focused on the Geg.

"There's always Limbeck and his WUPP's. They'd fight to save us, or, if not us, their leader."

Hugh glanced at him dubiously. "Do you think so? I always heard Gegs had the fighting spirit of a flock of sheep."

"That may be true now, but it didn't used to be so. Not in the old days. Once, long ago, the dwarves were a fierce, proud people."

Hugh, returning his gaze to Limbeck, shook his head.

The Geg sat huddled in a corner, his shoulders slumped,

arms dangling limply between his knees. The child was talking at him; the Geg was completely oblivious of the conversation.

"He's been walking along with his head in the clouds," said Haplo. "He didn't see the ground coming and got hurt in the fall. But he's the one to lead his people."

"You're really caught up in this revolution of theirs," observed Hugh. "Some might wonder why you care."

"Limbeck saved my life," answered Haplo, lazily scratching the ears of the dog that was stretched out at his side, its head resting in his lap. "I like him and his people. As I said, I know something about their past." The mild face darkened. "I hate seeing what they've become. Sheep, I believe, was how you put it."

Hugh sucked thoughtfully, silently on his empty pipe. The man sounded good, but Hugh found it difficult to believe this Haplo was that concerned about a bunch of dwarves. A quiet, unassuming man, you tended to ignore him, forget he was around. And that, said Hugh to himself, might be a very big mistake. Lizards that blend in with the rocks do so to catch flies.

"Somehow we've got to get some backbone into your Limbeck, then," remarked Hugh. "If we're going to save ourselves from the elves, we'll need the Gegs to help us."

"You can leave him to me," said Haplo. "Where were you headed, before you got caught up in all this?"

"I was going to return the kid to his father, his real father, the mysteriarch."

"Damn nice of you," commented Haplo.

"Hunh," Hugh grunted, his lips twisting in a grin.

"These wizards who live in the High Realm. Why was it they left the world below? They must have enjoyed a large amount of power among the people."

"The answer to that depends on who you ask. The mysteriarchs claim they left because they'd advanced in culture and wisdom and the rest of us hadn't. Our barbaric ways disgusted them. They didn't want to bring up their kids in an evil world."

"And what do you barbarians say to all this?" asked Haplo, smiling. The dog had rolled over on its back, all four feet in the air, its tongue lolling out of its mouth in foolish pleasure.

"We say"—Hugh sucked on the empty pipe, his words coming out between the stem and his teeth—"that the mysteriarchs were afraid of the growing power of the elven wizards and beat it. They left us in the lurch, no doubt of it. Their leaving was the cause of our downfall. If it hadn't been for the revolt among their own people, the elves'd be our masters still."

"And so these mysteriarchs wouldn't be welcome, if they returned?"

"Oh, they'd be welcome. Welcomed with cold steel, if the people had their way. But our king maintains friendly relations, or so I've heard. People wonder why." His gaze shifted back to Bane.

Haplo knew the changeling's story. Bane himself had proudly explained it to him. "But the mysteriarchs could come back if one of them was the human king's son."

Hugh made no response to the obvious. He removed the pipe from his mouth, tucked it back in his doublet. Crossing his arms over his chest, he rested his chin on his breast and closed his eyes.

Haplo rose to his feet, stretched. He needed to walk, needed to work the kinks out of his muscles. Pacing the cell, the Patryn thought about all he'd heard. He had very little work to do, it seemed. This entire realm was overripe and ready to fall. His lord would not even have to reach out his hand to pluck it. The fruit would be found lying, rotting, on the ground at his feet.

Surely this was the clearest possible evidence that the Sartan were no longer involved in the world? The child was the question. Bane had evinced a magical power, but that might be expected of the son of a mysteriarch of the Seventh House. Long ago, before the Sundering, the magics of those wizards had reached the lower level of both Sartan and Patryns. After all this time, they had likely grown in power.

Or Bane could be a young Sartan—clever enough not to reveal himself. Haplo looked over to where the boy sat talking earnestly to the distraught Geg.

The Patryn made an almost imperceptible sign with his wrapped hand. The dog, who rarely took his eyes from his master, immediately trotted over to Limbeck and gave the Geg's limp hand a swipe with his tongue. Limbeck looked up and smiled wanly at the dog, who, tail wagging, settled down comfortably at the Geg's side.

Haplo drifted over to the opposite end of the vat to stare in seeming absorption at one of the air shafts. He could now hear clearly every word being said.

"You can't give up," said the boy. "Not now! The fight's just beginning!"

"But I never meant there to be a fight," protested poor Limbeck. "Gegs attacking each other! Nothing like that has ever happened before in our history, and it's all my fault!"

"Oh, stop whining!" said Bane. Scratching at an itch on his stomach, he looked around the vat and frowned. "I'm hungry. I wonder if they're going to starve us. I'll be glad when the Welves get here. I—"

The boy fell suddenly silent, as if someone had bidden him hold his tongue. Haplo, glancing surreptitiously over his shoulder, saw Bane holding the feather amulet, rubbing it against his cheek. When he spoke again, his voice had changed.

"I've got an idea, Limbeck," said the prince, scooting forward to be very near the Geg. "When we leave this place, you can go with us! You'll see how well the elves and the humans live up above while you Gegs slave down here below. Then you can come back and tell your people what you've seen and they'll be furious. Even this king of yours will have to go along with you. My father and I will help you raise an army to attack the elves and the humans—"

"An army! Attack!" Limbeck stared at him, horrified, and Bane saw that he had gone too far.

"Never mind about that now," he said, brushing aside world warfare. "The important thing is that you get to see the truth."

"The truth," repeated Limbeck.

"Yes," said Bane, sensing that the Geg was, at last, impressed. "The truth. Isn't that what's important? You and your people can't go on living a lie. Wait. I just got an idea. Tell me about this Judgment that's supposed to come to the Gegs."

Limbeck appeared thoughtful, his misery fading. It was as if he'd put on his spectacles. Everything that was blurry, he could now see clearly—see the sharp lines and crisp edges. "When the Judgment is given and we are found worthy, we will ascend to the realms above."

"This is *it*, Limbeck!" said Bane, awed. "This is the Judgment! It's all happened just like the prophecy said. We came down and found you worthy and now you're going to ascend into the upper realms!"

Very clever, kid, said Haplo to himself. Very clever. Bane no longer held the feather. Daddy was no longer prompting. That last had been Bane's own idea, seemingly. A remarkable child, this changeling. And a dangerous one.

"But we thought the Judgment would be peaceful."

"Was that ever said?" Bane countered. "Anywhere in the prophecy?"

Limbeck turned his attention to the dog, patting its head, attempting to avoid answering while he tried to accustom himself to this new vision.

"Limbeck?" pushed Bane.

The Geg continued to stroke the dog, who lay still beneath his hands. "New vision," he said, looking up. "That's it. When the Welves come, I know just what to do."

"What?" asked Bane eagerly.

"I'll make a speech."

Later that evening, after their jailors brought them food, Hugh called a meeting. "We don't want to end up prisoners of the elves," explained the assassin. "We've got to fight and try to get away, and we can—if you Gegs will help us."

Limbeck wasn't listening. He was composing.

" 'Welves and WUPP's, wadies and gentle . . . No, no. Too many 'wahs.' '. . . Distinguished visitors from another realm' —that's better. Drat, I wish I could write this down!" The Geg paced up and down in front of his companions, mulling over his speech and pulling distractedly on his beard. The dog, trotting along behind him, looked sympathetic and wagged its tail.

Haplo shook his head. "Don't look for help there."

"But, Limbeck, it wouldn't be much of a battle!" Bane protested. "The Gegs outnumber the elves. We'll take them completely by surprise. I don't like elves. They threw me off their ship. I nearly died."

"Distinguished visitors from another realm—"

Haplo pursued his argument. "The Gegs are untrained, undisciplined. They don't have any weapons. And even if they could get weapons, we don't dare trust them. It'd be like sending in an army of children—ordinary children," Haplo added, seeing Bane bristle. "The Gegs aren't ready *yet*." He put an unconscious emphasis on the word that caught Hugh's attention.

"Yet?"

"When father and I return," struck in Bane, "we're going to whip the Gegs into shape. We'll take on the elves and we'll win. Then we'll control all the water in the world and we'll have power and be rich beyond belief."

Rich. Hugh twisted his beard. A thought occurred to him. If

it came to open war, any human with a ship and the nerve to fly the Maelstrom could make his fortune in one run. He would need a watership. An elven watership and a crew to man it. It would be a shame to destroy these elves.

"What about the Gegs?" suggested Haplo.

"Oh, we'll take care of them," answered Bane. "They'll have to fight a lot harder than what I've seen so far. But—"

"Fight?" repeated Hugh, interrupting Bane in mid-dictatorship. "Why are we talking about fighting?" Reaching into his pocket, he drew forth his pipe and clamped his teeth down on it. "How are you at singing?" he asked Haplo.

CHAPTER ♦ 37

THE RESTING PLACE,

LOW REALM

♦

JARRE'S HAND SLID NERVELESSLY FROM ALFRED'S. SHE COULD NOT MOVE; the strength seeped from her body. She shrank back against the archway, leaning on it for support. Alfred never seemed to notice. He walked ahead, leaving the Geg, shaken and trembling, to wait for him.

The chamber he entered was vast; Jarre couldn't recall ever seeing such a huge open space in her life—a space not inhabited by some whirly, clanging, or thumping part of the Kicksey-winsey. Made of the same smooth, flawless stone as the tunnels, the walls of the chamber glowed with a soft white light that began to shine from them when Alfred set his foot inside the archway. It was by this light that Jarre saw the coffins. Set into the walls, each covered by glass, the coffins numbered in the hundreds and held the bodies of men and women. Jarre could not see the people closely—they were little more than silhouettes against the light. But she could tell that they were of the same race as Alfred and the other gods who had come to Drevlin. The bodies were tall and slender and lay resting with arms at their sides.

The floor of the chamber was smooth and wide, and the coffins encircled it in rows that extended up to the high domed ceiling. The chamber itself was completely empty. Alfred moved slowly, looking all around him in wistful recognition, as does someone returning home after a long absence.

The light in the room grew brighter, and Jarre saw that there were symbols on the floor, similar in shape and design to the runes that had lit their way. There were twelve sigla, each carved singular and alone, never touching or overlapping. Alfred moved carefully among these, his gangly, ungainly form weaving its way across the empty chamber in a solemn dance, the lines and movements of his body appearing to imitate the particular sigil over which he was passing.

He made a complete circuit of the chamber, drifting across the floor, dancing to silent music. He glided close to each rune but never touched it, gliding away to another, honoring each in turn, until finally he came to the center of the chamber. Kneeling, he placed his hands upon the floor and began to sing.

Jarre could not understand the words he sang, but the song filled her with a joy that was bittersweet because it did nothing to lighten the terrible sadness. The runes on the floor glittered brightly, almost blinding in their radiance during Alfred's song. When he ceased, their gleaming light began to fade and, within moments, was gone.

Alfred, standing in the center, sighed. The body that had moved so beautifully in the dance stooped, the shoulders rounded. He looked over at Jarre and gave her a wistful smile.

"You're not still frightened?" He made a weak gesture toward the rows of coffins. "Nobody here can harm you. Not anymore. Not that they would have anyway—at least, not intentionally." He sighed and, turning in his place, looked long around the room. "But how much harm have we done unintentionally, meaning the best? Not gods, but with the power of gods. And yet lacking the wisdom."

He walked, slowly and with head bowed, over to a row of coffins that stood very near the entrance, near Jarre. Alfred placed his hand on one of the crystal windows, his fingers stroking it with an almost caressing touch. Sighing, he rested his forehead against another coffin up above. Jarre saw that the coffin he touched was empty. The others around it held bodies in them, and she noticed—her attention called to these because of him—that they seemed all to be young. Younger than he is, she thought, her gaze going to the bald head, the domed forehead carved with lines of anxiety, worry, and care that were so pronounced a smile only deepened them.

"These are my friends," he said to Jarre. "I told you about them as we were coming down here." He smoothed the crystal closure with one hand. "I told you that they might not be here. I told you that they might have gone. But I knew in my heart what

I told you wasn't true. They would be here. They will be here forever. Because they're dead, you see, Jarre. Dead before their time. I am alive long after!"

He closed his eyes, then covered his face with his hand. A sob wrenched the tall, ungainly body that leaned against the coffins. Jarre didn't understand. She hadn't listened to anything about these friends, and she could not and did not want to think about what she was seeing. But the man was grieving and his grief was heartbreaking to witness. Looking at the young people with their beautiful faces, serene and unmarred and cold as the crystal behind which they lay, Jarre understood that Alfred did not grieve for one but for many, himself among them.

Wrenching herself from the archway, she crept forward and slipped her hand into his. The solemnity, the despair, the sorrow of the place and of this man had affected Jarre deeply—just how deeply, she would not come to know until much later in her life. During that future time of great crisis when it seemed to her that she was losing all that was most valuable to her, everything he said—the story of Alfred and his losses and those of his people—would come back to her.

"Alfred. I'm sorry."

The man looked down at her, the tears glistening on his eyelashes. Squeezing her hand, he said something that she did not understand, for it was not in her language, nor in any other language that had been spoken for long ages in the realm of Arianus.

"This is why we failed," he said in that ancient language. "We thought of the many . . . and forgot the one. And so I am alone. And left perhaps to face by myself a peril ages old. The man with the bandaged hands." He shook his head. "The man with the bandaged hands."

He left the mausoleum without looking back. No longer afraid, Jarre walked with him.

Hugh woke at the sound. Starting up, pulling his dagger from his boot, he was on the move before he had completely thrown off sleep. It took him but an instant to collect himself, his eyes blinking back the blur of waking, adjusting to the dim glow of glimmerglamps shining from the never-sleeping Kicksey-winsey.

There was the sound again. He was heading in the right direction; it had come from behind one of the grilles located on the side of the vat.

Hugh's hearing was acute, his reflexes quick. He had trained himself to sleep lightly, and he was, therefore, not pleased to discover Haplo, fully awake, calmly standing near the air shaft as if he'd been there for hours. The sounds—scuffling and scraping— could now be heard clearly. They were getting closer. The dog, fur bristling around its neck, stared up at the shaft and whined softly.

"Shhst!" Haplo hissed, and the dog quieted. It walked around in a nervous circle and came back to stand beneath the shaft again. Seeing Hugh, Haplo made a motion with his hand. "Cover that side."

Hugh did not hesitate, but obeyed the silent command. To argue about leadership now would have been foolhardy, with some unknown something creeping toward them in the night and the two of them with only their bare hands and one dagger to fight it. He reflected, as he took up his stance, that not only had Haplo heard and reacted to the sound, he had moved so softly and stealthily that Hugh, who had heard the sound, had not heard Haplo.

The scuffling grew louder, nearer. The dog stiffened and bared its teeth. Suddenly there came a thump and a muffled "Ouch!"

Hugh relaxed. "It's Alfred."

"How in the name of the Mangers did he find us?" Haplo muttered.

A white face pressed against the grillwork from the inside. "Sir Hugh?"

"He has a wide range of talents," remarked Hugh.

"I'd be interested in hearing about them," returned Haplo. "How do we get him out?" He peered inside the grillwork. "Who's that with you?"

"One of the Gegs. Her name's Jarre."

The Geg poked her head beneath Alfred's arm. The space they were in was, seemingly, a tight fit, and Alfred was forced to scrunch up until he practically doubled in two to make room.

"Where's Limbeck?" Jarre demanded. "Is he all right?"

"He's over there, asleep. The grille's bolted fast on this side, Alfred. Can you work any of the bolts out from yours?"

"I'll see, sir. It's rather difficult . . . without any light. Perhaps if I used my feet, sir, and kicked—"

"Good idea." Haplo backed out of the way, the dog trotting at his heels.

"It's about time his feet were good for something," said Hugh, moving to the side of the vat. "It's going to make one hell of a clatter."

"Fortunately, the machine's doing an excellent job of clattering itself. Stand back, dog."

"I want to see Limbeck!"

"In just a moment, Jarre," came Alfred's mollifying voice. "Now, if you'll just scoot over there and give me some room."

Hugh heard a thud and saw the grillwork shiver slightly. Two more kicks, a groan from Alfred, and the grille popped off the side of the vat and fell to the ground.

By now, Limbeck and Bane were both awake and had come over to stare curiously at their midnight callers. Jarre slid out feet-first. Landing on the floor of the vat, she raced to Limbeck, threw her arms around him, and hugged him tight.

"Oh, my dear!" she said in a fierce whisper. "You can't imagine where I've been! You can't imagine it!"

Limbeck, feeling her trembling in his arms, somewhat bewilderedly smoothed her hair and gingerly patted her on the back.

"But, never mind!" said Jarre, returning to the serious business at hand. "The newssingers say the high froman's going to turn you over to the Welves. Don't worry. We're going to get you out of here now. This air shaft Alfred found leads to the outskirts of the city. Where we'll go once we leave here, I'm not quite certain, but we can sneak out of Wombe tonight and—"

"Are you all right, Alfred?" Hugh offered to help extricate the chamberlain from the shaft.

"Yes, sir."

Tumbling out of the air shaft, Alfred attempted to put his weight on his legs, and crumpled over in a heap on the ground. "That is, perhaps not," he amended from where he sat on the floor of the vat, a pained expression on his face. "I am afraid I've damaged something, sir. But it's not serious." Standing on one foot, with Hugh's help, he leaned back against the vat. "I can walk."

"You couldn't walk when you had two good feet."

"It's nothing, sir. My knee—"

"Guess what, Alfred!" interrupted Bane. "We're going to fight the elves!"

"I beg your pardon, Your Highness!"

"We're not going to have to escape, Jarre," Limbeck was explaining. "At least *I'm* not. I'm going to make a speech to the Welves and ask for their help and cooperation. Then the Welves will fly us to the realms above. I'll see the truth, Jarre. I'll see it for myself!"

"Make a speech to the Welves!" Jarre gasped, her breath completely taken away by this astounding revelation.

"Yes, my dear. And you've got to spread the word among our people. We'll need their help. Haplo will tell you what to do."

"You're not going to . . . fight anyone, are you?"

"No, my dear," said Limbeck, stroking his beard. "We're going to sing."

"Sing!" Jarre stared from one to another in blank astonishment. "I . . . I don't know much about elves. Are they fond of music?"

"What'd she say?" Hugh demanded. "Alfred, we've got to get this plan moving! Come here and translate for me. I have to teach her that song before morning."

"Very well, sir," said Alfred. "I assume, sir, you are referring to the song of the Battle of Seven Fields?"

"Yes. Tell her not to worry about what the words mean. They'll have to learn to sing it in human. Have her memorize it line by line and say it back to us to make sure she's got the words. The song shouldn't be too difficult for them to learn. Kids sing it all the time."

"I'll help!" Bane volunteered.

Haplo, squatting on the ground, stroked the dog, watched and listened, and said nothing.

"Jarre? Is that her name?" Hugh approached the two Gegs, Bane dancing at his side. The man's face was dark and stern in the flickering light. Bane's blue eyes gleamed with excitement. "Can you rally your people, teach them this song, and have them there at the ceremony?" Alfred translated. "This king of yours said the Welves will be here this day at noon. That doesn't give you much time."

"Sing!" Jarre murmured, staring at Limbeck. "Are you really going? Up there?"

Taking off his spectacles, Limbeck rubbed them on his shirt sleeve and put them on again. "Yes, my dear. If the Welves don't mind—"

" 'If the Welves don't *mind*,' " Alfred translated to Hugh, giving him a meaningful glance.

"Don't worry about the Welves, Alfred," interposed Haplo. "Limbeck's going to make a speech."

"Oh, Limbeck!" Jarre was pale, biting her lip. "Are you sure you should go up there? I don't think you should leave us. What will WUPP do without you? You going off like that—it will seem like the high froman's won!"

Limbeck frowned. "I hadn't thought about that." Removing his spectacles, he began to clean them again. Instead of putting them back on, he absentmindedly stuck them in his pocket. He looked at Jarre and blinked, as if wondering why she was all blurry. "I don't know. Perhaps you're right, my dear."

Hugh ground his teeth in frustration. He didn't know what had been said, but he could see the Geg was having second thoughts, and that was going to lose him his ship and probably his life. He looked impatiently at Alfred to help, but the chamberlain, limping on one foot, appeared undignified and storklike, also very sad and unhappy. Hugh was just admitting to himself that he might have to rely on Haplo when he saw the man, with a signal of his hand, send the dog forward.

Gliding across the floor of the vat, the animal came to Limbeck and thrust its muzzle in the Geg's hand. Limbeck started at the unexpected touch of the cold nose, and jerked his hand away. But the dog remained, looking up at him intently, the bushy tail slowly brushing from side to side. Limbeck's nearsighted gaze was drawn slowly and irresistibly from the dog to its master. Hugh glanced swiftly back at Haplo to see what message he was giving, but the man's face was mild and tranquil, with that quiet smile.

Limbeck's hand absently stroked the dog, his eyes fixed on Haplo. He sighed deeply.

"My dear?" Jarre touched him on the arm.

"The truth. And my speech. I must make my speech. I'm going, Jarre. And I'm counting on you and our people to help. And when I come back, when I've seen the Truth, then we'll start the revolution!"

Jarre recognized his stubborn tone, knew it was hopeless to argue. She wasn't certain she wanted to argue anyway. Part of her was stirred at the thought of what Limbeck was doing. It was the beginning of the revolution, really and truly. But he would be leaving her. She hadn't realized, until now, how much she truly loved him.

"I could come too," she offered.

"No, my dear." Limbeck gazed at her fondly. "It wouldn't do for both of us to be gone." He took a step forward, put his hands out to where it looked to his nearsighted eyes her shoulders were. Jarre, used to this, moved up to be right where he thought she was. "You must prepare the people for my return."

"I'll do it!"

The dog, afflicted by a sudden itch, sat down, scratching at its fur with a hind foot.

"You can teach her the song now, sir," said Alfred.

Alfred translating, Hugh gave Jarre his instructions, taught her the song, then bundled her back into the air shaft. Limbeck stood beneath it and, before she left, reached up to hold her hand.

"Thank you, my dear. This will be for the best. I know it!"

"Yes, I know it too."

To hide the trouble in her voice, Jarre leaned down and gave Limbeck a shy kiss on the cheek. She waved her hand to Alfred, who gave her a small solemn bow; then she hastily turned and began to climb through the air shaft.

Hugh and Haplo lifted the grille and put it back in place as best they could, hammering at it with their fists.

"Are you hurt very badly, Alfred?" asked Bane, struggling against sleepiness and an unwillingness to return to bed and possibly miss out on something.

"No, Your Highness, thank you for asking."

Bane nodded and yawned. "I think I'll just lie down, Alfred. Not to sleep, mind you, just to rest."

"Allow me to straighten your blankets, Your Highness." Alfred cast a swift sidelong glance over to Hugh and Haplo, pounding at the grille. "Might I trouble Your Highness with a question?"

Bane yawned until his jaws cracked. Eyelids drooping, he plopped down on the floor of the vat and said sleepily, "Sure."

"Your Highness"—Alfred lowered his voice, keeping his eyes fixed on the blanket that he was, as usual, clumsily twisting and knotting and doing everything but straightening—"when you look at that man Haplo, what do you see?"

"A man. Not very good-looking but not very ugly, not like Hugh. That Haplo's not very much of anything, if you ask me. Here, you're making a mess of that, as usual."

"No, Your Highness. I can manage." The chamberlain continued to maul the blanket. "About my question—that really wasn't what I meant, Your Highness." Alfred paused, licking his lips. He knew that this next question would undoubtedly start Bane thinking. Yet Alfred felt at this juncture he had no choice. He had to know the truth.

"What can you see with your . . . special vision?"

Bane's eyes widened, then narrowed, glistening with shrewdness and cunning. But the intelligence in them was gone so swiftly, masked by the bright gloss of innocence, that Alfred, if he had not seen it before, might not have believed he saw it then.

"Why do you ask, Alfred?"

"Just out of curiosity, Your Highness. Nothing more."

Bane regarded him speculatively, perhaps gauging how much more information he was likely to wheedle from the chamberlain, perhaps wondering whether he could gain more by telling the truth or lying or a judicious mixture of both.

Giving Haplo a wary sidelong glance, Bane leaned confidentially near to Alfred and said softly, "I can't see anything."

Alfred sat back on his heels, his careworn face drawn and troubled. He stared intently at Bane, trying to judge whether or not the child was sincere.

"Yes," continued Bane, taking the man's look for a question. "I can't see anything. And there's only one other person I've met who's the same—you, Alfred. What do you make of that?" The child gazed up at him with bright, shining eyes.

The blanket suddenly seemed to spread itself out, smooth and flat, without a wrinkle. "You can lie down now, Your Highness. We have, it seems, an exciting day tomorrow."

"I asked you a question, Alfred," said the prince, stretching out obediently.

"Yes, Your Highness. It must be coincidence. Nothing more."

"You're probably right, Alfred." Bane smiled sweetly and closed his eyes. The smile remained on his lips; he was inwardly enjoying some private joke.

Alfred, nursing his knee, decided that, as usual, he had made a mush of things. I gave Bane a clue to the truth. And against all express orders to the contrary, I took a being of another race into the Heart and the Brain and brought her back out again. But does it matter anymore? Does it really matter?

He couldn't help himself, his gaze went to Haplo, who was settling down for the night. Alfred knew the truth now, yet he resisted it. He told himself it was coincidence. The boy had not met every person in the world. There might be many whose past lives were not visible to him through the medium of his clairvoyance. The chamberlain watched Haplo lie down, saw him give the dog a pat, saw the dog take up a protective position at the man's side.

I have to find out. I must know for certain. Then my mind will be at rest. I can laugh at my fears.

Or prepare to face them.

No, stop thinking like that. Beneath the bandages, you will find sores, as he said.

Alfred waited. Limbeck and Hugh returned to their beds, Hugh casting a glance in Alfred's direction. The chamberlain pretended to sleep. The prince had drifted off, seemingly, but it might be well to make sure. Limbeck lay awake, staring up into the top of the vat, worrying, afraid, repeating to himself all his resolutions. Hugh leaned back against the vat's side. Taking out his pipe, he stuck it between his teeth and gazed moodily at nothing.

Alfred did not have much time. He propped himself on one elbow, keeping his shoulders hunched, his hand held close to his body, and faced Limbeck. Raising his index and middle fingers, Alfred drew a sigil in the air. Whispering the rune, he drew it again. Limbeck's eyelids lowered, opened, lowered, quivered, and finally shut. The Geg's breathing became even and regular. Turning slightly, keeping his movements smooth and stealthy, Alfred faced the assassin and drew the same sigil. Hugh's head dropped. The pipe slipped from between his teeth and fell into his lap. Alfred's gaze turned to Bane, and he made the same sign; if the child hadn't been asleep before this, he was now.

Then, facing Haplo, Alfred drew the rune and whispered the same words, only now with more concentration, more force.

The dog, of course, was most important. But if Alfred's suspicions were right about the animal, all would be well.

He forced himself to wait patiently a few more moments, letting the magical enchantment draw everyone down into deep sleep. No one moved. All was quiet.

Slowly and cautiously, Alfred crept to his feet. The spell was powerful; he might have run round the vat shouting and screaming, blowing horns and beating drums, and not a person there would have so much as blinked an eye. But his own irrational fears held him back, halted his steps. He sneaked forward, moving easily, without a limp, for he had been shamming the pain in his knee. But as slowly as he moved, the pain might have been real, the injury truly debilitating. His heart pulsed in his throat. Spots burst and danced in his eyes, obscuring his vision.

He forced himself on. The dog was asleep, its eyes closed, or he never would have succeeded in creeping up on its master. Not daring to breathe, fighting suffocating spasms in his chest, Alfred dropped to his knees beside the slumbering Haplo. He reached out a hand that shook so he could hardly guide it to where it must go, and he stopped and would have said a prayer had there been a god around to hear it. As it was, there was only himself.

He shoved aside the bandage that was wound tightly around Haplo's hand.

There were, as he had suspected, the runes.

Tears stung Alfred's eyes, blinding him. It took all his strength of will to draw the bandage back over the tattooed flesh so that the man would not notice it had been disturbed. Barely able to see where he was going, Alfred stumbled back to his blanket and hurled himself down. It seemed that he did not stop falling when his body touched the floor, but that he continued to fall and went spiraling down into a dark well of nameless horror.

CHAPTER ♦ 38

DEEPSKY,

ABOVE THE MAELSTROM

♦

THE CAPTAIN OF THE ELVEN SHIP *CARFA'SHON*[1] WAS A MEMBER OF THE royal family. Not a very important member, but a member nonetheless—a fact of which he himself was extraordinarily conscious and expected all others around him to be likewise. There was, however, one small matter of his royal blood that it was never wise to bring up, and this was an unfortunate relationship to Prince Reesh'ahn, the leader of the rebellion among the elves.

In the halcyon days of yore, the captain had been wont to state modestly that he was nothing less than a fifth cousin of the dashing young and handsome elven prince. Now, following Reesh'ahn's disgrace, Captain Zankor'el assured people that he was nothing more than a fifth cousin and that was stretching a cousin or two.

According to the manner and custom of all elven royalty, be they rich or poor, Captain Zankor'el served his people by working hard and energetically during his life. And, again in the manner and custom of those of royal lineage, he expected to continue serving them at the time of his death. The lords and ladies of the royal family are not allowed to slip peacefully into oblivion at their deaths. Their souls are captured before they can flutter away to spend days in eternal spring meadows. The royal

---

[1]Meaning, in elven, "at harmony with the elements."

souls are then held in stasis by the elven wizards, who draw upon the souls' energy to work their magic.

It is necessary, therefore, that wizards constantly attend the members of the royal family, ready at any time—day or night, in peace or during a raging battle—to grab up souls should death occur.[2] Wizards designated for such duty have a formal title, "weesham," by which they are referred to in polite society. Generally, however, they are known as "geir"—a word whose ancient meaning is "vulture."

The geir follow the royal elves from childhood to old age, never leaving them. A geir comes to the baby at his birth, watches his first steps, travels with him during the years of his schooling, sits beside the bed—even the bridal bed—every night, and attends him in the hour of his death.

Elven wizards who accept this duty that, to the elves, has become sacred, are carefully trained. They are encouraged to develop a close personal relationship with those over whom their wings spread a dark shadow. A geir is not allowed to marry, and thus the charge becomes his or her entire life, taking the place of husband, wife, and child. Since the geir are older than their charges—generally being in their twenties when they accept responsibility for infants—they frequently assume the additional roles of mentor and confidant. Many deep and abiding friendships grow between shadow and shadowed. In such instances, the geir often does not long outlive his charge, but delivers the soul to the Cathedral of the Albedo and then creeps away himself to die of grief.

And thus those of the royal family live, from birth on, with the constant reminder of their mortality hovering at their shoulders. They have come to be proud of the geir. The black-robed wizards mark royal status and symbolize to the elves that their leaders serve not only in life but also after death. The presence of the geir has the additional effect of increasing royal power. It is

---

[2]It is thought by some that the Order of the Kir Monks may have developed among humans as a corrupt form of the Elven Shadows. The Kir Monks, being a secret and closed organization, refuse to discuss their origins. Legend has it, however, that they were founded by a group of human wizards who were endeavoring to discover the secret of soul-capture. The wizards failed to achieve their goal, but the order they founded remained. Ordinary humans—those not possessing magical talents—were allowed to enter, and over the years, the monks gradually turned from the attempt to cheat death to a worship of it.

hard to refuse the elven king anything he wants with that dark-robed figure standing always at his side.

If the members of the royal family, particularly the younger members, are somewhat wild and foolhardy and live life with a devil-may-care attitude, it is understandable. Royal parties are often chaotic affairs. The wine flows freely and there is a frantic, hysterical edge to the merriment. A glittering, gaily dressed elf maiden dances and drinks and lacks for nothing that will give her joy, but, look where she will, she must see the geir standing, back to the wall, the geir's gaze never leaving the one whose life—and most important, death—is in the geir's trust.

The captain of the elven watership had his attendant geir, and it must be admitted that there were those aboard who wished the captain's geir godspeed in his work; the majority of those serving the captain expressing (quietly) the opinion that the captain's soul would be far more valuable to the elven king-dom if it was no longer attached to the captain's body.

Tall, slender, and handsome, Captain Zankor'el had a great personal regard for himself and none at all for those who had the distinct misfortune not to be of high rank, not to be of royal birth, and—in short—not to be him.

"Captain."

"Lieutenant." This was always spoken with a slight sneer.

"We are entering the Maelstrom."

"Thank you, lieutenant, but I am not blind, nor am I as stupid as perhaps was your last, late captain. Having seen the storm clouds, I was able to deduce almost instantly that we were in a storm. If you like, you may go pass the word around to the rest of the crew, who may, perhaps, not have noticed."

The lieutenant stiffened, his fair-skinned face flushed a deli-cate crimson. "May I respectfully remind the captain that it is my duty by law to inform him that we have entered dangerous skies?"

"You may remind him if you like, but I wouldn't, for he finds you to be teetering on the edge of insubordination," returned the captain, gazing out the portals of the dragonship, a spyglass to his eye. "Now, go below and take charge of the slaves. That is one duty, at least, you are fit for." These last words were not spoken aloud but, by the captain's tone, they were implied. The lieutenant—and everyone else on the bridge—heard them quite clearly.

"Very good, sir," responded Lieutenant Bothar'in. The crimson had drained from his face, leaving him livid with suppressed anger.

None of the other crew members dared catch the lieutenant's eye. It was absolutely unheard-of for the second in command to be sent down to the galley during a descent. The captain himself always took this hazardous duty, for control of the wings was essential to the ship's safety. It was a dangerous place to be during a descent—their former captain had lost his life down there. But a good captain placed the safety of ship and crew above his own, and the elven crew—seeing their lieutenant descend into the galley, their captain remaining at ease up top— could not forbear exchanging dark looks.

The dragonship dipped down into the storm. The winds began to buffet it about. Lightning flared, partially blinding them; thunder roared, nearly deafening them. Down below, the human galley slaves, wearing the body harnesses that connected them by cables to the wings, fought and wrestled to keep the ship upright and flying through the storm. The wings had been pulled in as far as possible to lessen the magic in order for them to descend. But the wings could not be drawn in completely, or else the magic would cease to work completely and they would plummet down, out of control, to crash upon Drevlin below. A delicate balance had to be maintained, therefore—not a difficult task in fair, clear weather but extremely difficult in the midst of a raging storm.

"Where's the captain?" demanded the overseer.

"I'm taking over down here," answered the lieutenant.

The overseer took one look at the lieutenant's pale, tense face, the clenched jaw and tightly drawn lips, and understood.

"It probably ain't proper to say this, sir, but I'm glad you're here and he ain't."

"No, it is *not* proper to say that, overseer," replied the lieutenant, taking up his position in the front of the galley.

The overseer wisely said nothing more. He and the ship's wizard, whose job it was to maintain the magic, glanced at each other. The wizard shrugged slightly; the overseer shook his head. Then both went about their business, which was critical enough to demand their full and complete attention.

Up above, Captain Zankor'el stood spread-legged, braced upon the heaving deck, staring through his spyglass down into the swirling mass of black clouds. His geir sat on a deck chair beside him; the wizard—green with sickness and terror—clung for dear life to anything he could get his hands on.

"There, weesham, I believe I can see the Liftalofts. Just a glimpse, in the eye of those swirling clouds." He offered the spyglass. "Do you want to take a look?"

"May the souls of your ancestors forbid!" said the wizard, shuddering. It was bad enough he had to travel in this frail and fragile contraption of skin and wood and magic, without having to look at where he was going. "What was that?"

The wizard reared up his head in alarm, his sharply pointed, beardless chin quivering. A crash had sounded from below. The ship listed suddenly, throwing the captain off his feet.

"Damn that Bothar'in!" Zankor'el swore. "I'll have him brought up on charges!"

"If he's still alive," gasped the pale-faced wizard.

"He better hope for his sake he isn't," snarled the captain, picking himself up.

Swift glances flashed about the crew, and one rash young elf actually opened his mouth to speak, but was nudged in the ribs by a fellow crewman. The midshipman swallowed his mutinous words.

For a terrifying instant the ship seemed to be out of control and at the mercy of the swirling wind. It plunged down sickeningly, was caught by a gust, and nearly flipped over. An updraft swept it high, then dropped it again. The captain screamed curses and contradictory orders in the direction of the galley, but took care never to leave the safety of the bridge. The geir crouched on the deck and seemed, by the expression on his face, to wish he had gone into another line of work.

At last the ship righted itself and sailed into the heart of the Maelstrom, where it was peaceful and calm and the sun shone, making the swirling clouds around it that much blacker and more threatening by contrast. Down below, on Drevlin, the Liftalofts winked brightly in the sunshine.

Having been purposefully built by the Mangers to be always directly in the eye of the ever-raging storm, the Liftalofts were the one place on the continent where the Gegs could look up and see the sparkling firmament and feel the warmth of the sun. Small wonder that, to the Gegs, this was a sacred and holy place, made even holier by the monthly descent of the "Welves."

After a brief interval, during which breath came easier and color returned to pale faces, the lieutenant made his appearance on the bridge. The rash young midshipman actually had the temerity to let out a cheer, which brought a baleful look from the captain, letting the young elf know that he wasn't likely to be a midshipman much longer.

"Well, what havoc have you wreaked down there, besides nearly killing us all?" demanded the captain.

Blood trickled down the lieutenant's face, his fair hair was clotted and matted with red, and his cheeks were ashen, his eyes dark with pain. "One of the cables snapped, sir. The right wing slid out. We have jury-rigged a new cable now, sir, and all is under control."

Not a word said about being slammed down onto the deck, about standing side by side with a human slave, both fighting desperately to drag the wing back in and save all their lives. No words were needed. The experienced crew knew of the life-and-death struggle that had been waged below their feet. Perhaps the captain knew too, despite the fact that he had never previously commanded a ship, or perhaps he saw it reflected in the faces of his crew. He did not launch into a tirade against the lieutenant's incompetence but said only, "Were any of the beasts[3] killed?"

The lieutenant's face darkened. "One human is very seriously injured, sir—the slave whose cable snapped. He was dragged off his feet and hurled into the hull. The cable wrapped around him, nearly cutting him in two before we could free him."

"But he's not dead?" The captain raised a finely plucked eyebrow.

"No, sir. The ship's wizard is treating him now."

"Nonsense! Waste of time. Toss him overboard. There's plenty more where he came from."

"Yes, sir," said the lieutenant, his eyes fixed on a point somewhere to the left of his captain's shoulder.

Once again, the almond eyes of the elven crew slid glances at each other. In all honesty, it must be admitted that none of them had any love for their human slaves. There was a certain amount of grudging respect for the humans, however, not to mention the fact that the crew perversely decided to like anyone their captain didn't. Everyone on the bridge—including Zankor'el himself— knew that the lieutenant had no intention of carrying out that order.

---

[3]A term used by elves to denote humans.

The ship was nearing its point of rendezvous with the Lifeline. Captain Zankor'el did not have time to make an issue of this now, nor could he really do so except to go below and personally see to it that his order was obeyed. To do that would lessen his dignity, however, and he might get blood on his uniform.

"That will be all, lieutenant. Return to your duties," said the captain, and, spyglass in hand, he turned to look out the portals, gazing upward to see if the waterpipe was in sight. But he had neither forgotten nor forgiven the lieutenant.

"I'll have his head for this," muttered Zankor'el to his geir, who merely nodded, closed his eyes, and thought about being violently ill.

The waterpipe was at last descried, descending from the sky, and the elven ship took up its position as guide and escort. The pipe was ancient, having been built by the Sartan when they first brought the survivors of the Sundering to Arianus, whose water was plentiful in the Low Realm but lacking on the realms above. The pipe was made of metal that never rusted. The alloy remained a mystery to the elven alchemists, who had spent centuries trying to reproduce it. Operated by a gigantic mechanism, the pipe dropped down a shaft that ran through the continent of Aristagon. Once every month, automatically, the pipe descended through Deepsky to the continent of Drevlin.

Although the pipe was capable of lowering itself, an elven ship was necessary to guide the waterpipe down to the Liftalofts, where it had to be connected to a huge waterspout. When the two were hooked up, the Kicksey-winsey, receiving some sort of mysterious signal, automatically turned on the water. A combination of magical and mechanical forces sent the liquid shooting up the pipe. Up above, on Aristagon, elves guided the flow into vast holding tanks.

Following the Sundering, elves and humans had dwelt in peace on Aristagon and the surrounding isles. Under the guidance of the Sartan, the races shared equally in the life-giving substance. But when the Sartan disappeared, their fond dream of peace shattered. The humans claimed the war was the fault of the elves, who had fallen increasingly under the control of a powerful faction of wizards. The elves claimed it was the fault of the humans, who were notoriously warlike and barbaric.

The elves, with their longer livespans, larger population, and knowledge of magical mechanics, had proved the stronger. They drove the humans from Aristagon—the Mid Realm source for water. The humans, with the aid of the dragons, fought back, raiding elven towns and stealing water or attacking the elven waterships that ferried the precious liquid to neighboring elven-held isles.

A watership such as the one flown by Captain Zankor'el carried on board eight huge casks made of rare oak (obtained from only the Sartan knew where) and bound by bands of steel. On an isle-run, the ship held the water in these casks. On this trip, however, the casks were filled with the junk that the elves gave as payment[4] to the Gegs.

The elves cared nothing about the Gegs. Humans were beasts. The Gegs were insects.

---

[4]Every month all the rubbish accumulated throughout the elven lands is transported by tier-drawn carts to the harbor. Here it is loaded on board the ship and sent down to reward the faithful, long-suffering Gegs without whom those in the Mid Realm would not long survive.

CHAPTER ◆ 39

WOMBE, DREVLIN,

LOW REALM

◆

THE SARTAN BUILT THE KICKSEY-WINSEY; NO ONE KNOWS WHY OR HOW. Elven wizards did an intensive study on the machine years ago and came up with a lot of theories but no answers. The Kicksey-winsey had something to do with the world, but what? The pumping of water to the higher realms was important, certainly, but it was obvious to the wizards that such a feat could have been accomplished by a much smaller and less complicated (albeit less marvelous) magical machine.

Of all the constructions of the Sartan, the Liftalofts were the most impressive, mysterious, and inexplicable. Nine gigantic arms, made of brass and steel, thrust up out of the coralite—some of them soaring several menka into the air. Atop each arm was an enormous hand whose thumb and fingers were made of gold with brass hinges at each of the joints and at the wrist. The hands were visible to the descending elven ships and it was obvious to all who saw them that the wrists and fingers—which were large enough to have grasped one of the enormous waterships and held it in a golden palm—were movable.

What were the hands designed to do? Had they done it? Would they do it still? It seemed unlikely. All but one of the hands drooped in limp stiffness, like those of a corpse. The only hand that possessed any life belonged to an arm shorter than all the rest. It stood in a vast circle of arms surrounding an open area corresponding roughly in size to the circumference of the eye of the storm. The short arm was located near the waterspout. Its hand was spread flat, the fingers together, the palm facing upward, forming a perfect platform on which any so inclined could stand. The interior of the arm was hollow with a shaft running up the center. A doorway at the base of the arm allowed entrance, and hundreds of stairs, spiraling upward around the center shaft, permitted those with long wind and strong legs to ascend to the top.

Apart from the stairs, an ornately carved golden door led into the shaft within the arm, and the Gegs had a legend which told that any who entered this door would be whisked to the top with the speed and force of the water that shot up out of the geyser. Thus the Geg name for the contraptions—Liftaloft—though no Geg in current memory had ever been known to dare open the golden door.

Here, on this arm, every month, the high froman and the head clark and such other Gegs deemed worthy gathered to greet the Welves and receive their payment for services rendered. All the Gegs of the city of Wombe and those making pilgrimages from neighboring sectors in Drevlin ventured out into the raging storm to gather around the base of the arms, watching and waiting for the monna, as it was known, to fall from heaven. Gegs were frequently injured during this ceremony, for there was no telling what might drop out of the barrels of the Welf ships. (An overstuffed velvet sofa with claw legs had once wiped out an entire family.) But all the Gegs agreed it was worth the risk.

This morning's ceremony was particularly well-attended, word having gone out among the newssingers and over the squawky-talk that Limbeck and his gods-who-weren't were going to be given to gods-who-were—the Welves. The high froman, expecting trouble, was considerably disconcerted when there wasn't any. The crowd that hastened across the coralite in a break during one of the storms was quiet and orderly—too quiet, thought the high froman, slogging through the puddles.

Beside him marched the head clark—his face a picture of self-righteous indignation. Behind him were the gods-who-weren't, taking this rather well, considering. They, too, were silent, even the troublemaker Limbeck. At least he appeared subdued and grave, giving the high froman the satisfaction of thinking that at last the rebellious youth had learned his lesson.

The arms could just be seen through the break in the scudding clouds, the steel and brass gleaming in the sunlight that shone only on this one place in all of Drevlin. Haplo gazed at them in undisguised wonder.

"What in the name of creation are those?"

Bane, too, was staring at them openmouthed and wide-eyed. Briefly Hugh explained what he knew of them—which was what he'd heard from the elves and amounted to almost nothing.

"You understand now why it's so frustrating," said Limbeck, roused out of his worries, staring almost angrily at the Liftaloft glistening on the horizon. "I know that if we Gegs put our minds together and analyzed the Kicksey-winsey, we could understand the why and the how. But they won't do it. They simply won't do it."

He irritably kicked a bit of loose coralite and sent it spinning across the ground. The dog, in high spirits, went chasing after it, leaping and bounding gleefully through the puddles and causing the coppers surrounding the prisoners to cast it wary, nervous glances.

"A 'why' is a dangerous thing," said Haplo. "It challenges old, comfortable ways; forces people to think about what they do instead of just mindlessly doing it. No wonder your people are afraid of it."

"I think the danger is not so much in asking the 'why' as in believing you have come up with the only answer," said Alfred, seeming almost to be talking to himself.

Haplo heard him and thought it a strange statement to come from a human, but then, this Alfred was a strange human. The chamberlain's gaze no longer darted to the Patryn's bandaged hands. Instead, he seemed to avoid looking at them and to avoid looking at Haplo if at all possible. Alfred appeared to have aged during the night. Lines of anxiety had deepened, smudges of purple discolored the folds of puffy skin beneath his eyes. He obviously had not slept much, if at all. Not unusual, perhaps, for a man facing a battle for his life in the morning.

Haplo tugged reflexively at the bandages, making certain the telltale sigla tattooed on his flesh were covered. But he was forced to wonder, as he did so, why it now seemed suddenly an empty, wasted gesture.

"Don't worry, Limbeck," shouted Bane, forgetting that they were walking out of range of the thumping and bumping of the great machine. "When we get to my father, the mysteriarch, he'll have all the answers!"

Hugh didn't know what the kid said, but he saw Limbeck

wince and look around fearfully at the guards, and saw the guards stare suspiciously at the prince and his companions. Obviously His Highness had said something he shouldn't. Where the hell was Alfred? He was supposed to be watching the kid.

Turning, he thumped Alfred in the arm and, when the man looked up, Hugh gestured toward Bane. The chamberlain blinked at Hugh as if wondering for a moment who he was, then understood. Hurrying forward, slipping and stumbling, his feet going in directions one would not have thought humanly possible, Alfred reached Bane's side and, to divert the boy's attention, began answering His Highness's questions about the steel arms.

Unfortunately, Alfred's mind was intent on last night's horrendous discovery, not on what he was saying. Bane was intent on making a discovery of his own, and using the chamberlain's unthinking answers, he was drawing very near it.

Jarre and the WUPP's marched behind the coppers, who marched behind the prisoners. Hidden beneath cloaks and shawls and long flowing beards were thunderers, jingers, a smattering of toots, and here and there a wheezy-wail.[1] At a meeting of the WUPP's called hurriedly and in secret late last night, Jarre had taught the song. Being a musical race—the newssingers had been keeping the Gegs informed for centuries—the WUPP's learned quickly and easily. They took it home and sang it to wives, children, and trustworthy neighbors, who also picked it up. No one was quite certain why they were singing this particular song. Jarre had been rather vague on this point, being uncertain herself.

Rumor had it that this was the way Welves and humans fought—they sang and tooted and jingled at each other. When the Welves were defeated (and they could be defeated, since they weren't immortal), they would be forced to grant the Gegs more treasure.

Jarre, when she heard this rumor spreading among the WUPP's, didn't deny it. It was, after all, sort of the truth.

Marching along toward the Lofts, the WUPP's appeared so eager and excited that Jarre was certain the coppers must be able to see their plans gleaming brightly in the flashing eyes and smug smiles (to say nothing of the fact that those carrying instruments jingled and rattled and occasionally wailed in a most

---

[1]Known to humans as bagpipes.

mysterious manner). There was, the Gegs felt, a certain amount of justice in disrupting this ceremony. These monthly rituals with the Welves were symbolic of their slavish treatment of the Gegs. Those Gegs who lived in Drevlin (mostly of the high froman's own scrift) were the ones who consistently received the monthly monna, and though the high froman insisted that all Gegs could come and share in it, he knew as well as the rest of Drevlin that the Gegs were bound to the Kicksey-winsey and that only a few—and then mostly clarks—could leave their servitude long enough to bask in the Welven eyes and share in the Welven monna. The Gegs, highly elated, marched to battle, their weapons jangling and ringing and wheezing in their hands.

Marching along, Jarre recalled the instructions she had given them.

"When the humans begin to sing, we swarm up the stairs, singing at the top of our lungs. Limbeck will make a speech—"

Scattered applause.

"—then he and the gods-who-aren't will enter the ship—"

"We want the ship!" cried several WUPP's.

"No, you don't," answered Jarre crossly. "You want the reward. We're going to get the monna this time. All of it."

Tumultuous applause.

"The high froman won't come back with so much as a hand-knit doily! Limbeck is going to take the ship and sail away to upper worlds, where he will learn the Truth, and come back to proclaim it and free his people!"

No applause. After the promise of treasure (particularly knit doilies, currently much in demand), no one cared about Truth. Jarre understood this and it saddened her, because she knew it would sadden Limbeck if he ever found out.

Thinking about Limbeck, she had gradually moved forward through the crowd until she was walking right behind him. Her shawl thrown over her head so that no one would recognize her, she kept her eyes and her thoughts fixed on Limbeck.

Jarre wanted to go with him—at least she told herself she did. But she hadn't argued very hard and had fallen silent completely when Limbeck told her she must stay behind and lead the movement in his absence.

In reality, Jarre was afraid. She had, it seemed, peeked through a crack and caught a glimpse of Truth down there in the tunnels with Alfred. Truth wasn't something you went out and found. It was wide and vast and deep and unending, and all you could hope to see was a tiny part of it. And to see that part and to mistake it for the whole was to make of Truth a lie.

But Jarre had promised. She couldn't let Limbeck down, not when this meant so much to him. And then there were her people—living a lie. Surely even a little of the Truth would help and not hurt them.

The Gegs marching around Jarre talked about what they would do with their share of the reward. Jarre was silent, her eyes on Limbeck, wondering if she was hoping they'd succeed or fail.

The high froman reached the door at the base of the arm. Turning to the head clark, he formally accepted a large key, nearly as big as his hand, which he used to open the opener.

"Bring the prisoners," he called, and the coppers herded everyone forward.

"Mind that dog!" snapped the head clark, kicking at the animal sniffing with intense interest at his feet.

Haplo called the dog to his side. The high froman, the head clark, several of the high froman's personal guard, and the prisoners crowded into the Liftaloft. At the last moment, Limbeck halted in the door and turned, his eyes scanning the crowd. Catching sight of Jarre, he looked at her long and earnestly. His expression was calm and resolute. He wasn't wearing his spectacles, but she had the feeling he could see her quite clearly.

Jarre, blinking back her tears, raised one hand in loving farewell. Her other hand, hidden beneath her cloak, clutched her weapon—a tambourine.

CHAPTER ♦ 40

THE LIFTALOFTS, DREVLIN,

LOW REALM

♦

"Captain," reported the lieutenant, peering at the ground below, "there are an unusual number of Gegs waiting for us on the Palm."

"They're not Gegs, lieutenant," said the captain, spyglass to his eyes. "They appear from the looks of them to be human."

"Human!" The lieutenant stared down at the Palm. His hands itched to snatch the spyglass away from his captain and see for himself.

"What do you make of it, lieutenant?" inquired the captain.

"Trouble, I should think, sir. I've served on this run a number of years, and my father served before me, and I've never heard of humans being found on the Low Realm. I might suggest—" The lieutenant caught himself and bit his tongue.

"Might suggest?" repeated Captain Zankor'el in a dangerous tone. "You *might suggest* to your captain? What might you suggest, lieutenant?"

"Nothing, sir. I was out of line."

"No, no, lieutenant, I insist," returned Zankor'el, with a glance at the geir.

"I might suggest that we do not dock until we find out what's going on."

This was a perfectly reasonable and logical suggestion, as Captain Zankor'el well knew. But it would mean discussion with the Gegs, and Zankor'el couldn't speak a word of Geg. The lieutenant could. Captain Zankor'el immediately came to the conclusion that this was just another trick of the lieutenant's to

make a mockery of him—Captain Zankor'el of the royal family—
in the eyes of the crew. The lieutenant had done so once already,
with his damn-fool heroics. The captain decided he would see
his soul in that small lapis-and-chalcedony-inlaid box the geir
carried with him at all times before he'd let that happen again.

"I didn't know you were quite so afraid of humans, lieutenant," responded the captain. "I cannot have a frightened man at
my side going into what might be a dangerous situation. Report
to your quarters, Lieutenant Bothar'in, and remain there for the
duration of the voyage. I'll deal with the beasts."

Stunned silence settled over the bridge. No one knew where
to look and so avoided looking at anything. A charge of cowardice leveled against an elven officer meant death once they returned to Aristagon. The lieutenant could speak in his own
defense at the Tribunal, certainly. But his only defense would be
to denounce his captain—a member of the royal family. Whom
would the judges believe?

Lieutenant Bothar'in's face was rigid, his almond eyes unblinking. A subdued midshipman said later that he'd seen dead
men look more alive.

"As you command, sir." The lieutenant turned on his heel
and left the bridge.

"Cowardice—a thing I won't tolerate!" intoned Captain
Zankor'el. "You men remember that."

"Yes, sir," was the dazed and halfhearted response from
men who had served under their lieutenant in several battles
against both humans and rebel elves and who knew, better than
anyone, Bothar'in's courage.

"Pass the word for the ship's wizard," commanded the captain, staring through the spyglass at the small group gathered in
the palm of the gigantic hand.

The word went out for the ship's wizard, who appeared
immediately. Slightly flustered, he glanced around the group on
the bridge as if endeavoring to ascertain if a rumor he'd heard on
his way forward was true. No one looked at him, no one dared.
No one needed to. Seeing the set faces and fixed eyes, the ship's
wizard had his answer.

"We're facing an encounter with humans, Magicka."[1] The

---

[1]Humans borrowed this word from the elven.

captain spoke in a bland voice, as if nothing was amiss. "I assume that all aboard have been issued whistles?"

"Yes, captain."

"All are familiar with their use?"

"I believe so, sir," replied the ship's wizard. "The ship's last engagement was with a group of rebel elves who boarded us—"

"I did not ask for a recitation of this vessel's war record, did I, Magicka?" inquired Captain Zankor'el.

"No, captain."

The ship's wizard did not apologize. Unlike the crew, he was not bound to obey the orders of a ship's officer. Since only a wizard could possibly understand the proper use of his arcane art, each wizard was made responsible for the magic aboard ship. A captain dissatisfied with the work of his ship's wizard might bring the wizard up on charges, but the wizard would be tried by the Council of the Arcane, not by the Naval Tribunal. And, in such a trial, it would not matter if the captain was a member of the royal family. Everyone knew who were the true rulers of Aristagon.

"The magic is functional?" pursued the captain. "Fully operational?"

"The crew members have but to put the whistles to their lips." The ship's wizard drew himself up, stared down his nose at the captain. The magus did not even add the customary "sir." His talent was being questioned.

The geir, a wizard himself, could see that Zankor'el had overstepped his authority.

"And you have done quite well, ship's wizard," intervened the geir in soft, oily tones. "I will be certain to pass on my commendation when we return home."

The ship's wizard sneered. As if it mattered to him what a geir thought of his work! Spending their lives running after spoiled brats in hopes of catching a soul. One might as well be a servant running after a pug dog in hopes of catching its droppings!

"Will you join us on the bridge?" asked the captain politely, taking the hint from his geir.

The ship's wizard had no intention of being anywhere else. This was his assigned station during battle, and though in this instance the captain was perfectly correct in making the invitation, the wizard chose to take it as an insult.

"Of course," he stated in clipped and icy tones and, stalking over to the portals, glared out at the Palm and its contingent of

Gegs and humans. "I believe we should make contact with the Gegs and find out what is going on," he added.

Did the ship's wizard know that this had been the lieutenant's suggestion? Did he know that this had precipitated the current crisis? The captain, thin cheeks flushing, glared at him. The ship's wizard, his back turned, did not notice. The captain opened his mouth, but catching sight of his geir shaking his head warningly, snapped it shut again.

"Very well!" Zankor'el was making an obvious effort to contain his anger. Hearing a noise behind him, he whipped around and fixed a baleful eye on the crew, but everyone was apparently engrossed in his duties.

The ship's wizard, bowing stiffly, took up a position in the prow, standing in front of the figurehead. Before him was a speaking cone carved out of the tooth of a grenko.[2] Across one end of this tooth was stretched a diaphragm made of the tier skin and magically enhanced to project a voice spoken into it. The sound boomed forth from the dragon's open mouth and was quite impressive even to those who knew how it worked. The Gegs considered it a miracle.

Bending near the cone, the wizard shouted out something in the uncouth language of the dwarves that sounds to elves like rocks being rattled in the bottom of a barrel. The captain maintained a rigid, stony-faced posture during the entire proceeding, expressing by his attitude that it was all errant nonsense.

From down below came a great squawking bellow—the Gegs were answering. The elven wizard listened and replied. Turning, he faced the captain.

"It is all rather confusing. As near as I can make out, it seems that these humans have come to Drevlin and told the Gegs that we 'Welves' are not gods but slavers, who have been exploiting the dwarves. The Geg king asks that we accept the humans as his gift and that, in return, we do something to reestablish our-

---

[2]Difficult to find, the grenko are large and savage beasts much prized for their teeth. Because of the animal's rarity, they are protected from hunting by strict elven law. Grenko shed their teeth annually. The teeth can be found strewn about the floor of any grenko cave. The challenge in gathering the teeth lies in the fact that the grenko leaves its cave only once yearly to go in search of a mate, and generally returns within a day's timespan. Highly intelligent, with a keen sense of smell, grenko will instantly attack anything found in their caves.

selves as divine. He suggests," the wizard added, "doubling the usual amount of treasure."

The elf captain had regained his good humor. "Human prisoners!" He rubbed his hands in satisfaction. "What's more, prisoners who have obviously been attempting to sabotage our water supply. What a valuable find! I shall be decorated for this. Inform the Gegs that we will be happy to comply."

"What about the treasure?"

"Bah! They'll get the same as usual. What do they expect? We don't carry more."

"We could promise to send another ship," stated the wizard, frowning.

The captain's face flushed. "If I made such an agreement, I'd be the laughingstock of the navy! Risk a ship to deliver more treasure to these maggots? Hah!"

"Sir, nothing like this has ever before occurred. It appears to me that the humans have discovered a way to descend safely through the Maelstrom and are endeavoring to disrupt Geg society to their own advantage. If the humans *could* manage to take control of our water supply . . ." The wizard shook his head, mere words apparently being unable to convey the seriousness of the situation.

"Disrupt Geg society!" Zankor'el laughed. "I'll disrupt their society! I'll go down and take control of their stupid society. It's what we should have done long ago anyway. Tell the grubs we'll take the prisoners off their hands. That should be enough for them."

The ship's wizard glowered, but there was nothing he could do—for the moment, at least. He could not authorize the sending of a treasure ship and he dared not make a promise that he could not keep. That would only make matters worse. He could, however, report this immediately to the Council and advise that action be taken—in regard to both the treasure and this imbecile captain.

Speaking into the cone, the wizard couched the refusal in vague and obscure terms intended to make it sound like an agreement unless anyone actually thought about it. Like most elves, he considered the Geg mental process to be tantamount to the sound of their language—rocks rattling around in a barrel.

The watership glided down on widespread wings, looking fearsome and majestic. Elven crew members, wielding spars, stood out on the deck and carefully pulled and pushed the

descending waterpipe into place above the geyser. When align-
ment was achieved, the magic was activated. Encased in a con-
duit of blue light that beamed up from the ground, water shot
forth and was sucked into the pipe and carried thousands of
menka above to the elves waiting for it on Aristagon. Once this
process was begun, the elven ship had completed its primary
task. When the holding tanks were full to capacity, the magical
flow of water would cease and the waterpipe would be drawn
back up. The watership could now drop its treasure and return,
or, as in this case, dock and spend a few moments impressing
the Gegs.

CHAPTER • 41

THE LIFTALOFTS, DREVLIN,

LOW REALM

◆

THE HIGH FROMAN DIDN'T LIKE IT—ANY OF IT. HE DIDN'T LIKE THE FACT that the prisoners were taking this much too docilely. He didn't like the words that the Welves were dropping on his head instead of more treasure. He didn't like the occasional musical note that emanated from the crowd below the Palm.

Watching the ship, the high froman thought he had never seen one move so slowly. He could hear the creaking of the cable drawing the gigantic wings inside the huge body, thus speeding the ship's descent, but it wasn't fast enough for Darral Longshoreman. Once these gods and Mad Limbeck were gone, life, he fondly hoped, would return to normal. If he could just get through the next few moments.

The ship settled into place, its wings trimmed so that it maintained enough magic to keep it afloat in the air, hovering near the Palm. The cargo bays opened and the monna fell onto the Gegs waiting below. A few of the Gegs began to clamor for it as it fell, those with keen eyes and good monetary sense latching onto the valuable pieces. But most of the Gegs ignored it. They remained standing, staring up at the top of the arm in tense, eager, (jingling) expectation.

"Hurry, hurry!" muttered the high froman.

The opening of the hatch took an interminable length of time. The head clark, oblivious of everything, was regarding the dragonship with his usual insufferable expression of self-righteousness. Darral longed to shove that expression (along with his teeth) down his brother-in-law's throat.

"Here they come!" The head clark chattered excitedly. "Here they come." Whipping around, he fixed a stern eye upon the prisoners. "Mind you treat the Welves with respect. They, at least, are gods!"

"Oh, we will!" piped up Bane with a sweet smile. "We're going to sing them a song."

"Hush, Your Highness, please!" remonstrated Alfred, laying a hand on Bane's shoulder. He added something in human that the high froman could not understand, and drew the boy back, out of the way. Out of the way of what?

And what was this nonsense about a song?

The high froman didn't like it. He didn't like it one bit.

The hatch opened and the gangway slid out from the bulwarks and was fixed firmly to the fingertips of the Palm. The elf captain emerged. Standing in the hatchway, surveying the objects before him, the elf appeared enormous in the ornately decorated iron suit that covered the thin body from toe to neck. His face could not be seen; a helmet shaped like the head of a dragon protected his head. Slung from his shoulder was a ceremonial sword encased in a jeweled scabbard that hung from a belt of frayed embroidered silk.

Seeing that all appeared in order, the elf clunked ponderously across the gangway, the scabbard rattling against his thigh when he walked. He reached the fingers of the Palm, stopped and stood gazing about, the dragon's-head helm lending him a stern and imperious air. The iron suit added an additional foot of height to the elf, who was already tall. He towered over the Gegs and over the humans as well. The helmet was so cunningly and fearsomely carved that even Gegs who had seen it before were awed. The head clark sank to his knees.

But the high froman was too nervous to be impressed.

"No time for that now," snapped Darral Longshoreman, reaching out to grab hold of his brother-in-law and get him back on his feet. "Coppers, bring the gods!"

"Damn!" swore Hugh beneath his breath.

"What is it?" Haplo leaned near.

The captain had clanked his way onto the fingers. The head clark had dropped to his knees and the high froman was tugging at him. Limbeck was fumbling with a sheaf of papers.

"The elf. See that thing he's wearing around his neck? It's a whistle."

"So?"

"Their wizards created it. Supposedly, when the elves blow into it, the sound it makes can magically negate the effects of the song!"

"Which means the elves will fight."

"Yes." Hugh cursed himself. "I knew warriors carried them, but not watership crews! And nothing to fight with except our bare hands and one dagger!"

Nothing. And everything. Haplo needed no weapon. Rip the bandages from his hands, and by his magic alone he could destroy every elf on board that ship or charm them to do his will or send them into enchanted slumber. But he was forbidden to make use of his magic. The first sigil whose fiery blaze he traced in the air would proclaim him a Patryn—the ancient enemy who had long ago very nearly conquered the ancient world.

Death first, before you betray us. You have the discipline and the courage to make that choice. You have the skill and the wits to make that choice unnecessary.

The high froman was ordering the coppers to bring the gods. The coppers started toward Limbeck, who firmly and politely elbowed them out of the way. Stepping forward, he rustled his papers and drew in a deep breath.

"Distinguished visitors from another realm. High Froman, Head Clark. My fellow WUPP's. It gives me great pleasure—"

"At least we'll die fighting," said Hugh. "With elves, that's something."

Haplo didn't have to die fighting. He didn't have to die at all. He hadn't expected it would be this frustrating.

The squawky-talk, designed to loudly transmit the blessings of the Welves, was now loudly transmitting Limbeck's speech.

"Shut him up!" shouted the high froman.

"—throw up your hackles. No, that can't be right." Limbeck stopped. Peering at the paper, he took out his spectacles and put them over his ears. "Throw off your shackles!" he shouted, now that he could see. The coppers surged forward, grabbed him by the arms.

"Start singing!" Haplo hissed. "I've got an idea!"

Hugh opened his mouth and began to boom out in a deep baritone the first notes of the song. Bane joined in, his shrill voice soaring above Hugh's in an ear-piercing shriek, heedless of tune, but never missing a word. Alfred's voice quavered, almost unheard; the man was pale as bleached bone with fear, and appeared on the verge of collapse.

> The Hand that holds the Arc and Bridge,
> The Fire that rails the Temp'red Span . . .

At the first note, the Gegs below let out a cheer and, grabbing their weapons, began to toot and jingle and wheeze and sing with all their might. The coppers above heard the singing below and became flustered and distracted. The elven captain, hearing the notes of the dreaded song, grasped the whistle that hung from around his neck, raised the visor of the helm, and put the whistle to his lips.

Haplo touched the dog lightly on the head, made a sweeping gesture with his hand, and pointed at the elf. "Take him."

> All Flame as Heart, surmount the Ridge,
> All noble Paths are *Ellxman*.

Sleek and swift and silent as a thrown spear, the dog cut through the tangled crowd and leapt straight at the elf.

The elven iron suit was ancient and archaic, designed primarily to intimidate, a remnant of olden days when such suits had to be worn as protection against the painful affliction known as "the bends" that struck those sailing swiftly up from the Low Realm to realms far above. By the time the elf captain saw the dog, it was airborne, aiming straight toward him. Instinctively he tried to brace himself for the blow, but his body, encased in the clumsy armor, could not react fast enough. The dog hit him square in the chest and the captain toppled over backward like a felled tree.

Haplo was on the move with the dog, Hugh not far behind. There was no song on the Patryn's lips. The assassin was singing loudly enough for both.

> Fire in Heart guides the Will,
> The Will of Flame, set by Hand,

"Servers unite!" shouted Limbeck, shaking off the annoying coppers. Immersed in his speech, he paid no attention to the chaos around him. "I, myself, ascending to the realms above, there to discover Truth, the most valuable of treasures—"

"Treasures . . ." echoed the squawky-talk.

"Treasure?" The Gegs standing below the Palm looked at each other. "He said treasure. They're giving more away! Up there! Up there!"

The Gegs, still singing, surged toward the door in the base of the arm. A few coppers had been detailed to guard the entrance, but they were overwhelmed by the mob (one was later discovered lying comatose, a tambourine around his neck). The singing Gegs raced up the stairs.

The Hand that moves *Ellxman* Song,
The Song of Fire and Heart and Land . . .

The first Gegs surged through the door at the top of the arm and dashed out onto the base of the golden Palm. The Palm's surface was slippery from the spray of the water shooting into the air. The Gegs slid and slithered and came precariously near hurtling over the edge. Hastening forward, the coppers attempted to stop them, trying without success to herd them back down the stairs. Darral Longshoreman stood in the center of the hooting, clanging crowd and watched, in mute anger and outrage, hundreds of years of peace and tranquillity go up in song.

Before Alfred could stop him, Bane raced excitedly after Hugh and Haplo. Caught up in the melee, Alfred struggled to try to catch the prince. Limbeck's spectacles were knocked off in the tussle. He managed to save them, but—getting knocked about in every direction—couldn't put them on. Blinking, bewildered, he stared around, unable to tell friend from foe, up from down. Seeing the Geg's predicament, Alfred caught hold of Limbeck by the shoulder and dragged him toward the ship.

The Fire born of Journey's End,
The Flame a part, a lightened call . . .

The elf captain, flat on his back on the Palm's fingers, struggled ineffectively with the dog, whose slashing teeth were trying to find their way between helm and breastplate. Reaching the gangway, Haplo glanced in some concern at an elven wizard hovering over the fallen elf. If the wizard used his magic, the Patryn would have little choice but to respond in kind. Perhaps, in the confusion, he could do it without being seen. But the wizard did not appear interested in fighting. He stood over the elf captain, watching keenly the battle with the dog. The wizard held in his hand a jeweled box; an eager expression lit his face.

Keeping one eye on this strange wizard, Haplo knelt swiftly at the battling elf's side. Making certain he kept clear of the dog's teeth, the Patryn slid his hand beneath the ironclad body, grappling for the sword. He grasped hold and pulled. The belt to which it was attached gave way and the weapon was his. Haplo considered the sword an instant. The Patryn was loath to kill in this world, particularly elves. He was beginning to see how his lord could make future use of them. Turning, he tossed the weapon to Hugh.

Sword in one hand, his dagger in the other, Hugh dashed across the gangway and through the hatch, singing as he ran.

"Dog! Here! To me!" Haplo called.

Immediately obeying the command, the dog bounded from the chest of the ironclad elf, leaving the captain floundering helplessly on his back, like an overturned turtle. Waiting for the dog, Haplo managed to catch hold of Bane as the child hurtled past him. The prince was in a state of wild excitement, shrieking the song out at the top of his lungs.

"Let me go! I want to see the fight!"

"Where the hell's your keeper? Alfred!"

Searching the crowd for the chamberlain, Haplo got a firm grip on the squirming, protesting boy and held on to him. Alfred was clumsily shepherding Limbeck through the chaos raging on the Palm. The Geg, struggling to keep his feet, was still pouring out his heart.

"And now, distinguished visitors from another realm, I would like to give to you the three tenets of WUPP. First—"

The mob closed around Alfred and Limbeck.

Releasing Bane, Haplo turned to the dog, pointed to the boy, and said, "Watch."

The dog, grinning, sat down on his hind legs and fixed his eyes on Bane. Haplo left them. Bane stared at the dog.

"Good boy," he said, and turned to enter the hatch.

Casually the dog rose to his feet, sank his teeth into the rear end of His Highness's trousers, and held him fast.

Haplo darted back across the gangway to Palm. He extricated Alfred and the speech-making Limbeck from the thick of the crowd and hustled them toward the ship. Several WUPP's, blowing their horns, surged after them, deafening any who tried to stop them. Haplo recognized Jarre among them and tried to catch her eye, but she was bashing a copper with a wheezy-wail and didn't see him.

Despite the confusion, Haplo attempted to keep an ear attuned for fighting on board the ship. He heard nothing except Hugh's singing, however, not even the sound of blowing whistles.

"Here, chamberlain, the kid's your responsibility."

Haplo freed Bane from the dog and thrust the kid toward a shaken Alfred. The Patryn and the dog raced across the gangway; Haplo assumed everyone else was following.

Coming into the dark ship from the sunlight glaring off the golden Palm, the Patryn was forced to pause and wait for his eyes to adjust. Behind him, he heard Limbeck cry out, stumble, and fall to his knees, the sudden absence of light and the loss of his spectacles combining to effectively blind the Geg.

Haplo's vision cleared quickly. He saw now why he had heard no sounds of fighting. Hugh stood facing an elf with a naked sword in his hand. Behind the elf ranged the rest of the ship's crew, armed and waiting. The silver war robes of a ship's wizard caught the sunlight, gleaming brightly from where he stood behind the warriors. No one spoke. Hugh had quit singing. He watched the elf narrowly, waiting for the attack.

" 'The sullen walk, the flick'ring aim . . .' " Bane trilled the words, his voice loud and jarring.

The elf's gaze slid toward the child, the hand grasping the sword shivered slightly, and his tongue flicked over dry lips. The other elves, ranged behind him, were seemingly awaiting his orders, for they kept their eyes fixed on him as their leader.

Haplo swiveled about. "Sing, dammit!" he shouted, and Alfred, jolted into action, raised his voice—a piping tenor. Limbeck was shuffling through his papers, trying to find the place where he'd left off.

There was Jarre, coming across the gangplank, more WUPP's behind her, all gleeful and eager for treasure. Haplo signaled frantically, and finally she saw him.

"Keep away!" he motioned, mouthing the words at the same time. "Keep away!"

Jarre halted her troop and they obediently (and a few literally) fell back at her command. The Gegs craned their heads to see, watching intently to make certain no one got a glass bead ahead of them.

" 'Fire leads again from futures, all.' "

The singing was louder now, Alfred's voice stronger, carrying the tune, Bane growing hoarse but never flagging. Certain now the Gegs would not interfere, Haplo turned from them to Hugh and the elf. Holding the same positions, swords raised, each watched the other warily.

"We mean you no harm," said Hugh in elven.

The elf raised a delicate eyebrow, glanced around at his armed crew, who outnumbered them twenty to one.

"No kidding," replied the elf.

But the Hand knew something of the ways of elves, apparently, for he continued without pause, speaking their language fluently.

"We've been stranded down here. We want to escape. We're bound for the High Realm—"

The elf sneered. "You're lying, human. The High Realm is banned. Ringed round by magical protection."

"Not to us. They'll let us pass," said Hugh. "This child"—he pointed at Bane—"is the son of a mysteriarch. He'll—"

Limbeck found his place. "Distinguished visitors from another realm—"

From outside came a clunking and clattering of iron.

"The whistles! Use the whistles, you fools!"

Two whistles screeched—the elf captain's and that of the wizard holding the box.

The dog growled, its ears pricked, its hackles bristled. Haplo stroked the animal reassuringly, but it wouldn't be calmed and began to howl in pain. The clunking noise and the whistling grew louder. A shadow appeared in the hatchway, blotting out the sunlight.

Alfred shrank back, pulling Bane behind him. Limbeck was reading his speech and didn't see the captain. An ironclad arm shoved the Geg roughly aside, knocking him into a bulkhead. The elf stood in the hatchway, blasting on his whistle. He had removed the helm. The eyes, glaring at his crew, were red with rage.

He took the whistle from his lips long enough to shout savagely, "Do as I command, damn you, lieutenant!" The wizard, box in hand, hovered at his charge's elbow.

The elf facing Hugh lifted the whistle with a hand that seemed to move of its own accord. The lieutenant's eyes went from his captain to Hugh and back to the captain again. The rest of the crew either lifted the whistles or toyed with them. A few blew tentative bleeps.

Hugh didn't understand what was going on, but he guessed that victory hung upon a note, so to speak, and so began to sing hoarsely. Haplo joined in, the captain blasted away on the whistle, the dog howled in pain, and everyone, including Limbeck, came out strong on the last two verses:

> The Arc and Bridge are thoughts and heart,
> The Span a life, the Ridge a part.

The lieutenant's hand moved and grasped the whistle. Haplo, marking an elven warrior near the officer, tensed, ready to jump the man and try to wrest away his weapon. But the lieutenant did not put the whistle to his lips. He gave the thong on which it hung a vicious jerk, broke it, and hurled it to the deck. There was ragged cheering among the elven crew, and many—including the ship's wizard—followed their lieutenant's example.

The captain's face flushed crimson with rage, blotches of white stood out on his thin cheeks, foam flecked his lips.

"Traitors! Traitors led by a coward! Weesham, you are my witness. They are mutineers, filthy rebels, and when we get back—"

"We're not going back, captain," said the lieutenant, standing straight and tall, his gray eyes cool. "Stop that singing!" he added.

Hugh had only a vague idea of what was going on; apparently they'd stumbled across some sort of private feud among the elves. But he was quick to recognize that it could turn to their advantage, and he made a motion with his hand. Everyone hushed, Alfred ordering Bane twice to keep silent and finally clapping his hand over the boy's mouth.

"I told you this man was a coward!" The captain addressed the crew. "He hasn't the guts to fight these beasts! Get me out of this thing!" The elf captain could not move in the iron suit. His geir laid a hand upon the armor and spoke a word. The iron melted away. Bounding forward, the elf captain put his hand to his side, only to discover his sword was gone. He found it almost immediately; Hugh was pointing it at his throat.

"No, human," cried the lieutenant, moving to block Hugh.

"This is my battle. Twice, captain, you have called me coward and I could not defend my honor. Now you can no longer hide behind your rank!"

"You say that very bravely, lieutenant, considering that you are armed and I am not!"

The lieutenant turned to Hugh. "As you can see, human, this is an affair of honor. I am told you humans understand such things. I ask that you give the captain his sword. That leaves you weaponless, of course, but you didn't have much chance anyway—being one against so many. If I live, I pledge myself to assist you. If I fall, then you must take your chances as before."

Hugh considered the odds, then, shrugging, handed over the sword. The two elves squared off, falling into fighting stance. The crew was intent on watching the battle between their captain and his lieutenant. Hugh edged his way near one of them, and Haplo guessed that the assassin wouldn't be weaponless for long.

The Patryn had his own worries. He had been keeping his eye on the riot raging outside the ship and saw that the WUPP's, having defeated the coppers, were blood-crazed and searching for trouble. Should the Gegs board the ship, the elves would think it was an all-out attack, forget their own differences, and fight back. Already Haplo could see the Gegs pointing at the ship, yammering about treasure.

Sword clashed against sword. The captain and lieutenant thrust and parried. The elf wizard watched eagerly, clutching the inlaid box he held to his breast. Moving swiftly but smoothly, hoping to attract as little attention as possible, Haplo made his way over to the hatch. The dog trotted along at his heels.

Jarre stood on the gangway, her hands grasping a broken tambourine, her eyes fixed on Limbeck. Undaunted, the Geg had climbed to his feet, adjusted his spectacles, found his place, and resumed speaking.

"—a better life for everyone—"

Behind Jarre, the Gegs were rallying, urging each other to go into the ship and grab the spoils of war. Haplo found the mechanism for raising and lowering the gangplank, and quickly studied it to understand how it operated. His only problem now was the female Geg.

"Jarre!" Haplo cried, waving his hand. "Get off the plank! I'm going to raise it! We've got to leave now!"

"Limbeck!" Jarre's voice was inaudible, but he understood the movement of her lips.

"I'll take care of him and bring him back to you safely. I promise!" That was an easy promise to make. Once Limbeck was properly molded, he would be ready to lead the Gegs and develop them into a united fighting force—an army willing to lay down their lives for the Lord of the Nexus.

Jarre took a step forward. Haplo didn't want her. He didn't trust her. Something had changed her. Alfred had changed her. She wasn't the same fiery revolutionary she'd been before she went off with him. That man, meek and inoffensive as he seemed, bore watching.

By this time the Gegs had goaded each other to action and were marching unimpeded toward the ship. Behind him, Haplo could hear the duel between the two elves rage on unabated. He set the mechanism, prepared to raise the gangway. Jarre would slip and fall to her death. It would look like an accident, the Gegs would blame it on the elves. He put his hand on the mechanism, ready to activate it, when he saw the dog dash past him, running across the plank.

"Dog! Get back here!"

But either the animal was ignoring him or, in the midst of the singing and the sword clashing, it couldn't hear him.

Frustrated, Haplo let go of the mechanism and started out onto the gangway after the animal. The dog had latched on to the sleeve of Jarre's blouse and was tugging her off the plank, herding her in the direction of the Palm.

Jarre, distracted, looked down at the dog, and as she did so, saw her people advancing on the ship.

"Jarre!" cried Haplo. "Turn them back! The Welves will kill them! They'll kill all of us if you attack!"

She looked back at him, then at Limbeck.

"It's up to you, Jarre!" Haplo shouted. "You're their leader now."

The dog had loosed its hold and was gazing up at her, its eyes bright, its tail wagging.

"Good-bye, Limbeck," whispered Jarre. Leaning down, she gave the dog a fierce hug, then turned and, shoulders squared, stepped off the gangway onto the fingers of the Palm. Facing the Gegs, she raised her hands and they halted.

"More treasure is being dropped. You must all go down below! There's nothing up here."

"Below? It's being dropped below?"

Hastily the Gegs whirled around and began to push and shove, trying to reach the stairs.

"Get in here, dog!" Haplo ordered.

The animal gamboled across the deck, its tongue lolling out of its mouth in an irrepressible grin of triumph.

"Proud of yourself, huh?" Haplo said, releasing the mechanism and pulling on the ropes, drawing up the gangplank as swiftly as possible. He heard Jarre's voice raised in command, heard the Gegs shout in support. The gangway slid inside. Closing the hatch, Haplo sealed it tight. The Gegs could no longer be seen or heard.

"Disobedient mutt. I should have you skinned," muttered Haplo, fondling the dog's silky ears.

Raising his voice about the clashing of steel, Limbeck carried on: "And in conclusion, I would like to say . . ."

CHAPTER ♦ 42

THE LIFTALOFTS, DREVLIN,

LOW REALM

♦

HAPLO TURNED FROM THE HATCH IN TIME TO SEE THE LIEUTENANT THRUST his sword through the elf captain's body. The lieutenant yanked his weapon free, and the captain slid to the deck. The crew was silent, no sound of either cheering or lamenting. The lieutenant, his face cold and impassive, stood back to allow the wizard room to kneel beside the dying elf. Haplo assumed that this wizard, who had been in attendance upon the captain, was a healer. The Patryn was surprised, therefore, to see the wizard make no gestures toward helping the dying. He held the inlaid box he carried up to the captain's lips.

"Speak the words!" the geir hissed.

The captain made some attempt, but blood gushed out of his mouth.

The wizard appeared angry and, propping up the elf's head, forced the rapidly dimming eyes to look at the box.

"Speak the words! It is your duty to your people!"

Slowly, with an obvious effort, the elf gasped out words that were, to Haplo, unintelligible. The captain sank back, lifeless. The wizard snapped the box shut and, glancing suspiciously at the other elves, guarded it jealously, as if he had just locked away some rare and priceless jewel.

"You dare not harm me!" he whined. "I am a weesham, protected by law! A curse will follow you all your days if you prevent me from carrying out my sacred task!"

"I have no intention of harming you," said the lieutenant, his lip curled in scorn. "Although what possible use the soul of that wretch can be to our people is best known to yourselves. Still, he died with honor, if he did not live with it. Perhaps that counts for something." Reaching down, he picked up the dead elf's sword and, turning, handed it—hilt-first—to Hugh.

"Thank you, human. And you." The elf glanced at Haplo. "I saw the peril we faced from the Gegs. Perhaps, when we have leisure to discuss such things, you can explain to me what is going on in Drevlin. Now we must prepare to swiftly take our leave." The elf turned back to Hugh. "What you said about the High Realm, is that true?"

"Yes." Hugh took the scabbard off the dead elf, thrust the sword into it. "The boy"—he jerked a thumb at Bane, who was standing mute, staring curiously at the corpse—"is the son of one Sinistrad, a mysteriarch."

"How came such a child to be in your care?" The elf was looking at Bane thoughtfully. Bane, his pale face almost translucent, caught the elf's gaze. Meeting the gray eyes, he smiled sweetly, bravely, and made a grave and graceful bow. The lieutenant was charmed.

Hugh's face darkened. "Never mind. It's not your affair. We were attempting to reach the High Realm when our ship was attacked by your people. We fought them off, but my ship was damaged and fell into the Maelstrom."

"Your ship? Humans do not fly dragonships!"

"Humans named Hugh the Hand fly what they please."

The elves murmured, the first sounds they had made since the commencement of the duel. The lieutenant nodded.

"I see. That explains much."

Withdrawing a lace-edged piece of cloth from the pocket of his uniform, the elf used it to wipe blood from his sword blade, then slid the weapon into its sheath. "You are known to be a human of honor—rather peculiar honor, but honor nonetheless. If you will excuse me, humans, I have duties to perform now that I am captain of this vessel. Midshipman Ilth will show you to quarters."

So might slaves be dismissed from the presence of the master, Haplo thought. The elf has chosen to side with us, but he has no love for us and apparently little respect. The elven midshipman motioned them to follow him.

Limbeck was kneeling beside the body of the dead elf.

"I was right," he said when he felt Haplo's hand on his shoulder. "They're not gods."

"No," said Haplo. "They're not. There are no gods in this world, as I've told you."

Limbeck glanced about, looking very much as if he had lost something and hadn't the vaguest idea where to begin searching for it. "Do you know," he said after a moment, "I'm almost sorry."

Following the midshipman off the bridge, Haplo heard one of the elves ask, "What do we do with the body, lieutenant? Throw it overboard?"

"No," said the lieutenant. "He was an officer and his remains will be treated with respect. Place the body in the hold. We will stop in the Mid Realm and deposit it and the geir with it. And from now on, mate, you will address me as captain."

The elf was moving swiftly to command his crew's respect, knowing that he must knit up the threads of discipline he himself had unraveled. Haplo awarded the elf silent commendation, and accompanied the others below.

The young elf placed them in what Hugh said was the shipboard equivalent of a dungeon. The brig was bare and cheerless. There were hooks on the walls where hammocks could be slung up at night for sleeping. During the day, they were stowed away to leave enough space to move about. Small portholes provided a view of outside.

Having informed them that he would return with food and water once the ship was safely through the Maelstrom, the midshipman shut the door and they heard the bolt slide home.

"We're prisoners!" cried Bane.

Hugh settled himself, crouching on his haunches, his back against a bulkhead. He appeared to be in a bad mood. Drawing his pipe out of his pocket, he clamped it between his teeth.

"You want to see prisoners, go take a look at the humans working below deck. They're the reason he's keeping us locked up. We could take over this ship if we freed the slaves, and he knows it."

"Then let's do it!" said Bane, his face flushed with excitement.

Hugh glowered at him. "You think you can fly this ship, Your Highness? Maybe like you flew mine, huh?"

Bane flushed in anger. Hand clutching the feather, the child swallowed his rage and marched across deck to glare out the portholes.

"And you trust him?" Alfred inquired somewhat anxiously. "This elf?"

"No more than he trusts me." Hugh sucked moodily on the empty pipe.

"So are they converted or whatever happens to elves when they hear that song?" asked Haplo.

"Converted?" Hugh shook his head. "I don't think so. Elves truly affected by that song lose all awareness of their surroundings. It's as if they've been transported to another world. This elf's doing what he's doing for himself. The lure of the reputed wealth of the High Realm and the fact that no elves have ever dared travel up there is what's drawing him."

"Wouldn't it occur to him that it would be easier just to toss us out into the storm and keep the kid for himself?"

"Yeah, maybe. But elves have a 'peculiar' honor. In some way—we'll probably never know how—we did this elf a service by delivering his captain into his hands. His crew witnessed it. He'd lose standing in their eyes by slaughtering us just to make things easier on himself."

"Honor, then, is important to the elves?"

"Important!" Hugh grunted. "They'd sell their souls for it, those souls the vultures don't get first."

Interesting to know. Haplo stored up the information. His lord was in the market for souls.

"So we're taking a boatload of elven pirates up to the High Realm." Alfred sighed, then began nervous fussing. "Your Highness, you must be tired. Let me put up one of these hammocks . . ." Tripping over a plank, the chamberlain sprawled facefirst on the deck.

"I'm not tired," protested Bane. "And don't worry about my father and these elves. My father'll take care of them!"

"Don't bother getting up," suggested Hugh to the prostrate chamberlain. "We'll be flying through the Maelstrom and then no one'll be on his feet. Everyone sit down and brace yourself."

Sound advice. Haplo could see the first storm clouds scudding past. Lightning flashed blindingly; thunder boomed. The ship began to pitch and buck. The Patryn relaxed in a corner. The dog curled up, nose to tail, at his feet. Alfred hunched miserably against the bulkhead and pulled a protesting Bane down by the seat of his pants.

Only Limbeck remained standing, staring entranced out the porthole.

"Limbeck," said Haplo. "Sit down. It's dangerous."

"I can't believe it," murmured the Geg, without turning. "There are no gods . . . and I am going to heaven."

CHAPTER ♦ 43

DEEPSKY,

MID REALM

♦

Lieutenant Bothar'in, now Captain Bothar'el[1], sailed the dragon-ship safely through the Maelstrom. Keeping clear of encounters with other elven ships, he steered for the Aristagonian port town of Suthnas—a safe haven recommended by Hugh the Hand. Here he planned to stop briefly to take on food and water and to rid his ship of the geir, the former captain's body, and the geir's little box.

Hugh knew Suthnas well; he had put up there when his ship needed the magic strengthened or repairs. He gave the elf captain the name because he, the Hand, intended to leave the ship himself.

The assassin had made up his mind. He cursed the day he met that "king's messenger." He cursed the day he had saddled himself with this contract. Nothing had gone right; now he had lost his own dragonship, almost his life, and damn near his self-respect. His plan to capture the elven ship had worked, but like everything else he touched these days, not the way it was supposed to. *He* was to have been the captain, not this elf. Why had he let himself get caught up in that damn duel? Why hadn't he just killed them both?

Hugh was shrewd enough to know that if he had fought, he and all the others would probably be dead right now. But he

---

[1]Suffixes attached to a name indicate rank. A captain's name ends with "el." A lieutenant's name ends with "in." A prince, such as Prince Reesh, adds the suffix "ahn" to his name.

ignored the logic. He refused to admit that he had done what he had done in order to save lives, to protect Alfred, Limbeck . . . the prince.

No! I did it for myself. Not for anyone else. No one else matters and I'll prove it. I'll leave them, disembark at Suthnas, let these fools go on to the High Realm and take their chances with a mysteriarch. Forget it. I'll write off my losses, toss in my cards, get up and leave the table.

The port of Suthnas was run by elves whose purses meant more to them than politics, and it had become a haven for water smugglers, rebels, deserters, and a few renegade humans. The prisoners had a good view of the town from the porthole and most, after seeing it, decided they were better off where they were.

The town was nothing more than a squalid assemblage of inns and taverns built near the harbor; the homes of the town's inhabitants bunched like a flock of sheep on the side of a coralite cliff. The buildings were shabby and run-down; a smell of cooked cabbage—an elven favorite—hung in the air, undoubtedly because mounds of it were rotting in the garbage-infested alleyways. But, because it stood in the sun, with blue sky above it, Suthnas was a beautiful and awe-inspiring sight to the Geg.

Limbeck had never seen streets drenched in sunlight, the firmament glittering like a million jewels in the sky above. He had never seen people strolling about aimlessly, not scurrying hither and yon on some business of the Kicksey-winsey. He had never felt a gentle breeze upon his cheek or smelled the smells of living, growing things, or even things that were rotting and dying. The houses that Hugh told him were hovels seemed to the Geg to be palaces. Limbeck looked on all this splendor, and it came to him that what he saw had been bought and paid for by the sweat and blood of his people. The Geg's face saddened, he became silent and withdrawn, and Haplo watched with a smile.

Hugh paced about the hold, staring out the portholes, fidgeting and inwardly fuming. Captain Bothar'el had given the assassin permission to leave if he wanted.

"You should all go," the captain said. "Leave now, while you have the chance."

"But we're going to the High Realm! You promised!" Bane cried. "You promised," he repeated, gazing up at the elf with pleading eyes.

"Yes," said the elf, staring at the child. Shaking his head, as if to break a hold, he turned to Alfred. "And you?"

"I stay with my prince, of course."

The elf turned to Limbeck, who, not understanding, looked at Haplo.

"I'm going to see the world, the whole world," said the Geg firmly when he heard the translation. "After all, it exists because of my people."

"I'm with him," said the Patryn, smiling and jerking a bandage-wrapped thumb in the direction of the Geg.

"So," said Bothar'el, turning to Hugh, "only you are leaving?"

"It looks that way."

Hugh didn't leave, however.

While they were docked, one of the midshipmen looked into the brig. "Are you still aboard, human? The captain is returning. You should go now, quickly."

Hugh didn't move.

"I wish you would come with us, Sir Hugh," said Bane, "My father would like very much to meet you and . . . thank you."

That cinched it. The kid wanted him. He'd leave right now. Right . . . now.

"Well, human?" demanded the midshipman. "Are you coming?"

Hugh fished around in a pocket, dragged out his last coin—payment for assassinating a child. Grunting, he tossed it at the elf. "I've decided to stay and find my fortune. Go buy me some tobacco."

The elves did not linger long in Suthnas. Once the geir reached civilized lands, he would report the mutiny and the *Carfa'shon* would be sought by all the ships of the line. Once in deepsky, Captain Bothar'el worked the human slaves, the crew, and himself to the point of exhaustion until the ship was, he believed, safely beyond possible pursuit.

Hours later, when the Lords of Night had cast their cloak over the sun, the captain found time to speak to his "guests."

"So, you heard the news," were the captain's first words, addressed to Hugh. "I want you to know that I could have made a nice profit off the lot of you, but I have a debt to repay to you. I consider at least part of it canceled."

"Where's my tobacco?" Hugh demanded.

"What news?" asked Alfred.

The captain raised an eyebrow. "Don't you know? I assumed that was the reason you didn't leave the ship." He tossed a pouch in the assassin's direction.

Hugh caught it handily, opened it, and sniffed. Removing his pipe, he began filling it.

"There's a reward out for your head, Hugh the Hand."

Hugh grunted. "Nothing new."

"A total of two hundred thousand barls."

The Hand looked up and whistled. "Now, that's a fine price. This has to do with the kid?" His glance shifted to Bane. The child had begged pen and paper from the elves and had done nothing but draw ever since he came on board. No one interfered with his latest amusement. It was safer than letting him pick berries.

"Yes. You and this man"—the elf gestured at Alfred—"are reported to have kidnapped the prince of Volkaran. There is a price of one hundred thousand barls on your head," he said to the horrified chamberlain, "two hundred thousand for Hugh the Hand, and the reward is good only if one or both are brought in alive."

"What about me?" Bane raised his head. "Isn't there any reward for me?"

"Stephen doesn't want you back," Hugh growled.

The prince appeared to consider this, then giggled. "Yes, I guess you're right," he said, and returned to his work.

"But this is impossible!" cried Alfred. "I . . . I am His Highness's servant! I came with him to protect him—"

"Exactly," said Hugh. "That's just what Stephen *didn't* want."

"I don't understand any of this," said Captain Bothar'el. "I hope, for your sakes, you are being honest about the High Realm. I need money to run this ship and pay my crew and I've just passed up a lot."

"Of course it's true!" cried Bane, lower lip thrust forward in a charming pout. "I *am* the son of Sinistrad, Mysteriarch of the Seventh House. My father will reward you well!"

"He had better!" said the captain.

The elf glanced around sternly at his prisoners, then stalked out of the hold. Bane, looking after him, laughed and returned to his scribbling.

"I can never go back to Volkaran!" murmured Alfred. "I'm an exile."

"You're dead unless we can figure some way out of this,"

said Hugh, lighting his pipe with a coal from the small magepot[2] they used to heat their food and to keep themselves warm at night.

"But Stephen wants us alive."

"Only so that he can have the pleasure of killing us himself."

Bane, looking up at him, smiled slyly. "So if you had gone out there, someone would have recognized you and turned you in. You stayed because of me, didn't you? I saved your life."

Hugh made no comment, preferring to pretend that he hadn't heard. He relapsed into a brooding, thoughtful silence. When his pipe went out, he didn't notice.

Coming back to himself sometime later, he noted that everyone—except Alfred—had fallen asleep. The chamberlain was standing beside the porthole, gazing out into night's gray gloom. The Hand, rising to stretch his stiff legs, wandered over.

"What do you make of this fellow Haplo?" Hugh asked.

"Why?" Alfred jumped, stared at the assassin fearfully. "Why do you ask?"

"No reason. Calm down. I just wanted to know what you made of him, that's all."

"Nothing! I make nothing of him at all! If you will excuse me, sir," Alfred interrupted when Hugh would have spoken, "I'm very tired. I must get some sleep."

Now what was that all about? The chamberlain returned to his blanket. He lay down, but Hugh, watching him, saw that Alfred was far from sleep. He lay stiff and rigid, rubbing his hands, tracing unseen lines upon the skin. His face could have been a mask in a play called *Terror and Misery*.

Hugh could almost pity him.

Almost, but not quite. No, the walls Hugh'd built around himself were still standing, still strong and unbroken. There had been a tiny crack, letting in a ray of light—harsh and painful to eyes accustomed to darkness. But he'd blocked it up, covered it over. Whatever hold the child had on him was magic—something beyond the assassin's control, at least until they came to the High Realm. Retreating to a corner of his cell, Hugh relaxed and went to sleep.

The flight to the High Realm took the elven dragonship almost

---

[2]An iron pot that holds magical glowstones. Used for light and heat.

two weeks, far longer than it should have, according to Captain Bothar'el's calculations. What he hadn't calculated on was that his crew and slaves all tired far too quickly. Magical spells cast by the ship's wizard enabled them to withstand the reduced air pressure, but he could do nothing to relieve the thinness of the air that left them always feeling as if they were short of breath.

The elven crew grew nervous, sullen, and uneasy. It was eerie, flying through the vast and empty sky. Above them, the firmament glittered and sparkled brightly by day, glistened with a pale sheen at night. Even the most gullible person aboard could see that the mysterious firmament was not made of jewels floating in the heavens.

"Chunks of ice," announced Captain Bothar'el, studying it through the spyglass.

"Ice?" The second in command appeared almost relieved. "That's stopped us, then, hasn't it, captain, sir? We can't fly through ice. We might as well turn back."

"No." Bothar'el snapped his spyglass shut. It seemed he was answering himself, replying to some inner argument rather than to the words of his mate. "We've come this far. The High Realm is up here somewhere. We're going to find it."

"Or die trying," said the second in command, but he said it to himself.

On they sailed, higher and higher, drawing nearer the firmament that hung spanning the sky like a monstrous radiant necklace. They saw no sign of life of any type, let alone a land where dwelt the most highly skilled of human magi.

The air grew colder. They were forced to wear every article of clothing they possessed, and even then it was difficult to keep warm. The crew began to mutter among themselves that this was mad folly, they would all perish up here, either of the cold or stranded in deepsky, lacking the strength to fly back.

After days passed with no sign of life, supplies running short and the cold growing almost unbearable, Captain Bothar'el went below to tell the "guests" he had changed his mind, they were returning to the Mid Realm.

He found the prisoners wrapped in every blanket they could get their hands on, huddled over the magepot. The Geg was deathly ill—either from the cold or the change in air pressure. The captain didn't know what kept him alive. (Alfred did, but took care no one should ask him.)

Bothar'el was just about to make his announcement when a shout hailed him.

"What is it?" The captain ran back to the bridge. "Have we found it?"

"I'd say, sir," said a stammering midshipman, staring with wide eyes out the porthole, "that *it's* found us!"

CHAPTER ♦ 44

CASTLE SINISTER,

HIGH REALM

♦

IRIDAL STOOD AT THE CASEMENT, GAZING OUT THE CRYSTAL WINDOW. The beauty of the sight before her was incomparable. The opal walls of her castle glistened in the sunlight, adding to the shimmering colors of the magical dome that was the High Realm's sky. Below the walls, the castle's parks and forests, carefully sculptured and tended, were traversed by pathways whose crushed marble was pricked by glittering gems. Its beauty could stop the heart. But it was long since Iridal had seen beauty in anything. Her name itself, meaning "of the rainbow," mocked her. All in her world was gray. As for her heart, it seemed to have stopped beating a long time ago.

"Wife." The voice came from behind her.

Iridal shivered. She had supposed she was alone in her room. She had not heard the silent padding of slippered feet or the rustling of silken robes that invariably announced the presence of her husband. He had not entered her room for many years and she felt the chill of his presence grip her heart and squeeze it tightly. Fearfully she turned around and faced him.

"What do you want?" Her hand clutched her gown tightly around her, as if the frail fabric might armor her against him. "Why do you come here to my private quarters?"

Sinistrad glanced at the bed with its flowing curtains and tasseled hangings, its silken sheets, smelling faintly of the lavender leaves scattered on them every morning and carefully brushed away each night.

"Since when is a husband forbidden his wife's bedchamber?"

"Leave me alone!" The chill in her heart seemed to have spread to her lips. She could barely move them.

"Do not worry, wife. For ten cycles I have not come here for the purpose you fear, and I do not intend to resume. Such doings are as repugnant to me as they are you; we might as well all be beasts, rutting in dark and stinking caves. However, it does bring me around to the subject I came to discuss. Our son is coming at last."

"*Our* son!" Iridal cried. "*Your* son. He is none of mine!"

"Let us rejoice," said Sinistrad with a pale, dry smile. "I am glad you take this view of the matter, my dear. I trust you will remember it when the boy arrives and that you will not interfere with our work."

"What could I possibly do?"

"Bitterness does not become you, wife. Remember, I know your tricks. Tears, pouting, little hugs for the child that you think I will not see. I warn you, Iridal, I *will* see. My eyes are everywhere, even in the back of my head. The boy is mine. You have pronounced it. Never forget it."

"Tears! Don't fear my tears, husband. They dried up long ago."

"Fear? I'm not afraid of anything, least of all you, wife," returned Sinistrad with some amusement. "But you could be an annoyance, confuse the boy's mind. I don't have time to fool with you."

"Why not just lock me up in the dungeon? I am already your prisoner in all but name."

"I had considered it, but the boy would take an undue interest in a mother he is forbidden to see. No, it will be far better if you appear and smile prettily at him, allow him to see that you are weak and spineless."

"You want me to teach him to despise me."

Sinistrad shrugged. "I do not aspire to that much, my dear. It will be far better for my plans if he thinks nothing of you at all. And, by good fortune, we have something that will ensure your proper behavior. Hostages. Three humans and a Geg are his traveling companions. How important it must make you feel, Iridal, to know that you hold so many lives in your hands!"

The woman's face went livid. Her knees gave way, and she sank into a chair. "You have sunk low, Sinistrad, but you have never committed murder! I don't believe your threat!"

"Let us rephrase that statement, wife. You have never known

me to commit murder. But then, let us both admit that you have never known me—period. Good day to you, wife. I will give you notice when you are to appear to greet *our* son."

Bowing, hand over his heart in the time-honored custom of husband and wife, turning even this gesture to one of disdain and mockery, Sinistrad left Iridal's chambers.

Shivering uncontrollably, the woman crouched in her chair and stared out the window with dry, burning eyes. . . .

". . . My father says you are an evil man."

The girl, Iridal, gazed out of a window in her father's dwelling. Standing quite near her, almost touching her, but never coming that close, was a young mysteriarch. He was the handsome, wicked hero of Iridal's nurse's romantic tales—smooth, pallid skin; liquid brown eyes that always seemed to be the repository of fascinating secrets; a smile that promised to share these secrets, if someone could only draw close enough to him. The black, gilt-edged skullcap that marked his standing as a master of discipline of the Seventh House—the highest rank attainable by wizards—dipped to a sharp point that came to the bridge of his thin nose. Sweeping upward between the eyes, the cap gave him an appearance of wisdom and added expression to his face that might otherwise be lacking—he had no eyebrows or eyelashes. His entire body was hairless, a defect of birth.

"Your father is right, Iridal," said Sinistrad softly. Reaching out his hand, he toyed with a strand of her hair, the nearest move to intimacy he ever made. "I am evil. I do not deny it." There was a touch of melancholy in his voice that melted Iridal's heart as his touch melted her flesh.

Turning to face him, she held out her hands, clasped his, and smiled at him. "No, beloved! The world may call you that, but it is because they don't know you! Not as I know you."

"But I am, Iridal." His voice was gentle and in earnest. "I tell you the truth now because I don't want you to reproach me with it later. Marry me, and you marry darkness."

His finger wound the strand of hair tighter and tighter, drawing her nearer and nearer. His words and the serious tone in which he spoke them made her heart falter painfully, but the pain was sweet and exciting. The darkness that hung over him—dark rumors, dark words spoken about him among the community of mysteriarchs—was exciting too. Her life, all its sixteen years, had been dull and prosaic. Living with a father who doted on her following her mother's death, Iridal had been raised by a grandmotherly nanny. Her father could not bear life's rough winds to blow too harshly against his daughter's tender cheek and he had kept her sheltered and cloistered, wrapped in a smothering cocoon of love.

The butterfly that emerged from that cocoon was bright and shining; its feeble wings carried it straight into Sinistrad's web.

"If you are evil," she said, twining her hands around his arm, "it is the world that has made you so, by refusing to listen to your plans and thwarting your genius at every turn. When I am walking by your side, I will bring you to the sunlight."

"Then you will be my wife? You will go against your father's wishes?"

"I am of age. I can make my own choice. And, beloved, I choose you."

Sinistrad said nothing, but, smiling his secret-promising smile, he kissed the strand of hair wound tightly around his finger. . . .

. . . Iridal lay in her bed, weak from the travails of birth. Her nurse had finished bathing the tiny infant and, wrapping him in a blanket, carried him to his mother. The occasion should have been one of joy, but the old nurse, who had been Iridal's own, wept when she laid the child in his mother's arms.

The door to the bedchamber opened. Iridal made a low moaning sound and clutched the baby so tightly he squalled. The nurse, looking up, smoothed back the woman's sweat-damp curls with gentle hands. A look of defiance hardened the wrinkled face.

"Leave us," said Sinistrad, speaking to the nurse, his gaze fixed upon his wife.

"I will not leave my lamb!"

The eyes of the mysteriarch shifted. The nurse held her ground, though the hand touching Iridal's fair hair trembled. Grabbing hold of the nurse's fingers, Iridal kissed them and bade her leave in a low and tremulous voice.

"I cannot, child!" The nurse began to weep. "It's cruel, what he means to do! Cruel and unnatural!"

"Get out," Sinistrad snarled, "or I will burn you to ashes where you stand!"

The nurse cast him a look of malice, but she withdrew from the room. She knew who would suffer if she did not.

"Now that this is over, she must go, wife," said Sinistrad,

coming to stand beside the bed. "I will not be defied in my own house."

"Please, no, husband. She is the only company I have." Iridal's arms clung to her baby. She looked up at her husband pleadingly, one hand plucking at the blanket. "And I will need her help with our son! See!" She drew the blanket aside, exhibiting a red, wrinkled face, eyes squinched shut, small fists bunched tightly together. "Isn't he beautiful, husband?" She hoped desperately, despairingly, that a glimpse of his own flesh and blood would change his mind.

"He suits my purpose," said Sinistrad, reaching out his hands.

"No!" Iridal shrank away from him. "Not my child! Please, don't!"

"I told you my intentions the day you announced your pregnancy. I told you then that I had married you for this purpose and this alone, that I had bedded you for the same reason, and no other. Give me the child!"

Iridal huddled over her baby, her head bowed, her long hair covering the boy in a shining curtain. She refused to look at her husband, as if looking at him gave him power. By shutting her eyes to him, she might make him vanish. But it didn't work, because with her eyes closed, she saw him as he had been that terrible day when her bright illusions of love were completely and irrevocably shattered. The day she had told him her joyous news, that she carried his child within her. That day he had told her, in cold and passionless tones, what he intended to do with the babe.

Iridal should have known he was plotting something. She did know, but wouldn't admit it. On her bridal night, her life had changed from rainbow dreams to gray emptiness. His lovemaking was without love, without passion. He was brisk, businesslike, keeping his eyes open, staring at her intently, willing her to something that she could not understand. Night after night he came to her. During the day, he rarely saw her, rarely spoke to her. She grew to dread the night visits and had once ventured to refuse him, begging that he treat her with love. He had taken her that night with violence and pain and she had never dared refuse him again. Perhaps that very night their child had been conceived. A month later she knew she was pregnant.

From the day she told him, Sinistrad never came to her bedroom again.

The child in her arms wailed. Strong hands grabbed Iridal by the hair and jerked her head back. Strong hands wrenched her child from her grasp. Pleading, the mother crawled from her bed and stumbled after her husband as he walked away, their crying infant in his arms. But she was too weak. Tangled in the blood-stained bedclothes, Iridal fell to the floor. One hand caught hold of his robes, dragging him back.

"My baby! Don't take my baby!"

He regarded her coldly, with disgust. "I told you the day I asked you to be my wife what I was. I have never lied to you. You chose not to believe me, and that is your own fault. You have brought this upon yourself." Reaching down, he grasped the fabric of his robe and jerked it from her feeble, clutching fingers. Turning, he left the room.

When he came back later that night, he brought another baby—the true child born to the wretched king and queen of Volkaran and Uylandia. Sinistrad handed it to Iridal as one might hand over a puppy found abandoned on the road.

"I want my son!" she cried. "Not the child of some other poor woman!"

"Do what you like with it, then," said Sinistrad. His plan had worked well. He was almost in a good humor. "Suckle it. Drown it. I don't care."

Iridal took pity on the tiny baby and, hoping that the love she lavished on it would be reciprocated on her child so far away, she nursed him tenderly. But the infant could not adapt to the rarefied atmosphere. He died within days, and something within Iridal died too.

Going to Sinistrad a month later in his laboratory, she told him calmly and quietly that she was leaving, returning to the house of her father. In reality, her plan was to go to the Mid Realm and take back her child.

"No, my dear, I think not," replied Sinistrad without looking up from the text he was perusing. "My marriage to you lifted the dark cloud from me. The others trust me now. If our plans to escape this realm are to succeed, I'll need the help of all in our community. They must do my will without question. I cannot afford the scandal of a separation from you."

He looked up at her then, and she saw that he knew her plans, he knew the secrets of her heart.

"You can't stop me!" Iridal cried. "The mysteries I weave are powerful, for I am skilled in magic, as skilled as you, husband, who have devoted your life to your overweening ambition. I will proclaim your evil to the world! They will not follow you, but rise up and destroy you!"

"You're right, my dear. I cannot stop you. But perhaps you'd like to discuss this with your father."

Keeping a finger on his place in the book, Sinistrad raised his head and made a gesture with his hand. A box of ebony drifted up from the table on which it stood, floated through the air, and came to rest near the wizard's book. Opening it with one hand, he lifted out a silver locket hanging from a rope of black velvet. He held out the locket to Iridal.

"What is it?" She stared at it suspiciously.

"A gift, my dear. From loving husband to loving wife." His smile was a knife, twisting in her heart. "Open it."

Iridal took the locket with fingers so numb and cold she nearly dropped it. Inside was a portrait of her father.

"Take care that you do not drop it or break it," said Sinistrad casually, returning to his reading.

Iridal saw, in horror, that the portrait was staring back at her, its trapped, living eyes pitying, helpless. . . .

Sounds outside the window roused Iridal from her melancholy reverie. Rising weakly and unsteadily from the chair, she stared out the casement. Sinistrad's dragon was floating through the clouds, its tail cutting the mist to wispy shreds that trailed away and vanished—like dreams, thought Iridal. The quicksilver dragon had come at Sinistrad's command and now circled round and round the castle, awaiting its master. The beast was huge, with shining silver skin, a sinuous thin body, and flaring red eyes. It had no wings, but could fly faster without them than could its winged cousins of the Mid Realm.

Nervous and unpredictable, the most intelligent of their kind, these quicksilver dragons, as they were known, could be controlled only by the most powerful wizards. Even then, the dragon knew it was enthralled and constantly fought a mental battle with the spell-caster, forcing the magus who enchanted it to be continually on his guard. Iridal watched it out the window. The dragon was always moving—one moment twisting itself into a gigantic coil, rearing its head higher than the tallest castle tower; the next, unwinding itself with lightning speed to wrap its long body around the castle's mist-shrouded base. Once Iridal had feared the quicksilver. If it slipped its magical leash, it would kill them all. Now she no longer cared.

Sinistrad appeared, and Iridal involuntarily drew back away from the window so that he would not see her if he happened to glance up. He did not look up at her chamber, however, being far more concerned with more important matters. The elven ship had been sighted; the ship carrying his son. He and the others in the Council must meet to make final plans and preparations. This was why he was taking the dragon.

As a mysteriarch of the Seventh House, Sinistrad could have transported himself mentally to the guildhall, dissolving his body and reforming it when the mind arrived at its destination. That had been his means of entry into the Mid Realm. Such a feat was taxing, however, and really impressive only if someone was there to see the wizard materialize, supposedly, out of thin air. Elves were much more likely to be terrified by the sight of a gigantic dragon than by the refined and delicate techniques of mental spell-casting.

Sinistrad mounted the quicksilver, which he had named Gorgon, and it soared into the air and out of Iridal's sight. Her husband had not once looked back. Why should he? He had no fear that she would escape him. Not anymore. There were no guards posted round the castle. There were no servants posted to watch her and report her doings to their master. He had no need of any, could any have been found. Iridal was her own guard, locked up by her shame, held captive by her terror.

Her hand clasped round the locket. The portrait inside was alive no longer. Her father had died some years ago. His soul trapped by Sinistrad, the body had withered away. But whenever Iridal looked at the image of her father's face, she could still see the pity in his eyes.

The castle was silent, empty, nearly as silent and empty as her heart. She must dress, she told herself drearily, taking off the nightclothes that she wore almost all the time now; the only escape she had was in sleep.

Turning from the window, she saw herself in a mirror opposite. Twenty-six cycles—she looked as if she had lived a hundred. Her hair, that had once been the color of strawberries dipped in golden honey, was now white as the clouds drifting past her window. Lifting a brush, she began to listlessly make some attempt to untangle the matted tresses.

Her son was coming. She must make a good impression. Otherwise, Sinistrad would be displeased.

CHAPTER ♦ 45

NEW HOPE,

HIGH REALM

♦

SWIFT AS ITS NAME, THE QUICKSILVER DRAGON BORE SINISTRAD TO NEW Hope, the capital city of the High Realm. The mysteriarch was fond of using the dragon to impress his own people. No other wizard had been able to exert a hold over the highly intelligent and dangerous quicksilver. It would not hurt, in this critical time, to remind the others, once again, why they had chosen him to be their leader.

Sinistrad arrived in New Hope to find that the magic had already been cast. Shining crystal, towering spires, tree-lined boulevards—he barely recognized the place. Two fellow mysteriarchs, standing outside the Council Chamber were looking extremely proud of themselves, also extremely fatigued.

Dipping down from the sky, Sinistrad gave them time to fully appreciate his mount; then he released it, ordering the creature to remain within call and await his summons.

The dragon opened its fanged mouth in a gaping snarl, its red eyes flamed with hatred. Sinistrad turned his back on the creature.

"I tell you, Sinistrad, someday that dragon's going to break free of the spell you've cast over him and then none of us will be safe. It was a mistake to capture it," said one of the wizards—an aged mysteriarch—eyeing the quicksilver askance.

"Have you so little faith in my power?" inquired Sinistrad in a mild voice.

The mysteriarch said nothing, but glanced at his companion.

Noting the look pass between them, Sinistrad guessed correctly that they had been discussing him before he came.

"What is it?" he demanded. "Let us be honest with each other. I have always insisted on that, you know."

"Yes, we know. You rub our noses in your honesty!" said the old man.

"Come, Balthazar, you know me for what I am. You knew what I was when you voted me your leader. You knew I was ruthless, that I would allow nothing to stand in my way. Some of you called me evil then. You call me that now, and it is an appellation I do not deny. Yet I was the only one among you with vision. I was the one who devised the plan to save our people. Isn't that so?"

The mysteriarchs looked at Sinistrad, glanced at each other, then looked away—one turning his gaze on the beautiful city, the other watching the quicksilver dragon vanish into the cloudless sky.

"Yes, we agree," said one.

"We had no choice," added the other.

"Not very complimentary, but then, I can do without compliments. Speaking of which, the work you have done is excellent." Sinistrad gave the spires, the boulevards, the trees a critical inspection. Reaching out his hand, he touched the stone of the building before which they were standing. "So good, in fact, I was forced to wonder if this wasn't all part of it as well! I was half-afraid to enter!"

One of the mysteriarchs smiled bleakly at the wizard's little essay into humor. The other—the old man—scowled, turned, and left him. Gathering his robes about him, Sinistrad followed his companions, ascending the marble stairs and passing through the glittering crystal doors of the Wizards' Guildhall.

Inside the hall, talking in solemn and hushed voices, were gathered about fifty wizards. Male and female, they were clad in robes similar to Sinistrad's in make and design, although widely varying in color. Each hue designated a wizard's particular devotion—green for the land, deep blue for the sky, red for fire (or magic of the mind), light blue for water. A few, such as Sinistrad, wore the black that stood for discipline—iron discipline, the discipline that admitted no weakness. When he strode into the room, those present, who had been conversing together in low, excited voices, fell silent. Each bowed and stepped aside, forming an opening in their ranks through which he walked.

Glancing about him, nodding to friends here, noting enemies there, Sinistrad moved without haste through the large hall. Made of marble, the Guildhall was bleak, empty, and unadorned. No tapestries graced its walls, no statues decorated its doorways, no windows admitted the sunlight, no magic dispelled the gloom. The dwellings of the mysteriarchs in the Mid Realm had been renowned throughout the world as the most marvelous of all human creations. Remembering the beauty from which they had come, the wizards found the starkness and austerity of the Guildhall in the High Realm chilling. Hands thrust into the sleeves of their robes, they stood well away from the walls and appeared to try to avoid looking anywhere except at each other or their leader—Sinistrad.

He was the youngest among them. Every mysteriarch there could remember him first entering the Guildhall—a well-built youth, inclined to be servile and sniveling. His parents had been among the earliest of the exiles to succumb up here, leaving him orphaned. The others felt sorry for the young man, but not unduly. There were, after all, many orphans at that time. Immersed in their own problems—which were monumental—no one had paid much attention to the young wizard.

Human wizards had their own version of history that was, much like any other race's history, distorted by their own perspective. Following the Sundering, the Sartan had brought the people—not first to Aristagon, as the elves would have it—but here, to this realm beneath a magical dome. The humans, particularly the wizards, worked extremely hard to make this realm not only habitable but beautiful. It seemed to them that the Sartan were never around to help, but were always off somewhere on "important" business.

On the infrequent occasions when the Sartan returned, they lent their assistance, utilizing their rune magic. Thus it was that fabulous buildings were created, the dome was strengthened. The coralite bore fruit, water was in abundance. The human wizards were not particularly grateful. They were envious. They coveted the rune magic.

Then came the day when the Sartan announced the Mid Realm below was suitable for habitation. Humans and elves were transported to Aristagon, while the Sartan remained above in the High Realm. The Sartan gave the reason for the move the fact that the domed land was getting too crowded. The human wizards believed that the Sartan had cast them out because the wizards were becoming too knowledgeable about the rune magic.

Time passed, and the elves grew strong and united under their powerful wizards and the humans turned into barbaric pirates. The human wizards watched the rise of the elves with outward disdain and inward fear.

They said to themselves, "If only we had the rune magic, then we could destroy the elves!"

Instead of helping their own people, therefore, they began to concentrate their magic on finding ways to return to the High Realm. At length, they succeeded and a large force of the most powerful magi—the mysteriarchs—ascended to the High Realm to challenge the Sartan and take back what they had come to see as rightfully their land.

This the humans called the War of Ascension, only it wasn't much of a war. The mysteriarchs woke one morning to find the Sartan gone, their dwellings empty, their cities abandoned. The wizards returned victorious to their people, only to find the Mid Realm in chaos—torn by war. It was all they could do to manage to stay alive, much less try to use their magic to move the people to the Promised Land.

Finally, after years of suffering and hardship, the mysteriarchs were able to leave the Mid Realm and enter the land their legends held was beautiful, bountiful, safe, and secure. Here, too, they hoped to discover at last the secrets of the runes. It all seemed a wonderful dream. It would soon turn to a nightmare.

The runes kept their secrets and the mysteriarchs discovered to their horror how much of the beauty and bounty of the land had depended on the runes. Crops grew, but not in the numbers needed to feed the people. Famine swept the land. Water was scarce and became scarcer—each family having to expend immense amounts of magic in order to produce it. Centuries of inbreeding had already weakened the wizards and further inbreeding in this closed realm produced frightful genetic defects that could not be cured with magic. These children died and, eventually, few children were born. Most horrifying, it became obvious to the mysteriarchs that the magic of the dome was fading.

They would have to leave this realm, yet how could they, without proclaiming their failure, their weaknesses? One man had an idea. One man told them how it could be done. They were desperate, they listened.

As time passed and Sinistrad did well in his magical studies, surpassing many of the elders in his power, he ceased to be servile and began to flaunt his abilities. His elders were displeased and disgusted when he changed his name to Sinistrad, but they thought little of it at the time. Back in the Mid Realm, a bully might call himself Brute or Thug or some other tough-sounding name in order to garner respect he hadn't earned. It meant nothing.

The mysteriarchs had ignored the name change, just as they had ignored Sinistrad. Oh, a few spoke out—Iridal's father being one of them. A few tried to make their fellows see the young man's overweening ambition, his ruthless cruelty, his ability to manipulate. Those who spoke the warnings were not heeded. Iridal's father lost his only loved daughter to the man, and lost his life in Sinistrad's magical captivity. None of the wizards knew that, however. The prison had been created so skillfully that no one ever noticed. The old wizard walked about the land, visited his friends, performed his duties. If any remarked that he seemed listless and sorrowful, all knew he grieved over his daughter's marriage. None knew that the old man's soul had been held hostage, like a bug in a glass jar.

Imperceptibly, patiently, the young wizard cast his web over all the surviving wizards of the High Realm. The filaments were practically invisible, light to the touch, barely felt. He didn't weave a gigantic web for all to see, but deftly wrapped a line around an arm, wound a toil around a foot, holding them so lightly that they never knew they were held at all until the day came when they couldn't move.

Now they were stuck fast, caught by their own desperation. Sinistrad was right. They had no choice. They had to rely on him, for he was the only one who had been smart enough to plan ahead and make some provision to escape their beautiful hell.

Sinistrad arrived at the front of the hall. He caused a golden podium to spring up from the floor and, mounting it, turned to address his fellows.

"The elf ship has been sighted. My son is aboard. In accordance with our plans, I shall go to meet and guide it—"

"We never agreed to allow an elven vessel inside the dome," spoke out a female mysteriarch. "You said it would be a small ship, piloted by your son and his oafish servant."

"I was forced to effect a change in plans," replied Sinistrad, his lips creasing in a thin and unpleasant smile. "The first ship was attacked by elves and crashed on Drevlin. My son was able to take over this elven vessel. The child holds their captain in thrall. There are no more than thirty elves on board the ship, and only one wizard—a very weak wizard, of course. I think we can deal with that situation, don't you?"

"Yes, in the old days," answered a woman. "One of us could have dealt with thirty elves. But now . . ." Her voice trailed away as she shook her head.

"That is why we have worked our magic, created the illusions." Sinistrad gestured toward the outside of the Guildhall. "They will be intimidated by the sight alone. We will have no trouble from them."

"Why not meet them at the firmament, take your son, and let them go on their way?" demanded the aged mysteriarch known as Balthazar.

"Because, you doddering fool, we need their vessel!" Sinistrad hissed, clearly growing angry at the questioning. "With it we can transport large numbers of our people back down to the Mid Realm. Before, we would have been forced to wait until we could either acquire vessels or enchant more dragons."

"So what do we do with the elves?" asked the woman.

Everyone looked to Sinistrad. They knew the answer as well as he did; they wanted to hear him say it.

He said it, without pause, without hesitation. "We kill them."

The silence was loud and echoing. The aged mysteriarch shook his head. "No. I won't be a party to this."

"Why not, Balthazar? You killed elves enough back in the Mid Realm."

"That was war. This is murder."

"War is 'us or them.' This is war. It is either us or them!"

The mysteriarchs around him murmured, seeming to agree. Several began to argue with the old wizard, trying to persuade him to change his stance. "Sinistrad is right," they said. "It *is* war! It can never be anything else between our races." And "After all, Sinistrad's only trying to lead us home."

"I pity you!" Balthazar snarled. "I pity you all! He"—pointing at Sinistrad—"is leading you, all right. Leading you around by the nose like fatted calves. And when he's ready to dine, he'll slaughter the lot of you and feed off your flesh. Bah! Leave me alone! I'll die up here sooner than follow him back there."

The old wizard stalked toward the door.

"And so you will, graybeard," muttered Sinistrad beneath his breath. "Let him go," he said aloud, when some of his fellows would have gone after the wizard. "Unless there are any others who want to leave with him?"

The mysteriarch cast a swift, searching glance around the room, gathering up the tendrils of his web and tugging it tighter and tighter. No one else managed to break free. Those who had once struggled were now so weak with fear, they were eager and ready to do his bidding.

"Very well. I will bring the elven ship through the dome. I will remove my son and his companions to my castle." Sinistrad might have told his people that one of his son's companions was a skilled assassin—a man who could take the blood of the elves on his own hands and leave those of the mysteriarchs clean. But Sinistrad wanted to harden his people, force them to sink lower and lower until they would willingly and unquestioningly do anything he asked. "Those of you who volunteered to learn to fly the elf ship know what you are to do. The rest must work to maintain the city's spells. When the time comes, I will give the signal and we will act."

He gazed at them all, studied each pallid, grim face, and was satisfied. "Our plans are progressing well. Better than we had anticipated, in fact. Traveling with my son are several who may be of use to us in ways we had not foreseen. One is a dwarf from the Low Realm. The elves have exploited the dwarves for centuries. It is likely we can turn the Gegs, as they call themselves, to war. Another is a human who claims to come from a realm beneath the Low Realm—a realm none of us previously knew existed. This news could be extremely valuable to all of us."

There were murmurs of approval and agreement.

"My son brings information about the human kingdoms and the elven revolution, all of which will be most helpful when we set about to conquer them. And, most important, he has seen the great machine built by the Sartan on the Low Realm. At last we may be able to unravel the mystery of the so-called Kicksey-winsey and turn it, too, to our use."

Sinistrad raised his hands in a blessing. "Go forth now, my people. Go forth and know that as you do so you are stepping out into the world, for soon Arianus will be ours!"

The meeting broke up with cheering, most of it enthusiastic. Sinistrad stepped down from the podium and it disappeared—

magic had to be carefully rationed, expended only on that which was essential. Many stopped him to congratulate him or to ask questions, clearing up small details about the plan of action. Several asked politely after his health, but no one inquired about his wife. Iridal had not been present at a council meeting in ten cycles, ever since the guild voted to go along with Sinistrad's plot—to take her child and exchange it for the human prince. The guild members were just as well pleased Iridal did not attend the meetings. They still, after all this time, found it difficult to look into her eyes.

Sinistrad, mindful of the need to commence his journey, shook off the hangers-on who crowded round him and made his way from the Guildhall. A mental command brought the quicksilver dragon to the very foot of the stairs of the hall. Glowering at the wizard balefully, the dragon nevertheless suffered the mysteriarch to mount its back and command it to do his bidding. The dragon had no choice but to obey Sinistrad; it was enthralled. In this the creature was unlike the wizards standing in the shadowy doorway of the Guildhall. They had given themselves to Sinistrad of their own free will.

CHAPTER ♦ 46

THE

FIRMAMENT

♦

THE ELVEN DRAGONSHIP HUNG MOTIONLESS IN THE THIN, CHILL AIR. Having reached the floating chunks of ice known as the firmament, it had come to a halt, no one daring to proceed further. Ice floes ten times larger than the vessel loomed above them. Smaller boulders circled the more massive chunks; the air glistened with tiny droplets of frozen water. The sun's glare off the floebergs dazzled the eye; no one could look at them directly without being blinded. How thick the firmament was, how far it reached, was anyone's guess. No one, except the mysteriarchs and the Sartan, had ever flown this high and returned to give an account of their journey. Maps had been drawn from speculation, and now everyone on board ship knew them to be inaccurate. No one had guessed the mysteriarchs had passed through the firmament to build their realm on the other side.

"Natural defense barrier," said Hugh, peering with narrowed eyes at the awful beauty outside the porthole. "No wonder they've kept their wealth undisturbed all these years."

"How do we get through it?" asked Bane. The child was standing on tip-toe to see.

"We don't."

"But we have to!" The prince's voice shrilled. "I have to get to my father!"

"Kid, one of the ice boulders—even a little one—hits us, and our bodies will be just another star twinkling in the daytime sky. Maybe you better tell daddy to come get you."

Bane's face smoothed, the flush of anger faded. "Thank you

for the suggestion, Sir Hugh." His hand clasped around the feather. "I'll do just that. And I'll be certain to tell him all you've done for me. All of you." His glance encompassed everyone from Alfred to a beauty-dazed Limbeck, to Haplo's dog. "I'm certain he'll reward you . . . as you deserve."

Skipping across the deck, Bane plunked himself down in a corner of the hold and, closing his eyes, apparently began to commune with his father.

"I didn't like that little pause he put in between 'reward' and 'deserve,' " remarked Haplo. "What's to keep this wizard from snatching his kid and sending us up in flames?"

"Nothing, I suppose," answered Hugh, "except that he wants something and it's not just his little boy. Otherwise, why go to all this trouble?"

"Sorry, you've lost me."

"Alfred, come here. Look, you said that this Sinistrad came to the castle at night, switched babies, and then left. How'd he manage that with guards all around?"

"The mysteriarchs have the power to transport themselves through the air. Trian explained it thus to His Majesty the king: the spell is done by means of sending the mind on ahead of the body. Once the mind is firmly established in a particular location, it can call for the body to join it. The only requirement to the spell-caster is that he must have previously visited the place, so that he can mentally call up an accurate picture of where he's going. The mysteriarchs had often visited the Royal Palace on Uylandia, which is nearly as old as the world."

"But he couldn't, for example, send himself to the Low Realm or the elven palace on Aristagon?"

"No, sir, he couldn't. Not mentally, at least. None of them could. The elves hated and feared the mysteriarchs and never allowed them in their kingdom. The wizards couldn't travel to the Low Realm that way either, since they'd never been there before. They'd have to rely on other means of transport . . . Oh, I see your point, sir!"

"Uh-huh. First Sinistrad tried to get my ship. That failed, and now he has this one. If he—"

"Hush, company," murmured Haplo.

The door to the brig opened and Captain Bothar'el, flanked by two crew members, entered. "You"—he pointed to Hugh—"come with me."

Shrugging, the Hand did as he was told, not sorry to get a

glimpse of what was going on above. The door slammed shut behind them, the guard locked it, and Hugh followed the elf up the ladder to the top deck. It was not until he arrived on the bridge that he noticed Haplo's dog trotting at his heels.

"Where did that come from?" The captain glared at the animal irritably. The dog gazed up at him, brown eyes shining, tongue lolling, tail wagging.

"I don't know. He followed me, I guess."

"Midshipman, get that thing off the bridge. Take it back to its master and tell him to keep an eye on it or I'll toss it overboard."

"Yes, sir."

The midshipman bent down to pick up the dog. The animal's demeanor changed instantly. Its ears flattened and the tail ceased wagging and began a slow and ominous brush from side to side. The lips parted in a snarl, a low growl rumbled in the chest.

"If you are fond of those fingers," the animal seemed to say, "you better keep them to yourself."

The midshipman took the dog's advice. Putting his hands behind his back, he looked questioningly and fearfully at his captain.

"Dog . . ." tried Hugh experimentally. The animal's ears lifted slightly. It glanced at him, keeping one eye fixed on the midshipman but letting Hugh know it considered him a friend.

"Here, dog," ordered Hugh, clumsily snapping his fingers.

The dog turned his head, asking him if he was sure about this.

Hugh snapped his fingers again, and the dog, with a parting snarl at the hapless elf, ambled over to Hugh, who patted it awkwardly. It sat down at his feet.

"It'll be all right. I'll watch him—"

"Captain, the dragon is closing on us," reported a lookout.

"Dragon?" Hugh looked at the elf.

Captain Bothar'el, in answer, pointed.

Hugh walked over to the ship's porthole and stared out. Threading its way through the firmament, the dragon was barely visible, appearing as a river of silver flowing among the floebergs— a river of silver with two flaming red eyes.

"Do you know its type, human?"

"A quicksilver." Hugh had to pause, to think of the elven word. "Silindistani."

"We can't outrun it," said Captain Bothar'el. "Look at its speed! It is well-named. We'll have to fight."

"I don't think so," offered Hugh. "My guess is we're about to meet the boy's father."

Elves dislike and distrust dragons intensely. The elf wizards' magic cannot control them and the knowledge that humans can has always throbbed like a rotting tooth in the elven mouth. The elves aboard the ship were nervous and ill-at-ease in the presence of the quicksilver dragon. It wound and writhed and twisted its long, shining body around their vessel. The elves shifted their heads constantly to keep the creature in view, or jumped in startlement whenever the head shot up in a place where it had not been two seconds earlier. Such nervous reactions appeared to amuse the mysteriarch standing on the bridge. Though the wizard was graciousness itself, Hugh could see the glint beneath the lashless eyelids, and a small smile flickered occasionally across the thin and bloodless lips.

"I am eternally in your debt, Captain Bothar'el," said Sinistrad. "My child means more to me than all the treasures of the High Realm." Looking down at the boy, who was clinging to his hand and gazing up at him in unfeigned admiration, Sinistrad enlarged his smile.

"I was glad to be of service. As the boy explained, we are now considered outlaws by our people. We must find and join the rebel forces. He promised us payment—"

"Oh, and you will receive it, in abundance, I assure you. And you must see our enchanting realm and meet our people. We have so few guests. We become quite weary of each other. Not that we encourage visitors," Sinistrad added delicately. "But this is a special circumstance."

Hugh glanced at Haplo, who had been brought to the bridge with the other "guests" upon Sinistrad's arrival. The assassin would have liked very much to get some indication of what Haplo thought of all this. They couldn't speak, of course, but even a raised eyebrow or a quick wink would tell Hugh that Haplo wasn't swallowing this honeyed fruit either. But Haplo was staring at Sinistrad so intently the man might have been counting the pores in the wizard's long nose.

"I will not risk flying my ship through that." Captain Bothar'el indicated the firmament with a nod of his head. "Give us what you have"—the elf's gaze fixed on several fine jewels adorning the fingers of the mysteriarch—"and we will return to our realm."

Hugh could have told the elf he was wasting his breath.

Sinistrad would never let this ship slip through his ruby-and-diamond-sparkling hands.

He didn't. "The journey might be the tiniest bit difficult, captain, but not impossible and certainly not dangerous. I will be your guide and show you the safe passage through the firmament." He glanced around the bridge. "Surely you will not refuse to allow your crew the chance to view the wonders of our realm?"

The legendary wealth and splendor of the High Realm, made real by the sight of the jewels the wizard wore with such careless ease, kindled a flame that burned up fear and—so Hugh saw in the crew's eyes—common sense. He felt a cool pity for the elven captain, who knew he was flying into a spiderweb but who could do nothing to stop himself. If he gave the order to leave this place and return home, *he'd* be the one returning—the hard way, head over heels through several miles of empty sky.

"Very well," Bothar'el said ungraciously. A cheer from the crew died out with the flash in the captain's eye.

"May I ride with you on the dragon, papa?" asked Bane.

"Of course, my son." Sinistrad ran a hand through the boy's fair hair. "And now, much as I would enjoy staying and talking further with all of you, especially my new friend Limbeck here" —Sinistrad bowed to the Geg, who bobbed awkwardly back— "my wife is waiting most impatiently to see her child. Women. What loving little creatures they are."

Sinistrad turned to the captain. "I have never flown a ship, but it occurs to me that the major problem you will encounter passing through the firmament is ice forming on the wings. I am certain, however, that this most skilled colleague of mine"—he bowed to the ship's wizard, who returned the courtesy respectfully, if guardedly—"can melt it."

His arm around his son, Sinistrad started to leave, using his magic to transport him the short distance back to the dragon. Their bodies had faded to almost nothing when he paused and fixed a glittering-eyed gaze upon the captain. "Follow the path of the dragon," he said, "exactly." And he was gone.

"So what do you think of him?" Hugh asked Haplo in an undertone as both men, plus the dog, Alfred, and Limbeck, were escorted back to the brig.

"The wizard?"

"Who else?"

"Oh, he's powerful," said Haplo, shrugging. "But not as powerful as I'd expected."

Hugh grunted. He'd found Sinistrad daunting. "And what did you expect—a Sartan?"

Haplo glanced sharply at Hugh, saw it was a joke. "Yeah," he answered, grinning.

CHAPTER 47

THE

FIRMAMENT

◆

THE *CARFA'SHON* SAILED THROUGH THE ICE FLOES, LEAVING A SPARKLING trail of crystals swirling and glittering in its wake. The cold was bitter. The ship's wizard had been forced to draw magical heat from the living and working areas of the ship and use it to keep the rigging, the cables, the wings, and the hull free of the ice that rained down on them with a rattling noise, sounding so Limbeck said, like millions of dried peas.

Haplo, Limbeck, Alfred, and Hugh huddled for warmth around the small brazier in the hold. The dog had curled up in a ball, its nose buried in its bushy tail, and was fast asleep. None of the four spoke. Limbeck was too awed by the sights he had seen and expected to see. What Haplo might be thinking was anybody's guess. Hugh was considering his options.

Murder is out. No assassin worth his dagger takes on the job of killing a wizard, let alone a mysteriarch! This Sinistrad is powerful. What am I saying? This man is power itself! He hums with it like a lightning rod in a thunderstorm. If only I could figure out why he wants me now, when he tried to kill me once before. Why am I suddenly so valuable?

"Why did you make me bring Hugh, father?"

The quicksilver dragon threaded its way through the ice floes. It was moving with unusual slowness, being held back by Sinistrad so that the elven ship could follow. The lethargic pace irritated the dragon, who, in addition, would have liked very much to dine on the sweet-smelling creatures inside the ship.

But it knew better than to challenge Sinistrad. The two had waged numerous magical battles before, and Gorgon had always lost. It hated the wizard with a grudging respect.

"I may need Hugh the Hand, Bane. He is a pilot, after all."

"But we have a pilot—the elf captain."

"My dear child, you have much to learn. So begin learning it now. Never trust elves. Though their intelligence is equal to that of humans, they are longer-lived, and tend to gain in wisdom. In ancient days, they were a noble race and humans were, as the elves are wont to sneer, little more than animals compared to them. But the elf wizards could not leave well enough alone. They were, in fact, jealous of us."

"I saw the wizard take the dead elf's soul," interrupted Bane, hushed with remembered awe.

"Yes." Sinistrad sneered. "That was how they thought to fight us."

"I don't understand, father."

"It is important that you do, my son, and quickly, for we will be dealing with an elven ship's wizard. Let me describe to you, briefly, the nature of magic. Before the Sundering, spiritual and physical magic—like all other elements in the world—were blended together in all people. After the Sundering, the world was split into its separate elements, at least so the legends of the Sartan tell us, and this happened with magic.

"Each race naturally seeks to use the power of magic to make up for its own deficiencies. Thus, elves, tending naturally toward the spiritual, needed magic to help enhance their physical powers. They studied the art of granting magical powers to physical objects that could work for them."

"Like the dragonship?"

"Yes, like the dragonship. Humans, on the other hand, were better able to control the physical world, and so sought additional power through the spiritual. To communicate with animals, to force the wind to do our bidding, the stones to rise up at our command—this became our greatest talent. And, because of our concern with the spiritual, we developed the ability of mental magic, of training our minds to alter and control physical laws."

"That's why I could fly."

"Yes, and if you had been an elf, you would have lost your life, for they do not possess such power. The elves poured all of their arcane skill into physical objects and studied the art of mental manipulation. An elven wizard with his hands bound is helpless. A human wizard, under the same circumstances, need simply tell himself that his wrists are shrinking in size and it will be true. Thus he can slip out of his bonds."

"Father," said Bane, looking backward, "the ship's stopped."

"So it has." Sinistrad checked an impatient sigh and reined in the dragon. "That ship's wizard of theirs must be nothing more than Second House if he can't keep the ice off their wings any better than this!"

"And so we have two pilots." Bane twisted around in the dragon saddle in order to get a better look at the ship. The elves had been forced to take axes to the ice that had formed on the cables.

"Not for long," said Sinistrad.

If he's going to use this vessel, the wizard needs a pilot. This question settled, Hugh took out his pipe and began to fill it sparingly with his dwindling supply of tobacco. *And now the wizard has two pilots—me and the elf. He can keep us both guessing, play us one off the other. Winner lives, loser dies. Or maybe not. Maybe he won't trust the elf at all. Interesting. I wonder if I should tip off Bothar'el?*

Lighting his pipe, Hugh gazed at the others from beneath hooded lids. *Limbeck. Why Limbeck? And Haplo. Where does he fit in?*

"The Geg you've brought, my son. You say he's the leader of his people?"

"Well, sort of." Bane squirmed uncomfortably. "It wasn't my fault. I tried to get their king—they call him the head foreman—"

"High froman."

"—but that other man wanted this Limbeck to come and"—the boy shrugged—"he came."

"What other man?" Sinistrad asked. "Alfred?"

"No, not Alfred," Bane said scornfully. "The other man. The quiet one. The one with the dog."

Sinistrad cast his mind around the bridge of the ship. He did recall seeing some other human but couldn't bring his face to memory. Nondescript, a kind of gray blur. That must be the one from the newly discovered realm.

"Perhaps you should have cast the enchantment over him, convinced him that he wanted what you wanted. Didn't you try?"

"Of course, father!" Bane said, his cheeks flushed with indignation.

"Then what happened?"

Bane ducked his head. "It didn't work."

"What? Could it be possible that Trian actually managed to disrupt the spell? Or perhaps this man has a charm—"

"No, he doesn't have anything except a dog. I don't like him. He came along and I didn't want him to but I couldn't stop him. When the enchantment went out to him, it didn't work like it does on most people. Everyone else sort of absorbs it, like a sponge sucking up water. With him—that Haplo—it just bounced right back."

"Impossible. He must have a hidden charm, or else it was your imagination."

"No, it wasn't either of those, father."

"Bah! What do you know? You're just a child. This Limbeck is the leader of some sort of rebellion among the people, isn't that right?"

Bane, head down, pouted, refused to answer.

Sinistrad brought the dragon to a halt. The ship was lumbering along behind, its wings brushing the edges of floebergs that could smash its hull into fragments. Twisting in the saddle, the mysteriarch caught hold of his son's jaw with his hand and jerked the boy's face upward. His grip was painful; Bane's eyes filled with tears.

"You will answer promptly any question I put to you. You will do my bidding without argument or back talk. You will, at all times, treat me with respect. I do not blame you for your lack of it now. You have been around those who did nothing to command it, who were not worthy of it. But that has changed. You are with your father now. Never forget that."

"No," whispered Bane.

"No, what?" The grip tightened.

"No, father!" Bane gasped.

Satisfied, Sinistrad released the boy, rewarding Bane with a slight widening of the thin, bloodless lips. He turned back to face forward, ordering the dragon on.

The wizard's fingers left white indentations on the boy's cheek, purplish marks on his jaw. Thoughtful, Bane was silent, trying to rub away the pain with his hand. His tears had not fallen and he blinked them back from his eyes, swallowed those in his throat.

"Now, answer my question. This Limbeck is leader of a rebellion."

"Yes, father."

"And so he could be useful to us. At the very least, he will provide information about the machine."

"I made drawings of the machine, father."

"Did you?" Sinistrad glanced behind him. "Good ones? No, don't take them out. They might blow away. I will look them over when we reach home."

Hugh puffed slowly on his pipe, feeling more relaxed. Whatever the wizard was plotting, Limbeck would provide him information and access to the Low Realm. But Haplo. Try to figure that one. Unless he just came along by accident. No. Hugh gazed at the man intently. Haplo was teasing the sleeping dog, tickling its nose with its tail. The dog sneezed, woke up, looked around irritably for the fly, and, not finding it, went back to sleep. Hugh thought back to their imprisonment on Drevlin, to the riveting shock he'd experienced seeing Haplo standing beside the grille. No, Hugh couldn't imagine Haplo doing anything by accident. This was by design, then. But by whose?

Hugh's gaze shifted to Alfred. The chamberlain was staring into nothing, his face the face of one who walks in a waking nightmare. What had happened to him in the Low Realm? And why was he here, other than that the kid wanted to bring along his servant? But Bane hadn't brought Alfred, Hugh remembered. The chamberlain had tagged along of his own accord. And was still tagging.

"And what about Alfred?" Sinistrad asked. "Why did you bring him?"

The mysteriarch and his son were nearing the edge of the firmament. The bergs were becoming smaller and the distances between them farther apart. Ahead of them, sparkling in the distance, shining through the ice like an emerald set amidst diamonds, was what Sinistrad said was the High Realm. In the distance, behind them, they could hear a ragged cheer lift from the elven ship.

"He found out about King Stephen's plan to have me murdered," Bane answered his father, "and he came along to protect me."

"He doesn't know more than that?"

"He knows I'm your son. He knows about the enchantment."

"All the fools know about it. That's what made it so effective.

They were so delightfully aware of their own helplessness. But that wasn't what I meant. Does Alfred know you manipulated your parents and that idiot Trian into thinking that they were the ones responsible for casting you out? Is that why he came?"

"No. Alfred came because he can't help himself. He has to be with me. He's not smart enough to do anything else."

"It will be handy to have him with you when you return. He can verify your story."

"Return? Return where?" Bane looked frightened. He clung to his father. "I'm going to stay with you!"

"Why don't you rest now? We'll be home soon and I want you to make a good impression on my friends."

"And on mother?" Bane settled himself more comfortably in the saddle.

"Yes, of course. Now, hold your tongue. We are nearing the dome and I must communicate with those waiting to receive us."

Bane rested his head against his father's back. He hadn't told quite all the truth about Alfred. *There had been that strange occurrence in the forest, when the tree fell on the boy. Alfred thought I was still unconscious, but I wasn't. I saw. Just what it was I saw, I'm not certain. Up here, I'm sure to find out. Perhaps, someday, I'll ask father. But not now. Not until I learn what he meant about "returning." Until then, I'll keep Alfred all to myself.*

Bane nestled closer to Sinistrad.

Hugh dumped the tobacco out of his pipe and, wrapping it carefully in its cloth, placed it snugly against his breast. He'd known all along he was making a mistake coming up here. But he couldn't help himself. The kid had ensorceled him. Hugh decided he could, therefore, quit thinking about his options.

He didn't have any.

CHAPTER 48

NEW HOPE,

HIGH REALM

◆

GUIDED BY THE MYSTERIARCH AND THE QUICKSILVER DRAGON, THE *Carfa'shon* sailed through the magical dome surrounding the High Realm. Elves, humans, and the Geg pressed their faces against the portholes, staring out at the marvelous world below them. They were dazzled by the extraordinary beauty, awestruck by the magnificence of what they saw, and each reminded himself uneasily just how powerful were the beings who created these marvels. Within seconds they had left behind a world of frozen, glittering ice and entered a sun-warmed green land with a shimmering rainbow-hued sky.

The elves shed the fur coats they had donned to combat the frigid cold. Hugh dumped the charwood out of the brazier into the firebox. The ice began to melt from the ship, pouring off the hull, falling to the ground below them like rain.

All hands not directly involved with the flying of the ship gazed in wide-eyed wonder at this enchanted realm. There must be water in abundance, was almost everyone's first thought. The ground was covered with lush vegetation, tall trees with green leaves dotted a landscape of rolling hills. Here and there, tall pearl spires stood against the sky; broad roads crisscrossed the valleys and vanished over the ridges.

Sinistrad flew before them, the quicksilver dragon streaking like a comet across the sun-drenched sky, making the graceful dragonship seem lumbering and clumsy by comparison. They followed his lead, and ahead of them, on the horizon, a cluster of spires appeared. Sinistrad aimed the dragon's head toward this location, and as the elven ship drew nearer, all on board saw it was a gigantic city.

Hugh had once, during his days as a slave, visited the capital city of Aristagon, of which the elves were very justly proud. The beauty of its buildings, which are made of coralite molded into artistic shapes by skilled elven craftsmen, are legendary. But the jewels of Tribus were common paste and glass when compared to the wondrous city that lay glistening before them—a handful of pearls scattered over green velvet with an occasional ruby or sapphire or diamond set among them.

A silence of profound awe, almost reverence, filled the elven ship. No one spoke, as if fearful of disturbing a lovely dream. Hugh had been taught by the Kir monks that beauty is ephemeral and all man's work will come to naught but dust in the end. He'd seen nothing yet in his lifetime to convince him otherwise, but now he began to think maybe he'd been wrong. Tears ran down Limbeck's cheeks; he was constantly forced to remove his spectacles and wipe them off so that he could see. Alfred appeared to forget whatever inner torment he was suffering and gazed out on the city with a face softened by what one might almost call melancholy.

As for Haplo, if he was impressed, he didn't show it, other than evincing a mild interest as he stared with the rest of them out the porthole.

But then, Hugh thought, scrutinizing the man carefully, that face of his never shows anything—fear, elation, worry, happiness, anger. And yet, if one looked carefully, there were traces, almost like scars, of emotions that had cut deep. The man's will alone had smoothed them out; almost, but not quite, erased them. No wonder he makes me want to keep putting my hand to my sword. I think I'd almost prefer an avowed enemy at my side than Haplo as a friend.

Sitting at Haplo's feet, gazing about with more interest than its master evinced, the dog suddenly ducked its head and gnawed at its flank, apparently driven to search out an elusive itch.

The elven ship entered the city. It drifted low over wide, flower-lined boulevards that wound among tall buildings. What these buildings were made of was anyone's guess. Smooth and sleek, they seemed to be created out of pearls—those gems that are sometimes found among the coralite and are rare and precious as drops of water. The elves sucked in their breaths and glanced at each other out of the corners of their almond eyes. A cornerstone of pearl alone would give them more wealth than their king himself possessed. Hugh, rubbing his hands, felt his spirits lift. If he got out of here alive, his fortune was made.

Dropping lower, they could see, beneath the vessel, upturned faces stare at them curiously as they passed. The streets were crowded; the city's population must number in the thousands, Hugh reckoned. Sinistrad guided the ship to a huge central park and indicated, by hand signals, that here they were to drop anchor. A crowd of wizards had gathered here, gazing at them curiously. Though none of the magi had ever seen a mechanical contraption such as this, they were quick to catch hold of the guy ropes tossed over the side by the elves and fasten them to trees. Captain Bothar'el caused the ship's wings to fold in almost completely, so that only a small bit of magic kept the vessel afloat.

Hugh and his companions were brought to the bridge and arrived there the same moment as Sinistrad and Bane appeared, seeming to step out of the air. The mysteriarch bowed respectfully to the captain.

"I trust your trip was not unduly difficult? Your ship sustained no damage from the ice?"

"Little, thank you," replied Captain Bothar'el, bowing in turn. "What damage we sustained we will be able to repair."

"My people and I will be most happy to furnish you with material: wood, rope—"

"Thank you, that will not be necessary. We are accustomed to making do with what we have." It was obvious that the beauty of this realm and all its wealth had not blinded Bothar'el's eyes. He was in alien lands, among an enemy race. Hugh was growing to like this elf. There was, he could see, no need to warn Bothar'el of his danger.

Sinistrad did not seem offended. Smiling a rictus smile, he said he hoped the crew would disembark and take in the pleasures of their city. Several of his people would come aboard and keep an eye on the slaves.

"Thank you. I, myself, and some of my officers may later be pleased to accept your invitation. As for now, we have work to do. And I would not want to burden you with responsibility for our slaves."

Sinistrad, it seemed, might have raised an eyebrow had he

had one. As it was, the lines in his forehead lifted slightly, but he said nothing, merely bowed again in acquiescence, the smile deepening and darkening. "I could make this ship mine in five seconds, if I wanted it," said the smile.

Captain Bothar'el bowed, and he, too, smiled.

Sinistrad's gaze slid over Hugh, Limbeck, and Alfred. It seemed they lingered for some time on Haplo, and the slight crease of a thoughtful frown appeared between the eyes. Haplo returned the inspection with his quiet, unassuming expression, and the frown line disappeared.

"You will have no objection, I hope, sir, to my taking these passengers of yours to meet my wife and to stay as guests in my house? We are most beholden to them for saving the life of our only child."

Captain Bothar'el replied that he was certain his passengers would enjoy escaping the dull routine of shipboard life. Hugh, reading between the words, figured that the elf was glad to be rid of them. The hatch opened, a rope ladder was thrown out. Sinistrad and Bane left the bridge in their usual airy style; the others descended via the ladder. Hugh was the last one to leave the ship. Standing in the hatchway, watching the others slowly and clumsily make their way down, he was startled by a light touch on his arm.

Turning, he looked into the eyes of the elf captain.

"Yes," said Bothar'el, "I know what he wants. I'll do my best to make certain he doesn't get it. If you come back with money, we'll get you out of here. We'll wait for you as long as we can hold out." The elf's mouth twisted. "I expect to be paid as promised—one way or the other."

A cry and thud from below announced that Alfred, as usual, had come to grief. Hugh said nothing. There was nothing to say. All was understood. He began to climb down the ladder. The others were on the ground already, Haplo and Limbeck tending a prone and unconscious Alfred. Standing next to Haplo, licking Alfred's face, was the dog, and it occurred to Hugh to wonder, as he descended, how the animal or its master had managed such a remarkable feat. Hugh had never heard of a four-legged animal being able to climb down a rope ladder. But when he asked the others, no one seemed to have noticed.

A group of twenty mysteriarchs—ten men and ten women—was on hand to welcome them. Sinistrad introduced them as mystagogues, teachers of the arcane and the ruling body of the city. They appeared to be of varying ages, though none were as young as Sinistrad. One couple looked to be ancient, their faces wizened masses of wrinkles nearly hiding eyes that were shrewd and intelligent and held in them knowledge amassed over who knew how many years. The others were in mid-life, with firm, unlined faces, hair thick and richly colored with only a few strands of silver or gray at the temples. They were pleasant and polite, welcoming visitors to their fair city, offering all in their power to make the stay memorable.

Memorable. Hugh had a feeling it would be that, at least. Walking among the wizards, hearing introductions, he looked into eyes that never looked into his, saw faces that might have been carved of the pearl substance around them, devoid of any expression other than polite and proper welcome. His sense of danger and unease grew and was made manifest by a peculiar incident.

"I was wondering, my friends, if you would care to walk about our city and view its wonders. My own dwelling is some distance away, and you may not have another opportunity to see much of New Hope before you have to leave."

All agreed and, having ascertained that Alfred was not injured—beyond a bump on the head—they followed Sinistrad through the park. Crowds of wizards gathered on the grass or sat beneath the trees to stare at them as they passed. But no one said a word, either to them or to a neighbor. The silence was eerie, and Hugh felt that he much preferred the thumping and banging of the Kicksey-winsey.

Reaching the sidewalk, he and his companions stood among the glittering buildings whose spires soared into the rainbow-shimmering sky. Arched doorways led to cool, shadowy courtyards. Arched windows gave glimpses of fabulous luxuries inside.

"These to your left belong to the college of the arcane, where we teach our young. Across are the dwellings of the students and professors. The very tallest building that you can see from here is the seat of government, where sit the members of the council, whom you have just met. Ah, I must warn you of one thing." Sinistrad, who had been walking with one hand resting lovingly on the shoulder of his son, turned around to face them.

"The material used in our buildings is made magically and therefore is not . . . How shall I put it so that you will understand? Let us say: it is not of this world. And so it would be a good idea if you, being of the world, did not touch it. Ah, there, what did I say?"

Limbeck, ever curious, had reached out his hand to run his fingers over the smooth, pearly stone. There was a sizzle, and the Geg yelped in pain and snatched back burned fingers.

"He doesn't understand your language," said Alfred with a rebuking glance at the wizard.

"Then I suggest that one of you translate," returned Sinistrad. "The next time, it might cost him his life."

Limbeck stared in awe at the buildings, sucking on the tips of his hurt fingers. Alfred imparted the warning to the Geg in a low voice and they continued on down the street, new wonders continually unfolding before their eyes. The sidewalks were massed with people, coming and going on their business, and all staring at them curiously and in silence.

Alfred and Limbeck kept pace with Bane and Sinistrad. Hugh was doing the same until he noticed Haplo lagging behind, walking slowly to assist his dog, which had suddenly developed a limp in one foot. Hugh, answering a silent request, paused to wait for them. They were a long time coming—the dog was in obvious discomfort—and the others drew well ahead. Haplo stopped and knelt down beside the animal, seemingly absorbed in its injury. Hugh joined him.

"Well, what's the matter with the mutt?"

"Nothing, really. I wanted to show you something. Reach out and touch that wall behind me."

"Are you crazy? You want to see me burn my fingers off?"

"Go ahead," said Haplo with his quiet smile. The dog was grinning at Hugh as if sharing a wonderful secret. "You won't get hurt."

Feeling very much like a boy who can't resist a dare though he knows he'll only end up in trouble, Hugh gingerly stretched out his hand toward the pearl-glistening wall. He cringed in expected pain when his fingers touched the surface, but he felt nothing. Absolutely nothing! His fingers went completely through the stone! The building was solid as a cloud.

"What the . . . ?"

"Illusion," said Haplo. He patted the dog on the flank. "Come on, the wizard's looking at us. Thorn in its paw," he called out to Sinistrad. "I removed it. The dog'll be all right now."

Sinistrad regarded them with narrow-eyed suspicion, perhaps wondering where the dog had managed to pick up a thorn in the middle of the city. He continued on, however, though it seemed that his speech about the wonders of New Hope was a bit forced, the descriptions delivered somewhat bitingly.

Hugh, mystified, nudged Haplo. "Why?"

Haplo shrugged. "There's something else, too," he said in a low voice, the words coming out of the corner of his mouth so that, if Sinistrad glanced back, they would not seem to be talking. "Take a close look at all these people around us."

"They're a quiet bunch. I can say that for them."

"Look at them. Closely."

Hugh did as he was told. "There *is* something strange about them," he admitted. "They look . . ." He paused.

"Familiar?"

"Yeah. Familiar. Like I've seen them somewhere before. But that's not possible."

"Yes, it is. If you're seeing the same twenty people over and over."

At that moment, almost as if he had overheard, Sinistrad brought the tour to an abrupt halt.

"It is time we traveled on to my humble dwelling," he said. "My wife will be waiting."

CHAPTER 49

CASTLE SINISTER,

HIGH REALM

♦

THE QUICKSILVER DRAGON CARRIED THEM TO SINISTRAD'S DWELLING.
They did not travel far. The castle seemed to float on a cloud,
and commanded, whenever the mists parted, a view of the city
of New Hope that was spectacular, breathtaking, and—to Hugh's
mind—disturbing. The buildings, the people—nothing but a dream.
If so, whose? And why were they being invited—no, forced—to
share it?

Hugh's first action on entering the castle was to take a sur-
reptitious poke at the wall. He noted Haplo doing the same, and
both exchanged glances. The castle, at least, was solid. This was
real.

And the woman descending the stairs . . . was she real?

"Ah, there you are, my dear. I thought you would be out
front, waiting impatiently to greet your son."

The castle's entry hall was enormous, its dominating feature
a grand staircase whose marble steps were so wide that a war
dragon could have flown up it, wings fully extended, and never
touched the sides. The interior walls were made of the same
smooth, pearlized opal as the outer, and shimmered in the sunlight shining softly through the shifting mists surrounding the
castle. Tapestries of rich and wondrous beauty adorned the walls.
Rare and valuable articles of furniture—massive wooden chests,
richly carved high-backed chairs—line the hallway. Ancient suits
of human armor made of precious metals, inlaid with silver and
gold, stood silent guard. The stairs were covered with a thick,
smooth carpet made of woven wool.

Halfway down the stairs, dwarfed by their massive size, they could see—once Sinistrad had drawn their attention to her—a woman. She stood frozen, staring at her child. Bane kept very near Sinistrad, the boy's small hand clinging tightly to the wizard's. The woman put her hand to a locket she wore at her throat and clasped her fingers round it. With her other, she leaned heavily against the balustrades. She had not stopped on the stair to make a grand entrance, to draw all eyes to her. She had stopped, Hugh saw, because she could go no farther.

Hugh had wondered, briefly, what kind of woman Bane's mother was. What kind of woman would participate in a baby-switching. He had thought he knew, and would not have been surprised to see someone as treacherous and ambitious as the father. Now, seeing her, he realized she was not a perpetrator but a victim.

"My dear, have you taken root?" Sinistrad appeared displeased. "Why don't you speak? Our guests—"

The woman was going to fall, and without pausing to think, Hugh ran up the stairs and caught the slumping body in his arms.

"So that's mother," said Bane.

"Yes, my son," remarked Sinistrad. "Gentlemen, my wife, Iridal." He waved a negligent hand at her motionless body. "I must apologize for her. She is weak, very weak. And now, sirs, if you will follow me, I will show you to your quarters. I am certain you will want to rest after your fatiguing journey."

"What about her—your wife?" Hugh demanded. He smelled the fragrance of crushed and faded lavender.

"Take her to her room," said Sinistrad, glancing at her without interest. "It's at the top of the stairs, along the balcony, second door to the left."

"Should I call a servant to care for her?"

"We have no servants. I find them . . . disruptive. She must care for herself. As must you all, I'm afraid."

Without looking to see if their guests were following, Sinistrad and Bane turned to the right and walked through a door that appeared, seemingly by the wizard's command, in a blank wall. The others did not immediately go after him—Haplo was idly looking around, Alfred was apparently torn between following his prince and attending to the poor woman in Hugh's arms, Limbeck looked with frightened round eyes at the door that had materialized out of solid rock and kept rubbing his ears, perhaps longing for a whoosh, zuzt, wham to break the oppressive silence.

"I suggest you follow me, gentlemen. You will never find your way alone. There are but few fixed rooms in this castle. The rest come and go as we need them. I deplore waste, you see."

The others, somewhat startled by this pronouncement, made their way through the door, Limbeck holding back until Alfred gently propelled him forward. Hugh wondered where the dog was, then, looking down, saw the animal at his feet.

"Get along!" Hugh snapped, shoving at the dog with a boot.

The animal dodged him neatly and remained standing on the stair, watching him with interest, head cocked to one side, ears erect.

The woman in Hugh's arms stirred faintly and moaned. No other assistance from his companions being forthcoming, the assassin turned and carried the woman up the stairs. The climb to the balcony above was long, but the burden he bore was light, far too light.

He carried her to her room, finding it without difficulty by the half-open door and the faint smell of the same sweet fragrance that clung to her. Inside was a sitting room, beyond that a dressing room, and beyond that her bedchamber. Passing through the various rooms, Hugh was surprised to see that they were almost devoid of furnishings, there were few decorations, and those that were visible were covered with dust. The atmosphere of these inner, private chambers was chill and barren. Far different from the warm luxury of the entry hall.

Hugh laid Iridal gently upon a bed covered with sheets of finest linen trimmed with lace. He drew a silken coverlet over her thin body and then stood gazing at her.

She was younger than he had first guessed on seeing her. Her hair was white but thick and as finely spun as gossamer. The face in repose was sweet, delicately molded, and unlined. Her skin was pale, so dreadfully pale.

Before Hugh could catch the dog, it slipped past and gave the woman's hand—hanging down beside the bed—a swipe with its tongue. Iridal stirred and woke. Her eyes fluttered open. She looked up at Hugh, and fear contorted her features.

"Go now!" she whispered. "You must go!"

. . . The sound of chanting greeted the sun in the chill morning. It was the song of black-robed monks descending on the village, driving away the other carrion birds:

each new child's birth,
we die in our hearts,
truth black, we are shown,
death always returns,

With . . . with . . . with . . .

Hugh and other boys trudged behind, shivering in their thin clothing, their bare feet stumbling numbly over frozen ground. They had come to look forward to the warmth of the terrible fires that would soon be burning in this village.

There were no living people to be seen; only the dead, lying in the streets where their relatives had tossed the plague-infested bodies, then gone into hiding against the coming of the Kir. At a few doors, however, stood baskets of food or perhaps—more precious—jugs of water, the village's payment for services rendered.

The monks were accustomed to this. They went about their grim business, gathering the bodies, hauling them to the large open area where the orphans they sheltered were already heaping up charcrystal. Other boys, Hugh among them, ran down the street gathering up the thank-offerings that would be carried back to the monastery. Coming to one doorway, he heard a sound and paused in the act of lifting a loaf of bread from a basket. He looked inside.

"Mother," said a little boy, starting to approach a woman lying on the bed. "I'm hungry. Why don't you get out of bed? It's time for our breakfast."

"I can't get up this morning, dear." The mother's voice, though gentle, apparently sounded strange and unfamiliar to the child, because it frightened him. "No, my sweet darling. Don't come near me. I forbid it." She drew a breath and Hugh could hear it wheeze in her lungs. Her face was already as white as those of the corpses lying in the street, but he saw that once she had been pretty. "Let me look at you, Mikal. You will be good while . . . while I'm sick. Do you promise? Promise me," she said weakly.

"Yes, mother, I promise."

"Go now!" the woman said in a low voice. Her hands clenched the blankets. "You must go. Go . . . fetch me some water."

The child turned and ran toward Hugh, who was standing in the doorway. Hugh saw the woman's body jerk in agony, then go rigid, then limp. The eyes stared up at the ceiling.

"I must get water, water for mother," the child said, looking up at Hugh. His back was turned; he had not seen.

"I'll help carry it," said Hugh. "You hold this." He handed the boy the bread. Might as well get the child accustomed to his new life.

Taking the little boy by the hand, Hugh led him away from the house. In the child's arms was the loaf of bread, baked by a woman just as she was probably beginning to feel the first symptoms of the disease that would shortly claim her. Behind him, Hugh could still hear the soft echo of the mother's command, sending her child away so that he would not see her die.

"Go now!"

Water. Hugh lifted a carafe and poured a glass. Iridal did not glance at it, but kept her gaze fixed on him.

"You!" Her voice was low and soft. "You are . . . one of them . . . with my son?"

Hugh nodded. The woman rose, half-sitting in bed, propped up on her arm. Her face was pale, there was a fever in her lustrous eyes. "Go!" she repeated, speaking in a low, trembling voice. "You're in terrible danger! Leave this house! Now!"

Her eyes. Hugh was mesmerized by her eyes. They were large and deeply set, the irises every color of the rainbow—a glistening spectrum surrounding the black pupils that shifted and changed as the light struck them.

"Do you hear me?" she demanded.

Hugh hadn't really. Something about danger.

"Here, drink this," he said, thrusting the glass toward her.

Angrily she knocked it aside. The goblet crashed to the floor, water running over the stone tiles. "Do you think I want your deaths, too, on my hands?"

"Tell me the danger, then. Why must we leave?"

But the woman sank back on the pillows and would not answer him. Drawing near, he saw that she was shivering with fear.

"What danger?"

He bent down to pick up the pieces of broken glass, looking at her as he worked.

The woman shook her head frenziedly. Her eyes darted about the room. "No. I've said enough, perhaps too much! He has eyes everywhere, his ears are always listening!" The fingers of her hands curled and closed in on the palms.

It had been a long time since Hugh had felt another's pain. It had been a long time since he'd felt his own. From somewhere buried deep inside him, memories and feelings that had been lying dead came to life, stretched out bony hands, and dug their nails into his soul. His hand jerked; a glass shard drove into his palm.

The pain angered him.

"What do I do with this mess?"

Iridal made a weak gesture with her hand, and the broken glass he was holding in his hands vanished, as if it had never been.

"I'm sorry you hurt yourself," she said in a dull, lifeless voice. "But that is what you must expect if you insist on staying."

Averting his face from her, he turned to stare out the window. Far beneath them, its silvery skin visible through the shifting mists, the dragon had curled its huge body about the castle and lay there murmuring to itself over and over of its hatred for the wizard.

"We can't leave," Hugh said. "That dragon's out there, guarding—"

"There are ways to avoid the quicksilver if you truly want to leave."

Hugh was silent, reluctant to tell her the truth, afraid of what he might hear in return. But he had to know. "I can't leave. I'm enthralled—your son has me under enchantment."

Iridal stirred fitfully, glanced up at him with pitying eyes.

"The enchantment works only because you want it to work. Your will feeds it. You could have broken it long ago, if you truly wanted. So the wizard Trian discovered. You care about the boy, you see. And caring is an invisible prison. I know . . . I know!"

The dog, which had stretched out, nose on paws, upon the floor at Hugh's feet, suddenly sat bolt upright and stared around fiercely.

Iridal gasped. "He's coming! Quickly, leave me now. You have been here too long."

Hugh, his face dark and foreboding, did not move.

"Oh, please leave me!" Iridal pleaded, stretching out her hands. "For my sake! *I* am the one who will be punished!"

The dog was already on its feet and heading for the outer chambers. Hugh, with a final glance back at the stricken woman, thought it best to do as she said—for now, at least. Until he could mull over what she had told him. Going out, he met Sinistrad in the door to the sitting room.

"Your wife is resting." Hugh forestalled any question.

"Thank you. I am certain you made her *very* comfortable." Sinistrad's lashless eyes flicked over Hugh's muscular arms and body; a knowing smile touched his thin lips.

Hugh flushed in anger. He started to push past the wizard, but Sinistrad moved slightly to block his way.

"You are hurt," said the mysteriarch. Reaching out, he took hold of Hugh's hand and turned it, palm-up, to the light.

"It's nothing. A broken glass, that's all."

"Tsk, tsk. I cannot have my guests injured! Allow me." Sinistrad laid fingers, thin and quivering like the legs of a spider, on Hugh's palm over the wound. Closing his eyes, the mysteriarch concentrated. The jagged cut closed. The pain—of the wound— eased.

Smiling, Sinistrad opened his eyes and looked intently into Hugh's.

"We're not your guests," said the Hand. "We're your prisoners."

"*That*, my dear sir," replied the mysteriarch, "is entirely up to you."

One of the few rooms of the castle to remain constantly in the castle was the wizard's study. Its location, in relation to other rooms in the dwelling, shifted constantly, depending upon Sinistrad's moods and needs. This day, it was in the upper part of the castle, the curtains drawn to catch the last light of Solarus before the Lords of Night snuffed day's candle.

Spread out on the wizard's large desk were the drawings his son had done of the great Kicksey-winsey. Some were diagrams of parts of the huge machine that Bane, personally, had seen. Others had been created with Limbeck's help and provided illustrations of the parts of the Kicksey-winsey that operated on the rest of the isle of Drevlin. The drawings were quite good and remarkably accurate. Sinistrad had instructed the boy on how to use magic to enhance his work. Picturing the image in his mind, Bane had only to connect that image with the motion of his hand to translate what he saw onto paper.

The wizard was studying the diagrams intently when a muffled bark caused him to raise his head.

"What is that dog doing in here?"

"He likes me," said Bane, throwing his arms around the dog's neck and hugging him. The two had been roughhousing on the floor, which tussle had occasioned the bark. "He always follows me around. He likes me better than he does Haplo, don't you, boy?"

The dog grinned, its tail thumping the floor.

"Don't be too certain of that." Sinistrad fixed the animal with a piercing gaze. "I don't trust it. I think we should get rid of it. In ancient times, magi used animals such as this to do their bidding, to go places they could not go and act as spies."

"But Haplo isn't a wizard. He's just a . . . a human."

"And one not to be trusted. No man is that quiet and self-assured unless he thinks he has things under his control." Sinistrad glanced sidelong at his son. "I don't like this exhibition of weakness I've discovered in you, Bane. You begin to remind me of your mother."

The child removed his arms slowly from around the dog's neck. Rising to his feet, Bane walked over to stand beside his father.

"We could get rid of Haplo. Then I could keep the dog and you wouldn't have to be nervous about it."

"An interesting idea, my son," answered Sinistrad, preoccupied. "Now, take the beast out of here and run along and play."

"But, papa, the dog's not hurting anything. He'll be quiet if I tell him to. See, he's just lying here."

Sinistrad looked down to see the dog looking up. The animal had remarkably intelligent eyes. The mysteriarch frowned.

"I don't want him in here. He smells. Run along, both of you." Sinistrad lifted one drawing, held it next to another, and regarded both thoughtfully. "What was it originally designed to do? Something this gigantic, this enormous. What did the Sartan intend? Surely not just a means of gathering water."

"It produces the water to keep itself going," said Bane, clambering up on a stool to stand level with his father. "It needs the steam to run the engines to create the electricity that runs the machine. The Sartan probably built this part of the machine" —Bane pointed—"to gather water and send it to the Mid Realm, but it's obvious that this wasn't the machine's central function. You see, I—"

Bane caught his father's eye. The words died on the boy's lips. Sinistrad said nothing. Slowly Bane slid down off the stool.

The mysteriarch, without another word, turned back to his perusing of the drawings.

Bane walked to the door. The dog, rising to its feet, followed eagerly after, evidently thinking it was time to play. In the doorway, the boy halted and turned back.

"I know," he said.

"What?" Sinistrad, irritated, glanced up.

"I know why the Kicksey-winsey was invented. I know what it was meant to do. I know how it can be made to do it. And I know how we can rule the entire world. I figured it out while I was making the drawings."

Sinistrad stared at the child. There was something of the boy's mother in the sweet mouth and the features, but it was his own shrewd and calculating eyes that stared fearlessly back at him.

Sinistrad indicated the drawings with a negligent wave of his hand. "Show me."

Bane, returning to the desk, did so. The dog, forgotten, plopped itself down at the wizard's feet.

CHAPTER ◆ 50

CASTLE SINISTER,

HIGH REALM

◆

THE TINKLING OF MANY UNSEEN BELLS CALLED SINISTRAD'S GUESTS TO dinner. The castle's dining room—no doubt having just been created—was windowless, large, dark, and chill. A long oaken table, covered with dust, stood in the center of the bleak chamber. Chairs draped in cloth ranged round it like guardian ghosts. The fireplace was cold and empty. The room had appeared right in front of the guests' noses, and they gathered within it, most of them ill-at-ease, to await the arrival of their host.

Sauntering over to the table, Haplo ran his finger through an inch of dust and dirt.

"I can hardly wait," he remarked, "to taste the food."

Lights flared above them, hitherto unseen candelabrum flamed to brilliant life. The cloth draped over the chairs was whisked away by unseen hands. The dust varnished. The empty table was suddenly laden with food—roast meat, steaming vegetables, fragrant breads. Goblets filled with wine and water appeared. Music played softly from some unseen source.

Limbeck, gaping, tumbled backward and nearly fell into a roaring fire blazing on the hearth. Alfred nearly leapt out of his skin. Hugh could not repress a start, and backed away from the feast, eyeing it suspiciously. Haplo, smiling quietly, took a bua[1]

---

[1]A fruit of which humans are particularly fond. Its tart purple skin covers an almost sickeningly sweet pink meat inside. Those with educated palates believe nothing compares to the subtle blending of flavors when skin and meat are consumed simultaneously. The wine made from this fruit is much coveted by the elves, who, however, scorn eating the bua itself.

and bit into it. Its crunch could be heard through the silence. He wiped juice from his chin. A pretty good illusion, he thought. Everyone will be fooled until about an hour from now when they'll begin to wonder why they're still hungry.

"Please, sit down," said Sinistrad, waving one hand. With the other, he led in Iridal. Bane walked at his father's side. "We do not stand on ceremony here. My dear." Leading his wife to the end of the table, he seated her in a chair with a bow. "To reward Sir Hugh for his exertions in caring for you today, wife, I will place him at your right hand."

Iridal flushed and kept her gaze on her plate. Hugh sat where he was told and did not appear displeased.

"The rest of you find chairs where you will, except for Limbeck. My dear sir, please forgive me." Switching to the Geg's language, the wizard made a graceful bow. "I have been inconsiderate, forgetting that you do not speak the human tongue. My son has been telling me of your gallant struggle to free your people from oppression. Pray, take a seat here near me and tell me of it yourself. Do not worry about the other guests, my wife will entertain them."

Sinistrad took his seat at the head of the table. Pleased, embarrassed, and flustered, Limbeck plunked his stout body into a chair at Sinistrad's right. Bane sat across from him, on his father's left. Alfred hastened to secure a seat beside the prince. Haplo chose to seat himself at the opposite end of the long table, near Iridal and Hugh. The dog plopped down on the floor beside Bane.

Taciturn and reticent as ever, Haplo could appear to be absorbed in his meal and could listen equally well to everyone's conversation.

"I hope you will forgive my indisposition this afternoon," said Iridal. Though she spoke to Hugh, her eyes kept sliding, as if compelled to do so, to her husband, seated opposite her at the table's far end. "I am subject to such spells. They come over me at times."

Sinistrad, watching her, nodded slightly. Iridal turned to Hugh and looked at him directly for the first time since he had taken his place beside her. She made an attempt at a smile. "I hope you will ignore anything I said to you. The illness . . . makes me talk about silly things."

"What you said wasn't silly," Hugh returned. "You meant every word. And you weren't sick. You were scared as hell."

There had been color in her cheeks when she entered. It drained as Hugh watched her. Glancing at her husband, Iridal swallowed and reached out her hand for her wine goblet.

"You must forget what I said! As you value your life, do not mention it again!"

"My life is, right now, of very little value." Hugh's hand caught hold of hers beneath the table and held it fast. "Except as it can be used to serve you, Iridal."

"Try some of the bread," said Haplo, passing it to Hugh. "It's delicious. Sinistrad recommends it."

The mysteriarch was, indeed, watching them closely. Reluctantly releasing Iridal's hand, Hugh took a piece of bread and set it down, untasted, on his plate. Iridal toyed with her food and pretended to eat.

"Then for my sake don't refer to my words, especially if you will not act on them."

"I couldn't leave, knowing I left you behind in danger."

"You fool!" Iridal straightened, warmth sweeping her face. "What can you do, a human who lacks the gift, against such as we? I am ten times more powerful than you, ten times better capable of defending myself if need be! Remember that!"

"Forgive me, then." Hugh's dark face flushed. "It seemed you were in trouble—"

"My troubles are my own and none of your concern, sir."

"I will not bother you anymore, madam, you may be certain of that!"

Iridal did not answer, but stared at the food on her plate. Hugh ate stolidly and said nothing.

Things now silent at his end of the table, Haplo turned his attention to the opposite.

The dog, lying by Bane's chair, kept its ears pricked, gazing up at everyone eagerly, as if hoping for a choice bit to fall its direction.

"But, Limbeck, you saw very little of the Mid Realm," Sinistrad was saying.

"I saw enough." Limbeck blinked at him owlishly through his thick spectacles. The Geg had changed visibly during the past few weeks. The sights he had witnessed, the thoughts he had been thinking, had, like hammer and chisel, chipped away at his dreamy idealism. He had seen the life his people had been denied all these centuries, seen the life they were providing, all the while not sharing. The hammer's first blows hurt him. Later would come the rage.

"I saw enough," Limbeck repeated. Overwhelmed by the magic, the beauty, and his own emotions, he could think of nothing else to say.

"Indeed, you must have," answered the wizard. "I am truly grieved for your people; all of us in the High Realm share your sorrow and your very proper anger. I feel we must share in the blame. Not that we ever exploited you. We have no need, as you see around you, to exploit anyone. But still, I feel that we are somewhat at fault." He sipped delicately at his wine. "We left the world because we were sick of war, sick of watching people suffer and die in the name of greed and hatred. We spoke out against it and did what we could to stop it, but we were too few, too few."

There were actually tears in the man's voice. Haplo could have told him he was wasting a fine performance, at least for his end of the table. Iridal had long since given up any pretense of eating. She had been sitting silently, staring at her plate, until it became obvious that her husband's attention was centered on his conversation with the Geg. Then she raised her eyes, but their gaze did not go to her husband or to the man seated beside her. She looked at her son, seeing Bane, perhaps, for the first time since he'd arrived. Tears filled her eyes. Swiftly she lowered her head. Lifting her hand to brush aside a stray lock of hair, she hastily wiped the drops from her cheeks.

Hugh's hand, resting on the table opposite him, clenched in pain and anger.

How had love's gilt-edged knife managed to penetrate a heart as tough as that one? Haplo didn't know and he didn't care. All he knew was that it was damned inconvenient. The Patryn needed a man of action, since he was barred from action himself. It wouldn't do at all for Hugh to get himself killed in some foolish, noble chivalric gesture.

Haplo began to scratch his right hand, digging down beneath the bandages, displacing them slightly. The sigla exposed, he casually reached for more bread, managing—in the same movement—to press the back of his hand firmly against the wine pitcher. Grasping the bread in his right hand, he returned it to his plate, brushed his left hand over the bandages covering the right, and the runes were hidden once again.

"Iridal," Hugh began, "I can't bear to see you suffer—"

"Why should you care about me?"

"I'm damned if I know!" Hugh leaned near her. "You or your son! I—"

"More wine?" Haplo held up the pitcher.

Hugh glowered, annoyed, and decided to ignore his companion.

Haplo poured a glassful and shoved it toward Hugh. The goblet's base struck the man's fingers, and wine—real wine—sloshed on his hand and his shirt sleeve.

"What the devil . . . ?" Hugh turned on the Patryn angrily.

Haplo raised an eyebrow, obliquely nodding his head in the direction of the opposite end of the table. Attracted by the commotion, everyone, including Sinistrad, was staring at them. Iridal sat straight and tall, her face pale and cold as the marble walls. Hugh lifted the goblet and drank deeply. From his dark expression, it might have been the wizard's blood.

Haplo smiled; he hadn't been any too soon. He waved a hunk of bread at Sinistrad. "Sorry. You were saying?"

Frowning, the mysteriarch continued. "I was saying that we should have realized what was happening to your people in the Low Realm and come to your aid. But we didn't know you were in trouble. We believed the stories that the Sartan had left behind. We did not know, then, that they were lying—"

A sharp clatter made them all start. Alfred had dropped his spoon onto his plate.

"What do you mean? What stories?" Limbeck was asking eagerly.

"After the Sundering, according to the Sartan, your people—being shorter in stature than humans and elves—were taken to the Low Realm for their own protection. Actually, as is now apparent, what the Sartan wanted was a source of cheap labor."

"That's not true!" The voice was Alfred's. He hadn't spoken a word during the entire meal. Everyone, including Iridal, looked at him in astonishment.

Sinistrad turned to him, his thin lips stretched in a polite smile. "No, and do you know what is the truth?"

Red spread from Alfred's neck to his balding head. "I . . . I've made a study of the Gegs, you see . . ." Flustered, he tugged at and twisted the hem of the tablecloth. "Anyway, I . . . I think the Sartan intended to do . . . what you said about protection. It wasn't so much that the dwarv . . . the Gegs were shorter and therefore in danger from the taller races, but that they—the Gegs—were few in number . . . following the Sundering. Then, the dwarv . . . Gegs are very mechanically minded people. And the Sartan needed that for the machine. But they never meant . . . That is, they always meant to . . . ."

Hugh's head slumped forward and hit the table with a thud. Iridal sprang from her chair, crying out in alarm. Haplo was on his feet and moving.

"It's nothing," he said, reaching Hugh's side.

Slipping the assassin's flaccid arm around his neck, Haplo lifted the heavy body from the chair. Hugh's limp hand dragged at the cloth, knocked over goblets, and sent a plate crashing to the floor.

"Good man, but a weak head for wine. I'll take him to his room. No need for the rest of you to be disturbed."

"Are you certain he's all right?" Iridal hovered over them anxiously. "Perhaps I should come—"

"A drunk has passed out at your table, my dear. There is hardly any need for concern," Sinistrad said. "Remove him, by all means."

"Can I keep the dog?" asked Bane, petting the animal, which, seeing its master preparing to leave, had jumped to its feet.

"Sure," said Haplo easily. "Dog, stay."

The dog settled happily back down at Bane's side.

Haplo got Hugh to his feet. Weaving drunkenly, the man was just barely able to stagger—with help—toward the door. Everyone else resumed his seat. Alfred's words were forgotten. Sinistrad turned back to Limbeck.

"This Kicksey-winsey of yours fascinates me. I believe that, since I now have a ship at my disposal, I will journey down to your realm and take a look at it. Of course, I will also be quite pleased to do what I can to help your people prepare for the war—"

"War!" The word echoed in the hall. Haplo, glancing back over his shoulder, saw Limbeck's face, troubled and pale.

"My dear Geg, I didn't mean to shock you." Sinistrad smiled at him kindly. "War being the next logical step, I simply assumed that you had come here for this very purpose—to ask my support. I can assure you, the Gegs will have the full cooperation of my people."

Sinistrad's words came through the dog's ears to Haplo, who was carrying a stumbling Hugh into a dark-and-chill corridor. He was just wondering which direction the guest rooms were located from the dining room when a hallway materialized before him. Several doors stood invitingly open.

"I hope no one walks in his sleep," Haplo muttered to his besotted companion.

Back in the dining room, the Patryn could hear the rustle of Iridal's silken gown and her chair scrape against the stone floor. Her voice, when she spoke, was tight with controlled anger. "If you will excuse me, I will retire to my room now."

"Not feeling well, are you, my dear?"

"Thank you, I am feeling fine." She paused, then added, "It is late. The boy should be in his bed."

"Yes, wife. I'll see to it. No need to trouble yourself. Bane, bid your mother good night."

Well, it had been an interesting evening. Fake food. Fake words. Haplo eased Hugh onto his bed and covered him with a blanket. The assassin wouldn't wake from the spell until morning.

Haplo retired to his own room. Entering, he shut the door and slid home the bolt. He needed time to rest and think undisturbed, assimilate all that he had heard today.

Voices continued to come to him, through the dog. Their words were unimportant; everyone was parting to rest for the night. Lying down on his bed, the Patryn sent out a silent command to the animal, then began to sort out his thoughts.

The Kicksey-winsey. He'd deduced its function from the flickering images portrayed on the eyeball held in the hand of the Manger—the Sartan flouting their power, proudly announcing their grand design. Haplo could see the images again, in his mind. He could see the drawing of the world—the Realm of Sky. He saw the isles and continents, scattered about in disorder; the raging storm that was both death-dealing and life-giving; everything moving in the chaotic manner so abhorrent to the order-loving Sartan.

When had they discovered their mistake? When had they found out that the world they created for the removal of a people after the Sundering was imperfect? After they had populated it? Did they realize, then, that the beautiful floating islands in the sky were dry and barren and could not nurture the life that had been placed in their trust?

The Sartan would fix it. They had fixed everything else, split apart a world rather than let those they considered unworthy rule it. The Sartan would build a machine that, combined with their magic, would align the isles and the continents. Closing his eyes, Haplo saw the pictures again clearly. A tremendous force beaming up from the Kicksey-winsey catches hold of the continents and the isles, drags them through the skies, and aligns them, one right above the other. A geyser of water, drawn from the constant storm, shoots upward continually, bringing the life-giving substance to everyone.

Haplo had figured out the puzzle. He was rather surprised that Bane had solved it as well. Now Sinistrad knew, and he had, most obligingly, explained his plans to his son—and to the listening dog.

One flick of the Kicksey-winsey's switch, and the mysteriarch would rule a realigned world.

The dog jumped up on the bed and settled itself at Haplo's side. Lazily, relaxed to the point of sleep, the Patryn stretched out his arm and patted the dog on the flank. With a contented sigh, the animal rested its head on Haplo's chest and closed its eyes.

What criminal folly, Haplo thought, stroking the dog's soft ears. To build something this powerful and then walk away and leave it to fall into the hands of some ambitious mensch.[2] Haplo couldn't imagine why they had done it. For all their faults, the Sartan weren't fools. Something had happened to them before they could finish their project. He wished he knew what. This was the clearest sign he could imagine, however, to prove that the Sartan were no longer in the world.

An echo came to him, words spoken by Alfred during the confusion of Hugh's drunken swoon, words probably heard only by the dog and transferred dutifully to the master.

"They thought they were gods. They tried to do right. But somehow it all kept going wrong."

---

[2] A word used by both Patryns and Sartan to refer to those less gifted with power than themselves. It is applied equally to elves, humans, and dwarves.

CHAPTER ◆ 51

CASTLE SINISTER,

HIGH REALM

◆

"Papa, I'm going with you to Drevlin—"

"No, and stop arguing with me, Bane! You must return to the Mid Realm and take your place on the throne."

"But I can't go back! Stephen wants to kill me!"

"Don't be stupid, child. I haven't time for it. In order for you to inherit the throne, Stephen and his queen must be dead. That will be arranged. In essence, of course, I will be the one who is truly ruling the Mid Realm. But I can't be in two places at once. I will be on the Low Realm, preparing the machine. Don't snivel! I can't abide it."

His father's words sounded over and over again in Bane's head like the screeching of some irritating nighttime insect that will not permit sleep.

I will be the one who is truly ruling the Mid Realm.

Yes, and where would you be now, papa, if I hadn't shown you how!

Lying on his back, stiff and rigid in the bed, the boy clutched handfuls of the fleecy blanket that covered him. Bane didn't cry. Tears were a valuable weapon in his fight against adults; he had often found them useful against Stephen and Anne. Tears, alone, in the darkness, were a weakness. So his father would think.

But what did he care what his father thought?

Bane gripped the blanket hard and the tears almost came anyway. Yes, he cared. He cared so much it hurt him inside.

Bane could remember clearly the day he had come to realize that the people he knew as his parents only adored him, they didn't love him. Having escaped from Alfred, he was loitering about the kitchen, teasing the cook for bites of sweet dough, when one of the stableboys ran in, wailing over a scratch from a dragon's claw. It was the cook's son, a lad not much older than Bane, who'd been put to work with his father—one of the dragon tenders. The cut wasn't serious. Cook cleaned it and bound it with a strip of cloth, then, taking the child in her arms, kissed him heartily, hugged him, and sent him back to his chores. The boy ran off with a glowing face, the pain and fright of his injury quite forgotten.

Bane had been watching from a corner. Just the day before, he'd cut his hand on a chipped goblet. There'd been a flurry of excitement. Trian had been summoned. He'd brought with him a solid silver knife passed through flame, healing herbs, and cobweb to stanch the bleeding. The offending goblet had been smashed. Alfred had come near being sacked over the incident; King Stephen shouted at the poor chamberlain for twenty minutes running. Queen Anne had nearly fainted at the sight and been forced to leave the room. His "mother" had not kissed him. She had not taken him into her arms and made him laugh to forget the pain.

Bane had derived a certain satisfaction from beating up the stableboy—a satisfaction compounded by the fact that the stableboy had been severely punished for fighting with the prince. That night Bane asked the voice of the feather amulet, the soft and whispering voice that often spoke to him during the night, to explain why his parents didn't love him.

The voice told him the truth. Stephen and Anne weren't his real parents. Bane was just using them for a while. His true father was a powerful mysteriarch. His true father dwelt in a splendid castle in a fabulous realm. His true father was proud of his son, and the day would come when he would call his son home *and they would be together always.*

The last part of the sentence was Bane's addition, not *I will be the one who is truly ruling the Mid Realm.*

Letting go of the blanket, the boy grasped hold of the feather amulet he wore around his neck and jerked hard on the leather thong. It would not break. Angrily, using words he'd picked up from the stableboy, Bane pulled at it again—harder—and succeeded only in hurting himself. Tears came to his eyes at last, tears of pain and frustration. Sitting up in bed, he pulled and tugged, and finally, after costing himself more pain by getting the thong tangled in his hair, managed to drag it up over and off his head.

Alfred was passing down the hallway, searching for his own bedchamber in the confusing, forbidding palace.

"Limbeck is falling under the sway of the mysteriarch. I can see the bloody conflict into which the Gegs will be drawn! Thousands will die, and for what—to gain an evil man control of the world! I should stop it, but how? What can I do alone? Or maybe I shouldn't stop it. After all, it was attempting to control what should have been left alone that brought tragedy on us all. And then there is Haplo. I know for certain who he is, but, again, what can I do? Should I do anything? I don't know! I don't know! Why was I left by myself? Is it a mistake, or am I supposed to be doing something? And if so, what?"

The chamberlain, in his aimless ramblings, found himself near Bane's door. His inner turmoil made the dark and shadowy hall swim before his eyes. Pausing until his vision cleared, wishing desperately his thoughts would do the same, Alfred heard the rustle of bedclothes and the child's voice crying and cursing. Glancing up and down the hall to make certain he was not seen, Alfred raised two fingers on his right hand and traced the sign of a sigil on the door. The wood seemed to disappear at his command, and he could see through it as if it were not there.

Bane hurled the amulet into a corner of the room. "No one loves me and I'm glad of it! I don't love them. I hate them, all of them!"

The boy flung himself down onto the bed, buried his head in the pillow. Alfred drew a deep and shaking breath. At last! It had happened at last, and just when his heart was despairing.

Now was the time to draw the boy back from the edge of Sinistrad's pit. Alfred stepped forward, forgetting the door, and narrowly missed bumping right into it, for the spell he had cast had not removed it, merely let him see through it.

The chamberlain caught himself and, at the same time, thought: No, not me. What am I? A servant, nothing more. His mother. Yes, his mother!

Bane heard a sound in his room and promptly shut his eyes and froze. He had the blanket pulled over his head, and he hastily dried his tears with a quick flick of his hand.

Was it Sinistrad, coming to say he'd changed his mind?

"Bane?" The voice was soft and gentle, his mother's.

The boy pretended to be sleeping. What does she want? he wondered. Do I want to talk to her? Yes, he decided, hearing once again his father's words, I think I do want to speak to mother. All my life people have used me to get what they wanted. Now I'm going to start using them.

Blinking sleepily, Bane raised a tousled head from the depth of the blankets. Iridal had materialized inside his room and was standing at the foot of his bed. Light slowly began to illuminate her, shining from within, and casting a warm and lovely radiance over the boy. The rest of the room remained in darkness. Looking at his mother, Bane knew, from the pitying expression that swept over her face, that she saw he had been crying. This was good. Once again he drew on his arsenal.

"Oh, my child!" His mother came to him. Sitting down on the bed, Iridal slid her arm around him and drew him close, soothing him with her hand.

A feeling of exquisite warmth enveloped the boy. Nestling into that comforting arm, he said to himself: I've given father what he wants. Now it's her turn. What does she want of me?

Nothing, apparently. Iridal wept over him and murmured incoherently about how much she had missed him and how she had longed for him to be with her. This gave the boy an idea.

"Mother," he said, looking up at her with tear-drenched blue eyes, "I want to be with you! But father says he's going to send me away!"

"Send you away! Where? Why?"

"Back to the Mid Realm, back to those people who don't love me!" He caught hold of her hand and hugged it tightly. "I want to stay with you! You and father!"

"Yes," Iridal murmured. Drawing Bane close, she kissed him on the forehead. "Yes . . . a family. Like I've always dreamed. Maybe there is a chance. Maybe I can't save him, but his own child. Surely he could not betray such innocent love and trust. This hand"—she kissed the child's fingers, bathing them with tears—"this hand might lead him away from the dark path he walks."

Bane didn't understand. All paths were one to him, neither dark nor light, all leading straight to the same goal—people doing what he wanted them to do.

"You'll talk to father," he said, squirming out of her grasp, feeling that, after all, kissing and hugging might get to be a nuisance.

"Yes, I'll talk to him tomorrow."

"Thank you, mama." Bane yawned.

"You should be sleeping," Iridal said, rising. "Good night, my son." She gently drew the blanket up snug around him and, leaning down, kissed his cheek. "Good night."

The magical radiance began to fade from her face. She raised her hands and closed her eyes, concentrating, and disappeared from his room.

Bane grinned into the darkness. He had no idea what kind of influence his mother might be able to exert; he could only judge by Queen Anne, who had generally been able to get what she wanted from Stephen.

But if this didn't work, there was always the other plan. In order to make that plan work, he would have to give away for free something he guessed was of inestimable value. He would be circumspect, of course, but his father was smart. Sinistrad might guess and rob him of it. Still, spend nothing, gain nothing.

Likely, he wouldn't have to give it up. Not yet. He wouldn't be sent away. Mama would see to that.

Gleefully Bane kicked off the smothering covers.

CHAPTER ♦ 52

CASTLE SINISTER,

HIGH REALM

♦

THE FOLLOWING MORNING, IRIDAL ENTERED HER HUSBAND'S STUDY. SHE found her son there with Sinistrad, the two of them seated at her husband's writing desk, poring over drawings made by Bane. The dog, lying at her son's feet, lifted its head when it saw her, its tail thumping the floor.

Iridal paused a moment in the doorway. All her fantasies had come true. Loving father, adoring son; Sinistrad patiently devoting his time to Bane, studying whatever the boy had done with an assumed gravity that was quite endearing. In that instant, seeing the skullcapped head bent so near the fair-haired one, hearing the murmur of the voices—one young and one old—caught up in the excitement of what she could only think was some childish project of her son's, Iridal forgave Sinistrad everything. Her years of terror and suffering she would gladly erase, banish from her memory, if only he would grant her this.

Stepping forward almost shyly—it had been many years since she had set foot in her husband's sanctum—Iridal tried to speak but couldn't find her voice. The choked sound caught the attention of both son and father, however. One looked up at her with a radiant, charming smile. The other appeared annoyed.

"Well, wife, what do you want?"

Iridal's fantasies wavered, their bright mist shredded by the chill voice and the icy gaze of the lashless eyes.

"Good morning, mama," said Bane. "Would you like to see my drawings? I made them myself."

"If I am not disturbing—" She looked hesitantly at Sinistrad.

"Come in, then," he said ungraciously.

"Why, Bane, these are marvelous." Iridal lifted a few pages and turned them to the light of the sun.

"I used my magic. Like father taught me. I thought of what I wanted to draw, and my hands took over and did it. I learn magic very quickly," said the boy, gazing up at his mother with wide-eyed charm. "You and father could teach me in your spare time. I wouldn't be any trouble."

Sinistrad sat back in his chair, the robes of heavy watered silk rustling dryly, like bat wings. His lips creased in a chill smile that blew the tattered remnants of Iridal's fancies from the skies. She would have fled to her chambers had not Bane been watching her hopefully, silently pleading with her to continue. The dog laid its head back down between its paws, its eyes moving alertly to whoever spoke.

"What . . . are these drawings?" She faltered. "The great machine?"

"Yes. Look, this is the part they call the wombay. Papa says that means 'womb' and it's where the Kicksey-winsey was born. And this part activates the great force that will pull all of the isles—"

"That will do, Bane," interrupted Sinistrad. "We mustn't keep your mother from the entertaining of our . . . guests." He lingered over the word. The look he gave her made her skin flush crimson and scattered her thoughts in confusion. "I assume you came here for some purpose, wife. Or perhaps it was just to make certain that my time was occupied so that you and the dark and handsome assassin—"

"How dare . . . ? What? What did you say?"

Iridal's hands began to shake. Hurriedly she laid the pages of drawings she'd been holding back on the desk.

"Didn't you know, my dear? One of your guests is a professional knife-man. Hugh the Hand is what he calls himself—a Hand stained in blood, if you will forgive my small jest. Your gallant champion was hired to murder a child." Sinistrad ruffled Bane's hair. "But for me, wife, your boy would never have come home to you. I thwarted Hugh's design—"

"I don't believe you! It's not possible!"

"I know it's shocking for you, my dear, to discover that we have a house guest who might murder us all in our beds. But I have taken every precaution. He did me a favor by drinking himself into a blind stupor last night. It was quite simple to transfer his wine-soaked body to a place of safekeeping. My son tells me that there is a price on the man's head, as well as that of the boy's treacherous servant. The amount will be just enough to finance my project in the Low Realm. And now, my dear, what was it you wanted?"

"Don't take my son from me!" Iridal gasped for breath, feeling as if cold water had been dashed over her. "Do whatever you want. I will not stop you. Just leave me my son!"

"Only the other morning, you disclaimed him. Now you say you want him." Sinistrad shrugged. "Really, madam, I can't subject the boy to your idle whims that change daily. He must return to the Mid Realm and take up his duties. And now I think you had better go. So nice that we could have this little chat, wife. We must do it more often."

"I do think, mama, that you might have talked this over with me first," interjected Bane. "I *want* to go back! I'm certain father knows what's best for me."

"I'm certain he does," said Iridal.

Turning, she walked with quiet dignity out of the study and managed to make it down the chill, shadowy hallway before she wept for her lost child.

"As for you, Bane," said Sinistrad, returning each of the drawings Iridal had disturbed to its proper place, "never try that with me again. This time I punished your mother, who should have known better. Next time, it will be you."

Bane accepted the rebuke in silence. It was refreshing to play the game with an opponent as skilled as himself for a change. He began to deal out the next hand, moving swiftly so that his father would not notice the cards were coming from the bottom of a prearranged deck.

"Father," said Bane, "I have a question about magic."

"Yes?" Now that discipline had been restored, Sinistrad was pleased at the boy's interest.

"One day I saw Trian drawing something on a sheet of paper. It was a letter of the alphabet, but yet it wasn't. When I asked him, he crumpled it up and looked embarrassed and threw it away. He said it was magic and I mustn't bother him about it."

Sinistrad turned his attention from the drawing he was perusing to his son. Bane returned the sharp-eyed, curious gaze with the ingenuous expression the child knew so well how to assume. The dog sat up and shoved his nose in the child's hand, wanting to be petted.

"What did the symbol look like?"

On the back of one of the drawings, Bane traced a rune.

"That?" Sinistrad snorted. "That is a sigil, used in rune magic. This Trian must be more of a fool than I thought, to be dabbling in that arcane art."

"Why?"

"Because only the Sartan were skilled in the use of runes."

"The Sartan!" The child appeared awed. "No others?"

"Well, it was said that in the world which existed before the Sundering, the Sartan had a mortal enemy—a group as powerful and more ambitious, a group who wanted to use their godlike powers to rule instead of to guide. They were known as the Patryns."

"And you're certain. No one else can use this magic?"

"Haven't I said so once? When I say a thing, I mean it!"

"I'm sorry, father."

Now that he was certain, Bane could afford to be magnanimous to a losing opponent.

"What does the rune do, father?"

Sinistrad glanced at it. "A rune of healing, I believe," he said without interest.

Bane smiled and petted the dog, which gratefully licked his fingers.

CHAPTER ♦ 53

CASTLE SINISTER,

HIGH REALM

♦

THE EFFECTS OF THE SPELL WERE SLOW TO WEAR OFF. HUGH COULD NOT distinguish between dream and reality. One moment the black monk was standing at his side, taunting him.

"Death's master? No, we are your masters. All your life, you have served us."

And then the black monk was Sinistrad.

"Why not serve me? I could use a man of your talents. Stephen and Anne must be dealt with. My son must sit on the throne of both Volkaran and Uylandia, and these two stand in his way. A clever man like you could figure out how their deaths could be accomplished. I've work to do, but I'll return later. Remain here and think about it."

"Here" was a dank cell that had been created out of nothing and nowhere. Sinistrad had carried Hugh to this place—wherever it was. The assassin had resisted, but not much. It's difficult to fight when you can barely tell the floor from the ceiling, your feet seem to have multiplied and your legs lost their bones.

Of course it was Sinistrad who cast the spell on me.

Hugh could vaguely remember trying to tell Haplo he wasn't drunk, that this was some terrible magic, but Haplo had only smiled that infuriating smile of his and said he'd feel better when he'd slept it off.

Maybe when Haplo wakes up and discovers I'm gone, he'll come looking for me.

Hugh held his pounding head in his hands and cursed himself for a fool. Even if Haplo does go looking for me, he'll never find me. This prison cell isn't located in the bowels of the castle, placed conveniently at the bottom of a long and winding stair. I saw the void out of which it sprang. It's at the bottom of night, the middle of nowhere. No one will ever find me. I'll stay here until I die . . .

. . . or until I call Sinistrad master.

And why not? I've served many men; what's one more? Or better yet, maybe I'll just stay where I am. This cell isn't much different from my life—a cold, bleak, and empty prison. I built the walls myself—made them out of money. I shut myself in and locked the door. I was my own guard, my own jailer. And it worked. Nothing has touched me. Pain, compassion, pity, remorse—they couldn't get past the walls. I even considered killing a child for the money.

And then the child got hold of the key.

But that had been the enchantment. It was his magic that made me pity him. Or was that my excuse? Certainly the enchantment didn't conjure up those memories—memories of myself before the prison cell.

The enchantment works only because you want it to work. Your will feeds it. You could have broken it long ago, if you truly wanted to. You care about him, you see. And caring is an invisible prison.

Perhaps not. Perhaps it was freedom.

Dazed, half-waking, half-dreaming, Hugh rose from where he'd been sitting on the stone floor and walked to the cell door. He reached out his hand . . . and stopped and stared. His hand was covered with blood. The wrist, forearm—he was smeared in blood to the elbow.

And as he saw himself, so must she see him.

"Sir."

Hugh started and turned his head. Was she real or was she only a trick of his throbbing mind that had been thinking about her? He blinked, and she did not go away.

"Iridal?"

Seeing in her eyes that she knew the truth about him, he glanced down self-consciously at his hands.

"So Sinistrad was right," Iridal said. "You are an assassin."

The rainbow eyes were gray and colorless; there was no light shining behind them.

What could he say? She spoke the truth. He could excuse himself, tell her about Three-Chop Nick. He could tell her how he had decided he couldn't harm the boy. He could tell her that he had planned to take the boy back to Queen Anne. But none of it made different the fact that he had agreed; he had taken the money; he had known, in his heart, he could kill a child.

And so he simply and quietly said, "Yes."

"I don't understand! It's evil, monstrous! How could you spend your life murdering people?"

He could say that most of the men he'd killed deserved to die. He could tell her that he had probably saved the lives of those who would have become their next victims.

But Iridal would ask him: Who are you to judge?

And he would answer: Who is any man? Who is King Stephen, that he can proclaim, "That man is an elf and therefore he must die"? Who are the barons, that they can say, "That man has land I want. He won't give it to me and therefore he must die"?

Fine arguments, but I agreed. I took the money. I knew, in my heart, I could kill a child. And so he said, "It doesn't matter now."

"No, except that I am alone. Again."

Iridal spoke softly. Hugh knew he hadn't been meant to hear. She stood in the center of the cell, her head bowed, the long white hair falling forward, hiding her face. She had cared for him. Trusted him. She had, perhaps, been going to ask him for help. His cell door swung slowly open, sunlight flooding into his soul.

"Iridal, you're not alone. There's someone you can trust. Alfred's a good man, he's devoted to your son." Far more than Bane deserves, Hugh thought, but didn't say. Aloud he continued, "Alfred saved the boy's life once when a tree fell on him. If you want to escape—you and your son—Alfred could help you. He could take you to the elven ship. The elf captain needs money. He'd give you passage in return for that and safe guidance out of the firmament."

"Escape?" Iridal glanced frantically around the cell walls, and then she buried her face in her hands. It was not Hugh's cell walls she saw, but her own.

So she, too, is a prisoner. I opened her cell door, offered her a glimpse of light and air. And now she sees it swinging shut.

"Iridal, I'm a murderer. Worse, I've murdered for money. I make no excuses for myself. But what I've done is nothing to what your husband's plotting!"

"You're wrong! He's never taken a life. He couldn't do such a thing."

"He's talking about world war, Iridal! Sacrificing the lives of thousands to put himself into power!"

"You don't understand. It's our lives he's trying to save. The lives of our people."

Seeing his puzzled expression, she made an impatient gesture, angry at being forced to explain what she thought must be obvious.

"Surely you've wondered why the mysteriarchs left the Mid Realm, left a land where we had everything—power, wealth. Oh, I know what is said of us. I know because we were the ones who said it. We had grown disgusted with the barbaric life, with the constant warring with the elves. The truth is, we left because we had to, we had no choice. Our magic was dwindling. Intermarriage with ordinary humans had diluted it. That's why there are so many wizards in this world of yours. Many, but weak. Those of us of pure blood were few but strong. To ensure the continuation of our race, we fled to someplace where we would not be—"

"Contaminated?" suggested Hugh.

Iridal flushed and bit her lip. Then, raising her head, she faced him with pride.

"I know you say that with contempt, but, yes, that is true. Can you blame us?"

"But it didn't work."

"The journey was difficult, and many died. More succumbed before the magical dome that protects us against the bitter cold and gives us air to breathe could be stabilized. At last all seemed well and children were born to us, but not many, and most of those died." Her pride drained from her, her head drooped. "Bane is the only child of his generation left alive. And now the dome is collapsing. That shimmer in the sky that you find so beautiful is, to us, deadly.

"The buildings are illusion, the people pretend to be a large population, so that you won't guess the truth."

"You have to return to the world below, but you're afraid to go back and reveal how weak you've grown," finished Hugh. "The changeling became the prince of Volkaran. And now he's going back as king!"

"King? That's impossible. They already have a king."

"Not impossible, madam. Your husband's planning to hire me to get rid of their king and queen, and then Bane—their son—will inherit the throne."

"I don't believe you! You're lying!"

"Yes, you believe me. I see it in your face. It's not your husband you're defending, it's yourself. You know what your husband's capable of doing. You know what he's done and what you haven't! Maybe it wasn't murder, but he would have caused two people down there in the Mid Realm less pain if he'd driven knives into them instead of taking their baby."

The dark, colorless eyes tried to meet his, but they faltered and fell. "I grieved for them. I tried to save their child . . . I would have given my life if their baby could have lived. And then there are the lives of so many others—"

"I've done evil. But it seems to me, Iridal, that there is equal evil in *not* doing. Sinistrad is returning to conclude his deal with me. Listen to what he has planned and judge for yourself."

Iridal stared at him, started to speak. Then, shaking her head, she shut her eyes and, in an instant, was gone. Her chains were too heavy. She couldn't break free.

Hugh sank back down, alone in his cell within a cell. Pulling out his pipe, he clamped it between his teeth and glared at the prison walls.

Walk the dragon wing.

If Sinistrad intended to startle him by his sudden appearance, the mysteriarch must have been disappointed. Hugh glanced up at him, but neither moved nor spoke.

"Well, Hugh the Hand, have you decided?"

"It wasn't much of a decision." Rising stiffly to his feet, Hugh carefully wrapped the pipe in its cloth and tucked it away near his breast. "I don't want to spend the rest of my life in this place. I'll work for you. I've worked for worse. After all, I once took money to kill a child."

CHAPTER ♦ 54

CASTLE SINISTER,

HIGH REALM

♦

Haplo wandered the corridors of the castle, idly wasting time, or so it seemed when anyone paid any attention to him. When no one was around, he continued searching, keeping account of everyone, as best he could.

The dog was with Bane. Haplo had overheard every word of the conversation between father and son. The Patryn had been caught off-guard by Bane's strange question about the sigil. Scratching the skin beneath his bandages, Haplo wondered if the child could have seen the runes. The Patryn tried to think back to a time when he might have slipped up, made a mistake. Finally, he decided he hadn't. It would have been impossible. What, then, was the boy talking about? Surely not some mensch wizard trying his hand at runes. Even a mensch had more sense.

Well, there's no use wasting brain power speculating. I'll find out soon enough. Bane—dog faithfully trotting along at the boy's side—had recently passed him in the hallway, searching for Alfred. Perhaps that conversation will give me a clue. Meanwhile, there's Limbeck to check up on.

Pausing before the door of the Geg's room, Haplo glanced up and down the hall. No one was in sight. He traced a sigil upon the door and the wood disappeared—at least to his eyes. To the Geg, sitting disconsolately at a desk, the door seemed as solid as ever. Limbeck had asked his host for writing materials and seemed to be absorbed in his favorite pastime—speech-composing. But Haplo saw that very little composing was being accomplished. Spectacles pushed up on his forehead, the Geg sat, head in hand, staring into a tapestry-covered stone wall that for him was a multicolored blur.

" 'My fellow Workers United . . .' No, that's too restricting. 'My fellow WUPP's and Gegs . . .' But the high froman might be there. High Froman, Head Clark, fellow WUPP's, brother Gegs . . . brother and *sister* Gegs, I have seen the world above and it is beautiful' "—Limbeck's voice softened—" 'more beautiful and wondrous than anything you can imagine. And I . . . I . . .' No!" He tugged violently on his own beard. "There," he said, wincing at the pain and blinking the tears from his eyes. "As Jarre would say, I'm a drugal. Now, maybe I can think better. 'My dear WUPP's . . .' No, there I go again. I've left out the high froman . . ."

Haplo removed the sigil, and the door took shape and form again. He could hear, as he continued down the corridor, Limbeck reciting to his crowd of one. The Geg knows what he has to say, thought Haplo. He just can't bring himself to say it.

"Oh, Alfred, here you are!" It was Bane's voice, coming to Haplo through the dog. "I've been searching all over for you." The child sounded petulant, put-out.

"I'm sorry, Your Highness, I was looking for Sir Hugh . . ."

He wasn't the only one.

Stopping at the next door, Haplo glanced inside. The room was empty—Hugh was gone. Haplo was not particularly surprised. If Hugh was even still alive, it was only because Sinistrad intended to make him suffer. Or, better yet, use him to make Iridal suffer. This jealousy Sinistrad was exhibiting over his wife was strange, considering he obviously didn't care for her.

"She's his possession," said Haplo to himself, turning back down the hallway and heading for Limbeck's room. "If Hugh'd been discovered making off with the spoons, Sinistrad would probably have been just as mad. Well, I tried to protect him. Pity. He was a bold fellow. I could have used him. Now, however, while Sinistrad is preoccupied with Hugh, would be an excellent time for the rest of us to leave."

"Alfred . . ." Bane was speaking in sugared tones. "I want to have a talk with you."

"Certainly, Your Highness."

The dog settled itself on the floor between them.

Time to leave, Haplo repeated. I'll collect Limbeck, we'll get back to the elf ship and take it, and leave this mensch wizard stranded on his realm. I don't have to put up with his meddling.

I'll transport the Geg back to Drevlin. Once that's done, I will have accomplished my lord's goals, except for bringing him back someone from this world to train as a disciple. I'd considered Hugh, but he's out, apparently.

Still, my lord should be satisfied. This world is wobbling about on the brink of disaster. If all goes well, I can nudge it over the edge. And I believe that I can safely say that there are no longer any Sartan—

"Alfred," said Bane, "I know you're a Sartan."

Haplo came to a dead stop.

It must be a mistake. He hadn't heard right. He'd been thinking the word and therefore heard it when in reality the boy had said something else. Holding his breath, almost wishing impatiently he could still the pounding of his heart so that he could hear more clearly, Haplo listened.

Alfred felt the world slide out beneath his feet. Walls expanded, the ceiling seemed to be falling down on top of him, and he thought for an awful, blessed moment that he might faint. But this time his brain refused to shut down. This time he would have to face the peril and deal with it as best he could. He knew he should be saying something, denying the boy's statement, of course, but he honestly didn't know whether or not he could talk. His face muscles were paralyzed.

"Come, Alfred," said Bane, regarding him with smug self-assurance, "there's no use denying it. I know it's true. Do you want to know how I know?"

The child was enjoying this immensely. And there was the dog, its head raised, watching him intently, as if it understood every word and it, too, was awaiting his reaction. The dog! Of course, it was understanding every word! And so was its master.

"You remember the time when the tree fell on me," Bane was saying. "I was dead. I knew I was dead because I was floating away and I looked back and saw my body lying on the ground, with the crystal pieces sticking right through me. But suddenly it was like a great big mouth opened and sucked me back. And I woke up and there weren't any crystals hurting me anymore. I looked down, and there on my chest I saw this." Bane held up the piece of paper he had removed from his father's desk. "I asked my father about it. He said it was a sigil, a rune. A rune of healing."

Deny it. Laugh lightly. What an imagination you have, Your Highness! You dreamed it, of course. That bump on your head.

"And then there was Hugh," Bane continued. "I know that I gave him enough hethbane to kill him. When he fell over, all in a heap, he was dead, just like me. *You* brought him back to life!"

Come, now, Your Highness. If I was a Sartan, what would I be doing earning my living as a servant? No, I'd live in a grand palace and you mensch would all flock to see me and fall at my feet and beg me to give you this and give you that and raise you up and cast your enemies down and offer me whatever I wanted except peace.

"And now that I know you're a Sartan, Alfred, you've got to help me. And the first thing we're going to do is kill my father." Bane reached into his tunic, pulled out a dagger that Alfred recognized as belonging to Hugh. "Look, I found this in my father's desk. Sinistrad's going to go down to the Low Realm and send the Gegs to war and fix the Kicksey-winsey and make it align all the isles, and then he'll control the water supply. All the wealth and power will go to him, and that's not fair! It was *my* idea! *I* was the one who figured out how the machine worked. And of course, Alfred, you probably know all about running the machine, since you and your people built it, and you can help me with that too."

The dog, with its far-too-intelligent eyes, was looking at Alfred, looking straight through him. Too late to deny. He'd missed his chance. He'd never been quick-thinking, quick-reacting. That was why his brain had taken to shutting down when confronted with danger. It couldn't cope with the constant war that raged inside him, the instinctive urge to use his wondrous powers to protect himself and others versus the terrible knowledge that if he did so he would be exposed for the demigod he was—and wasn't.

"I cannot help you, Your Highness. I cannot take a life."

"Oh, but you'll have to. You won't have any choice. If you don't, I'll tell my father who you are, and once my father finds out, he'll try to use you himself."

"And, Your Highness, I will refuse."

"You can't! He'll try to kill you if you don't obey him! Then you'll have to fight, and you'll win, because you're stronger."

"No, Your Highness. I will lose. I will die."

Bane was startled, perplexed. Obviously this was one move that had never occurred to him. "But you can't! You're a Sartan!"

"We are not immortal—something I think we forgot."

It was the despair that had killed them. The despair he was feeling now; a great and overwhelming sadness. They had dared to think and act as gods and had ceased to listen to the true gods. Things had begun to go wrong—as the Sartan saw it—and they had taken it upon themselves to decide what was best for the world and act accordingly. But then something else went wrong and they had to step in and fix it, and every time they fixed one thing, it caused something else to break. And soon the task became too large; there were too few of them. And they had realized, finally, that they had tampered with what should have been left undisturbed. But by then it was too late.

"I will die," repeated Alfred.

The dog rose to its feet, came over to him, and laid its head on his knee. Slowly, hesitantly, he reached out his hand to touch it, and felt its warmth, the well-shaped bones of the head hard beneath the silky fur.

And what is your master doing now? What is Haplo thinking, knowing that his ancient enemy is within his grasp? I can't begin to guess. It all depends, I suppose, on what Haplo is doing in this world in the first place.

The chamberlain smiled, much to Bane's frustration and ire. Alfred was wondering what Sinistrad would do if he knew he had *two* demigods under his roof.

"You might be ready to die, Alfred!" said Bane with sudden sly cunning. "But what about our friends—the Geg and Hugh and Haplo?"

At the sound of its master's name, the dog's plumy tail brushed slowly from side to side.

Bane came forward to stand at the chamberlain's side, the child's small hands clasped earnestly on his servant's shoulder. "When I tell father who you are and when I prove to him how I know who you are, he'll realize—like I do now—that we won't need any of these others. We won't need the elves or their ship, because your magic can take us where we want to go. We won't need Limbeck because you can talk to the Gegs and convince them to go to war. We don't need Haplo—we never did need Haplo. I'll take care of his dog. We don't need Hugh. Father won't kill you, Alfred. He'll control you by threatening to kill them! So you can't die!"

What he says is true. And Sinistrad would certainly realize it.

Expendable. I make them all expendable. But what can I do to save them, except kill?

"The truly wonderful part," said Bane, giggling, "is that at the end of it all, we won't even need father!"

It is the old curse of the Sartan, coming back to me at last. If I had allowed the child to die, as, perhaps, he was meant to, then none of this would have happened. But I had to meddle. I had to play god. I believed that there was good in the child, that he would change—because of *me*! I believed that *I* could save him! I, I, I! All we Sartan ever thought about was ourselves. We wanted to mold the world in *our* image. But perhaps that wasn't what was intended.

Slowly, gently thrusting aside the dog, Alfred rose to his feet. Walking to the center of the room, he lifted his arms into the air and began to move in a solemn and strangely graceful— for his ungainly body—dance.

"Alfred, what the hell are you doing?"

"I am leaving, Your Highness," said Alfred.

The air around him began to shimmer as his dancing continued. He was tracing the runes in the air with his hands and drawing them on the floor with his feet.

Bane's mouth gaped open. "You can't!" he gasped. Running forward, he tried to grab hold of the Sartan, but the magical wall Alfred had built around himself was now too powerful. There was a crackle when Bane's hand touched it, and the child, wailing, snatched back burned fingers.

"You can't leave me! No one can leave me unless I want them to!"

"Your enchantment doesn't work on me, Bane." Alfred spoke almost sadly, his body beginning to fade away. "It never did."

A large furry shape plummeted past Bane. The dog bounded through the shimmering shell and landed lightly at Alfred's side. Leaping, teeth snapping, the dog caught the chamberlain's ankle in its mouth and held on tightly.

A startled expression crossed Alfred's now-ghostlike face. Frantically he kicked his leg, trying to jerk it from the dog's mouth.

The dog, grinning, seemed to consider this a great game. It held on more tightly and began to growl playfully and tug back. Alfred pulled harder. His body had ceased to fade and was now gradually starting to regain its solidity. Going round and round in a circle, the chamberlain begged and pleaded, threatened and scolded the dog to let go. The dog followed him around and around, feet skidding as it sought to get a grip on the stone floor with its claws, its jaws clamped firmly around Alfred's leg.

The door to the room slammed open. The dog, looking over, wagged its tail furiously, but continued to keep its grip on Alfred.

"So you're leaving us behind, are you, Sartan?" inquired Haplo. "Just like the old days, huh?"

CHAPTER ♦ 55

CASTLE SINISTER,

HIGH REALM

♦

IN A ROOM DOWN THE CORRIDOR, LIMBECK FINALLY PUT HIS PEN TO
paper.

"My people . . ." he began.

Haplo had long imagined meeting a Sartan, meeting someone
who had sealed his people in that hellish place. He imagined
himself angry, but now even he could not believe his fury. He
stared at this man, this Alfred, this Sartan, and he saw the
chaodyn attacking him, he saw the dog's body lying broken,
bleeding. He saw his parents dead. It was suddenly hard to
breathe. He was suffocating. Veins, red against fiery yellow,
webbed his vision, and he had to close his eyes and fight to catch
his breath.

"Leaving again!" He gasped for air. "Just like you jailers left
us to die in that prison!"

Haplo forced the last word out between gritted teeth. Bandaged hands raised like striking talons, he stood quite close to
Alfred and stared into the face of the Sartan that seemed surrounded by a halo of flame. If this Alfred smiled, if his lips so
much as twitched, Haplo would kill him. His lord, his purpose,
his instructions—he couldn't hear any of them for the pounding
waves of rage in his head.

But Alfred didn't smile. He didn't blench in fright or draw
back or even move to defend himself. The lines of the aged,
careworn face deepened, the mild eyes were shadowed and
red-rimmed, shimmering with sorrow.

"The jailer didn't leave," he said. "The jailer died."

Haplo felt the dog's head press against his knee, and reaching down, he caught hold of the soft fur and gripped it tightly. The dog gazed up with worried eyes and pressed closer, whimpering. Haplo's breathing came easier, clear sight returned to his eyes, clear thought to his mind.

"I'm all right," said Haplo, drawing a shivering breath. "I'm all right."

"Does this mean," asked Bane, "that Alfred's *not* leaving?"

"No, he's not leaving," said Haplo. "Not now, at least. Not until I'm ready."

Master of himself once more, the Patryn faced the Sartan. Haplo's face was calm, his smile quiet. His hands rubbed slowly, one against the other, displacing slightly the bandages that covered the skin. "The jailer died? I don't believe that."

Alfred hesitated, licked his lips. "Your people have been . . . trapped in that place all this time?"

"Yes, but you knew that already, didn't you? That was your intent!"

Limbeck, hearing nothing of what was happening two doors down from him, continued writing:

"My people, I have been in the realms above. I have visited the realms our legends tell us are heaven. And they are. And they aren't. They are beautiful. They are rich—rich beyond belief. The sun shines on them throughout the day. The firmament sparkles in their sky. The rain falls gently, without malice. The shadows of the Lords of Night soothe them to sleep. They live in houses, not in cast-off parts of a machine or in a building the Kicksey-winsey decided it didn't need at the moment. They have winged ships that fly through the air. They have tamed winged beasts to take them anywhere they want. And all of this they have because of us.

"They lied to us. They told us that they were gods and that we had to work for them. They promised us that if we worked hard, they would judge us worthy and take us up to live in heaven. But they never intended to make good that promise."

"That was never our intent!" Alfred answered. "You must believe that. And you must believe that I—we—didn't know you were still there! It was only supposed to be a short time, a few years, several generations—"

"A thousand years, a hundred generations—those that survived! And where were you? What happened?"

"We . . . had our own problems." Alfred's gaze lowered, his head bowed.

"You have my deepest sympathy."

Alfred glanced up swiftly, saw the Patryn's curled lip, and, sighing, looked away.

"You're coming with me," said Haplo. "I'm going to take you back to see for yourself the hell your people created! And my lord will have questions for you. He'll find it hard to believe—as I do—that 'the jailer died.'"

"Your lord?"

"A great man, the most powerful of our kind who has ever lived. He has plans, many plans, which I'm certain he'll share with you."

"And that's why you're here," Alfred murmured. "His plans? No, I won't go with you." The Sartan shook his head. "Not voluntarily." Deep within the mild eyes, a spark kindled.

"Then I'll use force. I'll enjoy that!"

"I've no doubt. But if you're trying to conceal your presence in this world"—his gaze fixed on the bandaged hands—"then you know that a fight between us, a duel of that magnitude and magical ferocity, could not be hidden and would be disastrous to you. The wizards in this world are powerful and intelligent. Legends exist about Death Gate. Many, like Sinistrad or even this child"—Alfred's hand stroked Bane's hair—"could figure out what had occurred and would eagerly start to search for the entry into what is held to be a wondrous world. Is your lord prepared for that?"

"Lord? What lord? Look here, Alfred!" Bane burst out impatiently. "None of us are going anywhere as long as my father's alive!" Neither of the two men answered him or even looked at him. The boy glared at them. Adults, absorbed in their own concerns, they had, as usual, forgotten his.

"At last our eyes have been opened. At last we can see the truth." Limbeck found his spectacles irritating and pushed them back up on top of his head. "And the truth is that we no longer need them . . ."

"I don't need you!" Bane cried. "You weren't going to help me anyway. I'll do it myself." Reaching into his tunic, he drew out

Hugh's dagger and gazed at it admiringly, running his finger carefully over the rune-carved blade. "Come on," he said to the dog, still standing beside Haplo. "You come with me."

The dog looked at the boy and wagged his tail but did not move.

"Come on!" Bane coaxed. "Good dog!"

The dog cocked his head, then turned to Haplo, whining and pawing. The Patryn, intent on the Sartan, shoved the dog aside. Sighing, with a final, pleading glance back at its master, the dog—head down, ears flat—padded slowly over to Bane's side.

The child shoved the dagger in his belt and patted the dog's head. "That's a good boy. Let's go."

"And so, in conclusion . . ." Limbeck paused. His hand trembled, his eyes misted over. A blot of ink fell upon the paper. Pulling his spectacles down from on top of his head, he adjusted them on his nose and then sat unmoving, staring at the blank spot where the final words would be written.

"Can you truly afford to fight me?" Alfred persisted.

"I don't think you'll fight," answered Haplo. "I think you're too weak, too tired. That kid you pamper is more—"

Reminded, Alfred glanced around.

"Bane? Where is he?"

Haplo made an impatient gesture. "Gone somewhere. Don't try to—"

"I'm not 'trying' anything! You heard what he asked me. He has a knife. He's gone to murder his father! I've got to stop—!"

"No, you don't." Haplo caught hold of the Sartan's arm. "Let the mensch murder each other. It doesn't matter."

"It doesn't matter to you at all?" Alfred gave the Patryn a peculiar, searching look.

"No, of course not. The only one I care about is the leader of the Gegs' revolt, and Limbeck's safely shut up in his room."

"Then where's your dog?" asked Alfred.

"My people"—Limbeck's pen slowly and deliberately wrote down the words—"we are going to war."

There. It was done. Pulling off his spectacles, the Geg tossed them down upon the table, put his head in his hands, and wept.

CHAPTER ◆ 56

CASTLE SINISTER,

HIGH REALM

◆

Sɪɴɪsᴛʀᴀᴅ ᴀɴᴅ Hᴜɢʜ ᴡᴇʀᴇ sᴇᴀᴛᴇᴅ ɪɴ ᴛʜᴇ sᴛᴜᴅʏ ᴏꜰ ᴛʜᴇ ᴍʏsᴛᴇʀɪᴀʀᴄʜ. It was nearly midday. Light streamed in through a crystal window. Seeming to float on the mist outside the window were the glittering spires of the city of New Hope—the city that, according to what Iridal had told him, might as well be called No Hope. Hugh wondered if the buildings had been placed there for his benefit. Outside, coiled around the castle, dozing in the sun, was the quicksilver dragon.

"Let us see, what would be best?" Sinistrad tapped thoughtfully on the desk with his thin fingers. "We will transport the child back to Djern Volkain on the elven ship—taking care, of course, to make certain that the ship is seen by the humans. Then, when Stephen and Anne are discovered dead, it will be blamed on elves. Bane can tell them some rigmarole about how he was captured and escaped and the elves followed him and killed his loving parents as they tried to rescue him. You can make it appear that the elves murdered them, I suppose?"

The air around Hugh stirred, a cold breath swept over him, and icy fingers seemed to touch his shoulder. Iridal was working her own magic against her husband. She was here. She was listening.

"Sure, nothing's easier. Will the boy cooperate?" asked Hugh, tensing, yet doing his best to seem at ease. Now that she was faced with inescapable truth, what would she do? "The kid seems less than enthusiastic."

"He will cooperate. I have only to make him understand that

this is to his advantage. Once he knows how he can profit by this action, he will be eager to undertake it. The boy is ambitious, and rightfully so. After all, he *is* my son."

Invisible to all eyes, Iridal stood behind Hugh, watching, listening. She felt nothing at hearing Sinistrad plot murder; her mind, her senses, had gone numb. Why did I bother to come? she asked herself. There's nothing I can do. It's too late for him, for me. But not too late for Bane. How did the ancient saying go? "A little child shall lead them." Yes, there is hope for him. He is still innocent, unspoiled. Perhaps someday he will save us.

"Ah, here you are, father."

Bane entered the study, coolly ignoring Sinistrad's glaring frown. The child's color was heightened, and he seemed to glow with an inner radiance. His eyes gleamed with a feverish luster. Walking behind the boy, its nails clicking against the stone floor, the dog appeared worried and unhappy. Its eyes went to Hugh, pleading; its gaze shifted to a point behind the assassin, staring at Iridal so intently that she felt a panicked qualm and wondered if her spell of invisibility had ceased to work.

Hugh shifted uneasily in his chair. Bane was up to something. Probably—from that beatific expression on his face—no good.

"Bane, I'm busy. Leave us," said Sinistrad.

"No, father. I know what you're talking about. It's about me going back to Volkaran, isn't it? Don't make me, father." The child's voice was suddenly sweet and soft. "Don't make me go back to that place. No one likes me there. It's lonely. I want to be with you. You can teach me magic, like you taught me to fly. I'll show you all I know about the great machine, and I can introduce you to the high froman—"

"Stop whining!" Sinistrad rose to his feet. His robes rustled around him as he moved out from behind his desk to confront his son. "You want to please me, don't you, Bane?"

"Yes, father . . ." The boy faltered. "More than anything. That's why I want to be with you! Don't you want to be with me? Isn't that why you brought me home?"

"Bah! What nonsense. I brought you home so that we could put into action the second phase of our plan. Certain things have changed now, but only for the better. As for you, Bane, as long as I am your father, you will go where I tell you to go and do what I tell you to do. Now, leave us. I will send for you later."

Sinistrad turned his back on the child.

Bane, a strange smile on his lips, thrust his hand into his tunic. It came out holding a knife.

"I guess you won't be my father long, then!"

"How dare you—" Sinistrad whirled around, saw the dagger in the child's hand, and sucked in a seething breath. Pale with fury, the mysteriarch raised his right hand, prepared to cast the spell that would dissolve the child's body where he stood. "I can get more sons!"

The dog leapt, hit Bane square in the back, and knocked the child to the floor. The dagger flew from the boy's hand.

Something unseen struck Sinistrad; invisible hands clutched at his. Raging, he grappled with his wife, whose spell crumbled as she fought, revealing her to her husband.

Hugh was on his feet. Snatching up his dagger from the floor, he watched for his opportunity. He'd free her, free her child.

The wizard's body crackled with blue lightning. Iridal was flung aside in a thunderous shock wave that hurled her, dazed, against the wall. Sinistrad turned upon his child, only to find the dog standing above the terrified boy.

Teeth bared, hackles raised, it growled low in its throat.

Hugh struck, driving the dagger deep into the wizard's body. Sinistrad screamed in fury and in pain. The assassin jerked his dagger free. The body of the mysteriarch shimmered and faded and Hugh thought his foe was dead. Suddenly, the wizard returned, only now his body was that of an enormous snake.

The snake's head darted at Hugh. The assassin drove his knife again into the reptilian body, but too late. The snake sank its fangs into the back of Hugh's neck. The assassin cried out in agony, the poison surging through his body. He managed to retain his grip on the knife, and the snake—twisting and coiling— drove the blade deeper. It lashed out in its death throes, wrapped its tail around the assassin's legs, and both crashed to the floor.

The snake disappeared. Sinistrad lay dead, his legs wrapped around the feet of his killer.

Hugh stared at the corpse and tried feebly to rise. The assassin felt no pain, but he had no strength left in him, and he collapsed.

"Hugh."

Weakly he turned his head. It was pitch dark in the cell. He couldn't see.

"Hugh! You were right. Mine is the sin of *not* doing. And now it is too late . . . too late!"

There was a crack in the wall. A thin shaft of light gleamed brightly; he could smell fresh air, perfumed with the scent of lavender. Slipping his hand through the bars of his cell, Hugh held it out to her. Reaching out as far as she could from behind her own walls, Iridal touched the tips of his fingers.

And then the black monk came and set Hugh free.

CHAPTER ♦ 57

CASTLE SINISTER,

HIGH REALM

♦

A LOW RUMBLING SOUND CAUSED THE STONES OF THE PALACE TO QUIV-er on their foundation. It grew louder, like thunder heard in the distance, marching toward them, shaking the ground. The castle shifted; stone quaked and shuddered. A triumphant howl split the air.

"What the . . . ?" Haplo stared around him.

"The dragon's free!" murmured Alfred, eyes widening in awe. "Something's happened to Sinistrad!"

"It'll kill every living thing in this castle. I've fought dragons before. They're numerous in the Labyrinth. You?"

"No, never." Alfred glanced at the Patryn, caught the bitter smile. "It will take both of us to fight it, in the might of our power."

"No." Haplo shrugged. "You were right. I don't dare reveal myself. I'm not permitted to fight, not even to save my life. I guess it's up to you, Sartan."

The floor shook. A door down the corridor opened and Limbeck looked out. "This is more like home," he shouted cheerfully over the rumbling and thudding and cracking. Walking easily across the trembling floor, he waved a sheaf of papers. "Do you want to hear my spee—"

The outer walls split asunder. Alfred and Limbeck were flung from their feet, Haplo slammed up against a door that gave way behind him with a crash. A gleaming red eye the size of the sun peered through the ruptured wall at the victims trapped inside. The rumbling changed to a roar. The head reared back, jaws opening. White teeth flashed.

Haplo staggered to his feet. Limbeck was lying flat on his back, his spectacles smashed on the stone floor. Groping for them, the Geg stared up helplessly at the red-eyed silver blur that was the dragon. Near Limbeck lay Alfred, fainted.

Another roar shook the building. A silver tongue flickered like lightning. If the dragon destroyed them, Haplo would lose not only his life but also his purpose for coming here. No Limbeck to lead the revolution among the Gegs. No Limbeck to start the war that would lead to worldwide chaos.

Haplo ripped the bandages from his hands. Standing over the fallen, he crossed his arms and raised sigla-tattooed fists above his head. He wondered, briefly, where the dog had gone. He couldn't hear anything from it, but then, he couldn't hear much of anything at all over the bellowings of the dragon.

The creature dived for him, mouth open wide to snatch up the prey.

Haplo was right: he'd fought dragons before—dragons in the Labyrinth, whose magical powers made this quicksilver look like a mudworm. The hardest part was standing there, braced to take the blow, when every instinct in the body shrieked for him to run.

At the last instant, the silver head veered aside, jaws snapping on empty air. The dragon pulled back, eyeing the man suspiciously.

Dragons are intelligent beings. Coming out of enthrallment leaves them furious and confused. Their initial impulse is to strike back at the magus who ensorceled them. But even raging, they do not attack mindlessly. This one had experienced many types of magical forces in its lifetime, but never anything quite like what it faced now. It could feel, if it could not see, power surround the man like a strong metal shield.

Steel, the dragon could pierce. It might even pierce this magic, if it had time to work on it and unravel it. But why bother? There were other victims. It could smell hot blood. Casting Haplo a last curious, baleful glance, the dragon slid out of his view.

"But it'll be back, especially if it gets a taste of fresh meat." Haplo lowered his hands. "And what do I do? Take my little friend here and leave. My work in this realm is completed—or almost so."

He could hear, at last, and he heard what his dog was hearing. His brow furrowed, he absently rubbed the skin on his hands. From the sounds of it, the dragon was smashing in another part of the castle. Iridal and the boy were still alive, but they wouldn't be for long.

Haplo looked down at the unconscious Sartan. "I could send you into a faint that would last as long as I needed it to last, and transport you to my lord. But I've a better idea. You know where I've gone. You'll figure out how to get there. You'll come to me of your own accord. After all, we have the same goal—we both want to find out what happened to your people. So, old enemy, I'll let you cover my retreat."

Kneeling beside Alfred, he grabbed hold of the Sartan and shook him roughly.

"Come out of it, you craven scum."

Alfred blinked and groggily sat up. "I fainted, didn't I? I'm sorry. It's a reflex action. I can't control—"

"I don't want to hear about it," Haplo interrupted. "I've driven the dragon off for the time being, but it's only gone looking for a meal that won't fight back."

"You . . . you saved my life!" Alfred stared at the Patryn.

"Not your life. Limbeck's. You just happened to be in the way."

A child's thin wail of terror rose in the air. The dragon's howl cracked solid stone.

Haplo pointed in the creature's direction. "The boy and his mother are still alive. You'd better hurry."

Alfred swallowed hard, sweat beading on his forehead. Shakily he rose to his feet and, with a trembling hand, traced a sigil on his chest. His body began to fade.

"Good-bye, Sartan!" called Haplo. "For the time being. Limbeck, are you all right? Can you walk?"

"My . . . my spectacles!" Limbeck picked up bent frames, poked his fingers through the empty rims.

"Don't worry," said Haplo, helping the Geg to his feet. "You probably don't want to see where we're going anyway."

The Patryn paused a moment to run through everything in his mind.

Foment chaos in the realm.

His rune-covered hand closed fast over Limbeck's. I've done that, my lord. I'll transport him back to Drevlin. He will be the leader of the revolt among his people, the one who will plunge this world into war!

Bring me someone from this realm who will be my disciple. Someone who will spread the word—my word—to the people. Someone who will lead the people like sheep to my fold. It should be someone intelligent, ambitious, and . . . pliable.

Haplo, with his quiet smile, whistled for the dog.

Iridal had tamed dragons before in her girlhood, but only gentle creatures that would have almost done her bidding without enchantment. The dragon she faced now had always terrified her, perhaps as much because Sinistrad had ridden it as the dragon itself. She longed to be able to crawl into the corner of that safe, secure cell in which she had been hiding, but the prison was gone. The walls were beaten down, the door had swung open, the bars fallen from the windows. A chill wind tore at her; the light was blinding to eyes long accustomed to shadow.

The sin of not doing. Now it was too late for her, for the child. Death was their only freedom.

The dragon's roarings thundered above her. Iridal watched impassively as the ceiling split wide open. Dust and rock cascaded down around her. A fiery red eye peered in at them, a lightninglike tongue flicked in desire. The woman did not move.

Too late. Too late.

Crouched behind his mother, his arm clasped tightly around the dog's neck, Bane stared round-eyed. After his first cry of fear, he'd fallen silent, watching, waiting. The dragon couldn't reach them yet. It couldn't get its huge head into the small hole it had created, and was forced to rip more blocks from the castle walls. Driven by rage and a hunger for the blood it could smell, it was working rapidly.

The dog suddenly turned its head, looked back over its shoulder at the door, and whined.

Bane followed the dog's gaze and saw Haplo standing in the doorway, beckoning to him. Beside Haplo was Limbeck, peering dimly through the dust and rubble, gazing benignly at a horror he could not see.

The child looked up at his mother. Iridal was staring fixedly at the dragon. Bane tugged at her skirt.

"Mother, we must leave. We can hide somewhere. They'll help us!"

Iridal did not turn her head. Perhaps she had not heard him.

The dog whimpered and, gripping hold of Bane's tunic in his teeth, attempted to tug the boy toward the door.

"Mother!" the boy cried.

"Go along, child," said Iridal. "Hide somewhere. That's a good idea."

Bane grasped hold of her hand. "But . . . aren't you coming, mother?"

"Mother? Don't call me that. You're not my child." Iridal gazed at him with a strange and dreamlike calm. "When you were born, someone switched the babies. Go along, child." She spoke to someone else's son. "Run away and hide. I won't let the dragon harm you."

Bane stared at her. "Mother!" he cried out again, but she turned from him.

The boy grasped for the amulet around his neck. It was gone. He remembered: he had torn it off.

"Bring him!" Haplo shouted.

The dog got a grip on the boy's shirt and pulled. Bane saw the dragon thrust a taloned claw through the hole it had created in the ceiling and make a grab for its prey. Stone walls crashed down. Dust rose, obliterating his mother from his sight.

The claw groped, feeling for the warm flesh it could smell. A red eye peered inside, searching for its prey. Iridal fell back, but there was nowhere to hide in the rubble-strewn, partially collapsed chamber. She was trapped in a small area beneath the hole in the ceiling. When the dust cleared and the creature could see, it would have her.

She tried desperately to concentrate on her magic. Closing her eyes to blot out the fearsome sight, she formed mental reins and tossed them over the dragon's neck.

The infuriated creature roared and tossed its head. Jerking the reins out of her mental grasp, the dragon's opposing magic came near overthrowing the woman's reason. A claw slashed at Iridal's arm, tearing her flesh.

The ceiling gave way. Shards of stone fell all around her, striking her, knocking her down. The dragon, screeching in triumph, swooped on her. Gasping, choking in the dust, she crouched on the floor, her face averted from death.

Iridal waited almost impatiently to feel the sharp, searing pain, the talons piercing her flesh. Instead, she felt a gentle hand on her arm.

"Don't be afraid, child."

Incredulously, she raised her head. Bane's servant stood before her. Stoop-shouldered, his bald head covered with marble dust, the fringes of gray hair sticking out ludicrously, he smiled reassuringly at her, then turned to face the dragon.

Slowly, solemnly, and gracefully, Alfred began to dance.

His voice raised in a thin, high-pitched chant to accompany himself. His hands, his feet, traced unseen sigla, his voice gave them names and power, his mind enhanced them, his body fed them.

Burning acid dripped from the dragon's flicking tongue. Momentarily startled, feeling the man's magic and uncertain what it was, the creature drew back to consider the matter. But it had already been thwarted once. The lure of flesh and the memory of what it had endured at the hands of the detested wizard drove it on. Snapping jaws dived down, and Iridal shivered in terror, certain the man must be bitten in two.

"Run!" she screamed at him.

Alfred, looking up, saw his danger, but he merely smiled and nodded almost absentmindedly, his thoughts concentrating on his magic. His dance increased in tempo, the chanting grew a little louder—that was all.

The dragon hesitated. The snapping jaws did not close, but remained poised over their victim. The creature's head swayed slightly, in time to the rhythm of the man's voice. And suddenly the dragon's eyes widened and began to stare about in wonder.

Alfred's dance grew slower and slower, the chanting died away, and soon he came to a weary halt and stood gasping for breath, watching the dragon closely. The quicksilver didn't seem to notice him. Its head, thrust through the gaping hole in the castle wall, gazed at something only it could see.

Turning to Iridal, Alfred knelt beside her. "He won't harm you now. Are you hurt?"

"No." Keeping a wary eye on the dragon, Iridal took hold of Alfred's hand and held it fast. "What have you done to it?"

"The dragon thinks that it is back in its home, its ancient home—a world only it can remember. Right now it sees earth below and sky above, water in the center, and the sun's fire giving life to all."

"How long will the enchantment last? Forever?"

"Nothing lasts forever. A day, two days, a month, perhaps. It will blink, and all will be gone and it will see only the havoc that it wreaked. By that time, perhaps, its anger and pain will have subsided. Now, at least, it is at peace."

Iridal gazed in awe at the dragon, whose giant head was swaying back and forth, as if it heard a soothing, lulling voice.

"You've imprisoned it in its mind," she said.

"Yes," Alfred agreed. "The strongest cage ever built."

"And I am free," she said in wonder. "And it isn't too late. There is hope! Bane, my son! Bane!"

Iridal ran toward the door where she'd last seen him. The door was gone. The walls of her prison had collapsed, but the rubble blocked her path.

"Mother! I *am* your son! I—"

Bane tried to cry out again to her, but a sob welled up in his throat, shutting it off. He couldn't see her; the falling stone blocked his view.

The dog, barking frantically, ran around him in circles, nipping at his heels, trying to herd him away. The dragon gave a dreadful shriek and, terrified, Bane turned and ran. Halfway to the door, he nearly fell over Sinistrad's body.

"Father?" Bane whispered, reaching out a trembling hand. "Father, I'm sorry . . ."

The dead eyes stared at him, unseeing, uncaring.

Bane stumbled back and tripped over Hugh—the assassin paid to kill him, who had died to give him life.

"I'm sorry!" The child wept. "I'm sorry! Don't leave me alone! Please! Don't leave me alone!"

Strong hands—with blue sigla tattooed on the backs—caught hold of Bane and lifted him up out of the wreckage. Carrying him to the doorway, Haplo set the stunned and shaken boy on his feet next to the Geg.

"Both of you, keep near me," the Patryn ordered.

He lifted his hands, crossed his arms. Fiery runes began to burn in the air, one appearing after another. Each touched, yet never overlapped. They formed a circle of flame that completely encompassed the three of them, blinded them with its brilliance, yet did not harm them.

"Here, dog." Haplo whistled. The dog, grinning, leapt lightly through the fire and came to stand at his side. "We're going home."

EPILOGUE

"And so, Lord of the Nexus, that's the last I saw of the Sartan. I know you're disappointed, perhaps even angry, that I didn't bring him back. But I knew Alfred would never allow me to take the boy or the Geg, and as he said himself, I could not risk fighting him. It seemed to me to be a splendid irony that he should be the one to cover my escape. Alfred will come to us of his own accord, my lord. He can't help himself, now that he knows Death Gate swings open.

"Yes, my lord, you are correct. He has another incentive—his search for the child. Alfred knows I took the boy. I heard, before I left Drevlin, that the Sartan and the boy's mother, Iridal, had joined together to look for her son.

"As for the boy, I think you'll be pleased with Bane, my lord. There is potential in him. Naturally, he was shaken by what happened in the castle at the last—the death of his father, the horror of the dragon. It's made him thoughtful, so if you find him quiet and subdued, be patient with him. He is an intelligent boy and will soon learn to honor you, lord, as we all do.

"And now, to finish my story. When I left the castle, I took the boy and the Geg with me to the elven ship. Here we discovered that the elf captain and his crew were being held prisoners by the mysteriarchs. I made a deal with Bothar'el. In return for his freedom, he would take us back to Drevlin. Once there, he would hand over his ship to me.

"Bothar'el had little choice but to agree. He either accepted my terms or met death at the hands of the wizards—the mysteriarchs are powerful and desperate to escape their dying realm. I was, of course, forced to use my magic to free us. We could not have fought them successfully otherwise. But I was able to work my magic without the elves seeing me, they didn't notice the runes. In fact, they now believe that I'm one of the mysteriarchs myself. I didn't disillusion them.

"The assassin was correct in his estimation of the elves, my lord. You will find that they are people of honor, as are the humans in their own curious way. As he had agreed, Bothar'el flew us to the Low Realm. The Geg, Limbeck, was greeted by his people as a hero. He is high froman of Drevlin now. His first act was to launch an attack against an elven ship attempting to dock and take on water. In this, he was helped by Captain Bothar'el and his crew. A combined force of elves and dwarves attacked the ship and, singing that strange song I told you about, they managed to convert all the elves on it. Bothar'el told me before he left that he intended to take the ship to this Prince Reesh'ahn, leader of the rebellion. He hopes to form an alliance between the rebel elves and the dwarves against the Tribus Empire. It is rumored that King Stephen of the Uylandia Cluster will join them.

"Whatever the outcome, world war rages in Arianus, my lord. The way is prepared for your coming. When you choose to enter the Realm of Sky, the war-weary people will look upon you as a savior.

"As for Limbeck, he—as I predicted—has become a powerful leader. Because of him, the dwarves have rediscovered their dignity, their courage, their fighting spirit. He's ruthless, determined, not afraid of anything. His dreamy-eyed idealism broke with those spectacles of his, and he sees more clearly now than ever before. He has, I'm afraid, lost a girlfriend. But then, Jarre spent time alone with the Sartan. Who can say what strange notions he put into her head?

"As you can imagine, my lord, it took me some time to prepare the elven ship for its journey into Death Gate. I transported it and Bane down to the Steps of Terrel Fen, near where my own ship had crashed, so that I could work undisturbed. It was while I was performing the necessary modifications—using the Kicksey-winsey to assist me—that I heard about the Sartan and the boy's mother and their search. They had traveled as far as Drevlin. Fortunately, I was ready to leave.

"I sent the boy into a deep slumber, and made my way back through Death Gate. This time, I knew the perils I faced and was prepared for them. The ship sustained only minor damage, and I can have it repaired and refitted in time for the next journey. That is, my lord, if I have earned the right to be sent on another such mission?

"Thank you, my lord. Your praise is my greatest reward. And now I propose a salute. This is bua wine, a gift from

Captain Bothar'el. I think you will find its taste extremely interesting, and it seemed to me fitting that we should drink to the success of our next mission in what we might call the blood of Arianus.

"To Death Gate, my lord, and our next destination—the Realm of Fire."

MAGIC IN THE

SUNDERED REALMS

EXCERPT FROM A

SARTAN'S MUSINGS

◆

Magic is a thunder heard in each of the sundered realms. Its power reverberates through the foundations of all Existence. It echoes the lightning of creation itself. In its voice is heard the promise of life and death. It is a power to be coveted and feared.

Theorists tell us that magic draws its power from the original creation of the Omniverse. In the beginning, Elihn, God in One, stretched out his hand amid the Chaos. The motion of his hand ordered chaos into infinite possibilities of creation. This motion was the first Order out of Chaos. It is called the Wave Prime or more often simply the Prime.

Elihn saw in the Prime the creation of the ethereal and the physical, and the seeing of it made it so. In the creation of the spiritual and the physical, the Prime split into two sets of waves, each infinite in their possibilities. The two waves curved away from each other and back again. The waves crossed and where they crossed was created time and space. Thus was Reality woven from the forces of all possibilities.

With delight and wonder, Elihn looked again upon both waves. In the ethereal he saw the creation of Air and Fire; in the physical he saw Water and Stone . . . and the seeing of it made it so. Again, in its creation, the waves of ethereal and physical possibilities each split into four new waves, each with infinite possibilities of new creation. Elihn again wove these new possibilities together. In the intersection of the waves was born Life, Death, Power and Mind.

The longer Elihn looked upon the weave of Reality, the more

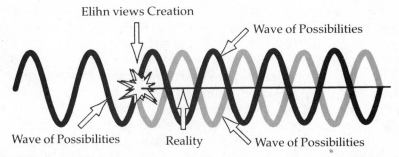

possibilities split into being. Stars, world, life—in short, all creation—was thus woven from infinite possibilities. So it was in the beginning and so it continues today.

Reality is simply the manifestation of intersecting waves of possibility. It is a vast and almost incomprehensible weave of solid physics in the midst of a myriad of infinite potentials. Science, technology and biology all use the woven rope of reality.

Magic, on the other hand, functions by reweaving the fabric of reality. A wizard begins by concentrating on the wave of probabilities rather than on reality itself. Through his learning and his powers, he looks out upon the myriad waves of infinite possibilities to find that part of the wave where his desired reality would be true. Then the wizard creates a harmonic wave of possibility to bend the existing wave so that what was once only possible becomes part of what is true. In this way the magician weaves his desire into existence.

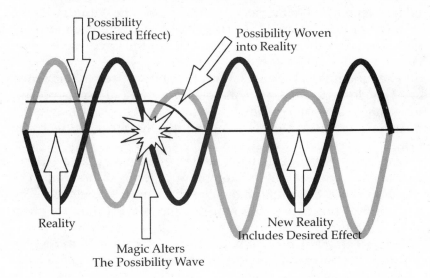

For example, a wizard stands on a field of battle against a great knight. The spell caster, wearing only his robes, is at the mercy of the armored and more powerful knight. This is reality and, if left alone, the knight will most likely slay the wizard without much resistance. However, the wizard knows from his study where the possibility (desired effect) of a protective shield exists on one of the countless waves of possibility. The wizard sets up a harmonic wave of possibility through his motions, thoughts, words, signs, and other aides. This magic alters the possibility wave so that what was once the possibility of a magical shield is woven into reality. The new reality includes the desired effect and so the magical shield now guards the wizard.

Although, to the outside observer, the protective field seems to spring up around the wizard from nothing, it would be more accurate to say that the possibility of such a field has been called into reality from the infinite possibilities of the Omniwave.

To use magic, one must be able to find and weave the appropriate portion of the Omniwave in some small degree. This is far from omnipotence or omniscience, even among those who see a vast section of the Wave. Being able to function in the discipline of magic does not explain why magic exists or its origins. It does not lead one to the reason for being. Just as knowing a rock will fall when dropped does not tell us why gravity exists or what intelligence brought such order out of chaos, so it is, too, with magic.

Only the Sartan and the Patryns understood magic to the fullest degree. Having seen magic from the center of the Omniwave, we mastered the art in the most elemental and powerful form. No others have seen as much of the Omniwave as we have.

The fundamental relationships of magic are seen in this drawing. The closer to the center the magic is, the greater its power. Rune magic, the most elemental and centered of all magics, is thus the most powerful and commands the most far reaching effects.

Each great level of understanding is designated as a House. Each of these houses can be thought of in terms of how much of the Omniwave the user of that level of magic perceives. The more central the house, the more of the Wave Prime they can perceive and use.

The greatest force of all is the magic of House Rune, which combines the waves of Life, Power, Mind and Death into a com-

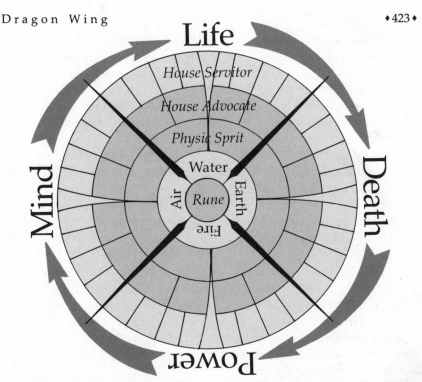

prehension of the central weave of reality and a clear picture of
the infinite possibilities of the Omniwave. Those who have mastered rune magic are said to have reached the Ninth Mastery or
the Final Mastery. The knowledge and potency of the Rune
Disciplines are all tied directly to the rune siglas which are used
in the casting of such spells. With the Sundering of Time, however, only we (the Sartan) and the Patryns (if they still exist) have
knowledge of rune magics.

The unified magic of House Rune is then divided into the
four Lesser Houses of Firmament (Air), Sun (Fire), Spring (Water), and Dark (Earth). Together they are known as the Sovereign
Masteries. The Sovereign Masteries represents the Eighth Mastery and are second only to rune magic in power. Each of the
Sovereign Masteries is then further divided equally into Spiritual
and Physical Masteries. The Spiritual masteries tend toward mental and emotional manipulation of the world about the magician.
The Physical Masteries tend to use and make use of physical
objects in the world about the wizard.

Both the Spiritual and Physical Masteries are further divided
into the Greater and Lesser Disciplines in each House. Greater
Disciplines are known as House Advocate while the Lesser Disci-

plines are referred to as House Servitor. House Advocate includes Fifth through Seventh Masteries while House Servitor is made up of First through Fourth Masteries. The terms 'greater' and 'lesser' are somewhat deceptive in that the Lesser Disciplines are the broadest based and most commonly used of the magics. The Greater Disciplines, while more powerful, also tend to be more specialized.

After the Sundering of Time, the Patryns vanished and the Sartan jealously guarded rune magic from mortal learning. This brought about the loss of any magic greater than Seventh Mastery in any of the realms as now constituted. Rune magic is now unknown among any of the mortal peoples of any realm. It remains a carefully guarded secret.

RUNE MAGIC

Rune magic is the most powerful manifestation of all the magics present in the realms. Rune magic weaves all the elements of the various House Sovereigns into a single magic whole. As such, rune magic touches on the fabric of all creation. It was this rune magic which was the instrument by which the unified creation was sundered into its current parts.

The key to rune (or runic) magic is that the harmonic wave that weaves a possibility into existence must be created with as much simultaneity as possible. This means that the various motions, signs, words, thoughts and elements that go into making up the harmonic wave must be completed as close together as possible. The more simultaneous the harmonic wave structure, the more balance and harmony will be maintained in the wave and the more powerful the magic itself. This is rather like the difference between throwing a warball[1] end over end and spiraling it. A wheel which is rolled straight will roll farther than one which is sent wobbling.

To attain this simultaneity, both the Sartan and the Patryns have developed magical languages and structures to convey their magic. Used only for magic, this language is unlike any other used in any of the realms. A second, more traditional language is used for standard communication by both of these races. The rune language is not so much spoken (although that is one element) as it is performed.

[1]Warball is a game popularized in ancient times and which is still played in a variety of forms in all of the realms. Warballs are generally cylindrical and oblong in shape, they are also generally weighted and balanced for aerodynamic flight when thrown.

The common element in both languages is their simultaneity. Traditional languages are sequential in their structure along single-channel, linear lines. When one reads words on a page, he reads letter after letter, word after word, sentence after sentence to build up a complete thought or meaning of the text. This means he is taking in the message through only one channel or source of experience at a time. When people watch a play, however, they are taking in several channels at one time (the words spoken, the gestures and poise of the actor, the lighting of the scene). One might also get multiple messages over a single channel at one time (seeing the actor, the actor's chair and the backdrop of the stage all at the same time). The play's messages are all hitting the audience simultaneously. For this reason the play is said to have simultaneity in its communication of ideas.

The complexity, balance and harmony of magic requires perfection in simultaneous communication of the magician's harmonic waves. This is generally conveyed through performance of the magic by the magician through words, tones, gestures and motion. In rune magic, the simultaneity is bound up in the concept of a non-linear written language.

The rune languages have evolved into two separate types along the lines of the Sartan and the Patryn cultures. Both operate the runic principles of the universe but their structure and methods are somewhat different.

SARTAN RUNE MAGIC

The Sartan use a hexagonal structure which is generally conveyed through six channels of communication at the same time. This involves the use of runes which are either drawn into or on an object or created in the air through performance art. In performance, the casting wizard is limited to three channels which include sound (auditory with complex harmonics), shape (gestures and dance positioning), mind (telepathic projections). The use of structured runes at the same time (sigla inscribed on objects such as staves, wands, rings, clothing, or any properly positioned object) can communicate the remaining three elements of the pattern.

All Sartan rune structures are built in a hexagonal pattern emanating from the Fountain or Root Rune. This rune is the source of the magic being cast and the point from which all the magical structure springs. The Fountain Rune determines the thrust of the spell structure. In rune magic, this Fountain Rune may be of any type from any of the Houses of magic. In complex spells, then, it is essential in the reading of the spell that one understands which rune is the Fountain Rune. Two separate spells which have identical runes in identical positions may have vastly different effects if they have different Fountain Runes.

ROOT STRUCTURES

Root structures bring the power of magic into the complex of the rune spell. These structures begin with Root itself: a rune which designates the source of magic coming from either Power, Mind, Life, or Death.

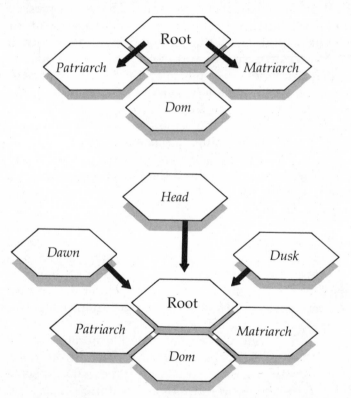

This Root Rune or, as it is more often called, the Fountain Rune, is flanked on its lower left side by its Patriarch (the rune preceding it as seen in the illustration). It is flanked on its lower right side by its Matriarch (the rune following the Patriarch for that Root). These support the Root and give direction to the power of magic welling up from the runes below it.

Directly below the Root is the Dom or Master. The top of the

Dom borders the bottom of the Root and touches on both the Patriarch and the Matriarch. This rune determines whether the nature of the power called forth will be Spiritual or Physical in nature and completes the Root Structure. Nearly always, other runes connect to the Dom from below to further define and amplify the power of the magic being cast.

The Fountain Rune is flanked on its upper left side by Dawn and on its upper right side by Dusk. These runes determine the amplitude (how much power) and vector (direction) to which the harmonic wave will be applied into the complex where the Root Structure is found.

Between the Dawn and Dusk runes is the Head which completes the Root structure. The head is part of a further complex of runes which transfers the elements of the Root structure into the general harmonic of the magic being called into existence.

THE FOUNTAIN RUNE: CENTER OF MAGIC
The Fountain Rune is both the center of the magical concept which is created when the spell is cast as well as the essential point of perspective from which rune magic is read and understood.

It is crucial to the proper reading of runes that the Fountain Rune be known and located in the structure. Similar rune structures take on completely different meanings when different Fountain Runes are chosen.

Here, by way of example, is a very simple rune structure.

There is no indication of the Fountain Rune. Which rune does one pick? Where does one begin? Here are two possible interpretations of this rune structure.

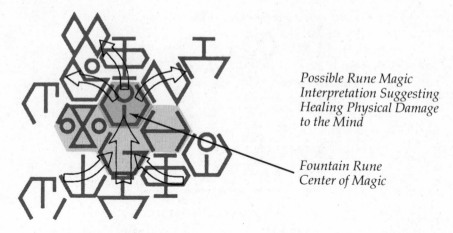

*Possible Rune Magic
Interpretation Suggesting
Healing Physical Damage
to the Mind*

*Fountain Rune
Center of Magic*

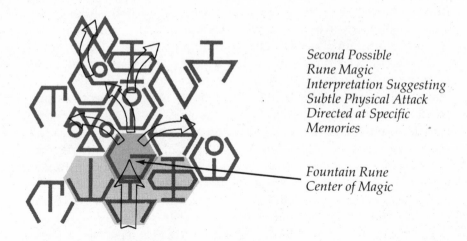

*Second Possible
Rune Magic
Interpretation Suggesting
Subtle Physical Attack
Directed at Specific
Memories*

*Fountain Rune
Center of Magic*

This is the great secret in rune magic. The location of the Fountain Rune is known only to those who learn its location from the rune's creator. Much of a wizard's training involves learning how to determine the Fountain Rune as well as simple rote memory of the locations of such runes. Without a Sartan to teach the location of these Fountain Runes, the chances of understanding our magical writings is negligible.

PATRYN RUNE MAGIC
Little is known about Patryn magic except that which may help identify them. By their magic runes we will know them should

any ever be seen entering the Sundered Realms from their place Beyond. Little more is known save by the Patryns themselves.

Like Sartan magic, Patryn rune magic also seeks the perfect balance in the harmonic wave. However, it does not find its balance through symmetry of structure. Patryn rune magic looks for balance in weighted opposites.

The Patryns use a series of interlaced octagons and squares to form the pattern of their magic. Octagons form the Source, Course, and Destiny of Patryn magic. Squares form the Branch, Juncture, and Cascade of the magic. Combinations of these elements create the magic along eight simultaneous channels of thought.

As with Sartan magic, the Fountain Rune is critical to the success of understanding and using the magic.

Patryn magic uses substructures—rather like runes within runes. Runes formed of other runes then imitate the concepts of Root, Stem, or other structures found in Sartan magic in a much more concise way. However, their nature is somewhat erratic and their use, unless carefully balanced, can lead to great lessening of the desired effect.

MAGIC BY REALM

House Rune works the same way in all the Realms. Each realm, however, specializes in a particular magic of the Sovereign Masteries. This is usually indicative of the general division of magic which took place at the sundering of the realms. The magic of House Firmament, for example, would be the primary magic ruling in the Sky realms while House Life would rule primarily in the Sea realms. Only the magic of House Life (that of Arianus) will be discussed here.

LADY OF THE FIRMAMENT (DISCIPLINES OF THE PHYSICAL MASTERY)

The Lady of House Firmament (Physical Masteries/Transportation and Motion Masters) are currently controlled by the Kenkari Elves of the Tribus Empire. These white-haired, slender creatures have formed the Tribus Empire on the Aristagon Continent. In conquest they have subjugated all of their own continent and are waging wars of conquest on several others. Their powerful magic is physical in nature, requiring the use of objects to channel, contain and direct their powers of magic. Despite their House, they have no powers of telepathy but do manifest telekinetic powers through their magics.

One power the Kenkari Elves have is the ability to weave complex messages into songs. This is an echo of the lost rune languages and a practical application of the more generally known magical languages which create rougher (unbalanced) spells in the magics of the Sovereign Masteries and below. The danger in these is that anyone can sing the song. Humans may be mildly inspired by these songs but to the elves such music communicates broad and deep elven feelings and messages. To gain full communication, the message of the song draws on genetic memories common among the elves—memories which the humans do not possess.

These disciplines utilize two channels to communicate the structure of the magic: verbal/tone (speaking the magic into auditory harmonics) and somatics (physical gestures of form to blend with the harmonics). If an elven wizard cannot speak or move freely, his magic will be crippled.

LORD OF THE FIRMAMENT (DISCIPLINES OF THE SPIRITUAL MASTERY)
The Vondekar humans know their magic as Vond—the Light—and, more formally, Vondreth—the Given Power. Those who are adept in its use are known as the Kyr-Vondreth (the Light Seers) and, when spoken to are addressed simply either as Vokar (Light-people) or as Kyr (Seer). Some are certainly more adept than others at Vond and its blessing seems to happen without pattern among the people.

The magic of the Vondreth is primarily spiritual in nature and derives its abilities from the manipulation of nature and natural spirit. The Vondreth can effect natural animals and call weather to their aide. They can communicate with and manipulate animals (in this way they handle the dragons). Though they have the capability to construct magic which would allow telepathy, the complexities of such magic with a more advanced mind have long since slipped from their understanding.

The Vokar have no formal schools—all teaching is done by master to apprentice. The Vokar have been aggressive in their magic since the threat of domination by the Kenkari elves. Vokar are used in battle to call natural infestations (plagues, skyrats, tornados, lightning and the like). The Vokar live for today and thrive on life and its pleasures.

The Kyr are far from their brother Vokar. This very disciplined order deals primarily with death. They see life as a punishment through which they must pass in order to gain their final reward in the Hvani (heaven) which is to come. They have developed magics of telempathy but consider feeling empathetic joy and happiness a sin. They also have developed natural magics of transportation in order to assist them in their work of gathering the dead, as well as protections against poisons and disease.

This magic uses two channels to communicate its structure: somatic gestures and mental projections of the concept. Speech is not needed to cast a spell in this mastery. It has earned the name of 'Silent Death' from the elves who have learned the hard way just how effective a magic which does not require shouting can be in combat. A bound Kyr is crippled in his magic—but can still make limited mental constructs which will function well to aide his escape.

Hand is Flame

Lyrics by Kevin Stein

Music by Janet Pack

The Hand that holds the Arc and Bridge, The Fire that rails the

Temp ---'red Span, All Flame as He–art Sur --- mount the Ridge,

All no -- ble Paths are Ell --- x -- man. Fire --- in Heart

gui – des the Will, The Will of Flame _____, set _____ by Hand,

The Hand that moves ——————— Ell–x–man Song, The Song of Fire and

Heart ——— and Land: The Fire ____ born of Jour ———— ney's End,

The Flame a part, a light ——— ened call, The sul – len walk, the

flick ——— 'ring aim, Fire leads a —— gain from fu ————— tures, all.

The Arc and Bridge are thou – ghts and heart, The Span a life, the

Ri – dge a part.